# WAITING
*for*
# UNCLE
# JOHN

JAMES OLIVER GOLDSBOROUGH

# WAITING

*for*

# UNCLE
# JOHN

*"Cuba Must be Ours"*

*A NOVEL*

PROSPECTA PRESS

Prospecta Press
An imprint of Easton Studio Press
P. O. Box 3131
Westport, CT 06880
(203) 571-0781

www. prospectapress.com

*Book and cover design by Barbara Aronica-Buck*
*Cover images by y-studio, ke77kz and subjug*

Hardcover ISBN: 978-1-63226-089-5
eBook ISBN: 978-1-63226-090-1

To James Oliver Crittenden,

another uncle who mattered

"I have ever looked on Cuba as the most interesting addition that could be made to our system of States."
 – Thomas Jefferson (1820)

"The annexation of Cuba will be indispensable to the integrity of the Union."
 – John Quincy Adams (1823)

"Cuba must be ours."
 – Jefferson Davis (1848)

"We mean to stop the horrible state of things in Cuba."
 – Senator Henry Cabot Lodge (1898)

"The United States may intervene for the preservation of Cuban independence."
 – Platt Amendment (1901)

"Until Castro, the American ambassador was the second most important man; sometimes more important than the Cuban president."
 – Earl T. Smith, former American ambassador to Cuba (1960)

# AUTHOR'S NOTE

*Waiting for Uncle John*, the story of the 1851 invasion of Cuba – the first U.S. invasion of Cuba – is true to the historical record. The principal characters, most especially Sen. John Jordan Crittenden, Col. William Logan Crittenden, Lucy Petway Holcombe and Gen. Narciso Lopez, are based on what their own accounts and letters reveal, plus the record. The principal Cubans and Spaniards are authentic. The military and political characters and events are true, as are the roles played by New Orleans newspapermen Laurent Sigur and James Freaner. The main fictional characters are composites of men and women found in the historical record.

A 1906 monograph by Anderson Quisenberry, written for the Louisville Filson Club (now Historical Society), was essential reading as background to the story. As Quisenberry states, prior to 1906, "no account whatever of the Bahia Honda expedition had ever been published." A 1915 Princeton dissertation by Robert Granville Caldwell expanded greatly on Quisenberry. The personal narrative of Maj. Louis Schlesinger, written after his escape from the mines of Ceuta, in Spanish Morocco, in 1852, self-serving as it is, added to the story.

The recent publication of the lost 1854 novel of Lucy Holcombe, *The Free Flag of Cuba*, sheds light on her love affair with Will Crittenden, the protagonist of my story, as does Elizabeth Wittenmyer Lewis's recent biography of Lucy, *Queen of the Confederacy*. The Cuban National Archives in Havana, where I spent considerable time, contain a wealth of documents on the Spanish and Cuban side of events. The best narrative account that I found is

Volume I of Ramiro Guerra's *Historia de Cuba*, with its revelations about the sinister Club of Havana.

Finally, there are *The Crittenden Memoirs*, compiled by Henry Huston Crittenden, Will Crittenden's nephew, and published by Putnam in 1936.

I met Uncle Huston, as he was called, when I was a small boy spending the summer on my grandfather's estate, Sucasa, in Sewickley, Pennsylvania, on the banks of the Ohio, a few miles downriver from Pittsburgh. H. H. Crittenden had come over from Kansas City for some business with his younger brother, William Jackson Crittenden, my grandfather. Both men were sons of Thomas T. Crittenden, former U.S. consul general to Mexico and Unionist governor of Missouri, famous for his role in the death of bandit Jesse James. Thomas T., like his brother Will, was a nephew of Senator John J. Crittenden of Kentucky, author of the 1860 Crittenden Compromise, the last-ditch effort to head off the Civil War.

In short pants, I was brought alone into Grandpa's paneled den to meet this distinguished-looking, white-haired gentleman in tightly buttoned-up vest over ample stomach. Beyond the windows stretched the magnificent lawns of Sucasa and the mighty Ohio River in the distance. Apart from the pungent whiff of the Cuban cigars that Uncle Huston had brought for his brother, I remember little of the encounter. But I remember *it*, which, I imagine, was the point. He shook my hand, and I lost myself in one of Grandpa's soft leather chairs for a few moments while the brothers talked. I was six years old. It was the only time I saw Uncle Huston.

*The Crittenden Memoirs* contain only a few pages on William Logan Crittenden, but Will's meeting with Ulysses Grant on the steamer to West Point is recounted, as is the famous West Point fight with Alexander Hays, who, like so many cadets of the era, went on to Civil War fame. Before the Civil War came the friendships, deaths, and glories of the Mexican War. Next along the road to Manifest Destiny lay Cuba. Will's two letters from Havana, to Lucien Hensley and to his Uncle John, U.S. attorney general at the time, are included in the memoirs, and once I read them I never forgot them. They are wrenching in their courage, determination, and clarity.

History has not given its due to the 1851 expedition, the outcome of which, so soon after the Compromise of 1850, drove the first nail into the coffin of the Whig Party, which was eventually destroyed by the Kansas-Nebraska Act of 1854. After that, any hopes of heading off a civil war were slim indeed. May this account at least partially rectify that oversight.

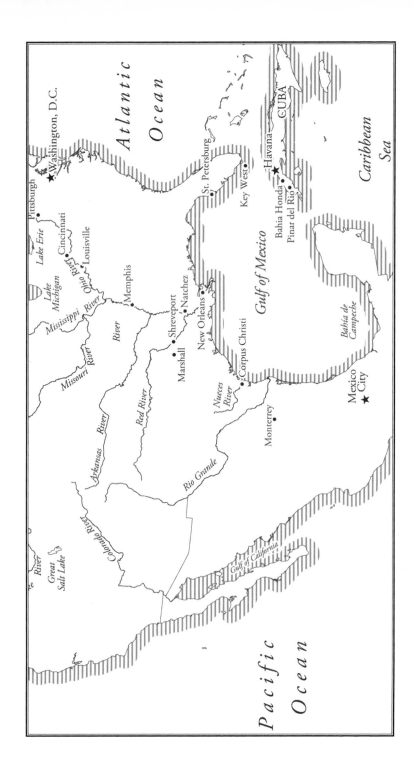

# PART ONE

✴

# INVITATION

# I

It began the night of the Christmas party at Uncle John's house in Frankfort. Will Crittenden, the nephew who'd resigned his army commission after the Mexican War and was a civilian for the first time in his adult life, had no inkling of what was coming. Had he known, he might have skipped the party. Of course, if he'd skipped it, he never would have met Lucy Holcombe, and there would be no story.

Coming down from his room, he stood on the stairs a moment to watch the glittering festivities below. Aunt Maria had decorated in a gallimaufry of bright holiday colors, and he let his eyes run over the greens and reds of wreaths, holly, mistletoe, and the eight-foot pine adorned top to bottom with the curious ornaments she'd been making and collecting all her life. The house was packed with guests who'd ridden and walked through a light snowfall to get to the house, many with pink cheeks from the snow, turned a shade rosier by the Christmas punch.

Christmas at Frankfort was gayer than at home in Shelbyville, mainly because Uncle John, a born politician, liked to politic, and Aunt Maria, a born politician's wife, liked to entertain. And what better time than Christmas? The fragrant smell of pine needles rose to greet him. It was a happy scene, a mixture of generations and politics and attitudes and people he knew and didn't know. For Will, the house was full of memories: of coming over as a boy from the Shelbyville farm for carefree summers, or with Ma and Pa to spend happy holidays with Pa's older brother, an important man in Kentucky.

Descending, he spied the bar across the room and determined to start his evening with a little Kentucky cheer.

Though the statehouse was just down one street and the governor's mansion just down another, the Crittenden house had long been the center of Frankfort political life. That was because John Jordan Crittenden had held just about every federal and state office the citizens of Kentucky had devised and was one of the few politicians in those perilous times with friends in both parties. At the time of the party, in honor of Mississippi Senator Jefferson Davis, it was 1849 and Uncle John was governor. He'd already been U.S. congressman, senator, and attorney general. He would soon be attorney general again and then senator again and turn down a nomination for president.

But that's getting ahead of the story.

Like its owner, the Crittenden house on Main Street was solid and unpretentious. It was classic colonial, two stories of red brick under a gray slate roof, running a full block in front and with gardens in back. As a boy, Will was lodged in a mansard area directly under the roof. Later, after Pa's murder and as Uncle John's children moved away, he occupied Cousin George's room on the second floor, next to Cousin Tom. As boys, Tom and Will would sit on the stairs evenings to observe the goings-on below. As they grew older, they were allowed to come down and mingle with the adults.

He'd met most of the great men of the day by the time he was fifteen. Evenings at Uncle John's were as lively as any theater and often ran a good deal later. The conversations filled several rooms and were mainly social, though the men found it hard to resist a little politics. The boys would move around together, staying out of the way but eavesdropping at every chance. Discussions were mostly good-humored. Though political chaos ruled in Washington, and Kentucky was divided as were few states in the Union, no one, no matter what his party, politics, or passions, dared raise his voice under a roof that wasn't his own, especially when it belonged to John Jordan Crittenden.

The women mixed with the men, which added to the civility. Little sandwiches with cakes and tea were served along with punch and Kentucky bourbon, and there was a great deal of bonhomie, especially at Christmastime. There was always a preacher or two present, most likely Presbyterians for the Crittendens were all Scotch-Irish. Preachers make good leavening for politicians, Aunt Maria liked to say, and it was rare at any party that the Rev. Browne of First Presbyterian wasn't somewhere near the punch bowl. Whatever might have happened up the street at the statehouse that day or at the governor's mansion, stayed up the street. Political quarrels between Whigs and Democrats, worsening each year and fueling an atmosphere of murder and mayhem in border states like Kentucky, were checked with hats and coats at the Crittenden door.

He saw Gov. John Quitman of Mississippi waving and crossing the room to greet him. Strange, he thought. Uncle John had told him that Quitman, who'd been one of the top generals in Mexico, had written that he was coming up with Sen. Davis. He said Quitman had inquired if his nephew would be at the party.

Will wondered at it. They'd served together during the Mexican War, but the paths of a general and a lieutenant don't cross much. Why would Quitman care to see him now that the war was over, now that both were civilians again? Quitman came no higher than his shoulders as they shook hands, but a high forehead and bushy hair made him seem taller. His flaxen beard exactly matched the length of his hair to give him a leonine look. His greeting was hearty, but the eyes were hard, not a man to trifle with.

"Your uncle informs me you've resigned your commission, Lieutenant," he said, still gripping his hand. "May I inform you, sir, from what I know of you in Mexico, that it is the army's loss."

He'd been a political general, not regular army, not West Point like Will, but the opinion was that he'd turned out better than most. His comment, more than generous, more than Will deserved, only deepened the mystery.

The party was two weeks before Christmas. The favorite nephew had come to visit while he figured out what to do with his life. Uncle John had urged him to stay in the army after Mexico, but what, he asked his uncle, is an army without a war? Many of his fellow West Pointers had stayed in, but the Indian Wars didn't interest him. The smell of civil war was in the air, but the politicians in Washington, led by Henry Clay of Kentucky and Daniel Webster of Massachusetts, were putting together a bill to head it off, the bill to be known as the Compromise of 1850.

Ma couldn't have been happier to have him back from Mexico. She knew what had happened to Henry Clay's son at Buena Vista. Will had written his ma regularly from Mexico, but that didn't keep her from worrying for two years that like young Clay, he wouldn't come back, at least not alive, that is. The Clays, Whigs like Uncle John, were close Crittenden friends.

He loved being at Frankfort, but couldn't be a guest forever. Lucien Hensley, an old Shelbyville friend, wrote him that he was thinking of moving his medical practice downriver to New Orleans. Will was going down with him to have a look around. He had friends in New Orleans.

He thanked Governor Quitman for the compliment and found himself being escorted across the crowded drawing room to the bar, where the bourbon, diluted for the ladies in punch, was flowing. Quitman chattered on about Mexico, treating him like they were old friends.

"You thought I didn't notice you in Mexico," he said, "but I did, and not just for your name. I meant to talk to you about your plans after the occupation, but had my hands full with the Mexicans. Freaner always mentioned you – you remember Freaner of the *Delta-News*, don't you?"

"How can I forget James Freaner – best damn whist player in Mexico."

Quitman smiled. "I thought that honor went to Trist."

"Ambassador Trist was second best."

"I don't play," said Quitman, a bit too abruptly.

Drinks in hand, they returned to the salon where the governor introduced him to his wife, Eliza, a redheaded woman of stunning Southern beauty probably not half her husband's age. She was dressed in green velvet with a low-cut bodice and held out a bangling hand to him. "An honah to meet you, suh," she said in her plantation accent. They'd heard he was coming to New Orleans, she said, and wondered if they might have the honor of his presence at Monmouth, their estate at Natchez, on his way down the Mississippi.

Stranger and stranger, he thought. He'd heard of Monmouth, just downriver from Jeff Davis's Brierfield plantation near Vicksburg. But just how would the Quitmans know he was traveling to New Orleans, a decision he'd only just made, and why would they care if they did? He had no idea the purpose behind the invitation beyond perhaps returning a kindness to Uncle John. Somehow there seemed more to it than that.

He knew something about John Quitman, a New Yorker who'd married a Natchez belle and become as Southern as Jefferson Davis himself. Quitman's manners were noticeably Southern, gracious but always with an edge. In Mexico City, when the fighting was over, he'd been appointed military governor during the U.S. occupation. He was a man with a future.

Aunt Maria, bustling about the room in finery with a holly corsage pinned to her breast, spied them and came up with the always courtly Congressman Andrew Johnson of Tennessee on her arm. "You are not going to infect this sweet young man with politics," she said to the Quitmans, laughing, "especially at Christmastime."

"We've invited him to Monmouth," said Eliza. "Now you be sure he comes to see us."

"By all means he will come – won't you, Will? Natchez makes for a nice break on that tedious river trip to New Orleans. How anyone sleeps on those shelves that pass for beds I'll never know."

They all laughed, including Johnson, a rough-hewn man who was said to carry a pistol at all times and who kept his talk flowing with steady doses of bourbon. Uncle John liked him because he was a Unionist, not a separatist like most in Tennessee. Johnson would support the Compromise of 1850, putting off talk of civil war a while longer. Most Southerners, led by John C. Calhoun of South Carolina, would bitterly oppose it.

One of those Southerners was Jefferson Davis of Mississippi, Calhoun's protégé and the man in whose honor the party was being held. Davis and Uncle John had nothing in common but a twenty-five-year-long friendship. The Davis clan was originally from Kentucky before moving downriver to Mississippi. Davis, a Democrat, had married President Zach Taylor's daughter, Sarah, a marriage that Taylor, a Whig, opposed. She died soon after the wedding; Taylor blamed Davis and the two men didn't speak until Colonel Davis's Mississippi Rifles saved General Taylor at Buena Vista, where young Henry Clay was killed. Davis and Buena Vista helped put old Zach in the White House. South and North were diverging, edging closer to taking up arms in the great war, but in Mexico everyone was on the same side.

In Will's mind, it was one of the stranger things about that war: how North and South, Yankees and Crackers, Democrats and Whigs, were able to forget everything that separated them — slavery and secession and tariffs and politics and the growing feeling on both sides that civil war was inevitable — and get on with the task of defeating the Mexicans. Strangest of all, he remembered, was how both sides had united against Kentucky — as if the worst sin was not slavery or emancipation, unity or secession, peace or war, but preferring compromise to a good fight.

Uncle John had spent the day in talks at the statehouse with Davis, Quitman, and Johnson, all Democrats, but whatever the topic, and it was surely political, it had stayed at the statehouse. The talk

that evening was a little about Taylor, who'd been elected president
the previous year, and a good deal about Charles Dickens's new book,
*Dombey and Son,* which everyone was reading in installments in
*Harper's Magazine.* Dickens had recently come down the Ohio River
on his American travels, and some at the party had heard him speak
at Galt House in Louisville. They took pleasure in pointing out that
while he hated most of America he'd had only kind words for
Louisville.

Well into the evening a knock came at the front door, but
instead of more guests being ushered in, the Negro butler entered
with a letter on a silver salver. It was special delivery for Governor
Crittenden and bore the seal of the federal government. Will watched
as Uncle John examined the envelope suspiciously, turned it over as
though not wanting to open it, finally slitting it open and reading
quickly. His shoulders slumped, and he dropped it to his side. His
long, undertaker's face, which no one had ever called handsome, lost
its Christmas conviviality and returned to its habitual state of solem-
nity. He was about to excuse himself when Aunt Maria came up, took
the letter from his hand, read it and whispered something.

He held the letter up.

"You'd know about it sooner or later, Maria says," he said, looking at the guests who had closed in on him. "It's from the secretary
of war. My son George has been arrested again. The secretary informs
me that the president is not inclined to let him escape court-martial
this time."

He was not going to hide it. Not again. Everyone knew Maj.
George Crittenden's record, brave in battle but with too many brawls
and too many arrests. George's mother, Uncle John's first wife, Sarah
Lee, was a first cousin of Zach Taylor, which made George and Zach
cousins once removed. George had served under Zach in Mexico.
Zach knew his reputation for drinking as well as anyone and might
have shown a little more compassion for his kinsman. Perhaps he
decided it was time for a family lesson.

"Don't worry, John," said Jeff Davis, laying a hand on Uncle John's arm. "George will not be court-martialed. I'll see to it."

"I'll write the president," said Uncle John.

"Let me handle it," said Davis. "George is a good officer. He just likes Kentucky bourbon a little too much. It's hard to blame him for that. In any case, I want to see the charges. For all we know he's innocent."

Uncle John actually smiled at that. "It would be nice to know that George Crittenden is innocent of a drinking charge."

Some people chuckled. Davis looked at the nephew, a wink in the eye of his thespian's face. "He didn't drink any more than the rest of us at Monterrey – did he, Lieutenant? And it wasn't Kentucky bourbon."

The whole room laughed, the tension lifted.

Will liked Jeff Davis, who seemed to like him, too, though maybe it was just the family connection. He knew Davis no better than he knew Quitman, senior officers in Mexico who'd been far ahead of him and who now were important politicians, but before the evening was over Davis informed him that he would be bringing Mrs. Davis – the second Mrs. Davis – to Monmouth while Will was visiting.

The information was as strange as the invitation: no date for Will's visit had yet been either proposed or accepted. Something was afoot that he did not comprehend. It would be no great displacement for Davis since his plantation at Vicksburg was just up the Mississippi from Quitman's at Monmouth. But why would he want to come?

No one ever knew if Davis's intervention with Zach Taylor helped George Crittenden or not, but it couldn't have hurt. The story is that after Buena Vista Zach Taylor apologized to Davis: "My daughter, sir, was a better judge of men than I was."

George was cashiered, but soon reinstated, just a slap on the wrist for the man promoted for bravery in Mexico. Perhaps old Zach was moved by a direct appeal from the man who married his daughter, saved his life at Buena Vista, and paved the way for him to enter the White House, which makes for a pretty big debt.

In any case, George went on drinking and soon afterward was involved in a duel that grew out of insults during another drinking row. Both men's shots missed.

"Avoid insults," Uncle John had told his nephew during a walk along the Kentucky River years before. The young man had asked him about dueling.

"Argue against the man's argument, not against the man," said the uncle. It was sound advice that the nephew, like Cousin George, found easier given than taken.

# II

It was three months after the Christmas party that Lucien Hensley was finally ready to leave on reconnaissance to New Orleans. Will waited impatiently on the Shelbyville farm, run by his brother John Allen since Pa's murder, while Lucien arranged for an intern to come down from Cincinnati to care for his patients. Mrs. Quitman sent him a sweet note reaffirming her invitation and requesting he give her notice before leaving so she could invite the people she wanted to meet him.

Such attention from people he scarcely knew was a mystery, but a pleasant one. In society, he had no experience outside a few West Point cadet balls and an occasional soiree at Frankfort and later in Mexico City during the U.S. occupation. His adult life, all of it military, had been regimented and confined to men. But he had no reason to refuse the lady's courtesy. Bound for what he hoped would be a new civilian life in New Orleans, he looked forward to the visit and many more such invitations to follow.

Once Lucien had his affairs in order, Will wrote Mrs. Quitman with the proposed date for their departure from Louisville, arriving in Natchez four days later. She wrote back that the timing was perfect, that the weather would be changed for the better on the river and that of course Dr. Hensley was welcome at Monmouth as well, both guests encouraged to stay as long as they desired.

It was early spring by the time they were under way and an easy enough trip downriver. Paddle wheelers don't like rough weather and will put in when things get ugly, but their Ohio journey was smooth going on a swift current all the way from Louisville. They fell in with other whist players, making time flow right along with the river. The woods and rolling empty countryside along the Ohio were brilliant green from spring rains, turning to low marshland and mudflats as they neared the confluence with the Mississippi. They pulled in at Cairo and awaited a change of boat.

Once on the Mississippi, the landscape turned flat and unspectacular. The Ohio River is clear enough that from the deck you can drop bottles down to catch and drink the water, but no one would ever take a swig from the Mississippi, which would be like drinking sludge. The river is more sewer than river with great islands of trees, roots, and debris from the upriver towns floating along with the current. If a boat collides with a big log at night the collision is enough to knock you off your perch. Each day they spent a few hours walking the deck, getting their exercise.

Lucien Hensley was a man of science who believed that good health depended more on good sense than on good medicine. "Get out of the chair and into the air," he told his patients, and for four days they followed that advice on the steamboats, ending each whist game with a walk around the decks, whatever the weather. Born in Shelbyville, obtaining his medical degree at Cincinnati's Medical College of Ohio, Hensley was too talented for Shelbyville but stayed on for his mother, who'd died the year before. He was good company, not greatly gregarious for he preferred his medical books, but overall a fine travel companion and a decent enough whist partner, though nothing like the players Will had in Mexico.

They put in along the way at Cairo, Memphis, and Vicksburg, changing boats at Cairo from the *Eclipse* to the *Natchez*. In Memphis, they docked for the night and Will had a taste of a place that he'd never cared for. Like most Kentuckians, he had no place in his heart for Tennessee, but especially for a slave center like Memphis. They walked through the city before dinner, pausing by the slave pens, which abutted Auction Square, where soon he would be returning. The pens were empty, awaiting a new shipment up from New Orleans.

Arriving in Natchez, they were met by the Monmouth carriage. Natchez called itself the cultural capital of the South, but a ride through town showed a noisy, dusty jumble of bales, barrels, mules, and wagons, more a place of commerce than of culture. Like Memphis, it was a slave center, and the streets were alive with Negroes. Making their way up from the river, they left clamor and dust behind and soon found themselves in a silent green paradise of broad lawns, cypresses, and magnolias leading to great houses hidden down long canopied avenues. Behind those houses lay the cotton and sugarcane fields. It was a different world from anything in Kentucky. He was pleased at the invitation from the Quitmans, pleased to look into the heart of the Deep South.

"Remind me again of these people and why you have been invited," Lucien said as the carriage rolled along.

He'd told him before, but the doctor, who had little mind for society, wanted to hear it again.

"Governor Quitman was a general officer in Mexico, where I served under him. Mrs. Quitman made the invitation at Uncle John's Christmas party. She says there are people I should meet."

Hensley nodded, as if taking in information for a diagnosis. "Ah, yes, I believe I remember now. Quite mysterious, isn't it, since you have no idea who these people are or why you should be meeting them. Be careful, my young friend. They clearly want something."

"And what do I have to offer people like the Quitmans?"

"You'll be finding out soon enough, I imagine."

He laughed. "Are all doctors as wary as you?"

"Caution is not only a virtue in medicine."

"I know some generals who would disagree."

Lucien smiled.

It was late afternoon when they came to one more avenue off

the main road and after a few bends and curves Monmouth surged from the woods before them, its cornice and tall pillars breaking through the willows like a steamship from the river mists. A liveried slave came out, followed by Mrs. Quitman, the belle of Natchez, ravishing in white lace cinched in all the right places.

"How wonderful to see you again, suh – and this must be Doctah Hensley. Welcome to Monmouth, gentlemen!"

The story was that the Natchez belle was swept off her feet by the dashing young man from New York, who fell in love simultaneously with her and the South. Perhaps the plantation didn't hurt either. Will had no idea what had brought Quitman to Natchez, but understood, after gazing again on the former Miss Eliza Turner, why he had stayed.

A butler led them down the main hallway, past the salon, which already showed signs of activity. They glimpsed a second staircase, larger, grander, leading up to an inside balcony. On the far side of the salon, double doors opened onto a ballroom. They were taken up a rear set of stairs to their rooms in back, overlooking the plantation. A copse of cypresses shut out view of the fields just beyond the lawns, but they could see that the plantation stretched to the horizon.

"Hundreds, maybe thousands of slaves out there somewhere," muttered Lucien. "Nothing like it in Kentucky."

They had more than an hour to rest, wash, and dress for the evening, and came down shortly after six. A string quartet was playing, and tables were set up around the ballroom and on the enclosed veranda.

What was the occasion, he wondered? Or did they entertain at Monmouth every night? John Quitman was, after all, governor of the state. But so was Uncle John governor of Kentucky, and he could not remember musicians playing at Frankfort, perhaps because there was no ballroom in the house. In any case, Aunt Maria wasn't that fond of music, which she said interfered with good conversation.

Already the house was abuzz. Guests descended from their rooms, carriages dropped off passengers up from the city, and the good people of Natchez were ushered in to be met by the governor and his lady. Crinoline rustled and jewelry sparkled. Despite the bustle and conviviality, despite the confusion of being among people he did not know or know well, he somehow felt at the center of things. Lucien remarked on it.

Mrs. Quitman kept him close. People came up as they arrived, paying him more attention than he deserved at such a gathering. Cool drinks with bourbon were served, and guests moved freely from ballroom to salon to the veranda and lawns beyond. It was a lovely evening, the countryside still lighted by the sinking sun, the weather gentle, the chill of winter passed and the stifling heat of Mississippi summer not yet arrived.

Soon after the last guests had arrived, Mrs. Quitman took him by the hand and led him across the room toward a young woman he'd already remarked from a distance. Earlier, she'd come down the main staircase with two other women of similar but not quite so spectacular appearance in a great flurry of silk and satin that commanded, as intended, everyone's attention.

She was standing off with Jefferson Davis and his lady and a silver-haired gentleman in a military uniform, whom he did not immediately recognize. The group was deep in conversation. The man is her father, he thought as they approached, though he'd not seen him come down with the ladies. But, no – the man was swarthy and the lady pale. Surely he was not a suitor.

He bowed, the lady curtsied, and he touched Lucy Holcombe's soft hand for the first time. "So happy to meet you, sir," she said in an accent that was Southern, but not too much. Her eyes held his until he thought it best to look away.

It was how Cleopatra must have been, he thought as the other introductions were made, blue eyes and full red lips and jet black hair swept back in a severe coif, a deadly combination of red, black and blue, not the happiest of colors. She was composed and commanding, even in the company of officers and high officials, a young woman who understood the power of her gifts. Golden dangles fell from her ears and were matched by a pendant hung from black velvet at her neck. She turned her attention from one man to the other as they spoke, each speaking as if desiring her attention alone. When she spoke she was bold and direct, offering strong opinions quite unlike anything he'd ever heard from a young woman.

The man beside her was introduced as Gen. Narciso Lopez, short and bull-chested in a well-tailored uniform that carried Spanish decorations. He'd heard of Lopez, of course. Southern newspapers were full of accounts of his exploits, a former Spanish general who'd turned against Spain for mysterious reasons to fight for the liberation of Cuba. He'd been put on trial by the U.S. government for a previous endeavor in Cuba and was said to be preparing a second one. The Southern press beat the drums for him, urging him to take Cuba, strengthen slavery and the American South. The young man searched his memory, recalling that Governor Quitman was somehow associated with him.

"You will of course join us when we are in Havana," Lopez remarked to the lady when the conversation resumed.

"We will come, General, of course we will come."

"We will *all* come," said Jeff Davis, taking Will's arm. "Isn't that right, Lieutenant?"

He nodded. "By all means. On to Cuba! It's what the army has been saying since Mexico City."

"I must speak to President Taylor," said Davis, smiling, squeezing his arm, pleasing the young man with his comradely familiarity.

Governor Quitman and some others came up to join them, Will recognizing one of the men, though doubting he was recognized in return. It was Gen. William Jenkins Worth, commander of Lt. Crittenden's 1st Division, 5th Infantry, ordered to take Casa Mata and Molino del Rey in the battle for Mexico City, the slaughter where so many comrades fell. A man of severe aspect, Worth was not in uniform but still formidable in black frock and white muttonchops and stiff military bearing. He was not a tall man, but known to be, as is said of some generals, "tall in the saddle."

"I believe we have met before," Worth said with a slight bow, "though perhaps not formally."

So he *was* recognized. Another pleasure. They both remembered the incident. Was Worth one of those invited for him to meet? But why would he be?

A second man was introduced as Sen. Laurent Sigur, owner of the New Orleans *Delta-News*, the newspaper where James Freaner, his whist-playing friend from Mexico, worked as a reporter. Could Freaner be here as well? But Freaner was not the sort to be found in such sparkling company. Sigur was introduced as "Senator," though to which senate he belonged was not specified. He would turn out to be one of Lopez's principal backers. The others in the group, all Cubans, were part of Lopez's New Orleans entourage.

He followed the amiable chatter, saying as little as possible, nodding appropriately, learning from the conversation as he got his bearings, glancing at Lucy Holcombe from time to time and finding her always ready to return his glance. He searched the room for Lucien, finding him – as he often did at social gatherings – surrounded by people pointing out their ailments.

As the conversation proceeded, lubricated by good Kentucky bourbon, he came to understand that this was no routine Monmouth gathering; that the illustrious assemblage had been summoned only after he'd communicated his travel plans to Eliza Quitman. Some had come only short distances, up from Natchez or, like Jefferson Davis, downriver from his plantation near Vicksburg, but others had come longer distances – Lopez, Sigur, and the Cubans from New Orleans; General Worth and the Holcombes from Texas.

If it had been arranged as a courtesy to Uncle John, it was a spectacular one. He would write his uncle about it.

"We will celebrate on the Malecon," Lopez was saying, in his soft Spanish accent. "There is a bandstand on Plaza de la Punta at the entrance to Havana Harbor. We will engage Havana's finest musicians to play as we dance."

"My dear General, how poetic you make it sound!" said Lucy. "I shall write it down in my notebook tonight." She laid her hand on Will's sleeve. "And perhaps this handsome gentleman with the famous name will offer me the pleasure of a dance."

Will bowed and offered the lady his arm.

"Oh, not now, sir, later, I mean."

He must have worn a puzzled look, for the others laughed.

Davis, ever courtly beside his young wife – he'd married again after a long period of mourning following the death of Sarah Taylor – did most of the talking. He'd recently returned from Cuba where he'd been treated rudely by the Spaniards, and he did not hide his antipathy toward them. Lopez listened and watched Davis, but paid even more attention to Miss Holcombe. Sigur mostly listened, nodding his approval. Worth kept his eyes on Davis. Worth had been Davis's military superior in Mexico, but saw, as did most people, that there was more to Davis than his military career. As for Worth, there was probably less.

A butler with a gong announced dinner. Miss Holcombe took the hands of Lopez and Worth and joined them together. "Our success is sealed tonight, gentlemen, is it not? With these two generals in command and with Governor Quitman and Senator Davis tending to affairs at home, how can we fail?"

How odd, he thought. She cannot be past twenty years old, is a guest at Monmouth and yet stands among high officials and general officers offering advice and encouragement for an operation not only audacious but illegal!

How can *we* fail, she said?

But what is her interest in the business?

She turned to him, offering her arm. "And perhaps you, sir, will be kind enough to escort me to the dining room."

# III

Of course she'd agreed to come to Monmouth with her mother and sister! She adored Monmouth. She adored the Quitmans.

Anyway, she would do anything to get out of East Texas, which she already loathed. She'd met General Lopez on a previous visit to Monmouth, and the idea of that magnificent man taking Cuba back from Spain had been with her ever since. How glorious, she thought, her mind going to *Ivanhoe*, which she'd first read at the Philadelphia seminary and still kept close at hand. Brave warriors going off to do the grand thing. Exactly so!

"Eliza Quitman wants you to come, especially," Maman had said, as if there was any chance she'd let them go without her. Daddy had done everything to make Wyalusing a lovely home, but unfortunately had built it in East Texas.

It had not been difficult for Lucy to find out why Mrs. Quitman wanted her "especially": There was a young man she was to meet. Lucy must have frowned at her mother's mention of it. Eugenia more or less understood what her younger daughter thought of young men, for she quickly added: "It has something to do with General Lopez."

Lucy Holcombe did not like young men. She found them short on taste and education and long on posing and mooning – in short, *pas serieux*; in short, boring. Not that she'd known many young men, certainly none at the Moravian Seminary in Pennsylvania and none she cared to remember at home in La Grange, Tennessee. In their brief time in Marshall, after being required to leave La Grange against their better judgment, she'd encountered quite enough idiocy among the young squires of East Texas to fortify her distaste. Her sister Anna Eliza had engaged herself to a Tennessean before they left for Marshall, but Anna was two years older than Lucy and not at all as picky. If she had been, would she have accepted someone like Elkanah Greer?

It was Lucy's opinion that it took older men to appreciate young women as people, not just objects of desire some of which came equipped with handsome dowries. The young men of Marshall regarded her as they might regard a young mare being sized up for their best stallion. When she tried out a political opinion on them, something for example on the doings in the White House since Zach Taylor and the Whigs had moved in, they looked at her as if to say, "What business is that of a woman?" As for literature, which along with politics was Lucy's driving passion, they knew nothing at all. Most young men she'd met had never read a novel. She had no intention of talking down to them and so determined not to talk to them at all.

It was to be her third visit to Monmouth, which was certainly not New Orleans or Philadelphia, but neither was it Marshall. The Quitmans had done their best to bring culture and refinement to the lower Mississippi and always had interesting guests to meet. And there was Governor Quitman himself, who in addition to being a distinguished soldier and politician, was a scholar, an educated New Yorker who cared enough about literature to have gone to Louisville to meet Dickens when he came through. They both were reading *Dombey and Son*, serialized in *Harper's,* and had a lively discussion of it on her last visit to Monmouth – when they were not talking about Lopez and Cuba, that is.

Eliza Quitman, with a gentle smile of feminine complicity, had taken Lucy aside a day before the other guests arrived. Neither Eugenia, who had no interest in politics, nor Anna Eliza, already engaged to be married, had an interest in the Cuba enterprise or the young man in question, subjects which Mrs. Quitman preferred to discuss in tête-à-tête with Lucy. The young man was the nephew of John

Jordan Crittenden of Kentucky, she explained as they sat alone in the drawing room. He was invited to Monmouth to meet General Lopez, though he didn't yet know it. The Quitmans had met him at Yuletide during a visit with Governor Crittenden in Frankfort. Both Senator Davis and Governor Quitman believed young Crittenden to be the ideal recruit for their endeavor, not only because he was a West Point graduate and veteran of the Mexican War, but because his name would be important for attracting other young veterans of Mexico. General Worth particularly remembered Lieutenant Crittenden from Mexico.

The young man had left the army and was on his way to a civilian post in New Orleans, said Eliza. The hope was that Lucy, with her enthusiasm for Governor Quitman, General Lopez, and their project (she did not mention Lucy's other advantages), could help persuade Lieutenant Crittenden to alter his plans.

A surprisingly pleasant young man, Lucy reflected as she and Will entered the dining room together – handsome, courteous, commanding in appearance but modest in demeanor, quite the perfect combination! In the salon he'd stood listening, observing, nodding, smiling, never interrupting, exceedingly well educated, well trained, she thought. They'd locked eyes several times until something – shyness, she supposed, or inexperience with women, caused him to look away.

She, however, had not looked away, but examined him closely: pale blue eyes, a sensual (if somewhat petulant) mouth, lock of sandy hair falling across a high forehead. Taller and better formed than the others, he was dressed simply enough in dark frock coat and tie, but maintained himself so still and so erect that he stood out even among the more elegantly attired senators, governors, and generals. Such carriage, she knew, came only from family and education.

Perhaps she'd stared too long, but she was quite dumbfounded. The young man was exactly what she was looking for – not for herself, of course, but for her story. She'd told no one (except her sister Anna Eliza who knew everything), but she had a novel firmly in mind, a novel about the coming adventure: about Narciso Lopez and the taking of Cuba from degenerate Spain, finally joining Cuba, the marvelous "sugar island," to the Southern United States, where it belonged.

As they circled the table seeking places and waiting for the governor and Mrs. Quitman to return from making goodbyes, his heart gave a little leap when he found himself seated next to her. His eyes swept the table. They would be twenty-two at dinner, ten to a side with the host and hostess at each end. Portraits of great men hung the walls, and his eyes went to one in particular: an oil painting of a white stallion reared on his hind legs, with Gen. John A. Quitman, unmistakable with his ring of flaxen beard and raised sword, firmly in the saddle. Chapultepec Castle jutted up from the Mexico City woods in the background. A Mexican flag lay trampled under the horse's feet. The scene was still vivid in his mind.

Dinner was served with great ceremony; plates and crystal were constantly changed, wines decanted, a servant designated to brush crumbs from the tablecloth onto a silver salver between courses. If Natchez lacked the elegance of New Orleans it was not the fault of the governor of Mississippi and his lady. Two glittering chandeliers each with several dozen candles lighted the room. The talk was lively, stimulated by the wines, and the din made it impossible to talk to anyone but your neighbor. He was too polite to have ignored the large, garrulous lady on his right, but she, fortunately, was engaged with the gentleman on her right. He could give full attention to the young lady on his left.

"I understand you are on your way to New Orleans, Lieutenant," she said as a creamy, chilled vichyssoise was served. "You are a fortunate man."

"You have been to New Orleans, Miss Holcombe?"

"Indeed I have, and you will do me the honor to call me Lucy, sir."

"If you will call me Will."

"That I will, Will." She laughed. "Or perhaps – that I shall, Will, is better put."

It was a happy, infectious laugh, the first time he'd heard it.

"Tell me about New Orleans."

"It is a place I would die to live. But alas . . ."

He looked down the table to see Lucien in conversation with a lady pointing to her shoulder.

"*Alas* . . . ?"

"I'm afraid there's no chance for that – but we visit often."

"With your mother and sister?"

"My sister, Anna Eliza, is to be married, you know. We shall come to New Orleans for the fittings."

"And the wedding?"

"I'm afraid will be in Tennessee."

"You are from Tennessee?"

"Yes. But Daddy has taken us to East Texas, where we have a plantation."

He racked his mind, but could not remember ever being seated next to so ravishing a creature. The sleeves of her dark silk dress ended at the elbows, leaving her lower arms bare, and as he could not stay constantly turned to regard her directly, he watched her hands with their fine nails and rings that looked like onyx. Turning slightly, he followed her arms up and found her staring at him in a manner that, after a moment, caused him to look away.

He held my gaze a little longer this time, she thought, fully aware of her effect on young men. She posed her spoon as the butlers came for their plates.

She smiled at him. "I'd do anything to get away."

"Ah," he said, looking at her, and this time did not look away.

"You have found lodgings in New Orleans?" she asked after a moment.

"No, ma'am. I'm on a visit of acquaintance with Dr. Hensley, who sits across from us next to the lady who I believe is your mother and who perhaps has a problem with her shoulder. But I have every intention of remaining in New Orleans, as does Lucien."

Her mind was drifting. If he joined the mission to Cuba she would have found her protagonist, her Ivanhoe. Lopez and Worth were far too old for the role.

The butlers came bearing plates of roast duck, succotash, and mashed potatoes, plates prepared at several rolling tables set against the wall.

"You have left the military then?"

"I have. I carry a letter of introduction to the customhouse in New Orleans."

"And your service to the country?"

The question stopped him. He looked over and saw her eyes sparkling with light from the candles. Was she mocking him? The woman was magic. He felt oddly short-circuited.

"Perhaps at the customhouse I can be of some small service . . ."

"Perhaps you would prefer to be of a larger service?"

"That I have been, ma'am, Miss . . . Miss Lucy . . . for eight years."

She bit ravenously into the duck, soft and juicy with the kind of crisp skin she loved, skin obviously plucked with skill and care.

She saw his discomposure. She was used to male discomposure. She set down her fork, sipped wine, and posed the glass, touching his hand gently, just for a moment, a natural feminine gesture, almost inadvertent, to show she was not chiding, just interested, gently probing.

"It is my view, sir, that one's service to one's country never ends."

What for her may have been a natural feminine gesture for him was a jolt as if struck by a bolt. His hand still tingled and he must have colored for he felt others looking their way. How long had they been watching? Governor Quitman was leaning toward Mrs. Davis on his left, whispering to her but looking at Lucy with a rare smile on his lips.

It took a moment for him to respond.

"I believe you are right about that, Miss Lucy."

The truth is that as sophisticated as they were – Lucy had traveled and studied a good deal for someone still but twenty years old – they were equally naïve in matters of the heart. Lucy could say she didn't like young men because she'd never really known one, certainly not during her formative years at the Moravian Girls' Seminary, which she preferred in conversation to transplant to nearby Philadelphia from its actual location in Bethlehem, Pennsylvania.

Gentle, vigorous folk who'd opened the school in 1742 and for a century dedicated themselves to teaching young girls to develop mind, body, and spirit, the Moravians were known for Spartan living. For Lucy, the seminary was no less than an awakening, taking her away from all that had been dull and dreary about life in La Grange, Tennessee, and exposing her to a world of new people, ideas and interests, including Cuba, for the Moravians had established a mission on the island.

She'd flourished, but it was a strictly feminine flourishing, devoid of men other than the teachers, who were mostly monks. Days started at five and ended seventeen hours later. If the Moravians gave her a passion for life, it was a distant, German kind of passion, more of mind than of body. She knew nothing of physical passion.

As for him, he knew nothing at all of young women. Eight years as a cadet and soldier had taken him away from mixed society. Beyond the cantina girls of Mexico and a short friendship with a well-born Mexican girl in Mexico City that ended with the U.S. occupation, he was unschooled in the ways of young women.

In short, in different ways, both were susceptible to the encounter arranged for them by their elders at Monmouth. If some guests, including General Lopez, snuck discreet glances their way as dinner went on, they were laboratory glances, the kind that scientists sneak at caged mice from time to time to see if the experiment is proceeding according to plan.

# IV

Dinner over, the women retired to the salon while Governor Quitman led the men onto the veranda for cigars, coffee, and brandy. Night had fallen, lanterns were aglow, and a log fire was lit to drive the chill from the night air. The room had been altered since earlier, chairs brought back from the walls to place around the hearth. The governor's writing table and highboy abutted one of the walls, another was taken with tall bookshelves. The exterior side of the room consisted of two French doors and windows that could be opened or closed according to the weather. Thrown open before dinner, the doors, but not the windows, were now closed.

Outside, the crickets were in full song. It was a friendly, open, masculine space, one to which the governor was accustomed to repair for intimate, postprandial, masculine conversation. The cigars were Cuban, the brandy French, and the demitasse strong. As they sat in a large semicircle, Will tried to concentrate on the conversation, which, given his state of mind, was not easy. The talk was convivial, and with brandy following on wines at dinner, spontaneous and good-humored, or as Governor Quitman liked to put it for his Cajun guests, *à bâtons rompus*.

After snifters were filled a second time, the governor sought to corral the talk, calling on his Cuban guests to speak of the challenges facing their country. Each of them, Cirilo Villaverde, Miguel Teurbe Tolón, Ambrosio José Gonzales, and Domingo Goicuría by name, was a prominent member of a group called the Club of Havana. Each man was dignified and impressive, eloquent in English, explaining briefly but with bravura his people's hard history under Spain's iron hand and their desire to be liberated. Each man was an exile and faced arrest and execution for treason should he return to the island. General Lopez hung on every word, the look of stern professional approval on his face never changing.

None of them spoke of independence, though surely the desire for independence must be as strong as that for annexation. Listening to them, the young man recalled Major Desmoulins at West Point, who'd tutored him in French, whom he'd helped to translate Napoleon's memoirs and who insisted that Texas could be the model. Texas declared independence from Mexico and became a republic only to be annexed ten years later in return for having its debts assumed by Washington and being admitted to the Union as a slave state. Why not a similar arrangement for Cuba, argued the major?

Seated next to Senator Sigur, across the semicircle from General Lopez, whose eyes drifted inscrutably to his own from time to time, Will felt dreamily addled, glancing over to Lucien, his one link to reality. More than anything, he desired to bolt out the door and escape into the freedom of the night. He needed time to organize the ocean of new thoughts and feelings sweeping over him. He wanted to jettison smoke and talk and brandy and Cubans and inhale the sweet scents of the grass and cotton and commune with the crickets hiding in fields. He thought of searching for Lucy to ask her to dance with him in the moonlight.

Never before had he spent an evening in conversation with such a woman. Was she one of those invited to meet him? But why? What had he to offer such a woman? What was it all about? He was not intimidated by rank and high position, how could he be when he'd been around Uncle John and Kentucky political society for so long? But previously his role had been as a junior, as an onlooker or subordinate. At Monmouth they'd welcomed him as an equal. It was a mystery.

Postprandial ended, Lopez, accompanied by Sigur, came up to

ask if he might have the privilege of calling on him in New Orleans. He assented immediately – why wouldn't he? It was an honor. He advised the general to contact him through the customhouse. Sigur, a man of oppressive dignity, said something, but Will caught only the word "Freaner."

"And how is Freaner these days, Senator?" He'd learned that Sigur was a member of the Louisiana State Senate.

"Bored," replied the Creole, who spoke in a French Louisiana accent. "After Mexico, he needs another war to cover, Lieutenant." He smiled and glanced at Lopez. "Perhaps General Lopez and General Worth will provide him with one."

Will smiled with the others.

Unobtrusively, in his scientific way, Lucien Hensley had observed everything, beginning to end. Back in their room, in night-shirts preparing for sleep in real beds for the first time in days, he recreated the evening, describing the many expressions he'd observed on his friend's face as though diagnosing the symptoms of a disease.

"The young lady has a way with her – has a way with *you*, does she not, my friend?"

He didn't want to hear it, wanted to sleep, wanted to sleep it off, but Lucien droned on. Governor Quitman, he opined, was the mastermind of the operation. Jeff Davis might have done it, but Davis, unlike Quitman, had put his military career behind him. Lopez would serve under Worth.

"And what operation would that be?" Will inquired.

"Good God, man, were we at the same party? These people are bent at making war with Spain over Cuba. Surely you understand that."

"I suspect you are right about that," he answered dreamily, his mind on Lucy. "But I understand that Quitman is done with the military as well. I believe he is governor of the State of Mississippi – or am I mistaken?"

"The one thing does not exclude the other. Did you not hear

him at the end – probably not with that moony look you had on your face. I thought at moments we were in Havana, not Natchez, especially after dinner. I would not be surprised if Quitman took charge of the military operation himself, pushing Worth aside."

"I am impressed. And all the time I thought you were talking about gout and lumbago."

"Perhaps I had fewer diversions than you. One gentleman did have a rather bad case of the gout, but that did not prevent him from informing me that it was a surprise to find Jefferson Davis at Monmouth. Apparently the governor and senator of Mississippi are not close."

"But I saw them together in Frankfort."

"They were on a mission."

"And what mission would that be?

"*You*, my young friend. Davis is here because of you. As is the young lady."

The statement brought him back from the romantic mists.

"What complete rot."

Lucien was up on an elbow, looking through the candlelight at his friend. "Do you still not understand why you are here?"

Of course he did. Respect for Uncle John. Had his uncle not visited Monmouth himself? Whigs and Democrats were cooking something up. Was that not the reason for their meetings in Frankfort at Christmastime? Why should he not play his role?

"I see you are not responding," said Lucien, still eying him through the candle, "so perhaps I will assist you. You, my young friend, are being recruited."

"*Recruited . . . ?*"

"Recruited for their mission to Cuba."

Now he came up on an elbow. "Lucien, you are hallucinating. How could anyone think I'd be interested in such an adventure?"

"My friend, the entire evening was arranged for your benefit. They were subtle about it, nothing like a direct solicitation, nothing so crass, but they kept their eyes on you like the fatted calf. You might have caught on had you been a little less intoxicated with the young lady. Or was it the bourbon? Or both, probably. I tried to catch some of your conversation with her but could not with the infernal Mrs. Holcombe talking so much about her joints. Did she say nothing directly to you about Cuba?"

"Miss Lucy? She did not. She merely asked if I was finished with service to my country."

"And you responded . . . ?"

"Something about the customs office, I think."

"She will be returning to the subject, believe me."

"You seemed distrait after dinner," said Anna Eliza, "hardly adding a word to the conversation. It is not like you."

"Ladies' conversation can be a bit boring, don't you think?"

"I don't think so at all. I quite enjoyed listening to Mrs. Quitman and found Mrs. Davis interesting as well. With the plantation at Vicksburg they are almost neighbors with the Quitmans."

"Yes," said Lucy, who was busy writing in her notebook under light from the candles. "I like Mrs. Davis. I believe she has helped Senator Davis recover from the loss of Sarah Taylor."

"Surprising that she'd not been a guest at Monmouth before."

The girls occupied a bedroom at the end of the front hall, just off the main staircase, far from the rear bedrooms where the gentlemen lodged. Their room was part of a suite opening onto Eugenia's room, and Maman had slipped in a short time before to wish them good night, ask them to douse their flame and make them promise not to wake her in the morning. After such an evening she intended to sleep late, recommending that her daughters do the same.

None of the ladies was in a hurry to return to East Texas.

Like the gentlemen in the rear bedrooms, the girls lay on twin beds separated by a nightstand and a candle, which was extinguished after Lucy laid aside her notebook. It had been a full evening that ran past the usual bedtime for girls more used to the rigors of seminary life than to high Mississippi society.

"You didn't have much to say either," said Lucy.

"I'm not the talker in the family, nor the writer."

Lucy pulled the comforter up to her chin.

Anna Eliza rolled toward her sister trying to make her out, but her vision had not yet adjusted to the dark. Though two years older and, according to many the prettier sister, Anna Eliza was also shier. It was rare that she challenged her sister.

"You seemed to have eyes tonight only for the young man."

"Indeed – *what* young man?"

"Lucy, don't be coy. I know you too well."

She rolled onto her stomach and did not answer. Her mind was in too turbulent a state to be cross-examined.

"Lucy, do answer, please. What have you been so madly writing if not about the young man?"

"You have the wrong idea, dear Anna," she said, her voice muffled in the pillow. "I have simply been asked by Mrs. Quitman to help make the gentleman's stay at Monmouth a pleasant one."

Anna could not stifle a titter. "I do believe he's helping to make your stay a pleasant one as well."

"You exaggerate, you know."

"I don't believe that I do. I've observed you for too many years. You were, dear Lucy, radiant as seldom before."

"How you exaggerate! And even if I was – why not? I took some wine. It was a splendid evening. You looked quite radiant yourself."

"I imagine my complexion was several shades lighter than yours."

With that, Lucy flipped over onto her back. "Just what do you mean by *that?*"

"I've never seen you with such high color – not even on cold winter mornings at the seminary."

"Anna, please stop," she said, annoyed. "How can you reproach me for being cordial to the gentleman? Isn't that how the monks taught us?"

Later, when he knew more, knew everything, he could reconstruct:

Governor Quitman was brought to Uncle John's Christmas party by Jefferson Davis with the intention of inviting him to Monmouth to sign on to their Cuba enterprise. They were in search of a West Point officer with experience in Mexico who had left the army. General Worth suggested Crittenden, whom he remembered from an incident in Mexico City. The name Crittenden appealed to all of them.

Uncle John knew nothing of any of it. Had he known, things would have turned out differently.

Worth's presence at Monmouth was not because he and Quitman were close (they were united in Freemasonry but had been fierce military rivals in Mexico), but because Worth had agreed to lead the expedition, which Quitman, as Mississippi governor, could not. Worth had given his word to the Club of Havana, a Freemason organization of white plantation owners and other prominent Cubans that feared Spain would soon free its slaves, as France and Britain had recently done. The Club looked on emancipation as disaster for the plantations and for the island. The Dessalines slave massacre of whites in Haiti was known to every Creole in Cuba.

The Cubans were present because they backed Lopez. Sigur was there because in addition to being a Freemason and member of the Club of Havana, he was Lopez's chief financier.

Finally, Lucy Holcombe was present because Eliza Quitman had invited her oldest friend, Eugenia Holcombe, to the party. Mrs. Quitman could hardly have invited her oldest friend's daughter without inviting her oldest friend.

# PART TWO

✳

# ORIGINS

# V

None of it would have come about without West Point, which was Uncle John's doing. As a boy, the nephew's school grades weren't bad, but neither were they up there with the girls, who tended to have less interest in getting back into the fields each day. In any case, girls didn't go to West Point nor did that many boys from Kentucky, who preferred farming to moving to New York for four years to learn how to fight Indians, which most of them thought they knew how to do anyway.

The idea came up when Uncle John came over from Frankfort for Pa's funeral. It wasn't that he paid more attention to Will than to the others during the arrangements, but that Will seemed to need more comforting than the others. Ma said he hadn't spoken a word since news came that Pa was killed at Hawkins's dry goods store. Will was ten years old the summer of '33, and Ma said he took Pa's death hardest because of his age.

It was after supper the day after the funeral that he took his nephew by the arm and said, let's take a walk. They headed down the road toward Shelbyville, the same road he'd ridden in on from Frankfort two days earlier dressed all in black, legs pumping down on the white horse like steam pistons. John Allen, Will's older brother, had spied him first and his yelps brought everyone running in from the hemp fields and out from the house.

"Let's talk about it, Nephew," he said in that reasonable way of his. It was still hot after supper as they set out; there'd been showers, and the fields were steaming. Locusts were chirping and a few fireflies already at work. "It's hard for me, too, you know; as hard to lose a brother as to lose a father."

Will wondered about that, but wasn't going to argue. It was as good way as any to start. The boy had let the others talk for two days because he knew if he started in he would start blubbering, a damnable thing for a boy already past ten. Even his sisters held it in. With his uncle it was just easier.

"It's not fair, Uncle. What did Pa ever do to John Waring? He hardly even knew the man."

"Life isn't fair," he said. "It's our job to make it fairer."

"Won't bring Pa back."

"No, but my brother did his duty: testified against a horse thief. Waring will hang for the crime."

That was Uncle John, a man of law and order. He'd left college to study law and never regretted it. The law was the best foundation for politics, he said, the business of which is making laws.

They were about a half mile down the road under the beech trees when he told his uncle he'd decided to become a soldier.

Not a word. Uncle John just kept on walking.

"Now, where'd you get that idea?" he said after a while.

"Just came."

He always walked with a stick, and the boy saw that he'd taken his Pa's favorite stick from the wooden butter churn by the door.

"Well," he said, looking down at him, "it's true we've had soldiers in the family: Your grandpa, Major John Crittenden, served under General Washington. On your mother's side there was Colonel John Allen, killed at the battle of River Raisin, War of 1812, killed because of an incompetent commander, James Wilkinson, a traitor, a criminal, like his friend Aaron Burr. With the academy at West Point there's no longer any excuse for military incompetence. My son George graduates this year. Do you want to go to West Point?"

Before the boy could answer, his uncle stopped and took his arm. "If your grades are up, that is."

They'd walked a mile down the road before turning back. Uncle John had made the same walk with John Allen, the oldest boy, who would take over the farm with Pa gone, and would make it again with Henry Jr. before leaving. He'd have to wait to make it with Tommy, the baby. But Will knew that his walk was special: If he kept his grades up he'd be going to West Point.

"I was destined for politics," he said. "I knew it and my father knew it and always supported me. I like the clash of ideas, the clash of good minds. You, Nephew, on both sides, have military blood, the clash of swords. It was never my choice, but it is a necessary and honorable profession."

Before the boy could agree, his uncle stopped again.

"*Why* do you want to be a soldier, Nephew?"

"*Why?*"

"That is the question."

"To fight the enemy, Uncle."

"Who is the enemy?"

The answer came in an instant. "Whoever challenges you is the enemy. John Waring is the enemy. Pa should have killed him first."

"*Killed him first . . ?* Then it would be your Pa who was hanged."

"Kill him in a duel, in a fair fight. Not a stab in the back."

The silence, except for the locusts, crept back in. His uncle stared down hard at him. They resumed walking.

"I hate dueling, Nephew," he said, "hate it like the plague. There was an affair involving two colleagues in Congress, Graves and Cilley. Graves challenged Cilley and asked me to be a witness to their duel. I turned him down. He implored me as a fellow Whig and Kentuckian. Finally, I agreed."

He fell silent, and the boy listened to the tapping of his stick.

"I shall regret that decision until the end of my days."

He was walking faster now, speeding up to keep pace with his thoughts, to keep pace with the stick that was poling him ahead. The boy looked up at him and could almost see the wheels of his mind turning.

"There was no animosity between those two men. The insult involved a third party, a New York newspaper publisher, Webb, a scoundrel. Manipulated the whole thing to get at Cilley, a New Englander. Said abolitionists like him were marrying their daughters off to Negroes. Cilley denounced Webb for the lie, and Graves interceded for Webb. He had no reason to do so. Those two men had no quarrel with each other – a perfect illustration of the insanity of the thing."

He fell silent again. They went on a good fifty more yards before the boy realized his uncle was reliving the duel in his mind.

"Uncle?"

"Yes, yes, I'm coming to it. I've not talked about it since, but I want you to know the truth about this business. Dueling is illegal in the capital so they met in Maryland. Used rifles at fifty yards. Hit Cilley in an artery and he bled to death. Graves was a marksman. Cilley had no chance. They missed the first two shots and should have stopped but Graves insisted on going on. No more than an excuse for cold-blooded murder. He should have been hanged."

Suddenly he pulled up and grabbed the boy by the arm. He didn't mean to hurt him, but the grip was surprisingly tight.

"Let me tell you something, Nephew: Violence is part of the culture down there, a culture of cotton and slavery – and yes, dueling – that they would spread all the way to the Pacific if we let them."

"But, Uncle, you said Graves was from Kentucky."

"I'm ashamed to say that he was. He never returned to Congress. Thrown out. Good riddance."

His best friend was Jude Freeman, born on the Shelbyville farm the same day he was born, May 31, 1823. At the time, he was known simply as Jude.

There was something predestined about the two boys. Josie, a handsome Negro woman, was brought into the big house to work during her pregnancy and Ma taught her to read. Josie was lightning quick at everything she did and when Ma saw that Josie shared her piety and already knew scripture from the Negro services, a bond was formed. Ma had particular feelings about slavery and passed them on to her children. When both women gave birth on the same day at the same time, it was a sign the bond would extend to the boys as well. Josie chose the name Jude, which means "in praise of the Lord."

Jude was tough as a mule and didn't spend much time thinking about being a slave. When they were nine they discovered a little lake hidden in the woods about two miles north of the farm and began sneaking away to fish. Jude's father, Elias, was illiterate, but Josie could read and soon had Jude reading. It's illegal to teach slaves to read, but it wasn't a law anyone bothered much with in Kentucky.

When Pa started his bagging and rope business the boys worked together in the sheds. At sewing, Jude was the best – faster and cleverer with his hands even than the women. Kentucky was never a cotton or rice state, wasn't the Deep South. There were no plantations in Kentucky, no need to float down to New Orleans looking for slaves of a particular tribe or region of Africa that you knew would be good in the rice or cotton fields. Kentucky needed farm labor, and so owners looked for healthy people who would exchange honest work for a decent life. Families were kept together, some paid their slaves, and manumission was common.

"Don't bring your pole."

It was a muggy, mid-summer Kentucky day of '41, the kind of day you're happy to be working in the shade of the sheds. Will had come over from Cloverport, where he'd gone to live with his brothers and sisters after Ma married Col. John Murray of Cloverport a few years after Pa's death. He was working on the farm that summer for his brother John Allen and awaiting the letter that would decide his fate. He'd crept up behind him and stood a moment watching his flying fingers. Jude could spin hemp fibers into yarn and make yarn into rope and bags faster than any two people, maybe three.

Jude understood. They'd been to the lake maybe a hundred times over the years, but never without poles. Jude knew what the letter said before Will told him. And he had his own surprise.

They trekked through the woods without a word, Indian file along the path of matted grass and pine needles they'd worn themselves. They carried hemp bags and checked on the wild blueberries and raspberries they'd pick on the way back. They both had something to tell but were in no hurry.

"I know what you're going to say," Jude said when they reached the lake and flopped in the shade of a sassafras tree.

He was a big boy, bigger even than Will. Elias was probably the biggest slave in Shelby County and Jude showed every sign of outgrowing his father. As boys, they'd wrestled for fun, both knowing it was more than just fun. They didn't hurt each other until Elias decided it was time to learn boxing. He made gloves out of hemp, and a good hook or jab would leave some blood. They'd get mad but then start laughing. Will reckoned he hurt Jude more than the other way around for Jude's heart was not in the thing. He didn't mind losing, at least not to his friend.

Will's grin didn't hide much. "I've been accepted."

Jude punched him. "Did you ever doubt it?"

"Uncle John helped."

"G'wan – you'd have made it anyway."

He looked away. "I'm going to miss you, you know."

Jude was quiet for a while after that. They were back on their elbows under the sassafras, wishing suddenly they had their poles, something to talk about that made it easier. Boys keep from crying through bluster, and he'd violated the code. His eyes watered up. He deeply loved Jude but hated showing it. When he looked back Jude was looking away. He didn't want to embarrass his friend.

"I'm leaving too," Jude said after a while.

Will knew, but wanted to hear it from him.

"John Allen agreed on manumission for all of us, but Ma and Pa won't go. Mary Jane's too little."

"They're better off here."

Jude glanced up at him but said nothing.

"What's your plan?"

The hot, humid weather was a drug, slowing the heartbeat, pulling down on your eyelids, slowing the mind to a crawl. The still water of the lake was hypnotizing. Everything wanted to sleep except the insects. Water bugs flitted. A dragonfly, frantic from the glint off the water, bounced along like a skipping stone. Tadpoles shimmied and wriggled under the surface, anxious to grow up and take their place with their elders on a sunny lily pad.

It was a big decision for a Negro to strike out, understanding the risk of never coming home, of going where you didn't know a soul and were easy prey for bounty hunters. Negroes were free in the North, but that didn't mean they were welcome. States like Indiana had border guards to make sure they stayed away. White bounty hunters roamed the north looking for runaway slaves. It was an easy matter to tear up a freeman's papers and send him downriver, back into slavery.

Suddenly he sat up. "You read about those riots in Cincinnati? Those were all freemen. Damn Black Laws! They hate us up there more than here."

He was mad, rare for him. He wasn't a boy anymore. Little crows' feet were etched where his face had always been smooth. A fine beard was growing. They were talking about things they'd never talked about before. Black Laws in states like Ohio were an abomination, restricting the freedom of black freemen. It was their first time at the lake as men.

"Stay here then, stay where you're wanted. Stay with your people. Stay with John Allen. Stay where I know where you are."

"It is God's will."

He turned away so Jude wouldn't see him frown. He hated the whole business of God's will. Why was it when their ma's were both religious and they'd read and recited the verses together every day as children, why had it stuck with Jude and not with him? Jude still read his Bible. Everything had been the same for them, but nothing had stuck for Will.

"You need a plan."

"I have a plan."

"Which is . . . ?"

"New Orleans."

"You're going *south*?"

He was scarcely listening. "New Orleans is different. Saw a case in the paper – maybe you didn't see it. Bounty hunter stole a freeman's papers and got caught. They sent the bounty hunter to jail, not the freeman. A lot of New Orleans people have Negro blood. They've banded together. Call themselves gens de couleur."

Will laughed. "So when I come down to see you we'll speak French. How do you know so much?"

"Ma knows something about New Orleans."

"She's been there?"

"She was born there. Has a recollection of it before she ended up in Memphis. Lost track of her ma."

"Say, did you know there were Negro soldiers in the Revolutionary War?"

"You going to get me into West Point?"

They laughed together. "Uncle John told me that. They served in place of their masters and won their freedom – if they weren't killed, that is."

"Maybe that was a kind of freedom too."

# VI

He had his first friend at West Point before even arriving.

It was August, 1841, and Colonel Murray, his stepfather, was escorting him to the academy for the first time. They boarded at Louisville and were idling on deck watching the quiet Ohio countryside drift by when a young man who boarded at Cincinnati came up and stood beside them. Will hardly noticed him. He was deep in his own thoughts.

It was his first trip east, first time out of Kentucky, second day on deck watching the passing scenery, which already had some surprises. He'd expected to see civilization along the river like they had around Louisville, but instead saw raw land that except for a few clearings and stumps of cut or burned trees and log cabins set back from the river was not changed from what it had always been. They'd travelled miles without seeing a living soul on shore and aside from an occasional blue jay or robin no life at all. The woods and trees grew right down to the river as they headed upriver for Pittsburgh, the clearings sometimes marked by an Indian mound, though the Shawnees had moved west by then.

He was dreaming of his new life. They'd sent him pictures of the academy, and already he saw himself marching along the parade grounds above the Hudson in his cadet's uniform with the high hat and braid and silver scabbard. He'd dreamt of it so long it had already become reality. Everyone in Kentucky said he'd been useless since the letter of appointment came.

The letter was no surprise, not with Uncle John in his corner.

His uncle wrote immediately that getting into West Point and staying in were two different matters. Many boys arrived with far better schooling than he'd had and still didn't make it. It was designed to be an ordeal, to weed out the wheat from the chaff, and as many cadets dropped out on their own as were sent home. It was no shame not to make it. Better to decide it's not the life for you than to waste everyone's time and money. He wasn't trying to discourage him, he said, just wanted him to have the courage to come home if he saw it wasn't right for him.

Will understood the letter. His uncle was a politician, not a soldier.

He'd have paid more attention to their new shipboard companion if he'd been in uniform, but the young man was dressed as plainly as any farm boy, and his person was no more imposing than his clothes. There was no conversation at first, just a nod to this fellow who'd tipped his hat to Colonel Murray and stood quietly beside them a while, a goodly while really, as they all gazed out at the river. But Colonel Murray was a sociable man and before too long he started up a conversation that produced the information that the young man's name was Grant and that he was a cadet returning to West Point. He'd gone home for a spell to help with the family business, which was tanning.

He was a serious, country-looking fellow of reddish hair and slight build and no pretensions. Will looked over when Colonel Murray let drop that they, too, were heading for West Point, and found him staring hard back at him. Grant had to look up, for Will was a head taller. The boy was struck by his eyes, a deep, penetrating blue, which did not fit with the primary aspect of the man, which was drab. He set those eyes on you and hardly blinked.

It was extraordinary how he listened, never changing expression, never interrupting, thin lips set in a line like they'd been drawn on his face. He was so quiet you'd think he had nothing to say except that when he did speak it was worth hearing. Meeting him that first day and with Grant two years ahead of him Will had no idea their paths would ever cross again. Coming to know him later in Mexico, he saw something in him of Uncle John himself, a no-nonsense directness that shunned ceremony and complication and circumlocution.

The Grants were from Ohio and Pennsylvania, the boy's father a Whig who liked Henry Clay but supported Andrew Jackson, admiring two politicians who hated each other. Grant, he would learn, had some of the same quality, able to hold opposing ideas simultaneously, something totally foreign to Will himself. He said his father was a great admirer of John J. Crittenden, had been pleased when he was named attorney general and disappointed when he resigned and returned to the Senate after President Harrison died and Tyler took over. John Tyler was a Southern slave-owner. Most all the Whigs in the cabinet resigned.

They talked all the way to Pittsburgh, a slow journey only possible for big boats since the steam engine came onto the Ohio. Prior to that, all heavy traffic was downriver. At Pittsburgh, they changed onto a barge boat that took three more days to make Harrisburg along the Pennsylvania Canal, a monumental feat of engineering for which Grant had fulsome praise.

Colonel Murray was less enthusiastic about the barge, especially at night, when their sleeping arrangements consisted of shelves more fitting for books than for people. Colonel Murray fell off his shelf the first night, but fortunately had taken a lower one. During the day, they got off to walk along the towpath ahead of the horses, observing, as they had along the Ohio, tree stumps and an occasional log cabin and corn fields, but mostly vast empty woods stretching as far as you could see. The Indian tribes, by treaty and force of arms, had been driven out by then.

They switched from barge to horses to cross the Alleghenies and came down on the far side to join the canal again. At Harrisburg the canal ended and they rented horses to ride to Philadelphia to catch the steamer to New York and make the boat change that took them up the Hudson to West Point.

Colonel Murray and Cadet Grant did most of the talking. Listening, the young man felt at moments like getting off the boat and starting for home, for neither of his companions had a high opinion of soldiering. Colonel Murray hadn't wanted his stepson to become a soldier. He wasn't the kind to make a fuss or try to impose himself, but Will knew that for Ma's sake he'd hoped the appointment wouldn't come through.

As for Grant, Will wondered why, if he hated soldiering that much, he'd even gone to West Point, though maybe soldiering wasn't any worse than tanning.

He lost track of Jude, his birth brother, until his third year at West Point. Thanks to Ma and Josie they got back in touch, starting a correspondence that was more regular on Jude's part than his own. Jude had married and already passed from apprentice to journeyman tailor in the Vieux Carré, the old part of New Orleans. His wife, Dominique, was a Cuban come to New Orleans with her mother and wrapped in an enigmatic past. Not to be outdone by Cadet Crittenden, Jude informed him he'd become a member of the New Orleans Battalion of Free Men of Color.

"Don't worry," he wrote, "we spend our time mostly working on the levees."

He often thought of Jude and their treks to the lake, but had enough trouble staying in school to be much of a correspondent with anyone, including Ma. Besides, what did he have to recount except studies and drilling and demerits? In three years he'd only left the academy grounds for summer bivouacs up the Hudson.

He was a decent enough student and figured it was as much thanks to Ma as to Kentucky schooling. But the demerits kept accumulating. The slavery thing was always with them. Cadets were forbidden to talk about it – cadets and instructors alike – but it was on everyone's mind and sometimes came bubbling out. They might keep it from the classrooms and off the drill field, but no one could remove it from the minds of young men who'd had it drummed into them at home all their lives. Close to half the cadets came from the South, and for most of them it was their first time in the North, where they weren't always welcomed.

With his name and state and size and temper, Will was destined to be in the middle of things, just like Kentucky. They gave him a hundred demerits for marking a coxcomb from Massachusetts named George Derby with his saber and it took a letter from Uncle John to Superintendent Delafield and promises all around to keep him at the academy. When an unavoidable quarrel with Cadet Winfield Scott Hancock escalated into a challenge not many months after the Derby incident, he feared his military days were over.

A foppish Pennsylvanian a year and a rank ahead of him, Hancock had been named after General Winfield Scott, the "grand old man of the army," and figured his name and rank as cadet sergeant carried certain rights and privileges. "What are you looking at, bumpkin?" Hancock remarked when he found Will staring at him too long. "Rustics like you have no business at the academy. The whole bunch of you. Take your slaves and get out of the Union."

It was deliberate. Will knew it. The Derby incident had made him a marked man with certain Northerners. He tried to move on, but his way was blocked. Hancock, a puny thing who had no business trying to provoke someone Will's size, spat, some of the spittle landing on his prey. Will pushed him out of the way. Others witnessed the scene, and so the challenge became inevitable. In private life, it would have been with sabers or pistols, but at West Point it was just fists. As Uncle John said, you go to the academy to learn to kill the enemy, not each other.

It was a damnable situation, one where he felt he could neither back down nor go ahead. Because of the delicate cadet balance between North and South, challenges were frowned upon. In addition, with Hancock hardly reaching his shoulders, it would be an unfair fight and would be so seen by the superintendent when word reached him, as it inevitably would.

That evening, Cadet Alexander Hays, a big, melancholy Pennsylvanian with whom he had hardly ever spoken, approached him with a message from Hancock. "As a fellow Pennsylvanian, I have been asked by Cadet Hancock to step in for him," he said, stiffly. "If that is agreeable to you, of course."

Will's laugh was infectious, and Hays could not help smiling. They shook hands on it. Hays was fully Crittenden's size. It would be a fight between equals.

The second surprise was that when Superintendent Delafield got wind of it he decided to let it go ahead. Whatever he thought of the Derby affair (and the correspondence with Uncle John), he determined that Crittenden and the South had been unjustly insulted by Hancock, and that Crittenden had handled himself correctly in accepting Hays as a stand-in. It was as good a way as any, he decided, for cadets to vent the steam accumulated by the North-South tensions.

They set up the ring on the parade grounds. The whole corps – cadets, instructors, and administration – came out to watch, all fifty cadets allowed to whoop and holler for their man. It turned out not to be a North-South thing at all because private bets had been laid, and so the men cheered more for their wallets than for their hearts. In any case, no one quite knew where Kentucky stood in the quarrel anyway.

They said Hays looked worse than he did when it was over, though both of them took considerable patching up. Hays put him down, down and right back up, and they judged it a trip. It was a long fight, over an hour, and he had time to thank Elias more than once for the sessions with Jude. Hays was quick for a big man and a good fighter, less melancholy with his fists than with his demeanor, surely someone to go places in the army. The judges ruled it a draw, something that did not go down well with the bettors.

He got along with Hayes well enough afterward. They ended up together in Mexico City and laughed about it when they ran into each other. They took pride that the fight had become a legend at the Point, used by the administration to show that cadets could settle arguments in a civilized way – boxing being regarded as a gentleman's activity.

# VII

"Will, my boy, you are naïve. Impossible to compromise something like slavery. You have it or you don't. Fundamental differences."

George Crittenden made him squirm, always had. Growing up, Will had never seen that much of his cousin, who was ten years older, but what he saw of him was more than enough. He was a bully. The eldest son of Uncle John's first wife, George's shadow hung over the house in Frankfort long after he was gone. After West Point he resigned his commission to become a Texas Ranger and turned his back on family and country. As hard as the father sought to head off a great war, the son lusted for the war that would settle matters between North and South. He made no secret where his sympathies lay.

He disliked everyone, which is why he'd left for Texas. With the war against Mexico, his Rangers had joined up with the U.S. Army, and together they'd marched into Mexico for the war President Polk had worked so hard to provoke. It was called Manifest Destiny, and they went to Mexico in pursuit of it, every West Point class for the past twenty years. Polk wanted Texas and California, and Congress would take Mexico as well if it could have its way. Then it was on to Cuba, next stop on the road to Manifest Destiny, whatever that meant.

"Your father wouldn't agree," said Will, annoyed the conversation had drifted onto slavery, a subject they normally sought to avoid. Raising it came with risks.

George's eyes bore into his cousin's. "The hell, you say."

Will glanced around the table at La Madriguera, the Monterrey cantina where George had a table. The others, knowing George, watching him bait his cousin, wondered what was coming. He was the only captain at the table, even though it was the Rangers. Will studied his cousin's dark face, the stubble, the hard eyes, the smirk, the droopy mustache. George liked to fight, liked to fight drunk, liked to duel, holding that Zach Taylor, his dead mother's first cousin and their commander in Mexico, would get him out of anything.

Six of them were there. Two near-empty bottles of mescal sat before them along with empty plates formerly filled with tortillas, chiles and beans. Nothing fancy about the place, wooden tables and chairs, and sawdust on the floor. A few such Monterrey places had been taken over by Americans, but Madriguera still had its Mexican clientele. There was always something in the air at Madriguera, tension going up as mescal went down. The owner was the Monterrey mayor.

They'd been sitting on their bayonets for a month, anxious, frustrated, peevish, sick of each other's company. No one had any idea what came next – advance or retreat, south to Mexico City or north back to the Rio Grande. Following a Monterrey armistice, the townspeople drifted back to discover that maybe the Yankees were no worse than the Mexican troops had been – and they didn't rob them. General Taylor put his own informal touch on things, slouching around town sans sword and uniform, exchanging drinks and cigars with town leaders, assuring them there would be no incidents. As a soldier, Zach Taylor was a born politician.

The six present at La Madriguera were three Crittendens: Will, George, and Lieutenant Tom, George's little brother, an amiable Frankfort lawyer who'd been handed a political commission. The other three were Lt. Col. Henry Clay Jr., Lt. Ulysses Grant, and Lt. George Pickett. Pickett, a Virginian, and Will shared the distinction of being last in their class, proud members of West Point's goat fraternity. Pickett, a year behind him, had come in the week before with the rest of the West Point class of '46. Clay had marched in that very day at the head of his regiment of Kentucky volunteers, which included Tom Crittenden. Will and George Crittenden had been with Zach Taylor's army since it crossed the Rio Grande in January of '46.

Others besides George might have agreed on the inevitability of conflict over slavery, but in Mexico they sought to put it from their minds. They knew their differences, had known them long before West Point, but for now they were on the same side and tolerated each other's company. That Yankee or Cracker you disagreed with might kill the Mexican who was trying to kill you.

Heavy fighting had led to the surrender of the Monterrey garrison. An invading army of 6,500 men in three divisions under General Taylor occupied the city and awaited its marching orders. Six months after leaving Corpus Christi they were two hundred miles into Mexico, had fought battles at Palo Alto, Resaca de Palma, and Monterrey. Taking Monterrey had led to the worst losses of the war, one third of their forces dead or wounded.

"Fundamental differences," repeated George, eyes still locked on his cousin. The others watched, edgy. Nobody trusted George Crittenden. "Different cultures, different politics, different values," he said. "My God, some Whigs didn't even want Texas in the Union . . . think of it!"

"Like your father," Will said again, cactus juice warming his blood, turning the screw back at him.

"And *my* father," said young Clay, trying to ease the tension. "We don't need another slave state in the Union."

"Two Kentuckians," muttered George, looking around the table. "What do you expect? I've never understood if Henry Clay was a man of the North or of the South."

"And what are you, George?" asked Clay.

Henry and George had grown up together, caroused together as children whenever Uncle John and Henry Clay visited each other.

The Clays lived in a fine old brick house in Lexington, just down the road from Uncle John's house in Frankfort. Will didn't remember much of it because he mostly wasn't born yet. He might have said that Henry was George's oldest friend, but George didn't have any friends.

"You know damn well I'm a Texan."

Differences in rank meant nothing to George. In any case, in his eyes a West Point captain outranked a political light colonel from Kentucky.

As a soldier who'd been around – West Pointer who'd quit the army for the Texas Rangers and come back into the army to fight Mr. Polk's war – George Crittenden knew many people. His reputation was that of a difficult officer whose drinking made him unpredictable – not always a bad quality in an officer. But the information he brought that night to La Madriguera was a surprise.

"I hear that General Winfield Scott is on his way," he offered.

The conversation stopped dead. "Where did you hear it, George?" Clay asked.

George pulled at his mustache, enjoying the attention. "Never mind that. Take it as gospel."

It made sense. When news reached Washington that General Taylor had accepted the surrender of Monterrey on condition the Mexican army vacate the city, Polk went into a rage, blaming Taylor and splashing it across the newspapers. He had the enemy trapped and let it escape, the president charged. Of course Polk wanted to discredit Taylor, already mentioned as the Whig candidate for '48. What did Polk care that they'd lost two thousand men trying to take Monterrey's twin fortresses?

Polk couldn't stand that the nation had acclaimed Taylor for the "glorious days of Monterrey," the acclaiming led by none other than Sen. John J. Crittenden. In Taylor, Uncle John saw the man who could defeat Polk in the '48 election, succeed where Henry Clay had failed in four previous elections. It didn't hurt that Uncle John was related to Zach through Sarah Lee, his first wife. Taylor, not Clay, would be the man finally to rid the White House of the Tennesseans.

"Polk wants to get Taylor out of the headlines," said Tom. "Doesn't he know that Scott wants to be president worse than Taylor?"

Pickett, an inebriated smile on his pink face, laughed out loud. "The only Winfield Scott who's going to be elected president is Winfield Scott Hancock."

Laughing, they looked from Pickett to Will. They all knew Will's history at the Point with Hancock. Hancock had a history of histories, including with Pickett, whom he loathed, a feeling fully returned. Will laughed along with them.

"Hancock will be arriving with Scott, who likes having a namesake," said George. "As will Bobby Lee. As will Jeff Davis and his Mississippi Rifles. Looks like Polk wants this war over sooner rather than later."

"I believe only generals have the habit of running for president," said Will.

"Ah," said George, "but Hancock intends to make general first."

"He'll need a better war than this one," said Pickett.

"And by God he'll have it!" said George, banging the table.

The mayor glanced over. The Mexicans at the bar turned around.

"Serious business, George," said Grant, quietly, "not cactus juice talk."

George's dark eyes closed in on Grant. "Ain't cactus juice talking."

"Why avoid it?" said Pickett. "George is right . . . better for everyone if we go our separate ways."

"Which way does Kentucky go?" asked Tom.

"No," said Grant, loudly for once, looking up from his drink. "Theoretically maybe . . . practically is another matter."

"What the Hell does that mean?" demanded George.

Grant ignored him. He was addressing Pickett. "Forget Kentucky, what of your state, Pickett – Virginia, cradle of independence, home of the founding fathers, the state bordering the federal capital. Which way does Virginia go, Lieutenant?"

Pickett smiled. "No choice. We are a plantation state, a slave state."

Grant took a moment to respond in that flat voice of his. He'd been enjoying the mescal as much as anyone, smoking his cigar and keeping to himself. But the conversation clearly bothered him.

"Understand, Pickett, if it comes to war it won't be like Mexico where the job is to kill people we don't know. In civil war, half of us here will be charged with killing the other half. I might have to kill you, Pickett. And once it starts, where will it end? How many thousands, tens of thousands, hundreds of thousands, will die? Who will give in – you, us? Families will disintegrate. The nation will disintegrate."

Pickett laughed. "West Point will disintegrate."

"So which way does Virginia go, Pickett?" said Grant, still stalking his prey. "West Point is in New York, if I'm not mistaken. Secede and there'll be no more Virginians at the Point. No more Bobby Lees. No more George Picketts."

"I can't speak for Bobby, but in my case, no great loss."

"I believe Mr. Lee's father served with General Washington," said Grant, deadly serious. "I believe he served in the Continental Congress. I cannot imagine his son turning his back on the Republic."

"Grant, you are hopeless," said George, standing, waving the mayor over and handing him a fistful of dollars. "Funny business this: Jeff Davis coming down with Scott to replace Zach Taylor. Jeff Davis is Zach Taylor's son-in-law."

"*Was* his son-in-law," said Clay. "I believe the lady died."

Will was celebrating something else that night besides the arrival of Henry Clay's Kentucky Volunteers and Cousin Tom. Watching them march into camp in their blues and slouched hats, he'd been on the lookout for a tall, strapping corporal he'd known always in denims, never in uniform. Jude had written that he'd left his Louisiana Battalion of Free Men of Color to join Henry Clay's Kentucky unit. "Dominique is fit to be tied," he wrote, "but I told her there's nothing to be done. I'm tired of building levees."

There'd been some muttering as the Vols marched in with their sprinkling of dark faces, but that was it. After the heavy losses taking Monterrey they needed all the help they could get. The two friends embraced when the Vols fell out. Neither cared who saw them.

# VIII

Nearly two years after crossing the Rio Grande, the great beast of an invading army had reached the outskirts of Mexico City, where it waited for the order to take the capital. They had been bloodied at Monterrey, nearly beaten outside Puebla, blocked at Churubusco where they kept going thanks to the engineering genius of Capt. Robert E. Lee and the bravery of men like Capt. George Crittenden, who won a commendation for bravery and was promoted to brevet major. U.S. casualties already surpassed ten thousand. The Mexicans were tenacious.

In hundreds of tents spread out across the hill called Tacubaya, the invaders looked down on the capital and waited – days running into weeks, then a month and more. The Valley of Mexico spread out under them, lush trees and plants thriving in the showers that fell each afternoon when the clouds turned dark, rain filling streams that rushed down the mountains and nourished the lakes. It was fine late-summer weather, the sun glinting each morning off Lake Texcoco, lighting in the distance the twin volcanoes, which to remind everyone of their presence from time to time sent up a loud burp. The beauty only added to their frustration.

"What exactly are we waiting for?"

It was a vague question Will put to no one in particular while waiting for Grant, who played cards like he talked, to take his turn.

Not sure what his partner meant, Grant looked up. Then he understood.

"I believe we are waiting for the man called Trist. Why take more casualties if the Mexicans want to make peace?"

Not wanting Scott to celebrate, as Cortéz had done, with another conquest of the place the Aztecs called Tenochtitlan, President Polk was seeking to seize glory back by sending Nicholas Trist, a diplomat, to Mexico with a peace treaty. Trist presented it to President Santa Anna, the "Mexican Napoleon," whom Polk had allowed to return from exile in Cuba on Santa Anna's assurance that he alone could persuade his people to make peace with the invader.

After three weeks, Santa Anna double-crossed Polk, rejecting the treaty and declaring the terms incompatible with Mexican honor. He countered with his own treaty. Without having won a single battle, he demanded that all U.S. troops be withdrawn not just from Mexico but from the New Mexico and California territories.

Exasperated and exceeding instructions – it took six weeks for mail to reach Washington – Trist countered by offering to set the Mexican border at the Nueces River, 150 miles north of the Rio Grande – *the very issue that had started the war!*

"Because it is a trick," said Pickett, replying to Grant after a long moment, playing an ace, taking the trick and grinning over his witticism.

"We will know soon enough," said an unsmiling Grant.

"It is a unique situation," said Kirby Smith, the only captain at the whist table that day. "A conquering army sitting on a hill overlooking a capital at its mercy and not permitted to enter."

Everyone loved Ephraim Kirby Smith, a serious, gregarious, literary man from a Connecticut family of soldiers, like the Crittendens in Kentucky, back to the Indian wars. For Pickett and Crittenden, Smith had a special appeal: he, too, was a goat, last in his class of '26. Only Grant prevented them from being a full table of goats at the whist table that day.

"Not *yet* permitted to enter," said Will.

"The Mexicans won't make peace," said Pickett. "What government surrenders its capital without a fight?"

"Who is this fellow Trist?"

"Democrat," said Smith. "Consul general to Cuba under Jackson. Made too many enemies and Daniel Webster got him fired. Jackson passed him on to Polk."

"Why is he here?"

"Too many casualties," said Grant. "Polk is worried. Election coming."

"With Zach Taylor back at his plantation rarin' to go," said Pickett. "Buena Vista will put him in the White House."

They'd all heard of Buena Vista, Zach Taylor's remarkable victory outside Monterrey after Polk had replaced him with Scott as commander in chief.

"From what I heard," said Smith, whose younger brother Edmund had been a West Point classmate of Will's, "Buena Vista will be studied for years at the Point. Mostly Jeff Davis's doing. Remarkable tactics, remarkable victory."

"Outnumbered three to one," said Grant.

"We've been outnumbered in every fight since we crossed the border," said Pickett. "So what?"

"I heard Henry Clay's son was killed at Buena Vista," said Smith. Will looked up quickly.

"Freaner says Clay's unit was beat up bad."

The thumping in his heart quickly reached his throat and he gasped. *Henry dead?* And what of Jude and Tom, both with Clay? Freaner would know of Clay, not of his men.

"Was that my name I heard?"

He emerged from the line of tents, moving around behind them, looking over their shoulders, checking their cards, clucking to himself. James Freaner was a reporter sent to cover the war for the New Orleans *Delta-News*. He played whist with the men and also in the more exalted company of Trist and Scott. He was a clever and industrious reporter and a devil of a whist player.

"If anyone drops out, I am available."

"I thought you only played with Scott and Trist," said Grant.

"They're not as good as you are, Lieutenant."

"Bad news if it's true," said Pickett.

"That true about Buena Vista?" Will asked, struggling to keep emotion from his voice. "Henry Clay killed?"

"Clay and a few hundred others – almost as many casualties as desertions. Men sick of it all. A few more victories like that and you won't have an army left. Arkansas and Kentucky units decimated. Mississippi Rifles carried the day."

"Any other news about the Kentuckians?"

"They're bringing the bodies back."

"So what else is new, Freaner?" asked Pickett.

He was a gawky, wheezy Yankee who'd been a reporter, soldier, and reporter again. Enlisted in the Louisiana Volunteers to join Taylor's army, he was discharged for health reasons. Hired by the *Delta-News* to cover the war, he'd run into Trist on the ship to Veracruz. With a shared passion for whist, they'd become inseparable. Story was they played cards even as the Mexicans took potshots at them in their carriage crossing the mountains on the way to Tacubaya.

Beyond whist, it was a relationship of mutual advantage: Freaner used Trist; Trist used Freaner. When Winfield Scott joined their whist table, he used them both. A Baltimorean transplanted to New Orleans, Freaner was informed and trustworthy and the best whist player around. A Northerner working for a Southern newspaper, he kept his politics to himself.

"Since you asked, Lieutenant," he said, drawling his words, addressing Pickett, "the news is this: don't make this game a long one."

They looked up as one. "Meaning?" said Smith.

"I'd write letters home tonight if I were you."

Smith's wife would publish the letters he wrote from Mexico, including the last one. He told her what he'd already told the others. He knew what was coming.

• • •

The wait had been awful, worse than Corpus Christi, worse than Monterrey. From their vast camp they looked down daily on the sinister low buildings of Molino del Rey and the mysterious hulk called Casa Mata. Farther on loomed the sheer stone heights of Chapultepec Castle, jutting up like a rugged man-o'-war from a sea of peaceful woods. An enormous Mexican flag fluttered from its highest tower.

By then, after two years of fighting, they were a real army, no longer slavers and abolitionists, Yankees and Crackers, West Pointers and volunteers. They were mean and mad, an army two years away from home, itching to finish the job and get out, but halted within sight of the prize. They all knew the problem, and it was not military: Polk did not want to give Scott the victory he'd denied to Taylor. Polk was a Democrat, Taylor and Scott Whigs. The '48 elections were a year away.

Scott called Molino del Rey "a skirmish," but the 116 Americans killed by Mexicans firing point blank down on them would have disagreed. Next came the thing called Casa Mata, a fortified hill that could have been pounded into gravel with artillery. Instead Scott ordered a second charge and they ran smack into a stone bunker carved into the rocks. Taking sheets of fire, the ground littered with fallen comrades, they were forced back until a charge from the rear by Colonel McIntosh's regiment turned them around again. Kirby Smith was hit in the face and fell with a scream at Will's feet. He hoisted his Connecticut friend onto his shoulders and turned into the raging face of Major Wright, waving his sword and shouting, "*forward, Lieutenant, forward!*"

He should have brought Smith back. It was his greatest regret. The choice was instantly clear to him: Saving this one man, this army captain and fellow goat who'd become his friend and confidante through countless games of whist, was more important than his presence in a fruitless charge against an impregnable rock. It was an instantaneous human reaction. Did Major Wright think he was afraid? They say the best officers know how to disobey.

They retreated amid heavy losses. Will lost half his company but survived without a scratch. Vicissitudes of war. Artillery was useless with so many men down in the field. They returned to their hillside, holding fire to give the Mexicans time to collect and tend the wounded.

They watched and waited, peering through spyglasses, finding the sudden silence strange. It was blazing hot. Birds began to chirp in the sunshine.

They watched the Mexicans emerge from their stone bunker. The Mexicans knew there would be no firing.

"*They're coming out!*" someone yelled.

Another voice: "*The Mexicans are coming out!*"

The shout went down the line. "*They're coming out! They're coming out!*"

The words tolled through his brain like church bells, never stopping.

"*The Mexicans are coming out! They're coming out!*"

The looked on in numbed silence as they paraded around in their blue blouses and black hats as though it were a stroll down the Alameda. At first they did nothing but stare down at the wounded Americans, turning around them, waiting for something. Hands reached out to them. Helplessly the Americans watched from their hill. Where were the orderlies? Where were the stretcher-bearers? Why didn't they give the wounded men water?

They heard a single shot, the signal to begin. The Mexicans gripped their sabers and fixed their bayonets, blue steel glinting in the sunshine. They began to run through the wounded men, who squirmed and reached out in a final gesture, protecting, beseeching. From the hill they heard the screams, saw the blue turn red.

"*They're killing 'em!*" shouted a voice, "*they're killing 'em!*"

"Colonel," the stunned young man shouted to Garland, the brigade commander. "Give me an assault group!"

"*Stand down, Lieutenant!*"

"We can bring them back, Colonel!"

"I can lose no more men, Lieutenant. *Stand down!*"

"It is our duty!" he shouted at the man.

*"Stand down or I will shoot you!"*

Mounted on a black steed directly behind Garland was the imposing figure of Gen. William Jenkins Worth, 1st Division commander, long white muttonchops accenting the pinkness of his severe face. Looking directly at Crittenden – neither could suspect that their paths would cross again – he slowly shook his head.

*"They've kilt Colonel McIntosh!"* someone shouted.

*"They've kilt Captain Smith!"* someone shouted.

*"They've kilt Sergeant McTavish!"* someone shouted.

He was furious. The hell with them all, he should have gone. It was the right thing to do. Watching those men murdered in cold blood – just as Pa was murdered – was the worst thing of his life.

"We're too nice with these damn people," Smith had said. "Better to fight the way they do."

It was a lesson he would not forget.


Winfield Scott called his general staff and chief engineers together that night to decide whether to press on to Chapultepec Castle. The losses had been enormous, nearly eight hundred Americans killed or wounded that day – and for what? Worth's 5th Infantry had lost forty percent of its men, fifty percent of its officers. Screams from the field hospital penetrated through the Tacubaya summer night to the little church where Scott had convoked his council of war.

Despite the day's losses, Scott told his men, he was inclined to go ahead with the assault on Chapultepec, symbol of Mexican independence. First, though, he wanted to hear from each of them. He owed them that.

They went around the room, each man echoing the last, not one of them agreeing with the commander: Chapultepec was impregnable, they said; Chapultepec was no more than a cadet academy, they said; Chapultepec could be bombarded or simply turned, they said; Chapultepec had no military value, they said. They had suffered too many losses.

Scott's top three generals, Worth, Quitman, and Twiggs, all opposed an attack on Chapultepec, as did Capt. Robert E. Lee, acting senior engineer.

They came to the last man, a lieutenant who wouldn't have been in the room except for the fact he was an engineer serving under Lee and held by some, including the lieutenant himself, to be at least as brilliant. P. G. T. Beauregard, a Louisianan and Creole legend at West Point, laid out his plan for feinting from the south and attacking Chapultepec from the west, scaling the steepest slopes of the fortress with ropes and ladders, something he alone believed could be done.

Scott had heard what he wanted. "Gentlemen," he announced, "we will attack from the west. This meeting is dissolved."

Ladders were thrown up and the scaling parties went up like so many spiders. Shooting straight down, the surprised Mexicans could not take good aim. A few hundred cadets waited at the top, but were quickly overrun. Remembering the butchering at Casa Mata, the Americans brought them down in hand-to-hand combat until General Bravo, the fortress commander, surrendered his sword. Astonished, horrified, the Americans watched as six cadets, holding hands, refusing to surrender, launched themselves over the precipice, becoming instant symbols of Mexican resistance and independence.

Santa Anna evacuated the city, and that evening the Americans who'd survived the slaughter rode in formation down the Alameda to take command of the Zócalo and city center. Santa Anna had lost 1,800 men that day; Scott half as many. But Scott was right: Chapultepec ended the war. Surely it would carry him on to the White House.

Santa Anna resigned within days, a new government was named and moved to the village of Guadalupe Hildalgo outside the capital where Nicholas Trist went to reopen peace negotiations. Scott named

John Quitman military governor, and Quitman moved into the National Palace on the Zócalo. Trist signed the Treaty of Guadalupe Hidalgo on February 2, 1848, giving Polk everything he wanted except Baja California. Trist had been fired weeks before as Polk shed anyone who might share credit with him, but because of the slow mails didn't know of his dismissal and so kept on negotiating. On February 16, Polk fired Scott.

Trist's whist-playing friend James Freaner carried the treaty back to Washington where the Senate ratified it after rejecting Jeff Davis's amendment to annex Mexico. Davis had been elected to the Senate from Mississippi upon his return in triumph from Buena Vista. On May 25, the Mexican Senate ratified the treaty and the Mexican flag once again fluttered over the national palace.

The triumphant army awaited the order from Polk to press on to Cuba. The "all Mexico" movement had given way to an equally powerful "all Cuba" movement. Manifest Destiny demanded no less. But Polk was ailing, decided not to run again in the fall, and the order for Havana never came. Zach Taylor was elected in November and showed no interest in Cuba. The army came home from Mexico and disbanded. The young man was a civilian again.

# PART THREE

✳

# PERSUASION

# IX

He arrived in New Orleans the ides of April, 1850. He arrived with Lucien Hensley to a city already home to Jude Freeman, who carried a bullet in him from Buena Vista. Now a journeyman tailor, Jude lived on Phillipa Street in the Vieux Carré with his wife, two daughters, sister, and mother-in-law. He arrived in the springtime to a bustling waterfront city that somehow seemed to be escaping the festering sectional discord infecting the rest of the nation. Thanks to Uncle John's letter of introduction, he was hired by the U.S. Customhouse, the most important Treasury office on the Gulf Coast, the primary source of revenue for the federal government.

Never had his spirits been higher or his prospects brighter. He did not believe he missed the army at all. When he thought back on those few days at Monmouth, it was not to think of Quitman or Lopez or Jeff Davis or the gaggle of Cuban patriots whose names had already faded from his mind. It was to think on one person only: the prodigious Lucy Holcombe, whose sparkling vision danced in his head days and nights. For the first time in his life he was in love.

He settled into his new life, finding rooms on St. Ann Street off Congo Square, only blocks from the customhouse on Canal Street. Lucien, happy with what he had discovered and getting ready to return to Shelbyville to hand over his practice, found comfortable lodgings around the corner on Royal Street. Jude was ten minutes away on Phillipa and worked at Dubois et fils on Chartres Street. They all lived and worked in the Vieux Carré, the French Quarter, and were physically as close as they'd been in Shelbyville. Personally, they had never been closer.

He loved visiting the Freemans, attracted by the informal hospitality and conviviality of the large family presided over by his friend. Jude had married well, no question, for Dominique was exotic and talented and wrapped in a mysterious Cuban past. She practiced Santeria, a strange Caribbean religion with even stranger practices, and read tarot cards, informing Will that the cards told her it was his destiny to come to New Orleans, just as it had been Jude's. When the subject got around to the island she would look to her mother, Liliana, who spoke little English. The two women would exchange a few words in incomprehensible Creole, smile demurely, and the subject would drop.

Mary Jane, Jude's sister, manumitted by John Allen two years after her brother, had been a welcome addition to the family, and the two young women bonded instantly. Jude's two little girls rounded out the household, which meant Jude was never out of the company of females, at home or at work.

As for himself, he was seldom *in* the company of females, something he sorely missed. Growing up, with Ma and his sisters and Jude's mother, Josie, he'd grown used to the company of women, easy company that did not require performing or competing or conforming, which is the life of men, especially in the military. On visits to Frankfort, Aunt Maria had always been there with her daughters. The thing he missed most in his life was women, one reason he found himself so often at the Freemans. Even when visiting them, Lucy was never long from his mind. He dreamt of having a warm and happy home like the Freemans, with children and laughter and a woman to greet him when his daily work was done.

But how could that woman be Lucy? How could he believe that Lucy Holcombe, a sophisticated child of seminaries and plantations who consorted with generals and governors, would be happy in upstairs rooms on St. Ann Street, living on the wages of a custom-house official? Something was badly wrong with his vision.

He brought the matter up with Lucien, his friend as well as his doctor. He was visiting Royal Street, in what were to be the doctor's new offices. Lucien listened to him attentively, his face a mask as it always was when assessing symptoms. Finished, the young man waited in awkward silence. The doctor offered no prognosis, the friend no encouragement.

"I am not competent to offer advice in such a matter," he said at length.

It was the first time, though would not be the last, that both the doctor and the friend disappointed him.

A word about Lucien:

If Dominique's tarot cards said it was Will's destiny to come to New Orleans, then Lucien Hensley, trading Shelbyville for New Orleans, country medicine for something more suitable to his skills, served that destiny. They'd been friends for years, ever since Lucien carved out his appendix on the kitchen table while Pa and John Allen held him down and he bit hard on a piece of wood.

They were fifteen years apart in age and there was even a time when he thought Lucien might become his stepfather. Maybe he fantasized because with eight children under the roof at Shelbyville some-one was always sick with something, and Lucien was always there. Maybe he fantasized because in the time between Pa's death and Colonel Murray's arrival, Lucien helped fill the void in many ways.

But it takes a certain type of man to marry a woman with eight children, and though Ma and Lucien were good friends he wasn't the type and maybe she wouldn't have had him for he wasn't religious. He was of good appearance, not what you'd call handsome, but open and honest and forthright. There was curiosity in his eyes, though not much humor. He was a serious man, a man whose opinion you could value, and not just in medical matters. He had never married, though it wasn't for lack of eligible women. Lucien Hensley was married to his work, and when there wasn't enough to keep him busy in Shelbyville he moved to New Orleans. At heart he was a congenital bachelor, happier in the company of men than of women. As for children, he saw enough of them in the delivery room and house calls to have his fill. He was a man comfortable in his skin who didn't need entertainments and diversions to be content. His work was his life.

With Lucy it was a *coup de foudre*. To be in love for the first time – and with such a woman! Waking each morning he was overcome with that most wonderful of feelings – the joy of being in love. To be sure, doubts crept in. Given his inexperience with women and modest situation, how could they not? But doubt only made the thing more exquisite. It's like combat, he thought: if it were easy there'd be no thrill to it. Marching unimpeded into Mexico City would have robbed them of the exhilaration of victory. A prize for the taking is no prize at all. Better a skirmish or two to test the strength of the thing.

In war he was an experienced officer, but in affairs of the heart still a plebe. He knew nothing of young women, could count on a few fingers those he'd known who were not his family. A few soirees at West Point was all; the spring formal when they would bring young ladies upriver from New York for a few hours of dances with girls they would never see again.

"Oh, you don't *look like* you're from Kentucky!" they would say, as if they expected a different species.

Could it be, he asked himself? But why not, came the answer? Anna Eliza was ready to marry and move away, and Lucy was only two years younger. He knew something of the man Anna was to marry, a man whose situation was not much different from his own. Lucy loved New Orleans, hated East Texas, said she'd do anything to get away from it. Something had passed between them at Monmouth, he was sure of it. He was a presentable man with an honorable past, a respectable job, a distinguished name. The question was not why would she, but why *wouldn't* she?

Thinking of it that way, his doubts abated, as though the thing, while difficult, was not impossible. This much he knew: it was something both exciting and frightening. He loved the feeling and feared it at the same time, and he was not a man accustomed to fear.

Was it coincidence that brought her to New Orleans only weeks after their meeting at Monmouth? They said it was for Anna Eliza's fitting, and he took them to Dubois et fils where Jude himself was to help sew the dress, though he sensed that the lady's wedding was for no time soon. Whatever the reason – and he could not help but think it was to see him again – he'd had the pleasure of escorting three Tennessee belles around the city he now called home. Thanks to Anna Eliza, who took her mother off for rounds of shopping in the Vieux Carré, he was able to be alone with Lucy. They sat over coffee and cakes on Jackson Square. He took her by the customhouse to meet his new colleagues. It was overpowering. She felt the same as he did, he was sure of it.

Afterward, Eugenia took her daughters back to Texas to join Mr. Holcombe at their new home in Marshall, up the Red River and across Caddo Lake from Shreveport. The women hated leaving civilized New Orleans, where they'd lodged at elegant Raynaud House with Eugenia's friend Victoria Raynaud, a former neighbor from Tennessee, but what choice did they have? He wrote Lucy immediately, was answered enthusiastically, and a correspondence began that became more intimate with each letter. She was amazing, including little poems and always having something to say about politics.

"Will dearest: Is there any reason a Democrat should not be president at the next election? I think I should prefer to have one – unless, of course, your distinguished uncle cares to run. What do you think?"

She never forgot to mention Narciso Lopez, the new Bolívar, ready to liberate Cuba from Spain just as Bolívar had done for South America. Whence the lady's enthusiasm for such an outlandish adventure, he wondered . . . but why not? She was a literary person, that was clear from her letters, influenced by the tales of Fenimore Cooper and Walter Scott and of course Dumas, whom she read in French, and thrilled by stories of love, cape, and sword. She kept her notebooks, talked of them often. She was a romantic in every sense of the word.

Eventually he received a letter from Mrs. Quitman. The young lady, quite smitten by the gallant lieutenant, bearer of the illustrious Kentucky name, would be returning to Monmouth with Mrs. Holcombe the following month. It was hoped the gentleman would be free to come at the same time.

He accepted immediately. It didn't hurt to be aided by people as distinguished as the Quitmans, and so far he'd found no way to nourish the courtship apart from correspondence. Lucy invited him to visit Wyalusing, the Holcombes' new home in East Texas, and a journey to Monmouth served his purposes for he could leave directly for East Texas without returning to New Orleans. He'd already arranged a short leave of absence with the customhouse. How he longed to see her again!

Jude came knocking one evening when he'd returned from the customhouse and was preparing to step out for supper. He heard rapping on the door below, and Madame Lucas, the Creole housekeeper, called up with the news that he had "un visiteur." Madame Lucas knew all the languages of New Orleans and used them indiscriminately, although snobbishly preferring French when she discovered that her new tenant knew the language.

He stepped into the hallway to hail his friend as he ascended, surprised by the unannounced visit.

He had a noticeable limp from the bullet he carried in him and used various devices to hide it, none of which worked well on a staircase. It would have been easier with a cane, but Jude was not the sort to use a cane. His habit was to carry an umbrella even on clear days, and he'd taken to walking with the gait of a flaneur, an amble, really, never missing a shop window or failing to lift his hat to a lady. He was proud of his war wound, proud of having fought for his country in the battle where Henry Clay Jr. fell, a battle carried by the audacity of Jefferson Davis and the Mississippi Rifles. Though he was not so proud as to go limping through life.

Jude Freeman had come a long way. The nimble fingers that once turned out hemp bags faster than any two people in Shelbyville now were employed by the highest-bred ladies of New Orleans and beyond to make the finest clothes. He lived in modest rooms with his large family; he walked to work each morning and home at night, moving perhaps slower than most in the crowd, but not so slow that anyone would notice.

"Pa's sick," he said as they settled onto the couch in his front room. "Got a letter from Ma."

"How bad?"

"Pretty bad. Trouble in the lungs. I've got to go home."

Hemp dust. Elias wouldn't be the first. He looked at his friend, the open, kind face marked by worry for his father. And there was something else to worry him: Free Negroes travelling alone on the river was dangerous business.

"Got anyone to go with you?"

Jude shook his head.

"I'd go if I could."

"You can't do that, Will. You're new at the customhouse."

It was true: He couldn't do it, not because he was new at the customhouse but because he'd already arranged the leave to visit Monmouth and go on from there to Wyalusing with Lucy.

"Wait – what of Lucien? Lucien's heading home to close up."

"I don't want to bother Lucien."

"*Bother*? He'd love the company. He still has plans to get that bullet out of your hip, you know."

# X

They met for lunch in the Pontalba on Chartres Street. It was some time since the party at Monmouth, and he'd forgotten the invitation, but a note from Lopez to the customhouse reminded him. He could hardly refuse. And his curiosity was aroused. Lucy had seen to that.

He was a gallant, a man of great courtesy and flourishes and obvious appeal to the ladies, who watched every move. He stood erect, chest thrust out under silk shirt and waistcoat, waist kept tight by white britches. A golden crucifix hung from his neck. Will looked for a pistol but saw no bulges. A lady's garrucha strapped under his coat, he speculated. He dared not wear his Spanish general's uniform in New Orleans. Too many enemies of Spain roamed the city for that.

He bowed and shook hands with the ease of a man aware of his strength. High cheekbones and a swarthy Latin face contrasted with the snow white of his hair and mustache. The eyes were deep-set and hard, lined around the edges, a man who'd seen a lot. He was a curious figure, a man from another time and world, fugitive of some ancien régime, an anachronism in America anywhere but in New Orleans. In the Vieux Carré he blended in perfectly with the multitude of other characters floating around, refugees washed up for unknowable reasons from unpronounceable places on the shores of the new American republic.

"So 'appy you could come," he said, trying for the *h* but not quite making it.

Sliced baguette arrived with their beers. They drank thirstily, ordered endive and cassoulet, and looked around for anyone they might know. He recalled Lopez well from Monmouth, not a tall man, but square and solid, giving the impression of bullish strength, both physical and moral. His English was good but accented. He talked not in the Latin manner with his hands, but with his eyes, widening and narrowing them as he spoke and listened. For all his bravura and celebrity, there was composure about the man.

He did not hide that he had come to talk of Cuba.

"It is," he said, "the most noble enterprise. It is what we aspire to all our life: to do the one great thing."

"Would that the U.S. Army had gone on from Mexico City."

"But it did not."

"A failure of leadership."

"Today there is more failure of leadership."

He nodded. It wasn't just President Taylor who opposed moving against Spain in Cuba, but Uncle John as well. He'd written his uncle about the evening at Monmouth, saying that Lucien Hensley was convinced it was arranged to recruit him to the cause, adding that Jefferson Davis was part of it.

"A fool's errand," came his uncle's testy reply, with an aside that Davis should have spoken to him first. "A clear violation of the Neutrality Act. You have what you want at the customhouse. Don't trust this man Lopez. Stay away from it!"

His uncle's opinion agreed with his own, but only in part. The liberation of Cuba from Spain had appealed to him since his time in Mexico, since seeing the poverty and cruelty of that badly governed place, so ripe for foreign takeover. But he held it to be the job of the U.S. government, not of a private army of men of dubious and conflicting motives.

The endive arrived. Lopez started in, calling for more beer and bread. Then: "General Worth is the leader now. I believe you knew him in Mexico."

"I served under General Worth."

"It was General Worth who recommended you."

The words stopped him. "Recommended me for what?"

Lopez ignored the question. "He remembered an incident."

The young man's mind went back to the terrible scene, and he nodded. "Yes. I, too, remember."

They fell to eating, silently reminiscing. A game was underway, each man playing out his hand. Lopez knew lunch was a courtesy. Crittenden had given no reason to believe he had any intention of joining the mission, on the contrary. But his curiosity and, yes, self-interest, made him susceptible.

"You will allow me to speak frankly, General?"

Lopez did not answer, only the slight lifting of an eyebrow indicated his full attention. Will's eyes swept the sprawling restaurant, taking in everything – the hum of voices, rattle of plates, bursts of laughter, waiters scurrying about with foaming mugs of beer and steaming platters of gumbo and bouillabaisse. In New Orleans he felt quite in his element.

"Is your mission not illegal?"

Eyes widening, Lopez posed his fork and looked across the table. "Under U.S. law, perhaps." A slight smile formed on the full Latin lips. "But does not natural law give every people the right to choose its own form of government? Is that not written in your own Declaration of Independence?"

"And that is what you will offer the Cuban people – the right to choose their own form of government?"

More beer arrived, followed by cassoulet in a steaming caldron. The waiter ladled out chunky morsels of sausage and Louisiana duck enveloped in a thick, rich sauce of beans, tomatoes, and onions. He refilled the bread tray and moved on.

"But of course, my dear sir. How else could it be?"

Certainly annexation was another way. But he'd come to lunch to inform himself of the project, not to argue over it. He thought back on what the Cubans had said at Monmouth: to land in Cuba, to arm the Creoles, to defeat the Spaniards. In victory, magnanimity.

Establish a provisional government and open negotiations for recognition with all the major powers, including the United States. Lopez had talked of Bolívar; how Bolívar prized a letter from Henry Clay congratulating him on his victories over Spain at Boyacá and Angostura in the name of liberty and democracy.

"I believe I understand your mission well enough," Will said, "but what is the ultimate objective?"

Lopez dabbed at his lips with a linen napkin and fixed the young man with a steady gaze. "I assume your question is directed at the ultimate status of Cuba."

"Indeed."

He nodded. "Permit me to inquire, sir: You who say you support U.S. military intervention in Cuba; what do *you* believe the U.S. interest to be?"

He'd turned the question back on him!

How often Cuba had come up among the self-appointed experts at West Point! Presidents back to Jefferson had called for taking Cuba, they said; Spain's time had passed, they said; U.S. control of the Gulf of Mexico was primordial; protection of our southern ports started in Cuba; an independent white Cuba could not exist; an independent Cuba would be a pawn of the great powers; taking Cuba was the best hope for North-South equilibrium. The arguments were endless.

But what was *Lopez's* objective? At Monmouth, he'd mentioned how Bolívar was inspired by Napoleon, and he, Lopez, inspired by Bolívar. Was it a personal thing for him? Angostura, Venezuelan city captured from Spain by Bolívar, was now called Ciudad Bolívar. Did he seek a new capital for Cuba called Ciudad Lopez? Why did Uncle John warn him not to trust Lopez? Were there things he didn't know?

"It will be up to the Cubans to decide their future, will it not?" the young man cautiously answered. "The plantation owners, for example: what do they think?"

Lopez recognized the evasion. "I am in complete agreement. I myself am a plantation owner – or should say, I *was* a plantation owner before the Spaniards confiscated my properties. But I am in contact with my former associates, especially in Pinar Province. You've heard of the Club of Havana?"

"I heard mention of it at Monmouth."

"The club represents plantation owners across the island, from Pinar to Santiago. I meet with their representatives constantly, from New Orleans to New York. Some came to Monmouth. They are with us to the man. Their voice will be strong in determining the future of the island."

He did not have to explain that Cuba's plantation owners, like those in America, depended on slave labor. He had his answer: Lopez's objective was to bring Cuba into the Union, moor it to the slave states of the American South.

"And the *independistas*? I do not believe their representatives were present at Monmouth. Do they agree that Cuba should be joined to the United States?"

The general started to answer and stopped. The waiter was back to clear the empty plates, gone and back in a flash with demitasse coffee, proffering Havana puros from a mahogany box. They lit up.

Lopez sat back, inhaling, mulling his answer. He exhaled, blowing out a perfect smoke ring. They watched it drift slowly upward, gradually losing shape, disappearing against the ceiling.

"*Independista*s, yes. They are like that smoke ring, no; something present one moment and gone the next, something, what is the word, evanescent, without substance? If they were a force, why would *we* exist at all? If they were capable of throwing Spain from the island without us, why haven't they done it? They've had enough time."

"They need help."

"Exactly."

"And then?"

"And then Cubans will have their say."

"Which is the objective."

"Self-determination. Yes."

• • •

Lunch was over. The waiter offered more coffee, which was declined. The restaurant began to empty. Will was pressed to return to the customhouse. Lopez reached for his billfold, extracting several bank notes.

But he was not done.

"You are with us of course, Colonel Crittenden. Given your views on Cuba, it could not be otherwise. I've known it from the beginning – though you have been discreet, understandably discreet, I might add. Your distinguished name will add luster to our enterprise."

The young man's eyes betrayed his astonishment. *Colonel Crittenden?*

"I beg your pardon."

"You can be sure that General Worth agrees with my decision. He has seen you in action. You will command a battalion."

The arrow whooshed, so close he could feel its wind. Every sound in the restaurant was instantly heightened: the chatter of people standing to leave, plates clanging, waiters calling, somebody had forgotten something and was returning, cries from the kitchen, the swoosh of a swinging door.

How long did it take to make colonel in the peacetime army? Grant was still lieutenant, as was Winfield Scott Hancock, despite his name. Hard to make general fighting Indians. Hays dropped out. Pickett disappeared. Cousin George was a forty-year-old former brevet major cashiered twice for boozing. Cousin Tom had gone back to lawyering in Frankfort. Pointless to stay in the corps.

His mind was whirling: Col. John Allen, Grandfather Allen, Ma's pa, the last colonel in the Crittenden family, killed at the battle of River Raisin, War of 1812, killed, said Uncle John, because of James Wilkinson, a traitor, a criminal, like his friend Aaron Burr . . . it all flashed back.

His face was flushed. He could do nothing about it. His mind flew to Lucy: How she would love the sound of it! *Colonel Crittenden?* Outrageous? Not at all: war enables the best men to advance quickly. Lee began the Mexican war a captain and came out a colonel.

"General, I am flattered. It is of course impossible. Surely you understand."

Lopez paid no attention. "A well-deserved promotion," he continued. "You have been educated at West Point and fought with distinction in Mexico."

He smiled. "Even a Spanish soldier knows what that means."

# XI

They came to his rooms on St. Ann Street. It was Sunday afternoon. He'd finished dressing and was about to go out to dinner when he heard the sharp rap of the knocker downstairs and Madame Lucas came bustling up to inform him of visitors. Ordinarily she stood at the bottom and called up, but this time, out of breath for she carried some weight, she delivered the message herself.

"*Deux demoiselles*," she said, pausing to catch her breath and speaking in a disapproving tone for she did not approve of her gentlemen receiving young ladies. "*Elles vous attendent.*"

He glanced downstairs to see Dominique and Mary Jane looking up at him with two little caramel faces peering out of prams beside them. He feared immediately. Calling on him alone, unexpected, it would not be a social visit.

Jude had returned to Shelbyville with Lucien, arriving shortly before Elias's death. They were in time to comfort him and bury him on the Crittenden farm, the land he'd worked most all his life. Will had letters from both Jude and Lucien, Jude specifically asking that he say nothing to his wife and sister, as he would shortly be home to inform them directly. He would not wait for Lucien, who had business to finish, but would catch the steamer in Louisville the coming week with the change in Memphis. Don't worry, he counseled his friend. He'd come down the Mississippi once before as a free man.

True enough, the young man thought, but in easier times. The presence of Texas in the Union had changed things drastically, especially on the river. Memphis was the easiest place for the new East

Texas plantations around Marshall to find slaves, buying or stealing them. Natchez was closer, but Governor Quitman had brought an order to the Natchez slave trade that did not exist in Memphis. Auction Square and the slave pens were no more than two hundred yards from the landing and easily visible. It was a bad place for free Negroes to be traveling alone, changing boats, but how else was Jude to get home?

The young women, the same age and build, looked remarkably alike, though Mary Jane was darker. Dressed identically in black high-buttoned shoes, white chiffon ankle-length dresses cinched tightly at the waist, and powder blue bonnets, they fit perfectly on the streets of the Vieux Carré. They carried matching yellow parasols. The children, whom they carried up the stairs, were well behaved, clearly intimidated. He showed them in. The girls had never been to his rooms before; their faces told him it was difficult.

Dominique sat on the divan watching him through dark eyes, a youngster tucked in closely on each side, pretty little things in calico print dresses and yellow ribbons tied in their hair. The children were free quadroons in the New Orleans classification. It was easy to see she'd been crying.

Mary Jane was more composed. "He should have come Friday at the latest," she said. "He's due back at the shop tomorrow. No other ships are due in. Something's wrong. We had no one else to turn to."

He nodded. "You've done the right thing."

Dominique's eyes welled up. He was embarrassed for her. She was the sweetest thing and could not be more in love. She knew she was lucky to get Jude back alive from Buena Vista and was not prepared to lose him again.

"It's what I told her," said Mary Jane. "She was afraid but I said there was no reason."

He was embarrassed in another way as well: He knew that Elias was dead but could tell neither daughter nor daughter-in-law, for the news was traveling with Jude, who had not come.

Dominique was beautiful, but her face was perpetually bathed in a kind of melancholy that even her love for Jude and occasional shy smile never completely erased. What he knew of her story came from Jude, and it was common enough – at least in its beginning: Liliana, an attractive mulatto slave girl and accomplished seamstress, was taken into the house of a Spanish plantation owner near Santiago de Cuba. Before long she was pregnant with Dominique.

What made the story unusual was that the Spaniard had brought mother and daughter to New Orleans, provided them with manumission papers and set them free. Jude believed it was because he did not want complications with his family, who might not desire a mulatto half-sister, but whatever his reasons, bringing them to New Orleans was a generous gesture, perhaps even a gesture of love. He could have sold them away.

Putting his dinner plans aside, he went to the kitchen, set the kettle on the oil burner, and came back with beaten biscuits and jam for the children. Their eyes went to their mothers.

"Will Crittenden," said Mary Jane, "please don't trouble yourself . . ."

"Truth is that I don't have that many visitors."

He stood a moment watching, smiling for the children, encouraging everyone to relax, trying to make it easier for them. At length Mary Jane leaned forward and began spreading jam on the biscuits.

"Do you have any ideas at all?" he asked.

"Ma wrote," said Mary Jane. "Pa's sick, you know, and Jude's been up there a spell. Ma wrote that Jude would catch the boat at Louisville Sunday a week ago. That would land him here on the Thursday steamer from Memphis, Friday latest. Here we are Sunday with no news."

He returned to the kitchen, took the kettle off, and poured hot water into the coffeepot, watching it start to drip. Just as well that he could say nothing about Elias, he reflected: one loss at a time. He watched them from the kitchen, two young women, timid, worried, whispering to each other. How long had they talked before Mary Jane convinced her sister-in-law they should come to him? So many barriers to cross. He needed a plan.

Nothing, he knew, could be more difficult. If Jude had missed the boat or was coming later he would have sent word. The assumption was that something had happened in Memphis, mostly likely that he'd been abducted, common enough for Negroes in Memphis, a hornet's nest of crime, misery and corruption, most likely taken by people who'd destroyed his papers and sold him away. Normally Jude was a careful man, but his life as a New Orleans freeman might have made him overconfident for a place like Memphis.

How anyone could have kidnapped someone of Jude's size and strength was hard to imagine unless they'd drugged or hurt him in some way. His limp might have made him seem an easier target. East Texas and its new plantation culture was the usual destination in such cases, a place where stolen Negroes were hard to trace, a situation soon to be made worse by the Fugitive Slave Act.

The trail had to start in Memphis, during the change of boats. The only other possibility was Natchez where he was not likely to have debarked. In any case, a plantation owner in Mississippi would be chary of dealing for a slave claiming to be a freeman, claiming to be a veteran of the Mexican War; one who had the wounds and papers and testimony to prove it. Lawless East Texas was another matter. He would write John Allen for copies of the manumission papers.

He set out cups on a tray and looked out the window toward Congo Square. Sunday afternoon and the Negroes had been congregating all day, dancing, singing, strutting, parading, making music on their strange handmade instruments with a few clarinets and cornets mixed in. He could see and hear it all – men, women, children in every kind of suit and costume, blacks, mulattoes, quadroons, octoroons, Creoles, slaves with Sunday afternoon off and freemen with their papers carefully sewn into their Sunday best. Only in New Orleans was such a scene possible.

He stood watching for some time. It was good fortune that he was taking leave from the customhouse for now he would have Jude to find. If he was right about Memphis there would be a ring of some kind operating, an organization involved, most likely with official cover. He'd likely have to pay, but someone would know something about it. Jude was not only a big man, he was a big man with a big limp. The bullet was still in him. He stood out.

As he poured the coffee, it suddenly hit him: *Lucy was in East Texas!* He put down the pot and returned to the window, his mind fixed hard on the woman he loved. It was Lucy's fate to have been taken to a place she told him in letter after letter she had loathed from first sight: flat, ugly, empty, and dull. Scintillating Lucy Holcombe with her seminary education, New Orleans tastes, and literary interests stuck in a rural backwater with nothing to do but write in her notebooks and hope the next visitor to Wyalusing would bring a copy of *Harper's* with the latest installment of *Dombey and Son*. She needed a challenge.

Southern belles, he'd heard it said too many times, made boring companions, had nothing to offer outside of bed and children. Lucy was not like that. Her letters were full of exciting ideas for changing things. The notion that woman's role was to sit idly by while men ran the world did not appeal to her, though oddly, he'd discovered, she was not a suffragist. Hers was a well-ordered traditional Southern world in which men fought the wars and ran the governments, and women, in turn, ran the men. They didn't need the vote to do that, just strong characters.

It's what he loved most about her. Feminine and beautiful as she was, she was cleverer and braver than the others and far more ambitious.

Idle and bored in a place she hated, Lucy could look into the matter of a limping, manumitted black freeman, veteran of the Mexican War, gone missing in Memphis and more than likely sold back into slavery somewhere in East Texas, center of the new Texas cotton plantation culture.

Even for a daughter of Tennessee, of the South, someone certain of the beneficence of slavery and ready to die for the Southern plantation way of life, such an injustice would be intolerable. He was certain of it.

# XII

He knew Texas. One bleak winter in a tent on the sands of Corpus Christi awaiting the order to take Mexico was enough Texas for a lifetime. From what Lucy told him he did not expect East Texas to be any better. As they steamed up the meandering Red River toward Shreveport they were heading for a part of Texas he'd only read about: cotton plantation Texas, a hard new place that was a law unto itself, where you didn't go unless you had a reason and were prepared.

He had a reason and was prepared. He'd packed his uniform and revolver, souvenirs from the U.S. Army and Mexico.

Lucy was more beautiful than ever and more exciting. Mrs. Quitman deserved his gratitude for arranging their second meeting at Monmouth, but whose idea had it been – hers, Lucy's, Eugenia's, Governor Quitman's? He had no way of knowing. In any case, the second meeting was just a small gathering of friends – no string quartet, no carriages from Natchez, no Jefferson Davis, no Narciso Lopez. If their goal remained to recruit him to the cause they were remarkably circumspect about it. The only reference to Cuba was when Governor Quitman commented at dinner that he'd heard General Worth was ailing and might not be recovered in time.

"You would take his place, I presume, Governor," Lucy said.

She is bold and relentless, Will thought, but Quitman's hard eyes actually twinkled at the comment and fixed on the young woman with affection. "Ah, but we are hardly there yet, dear lady. We must wait to have more information on General Worth's condition."

On the second day at Monmouth, Eugenia finally stopped hovering about and gave them time alone. He could not quite assess her opinion of him. Perhaps all mothers with marriageable daughters were like that, he thought, courteous toward presentable suitors but wary. It was not as if Lucy didn't have other prospects. She was a catch, though Eugenia would surely know she was too much for most men.

On the third day, Eugenia formally invited him to come on with them to Wyalusing, an invitation he readily accepted. Beverly Holcombe, her husband, often away on business, was playing host to another young veteran of the Mexican war, Elkanah Greer of Tennessee, Anna Eliza's fiancé, and it would please the girls to have both young men in attendance. Will knew something of Greer, who'd been with Jeff Davis's Mississippi Rifles at Buena Vista.

Her mother was happy to make the invitation, Lucy informed him, adding provocatively that Eugenia found Lieutenant Crittenden a pleasing young man from a distinguished Southern family and a definite improvement over Lieutenant Greer, who was respectable enough but boorish. Maman believed that Lieutenant Crittenden could have a career in politics. He was not, of course, to repeat any of it.

He was flattered, though reflected that Eugenia was likely thinking of his name, not his situation. She would assume that with the name Crittenden came expectations – lands and income, perhaps a family trust, a private fortune to enable him to pursue a gentleman's career in government and politics. For reasons he ignored, she already believed that his position at the customhouse was something more than it was. He expected to be thoroughly quizzed on his situation by Beverly before the visit was over. He had nothing to hide.

Eugenia could not know that his visit to East Texas would serve to do more than simply present him to her husband, or that the time Lucy and he spent alone together at Monmouth was not just to flirt:

*For she had found him!*

No sooner had he written about Jude's disappearance and the high likelihood he'd been taken to East Texas than she wrote back with the news. Cotton growing in Texas had begun with statehood only four years earlier and by 1850 amounted to no more than a half dozen plantations clustered just south of Marshall in Rusk County. The arrival of the Holcombes in Marshall to start a plantation was known up and down East Texas and it was no chore at all for the beautiful Lucy to be driven around on the pretense of slave-buying for the new Holcombe plantation.

She'd gone into the fields with the masters. She had no doubt that if Jude was there she would recognize him. He was, after all, one of the tailors at Dubois et fils working on her sister's wedding dress. Even bent over in a cotton field, a man Jude's size was unmistakable. When he walked, the limp was obvious.

She'd found him on a plantation just outside Henderson, southwest of Marshall. He'd seen her walking into the fields with the master, a man named Murchison, and stood up straight, as they all did as she passed.  He recognized her and knew why she was there and she moved her head slightly to indicate he was to show no sign of recognition, but he already knew that.

From Monmouth, Will and the Holcombe ladies caught the Natchez steamer to the Mississippi junction with the Red River, changed to a smaller boat and headed north for Shreveport. He'd never seen worse river land. Summer was fast giving way to early fall but still the land looked inhospitable. The few people they saw were mostly Caddo Indians, whose boats pushed out from the banks for fishing and whose villages spread out in the flat, marshy interior. The absence of white people in that part of Louisiana wasn't from fear of the Caddo, a peaceful tribe, Eugenia explained, but from the fact that most people didn't find the country hospitable.

"Texas is hardly better," Lucy whispered in his ear.

The river was slow-moving and shallow and filled with logs and other debris, not an impressive introduction to upper Louisiana and East Texas. Their boat terminated at a place called Natchitoches and they transferred to a still smaller craft to continue upriver to Shreveport, a town that was something more than Natchitoches but still not much of a place, probably not even a thousand people.

From Natchitoches they caught the ferry across Caddo Lake, a long, sinister body of water separating Texas from Louisiana and cluttered with hundreds of inlets and coves hidden under mossy cypresses and twisted willows and stretching through islands of floating vines and lily pads that looked like they'd been transported directly from prehistoric Mississippi bayous. Gators pushed out, eying them hungrily, eagles soared and water moccasins leapt from the water to snap up unsuspecting insects.

They continued on by carriage to Marshall, some twenty miles to the southwest. It was a memorable trip, their first one together, made more exciting by their growing affection, complicity in their secret, and the coming challenge.

Elkanah Greer, who'd made his reputation with Jeff Davis at Buena Vista, came down from the porch with Anna Eliza to greet the carriage. Eugenia kissed her elder daughter on both cheeks and offered her gloved hand to the young man to touch. The two lieutenants might well have met at Monterrey before the army split to send Will on with Winfield Scott to Mexico City and Elkanah with Zach Taylor and Jeff Davis to Buena Vista, but they had not.

"Very happy to meet you, suh," said Greer, a handsome if dull-eyed man in fine silk shirt and riding breeches. Nearly as tall as Will, though lankier, he examined the visitor with interest and extended his hand. "We shall have much to talk about."

Eugenia, exhausted from the journey, went inside to order preparation for an early supper. Beverly, master of the house, was nowhere to be found, nor was any reference to him made. The four young people walked the grounds, each man with his lady. Will observed that Elkanah and Anna Eliza did not have a great deal of conversation. As they walked, Lucy described the grounds to him without enthusiasm except for a small white belvedere she pointed to by a lily pond at the bottom of a winding path. It was the roof of a summerhouse she called her gazebo, the place she did her writing. She admired all that her father had built in Marshall, just not where he had built it.

Wyalusing was impressive in an East Texas kind of way, also oppressive, a massive imitation Grecian temple with columns. It was a place – like the Parthenon, like the Giza pyramids, like Monmouth – that owed its existence to slave labor. Situated on a hill above Marshall's main thoroughfare, Burleson Street, it looked down on the town like the Acropolis on Athens. Beverly Holcombe, fugitive from Tennessee, was lord of the lands, no question. No other house in Marshall stood near it; from what he had seen, no other house came close to it in size or pretension.

A wide front porch furnished with divans, small tables, and lounging chairs stretched along under Doric columns. The porch looked down the hill toward the town, which spread out in the distance beyond the lily pond and gazebo. On the opposite side of the hill from pond and gazebo were sheds for the slaves. Cotton fields stretched to the horizon.

From Lucy, Will learned that her father, fond of gaming and speculating, had abandoned the family home in Tennessee three years earlier over debts and come to Texas, like so many others, to start over. When the house was completed, Beverly sent for the family, which named the plantation Wyalusing, an Indian name meaning "wayfarer's home" that the girls had learned from the Moravians. The women were reluctant to leave civilized La Grange for remote Marshall but had no choice in the matter. Beverly had done well enough in East Texas to begin paying off his debts and return to the indulgent life to which he was accustomed.

Plantations would soon spread across East Texas as far south as Beaumont. Cotton from the region was of higher quality than Deep South cotton, finer and more in demand by Europe's clothiers. It sold as fast as they could grow it and they grew it as fast as the earth could produce it and the slaves could bring it in. East Texas bales were carted to the Gulf, shipped out of Port Arthur, crossed the Straits of Florida, and rode the Gulf Stream to the marketplaces of Europe.

They ate by candlelight the first night and afterward sat on the porch listening to the last crickets of summer. The evening air was oppressive and the conversation perfunctory. Eugenia was a modest, retiring sort of person, more so even than Anna Eliza. Whence Lucy got her verve and audacity was a mystery to him. Perhaps from the still-missing Beverly? The sisters had not seen each other since Lucy left for Monmouth, but if they had thoughts to exchange they were saving them for later. The men, content to smoke their cigars, made little conversation. If Elkanah knew anything of Will's mission in East Texas – though how would he? – he said nothing about it, which was just as well.

The bedrooms were on the second floor, those of Beverly and Eugenia at the top of the stairs along the main hallway, while the guest bedrooms were down a south wing and the sisters' rooms along the north wing. Each of the girls' rooms had a smaller room adjoined to it, one suitable for nanny, nurse, or child as the case might one day be. Their bedrooms were separated by a short passage, with a bathroom on one side and a walk-in closet on the other. The girls liked to visit each other before extinguishing their candles, as they'd done since they were old enough to have separate rooms.

Though different in all the ways that sisters can be, they were close, used to each other's company and rarely had been separated, though Anna Eliza's marriage would soon put an end to that. They would have disagreed on almost everything (starting with Wyalusing, of which Anna was fond and Lucy was not) if Anna had been more accustomed to making her opinions known.

It was Anna, bursting with curiosity, who knocked on her sister's door that night. Less enterprising than Lucy, she compensated for it with a vivid interest, some might say nosiness, in her sister's affairs. Being more private than Lucy and completely trustworthy, she was used to being taken into her sister's confidence. Only recently engaged to Elkanah, whom she'd met in Tennessee before the move to Marshall, she hoped Lucy would not be far behind.

"He is an Adonis," she said. "I quite understand why you are fond of him even if you won't admit it."

"Adonis? He is my warrior," said Lucy. "Think of him as Apollo, pure of mind, fighting to bring truth and light into a dark world."

"I see your novelist's mind at work."

The girls, in nightgowns, were propped on pillows at opposite ends of Lucy's brass bed. Lucy laughed. "Greek mythology is not my present interest."

"You'll never convince me that adventures in Cuba are your *only* interest."

"Since you insist, I grant that you are right: I am rather fond of him."

"Ha! You who don't like young men! I thank you for your candor. That's more than you admitted at Monmouth. I believe he is more than 'rather fond' of you; fondness has a way of becoming something more, you know."

"As it has for you and Elkanah."

Anna recognized the sarcasm. "I know you don't like Elkanah," she said, petulantly. "You don't do him justice."

"I only wish you'd stand up to him more."

She would not take the bait. "So which is it – the man or the island, the cause or the novel?"

"But it is all inseparable, dear Anna. My confusion is that he should come along at this very moment."

"The spider trapped in her own web."

"What an imagination you have! *You* should be the novelist."

Anna sat up suddenly. "Better than a spider: you are Emma Woodhouse, so busy manipulating others you don't see what's happening to you."

"*Manipulating*? Dear Anna, I am manipulating no one."

"Does he know of your intentions?"

"My *intentions*?"

"Does he know you intend to write a novel?"

It took a moment for Lucy to answer. She believed what she'd just said: Will Crittenden had appeared fortuitously at the precise moment her story needed a protagonist. If it was destiny, how could it be manipulation? Anna was insinuating that her feelings were somehow connected to her ambitions. It was unfair.

"He knows of my passion for writing."

Anna was not the sort to press an advantage. "I suppose your passion for the cause shouldn't surprise me."

"It should not. I've been interested in Cuba since the mission was founded."

"The Moravians did not establish the mission to go to war."

"As women, we cannot go to war, though I wish we could. Surely they could find some use for us near the battlefield. But until that day we can do no less than support just causes with all the passion we have. Lieutenant Crittenden has left the army for want of a cause. As yet he has shown little interest in Cuba."

"And you will light his fires."

"How vulgar you are!"

"I'm teasing. I do hope he and Elkanah will come to like each other."

"I sense," said Lucy, "some awkwardness between them. You didn't say a word about . . ."

"Of course not!"

"Then it's not that."

"Perhaps if they can spend some time together . . ."

"Lieutenant Crittenden will not stay past the weekend. He has his business to conclude and must be back to New Orleans."

"It is a difficult business."

"Very difficult."

"I hope it won't take him away for long. The two men should

come to know each other, don't you think? After all, one day they may be . . ."

Lucy pinched her sister's little toe. "That is all, dear Anna, return to your room and let me sleep. You are writing my novel far too fast."

# XIII

The immediate question facing him, one he contemplated alone in his room that night, was whether to undertake the mission alone or to invite the Rusk County sheriff to accompany him. He saw advantages and disadvantages either way, and they came down to the nature of the sheriff, a man, he learned from Lucy, named Sam Harris. No one but Lucy (and Anna Eliza) knew the true purpose of his visit to Wyalusing. With Elkanah Greer in residence, a man whose inclinations were obvious, he was reluctant to make too many inquiries. He suspected the sheriff would not appreciate the arrival of an outsider to take back property from a citizen of his county, but that property, a manumitted Negro named Jude Freeman, had been stolen. Even in Texas, theft was a crime.

He set out early the next morning before the household was up. He was in uniform and wore his revolver. There could be no mistake about his intentions. The slaves saddled up a fine horse for him, and he took another for Jude. It felt good to be armed and in uniform again and riding into battle. Had he gone to West Point to become a customhouse clerk? They'd done some good in Mexico, hadn't they?

The ride to Henderson was over miles of deserted, wide-open scrub, but in the cool of the morning made for a pleasant ride. The horses cantered along easily, and he had time to think about the new state of Texas. If the Southern rebellion came to pass, Texas, a slave state, would side with the rebels. The Texans had made that clear enough. But by what right would it do so? Even if you conceded that the South had the right to secede – and he agreed with Uncle John that there was nothing in the Constitution that denied it – Texas was a separate matter.

Texas was bought from Mexico and paid for with the blood and treasure of all Americans. Capt. Ephraim Kirby Smith, whose murdered bones lay buried in a blood-drenched grave at Casa Mata, came from Connecticut. Henry Clay Jr., whose body was carried back to Lexington, was a Kentuckian. Colonel McIntosh and Sergeant McTavish were Georgians whose bodies stayed buried in Mexico as did those of the thousands who fell at Resaca de Palma, Monterrey, and Cerro Gordo as they fought their way across Mexico. Jude Freeman, the man he'd come to take home, still carried a bullet in him from Buena Vista. Did these men fight so that Texas could turn its back on the men who paid in blood for its entry into the Union? The question stood heavy on his mind.

Sam Harris was at the rear of the stuffy jail in Henderson, the Rusk County seat, when he entered. In front, a boyish clerk looked up from his newspaper, studied the visitor briefly, and went back to his reading. The building was nondescript wooden frame, scrub pine, one large room with a corridor running off to one side with an empty cell. It looked like the Henderson jail hadn't been getting much action lately, probably a good thing. A spittoon by the sheriff's feet gave off a sour smell, attracting flies. A picture of Governor Wood hung over the desk. The Lone Star flag of Texas stood in a stand near a wall. Nothing in the room identified the building as part of the United States. Nor, for that matter, had anything he'd seen in the uninviting town called Henderson.

"Well now," said the sheriff, looking up, "welcome to Henderson, sonny. We don't see that uniform much in these parts. What can I do for you?"

He let the rudeness pass. He wanted this man on his side, which was why he was in uniform, which by rights he should not have been.

"Lieutenant Crittenden, Sheriff – just a visitor to your fine county, over from Kentucky. Staying up the road in Marshall with the Holcombes. Come here on some private business."

The friendly greeting and mention of the Holcombes seemed to soften him. He reached, they shook hands, and he offered the visitor a chair.

"Crittenden – you wouldn't by any chance be related to . . . ?"

"I am Governor Crittenden's nephew."

"You don't say. Well, what can I do for you? Judging from the looks of you, I gather this is not a social call."

He handed him the manumission document and watched as he read. He'd written to John Allen for a copy of the original, which Jude's kidnappers had surely destroyed. The sheriff's expression never changed. He handed it back.

"You want to tell me how this here piece of Kentucky paper affects your business in Henderson?"

"I believe this freeman was illegally abducted in Memphis. I believe he has been brought to the Murchison plantation near here, where he has been seen. I aim to go out there and take him back. I was wondering if you'd like to come with me."

The sheriff squinted, face darkening, eyes sizing the visitor up. He reached in his desk for a cigar, bit it, spat, and lit it with a few hard puffs. He did not offer one to the visitor, but blew the smoke in his direction. The clerk put down his newspaper and turned to watch.

The sheriff's pistols hung on the wall. Next to them was a closet that would be for ropes and rifles. The sheriff was agitated, no question, wondering what he'd done to earn this unwelcome intrusion on what had promised to be one more uneventful day in Rusk County.

Finally, he spoke: "That could be a mite dangerous, Lieutenant. People in these parts don't like outsiders coming around trying to take their property. Bobby Murchison least of all."

"The question, sir, is whether this man, Jude Freeman by name, is indeed his property. This paper I hold in my hand shows he is not. I aim to interview Mr. Murchison, Sheriff. I wonder if you shouldn't be there with me."

• • •

The plantation lay five miles outside Henderson. It was late morning and the sun close to as high as it would get as they rode up. From a distance he saw the slaves at work in the cotton fields, men and women bent over or hunched down, the men in wide-brimmed hats, women in bandanas. As they approached, some slaves stood up to look over at the soldier and the sheriff coming in with an extra horse, not a common sight on an ordinary East Texas morning. The distance was still too far for Will to recognize faces, which were shadowed by the hats.

The sheriff hadn't said much as they rode but it was clear he was of two minds about the matter. "Why not," he'd said to the clerk, "nothing else on the plate today, right, Billy?" Neither rider knew how Murchison had come to possess the man called Jude but he would have to have ownership documents, forgeries or not. Even in Texas, slaves, like cattle, had to be accounted for, though unlike cattle they weren't branded, just in case they had to be sold again.

They passed the main house, a large, white plains affair of slats and shingles fronted by a porch for evening sitting, a house without taste or pretension. Behind the house Will spied a grizzled man in a chair on the dirt outside the barn. A coffee cup perched on a cotton bale beside him. Stetson pushed back, stomach resting on his knees, piece of hay dangling from his mouth, he leaned forward toting up numbers. He'd heard them coming but didn't bother to look up.

"Morning, Bobby," the sheriff called as they dismounted.

Eventually he looked up, pulling his hat forward and sitting back to watch them approach. His face showed nothing. He treated the arrival of the sheriff and a U.S. Army officer, the officer leading an extra, saddled horse, as an event of no particular interest. He grunted something, let the hay drop from his mouth, and laid his pencil down. He did not stand.

"Bobby, this here is Lieutenant Crittenden, over from Kentucky, and he has brought me this here piece of paper. I want you to have a look at it."

Murchison eyed but did not greet the intruder. Sheriff Harris handed him the manumission, which he read slowly, leaning forward, lips moving ever so slightly.

He looked from the document to the horses. "What's this all about, Sam?"

"I believe it concerns one of your slaves, Bobby."

"And how would that be?"

"Sir," Will said, finally speaking, "you have a man working in your fields who is a freeman. This man, Jude Freeman by name, was a slave on my brother's farm in Shelbyville, Kentucky. He received manumission by my brother. He moved to New Orleans where his family resides. He was returning to New Orleans from Shelbyville, where his father had died, when he went missing in Memphis. He has been seen in your fields. He is a free man who has been illegally abducted and . . ."

"He ain't here, sonny . . . you got b-a-a-d information. What's all this babble about, anyway? Whoever he is, wherever he is, he's jes one more nigger, ain't he?"

The words were spat out like tobacco juice. Will was taken aback, taking a moment to gather himself. "Sir, you have interrupted me."

Murchison straightened, started to get up, but changed his mind. He'd heard the threat in the voice. He saw the pistol. The sheriff eyed the soldier uneasily.

"As I was saying, this man is a freeman. He has been kidnapped and seen in your fields. I have come to take him back with me."

Maybe he didn't need to add the last part, but he was angry. The man had shown his character, shown he didn't intend to make it easy. The sheriff needed to be pressed. They were at the scene of a crime. He didn't know if Murchison was a principal in the crime or merely a dupe and didn't much care.

In the back of the barn they heard voices and saw movement, difficult to make out in the shadows. Murchison turned and called out, waving the men to come up. Sheriff Harris, uneasy with men moving toward him in the dark, shifted his weight and tried to make out faces.

"Well, now, that's interesting, sonny – you coming out here to take property from me. I mean jes how you aim to do that all by yourself?"

Two men in dungarees, faces near black with sun and cotton dust, emerged silently from the shadows, carrying pitchforks. Frowning at what they saw, they stopped and leaned back against the barn.

"I am not by myself. I represent federal law and this man beside me represents Texas law. That should be sufficient."

The sheriff's face was a mask. He was looking around and waiting to see how things played out. Siding with either of them carried its risks.

Murchison's squinty eyes crusted with milkweed and hayseed squeezed down on Will. "Damn woman, warn't it?"

"Whatcha mean, Bobby?" said the sheriff.

"Man listed on this here paper don't work for me. Even if he did, you wouldn't git him, except maybe you offered the right price. If he was here, I mean. I've always got slaves for sale." The squinty eyes widened a little, and he looked to the men leaning against the barn. "Don't I, boys?"

"Oh, he's here all right," Crittenden said, "and if you take the sheriff and me into your fields I'll have no trouble identifying him. His description will match every detail on this manumission."

"You ain't goin' into my fields. Now git off my property."

"And if there is any doubt," he continued, "I will ask him to take a few steps to see if he has a limp, for you see, this man is a veteran of the Mexican War and was wounded at Buena Vista, fighting along-side Jefferson Davis and Henry Clay Jr. Were you in the war, sir? Or were you sitting here by your bale of cotton drinking coffee while the rest of us did the fighting to secure Texas's place in the Union?"

He meant to provoke and succeeded. The man turned beet red, stood up and took a step toward the soldier before turning to the sheriff. "Sam, I reckon I won't take you into my fields with this here Kentuckian. Git him off my property!"

It was always likely to come to that and just as well, which is why he wore the revolver. They all understood it, including the sheriff, who put one hand on his pistol. Whether it was just reflex or meant to send a signal to the men with the pitchforks, he didn't know, but they all saw it.

"Well, I think maybe as long as we've come all this way we might as well have a look, Bobby. What's the harm, anyway? Might save some unpleasantness."

So the sheriff had decided. Will pressed his advantage. "May I ask you, sir, how this freeman came into your possession?"

Scowling, furious, Murchison considered his answer, which would determine how things went. To admit anything would be to confess participation in a crime – whether it was kidnapping, forgery, or simple complicity in stolen property would be determined by a court – or more likely by the sheriff, who did not seem to be on his side. The man had no proof that could stand up against identification and legal manumission – even in East Texas. To start a fight with an armed U.S. Army officer and county sheriff was hardly a better option.

No one said another word. Murchison turned, nodded to the men, and walked away into the barn. They were led into the cotton fields. Jude was identified and brought in from the fields with no further mention of price and no charges brought against Bobby Murchison.

It was just one of those Texas things.

• • •

They dropped the sheriff at his office and started up the road to Marshall. Jude wore a smile on his face as they rode along.

"You must have been damn furious out there in the fields," Will said. "You a free man and all."

Jude looked over at him. He had the slouch hat pulled down and wore the slave denims. His beard had grown and had already some gray. He was twenty-seven years old. They both were.

"Oh, I knew you were coming."

"Because you saw Lucy."

"Oh, I knew before that."

Will laughed. "The cards, I suppose."

"That's it. The cards."

"It was Memphis, right? How'd they do it? Man your size doesn't hide easily."

"Drugged me. Between boats, I went to the market, saw a sign saying 'Colored-Eats,' sat down to drink some coffee. That's all I remember."

"Think you could find the place again?"

"Now, why would I want to do that?"

"Might save some other freeman from ending up at Murchison's."

"They were Negroes in there, too. It was a colored place."

"Everyone has his price, eh?"

"What kind of Negro sells free Negroes back into slavery?"

"Next time through Memphis I aim to find out."

"I'd leave it be if I were you."

"If you were me? I wonder if you would do that, Jude. I truly do."

# XIV

Lucy was in the garden when they rode in. Elkanah and Anna Eliza watched from the settee at the far end of the porch. Elkanah stared hard, wondering at what he saw – the uniform and the revolver and the big Negro coming in. The situation was difficult. Will was a guest of the Holcombes, Texas planters and slave owners. There was no way that Lucy, even if she'd cared to, could bring a colored man, free or not, into the house. Texas did not recognize free Negroes. Negroes were slaves. As for Elkanah, Will felt no call to give explanations.

He inquired if they might put him up at the hotel in Marshall, but Jude wanted no part of it. In any case, the hotel didn't take coloreds. There were no Negroes in Texas who weren't slaves. He might need his revolver just to get him back to New Orleans. Jude longed to get back to his family, but Will was a guest and they could not leave before the weekend was over. Jude headed around back to the slave quarters.

Dinner at Wyalusing was served at one o'clock except on Sundays when it was delayed until two to give everyone time for church and drinks. The later hour also gave Eugenia time to gather the slaves behind the kitchen after church and lead them in singing and prayer. There was no church in Marshall for slaves, Texas plantation life still too new for such refinements. Eugenia compensated by providing a homespun church of her own. She was a pious woman and saw no contradiction between slavery and piety as long as you treated your slaves with humanity. Slavery was condoned by the Bible. In her short time in Marshall already she'd become one of the town's leading church patrons. She'd asked Will about his religion and was pleased to learn that his family, like hers, was Presbyterian.

Sunday was his last full day in Marshall, and he accompanied the family to church, down the Wyalusing hill and along State Street. It was a pleasant promenade, people smiling and greeting each other as they did on Sunday-mornings-going-to-church across the country, able to forget for one day the separatist turmoil that had the nation straining at the seams. Lucy was unusually gay as she walked beside him, smiling and greeting people as if she loved the town as much as any native, of which there weren't many. Not yet a decade old, still a place of newcomers and drifters, Marshall was something of a boom-town thanks to the high quality of its cotton. A dozen or so stores, shut up for the Sabbath, lined up along State Street, with still more spreading down the side streets.

Eugenia pointed out their destination as they approached: a plain, redbrick edifice standing off by itself in a bare lot, the building obviously of recent vintage. The belfry was unfinished, the steeple yet unpainted, ivy trying to climb the walls but not succeeding. In the yard outside, a sign mounted on a wood post announced:

### FIRST PRESBYTERIAN CHURCH OF MARSHALL

Most of the congregation, Eugenia explained, consisted of Presbyterians obliged to attend Congregational services until they'd raised the money for their own church. Entering, he observed a simple interior of stained birch pews, a carved pulpit and chancel and no altar, demonstrating that they were good Scotch-Irish Presbyterians, not Episcopalians. It was a simple place, with plain, colorless windows – one day, Eugenia remarked, to be replaced by leaded stained glass. The new pastor, the Rev. Moses W. Staples, from Cincinnati, had been unable to resist their very generous offer, she told him, and the challenge of bringing the message of Calvin and Knox to the frontier. The Reverend and Mrs. Staples would be joining them afterward for lunch at Wyalusing.

The sermon was a well-argued homily on sin and salvation; the singing lively, though in the Presbyterian tradition, not too lively. The Holcombes occupied a front pew on one side of center aisle, marked by their name on a well-shined brass plate. Will and Elkanah sat by the sisters, whose simple beauty and elegance stood out among Presbyterians who try not to stand out. Beverly and Eugenia anchored the pew on the aisle. He heard some whispering after the sermon and saw Eugenia reminding her husband, who may have been dozing, to open his billfold for the passing plate. Will had not seen much of his host, who spent more time out of the house – riding the plantation, Lucy said – than at home. He was a tall, thin, pink-faced man with wispy dark hair, friendly enough in a dissipated way, though laconic, the kind of man who kept a flask handy, though probably not in church.

Accompanied by the Reverend Staples, his wife, and a few church friends, the family headed back up the hill after the service. While Beverly led most of the group onto the porch to prepare drinks, four of the party made their way to the back. Will looked around for Lucy, but found only Eugenia, Anna Eliza, and the Reverend Staples by his side. Already coming up the hill they'd heard singing, and rounding the house came upon a sea of black faces stretching across a grassy knoll reaching to the cotton fields behind. The congregation was at least a hundred strong – men, women, and children, all quietly listening to a clear-voiced contralto in colorful Sunday calico singing the gospel. Will spied Jude and slipped off to see him.

"You all right?"

"I'm the slave who doesn't work."

For two days he'd bunked and eaten with them. While they worked the fields, he read the Bible and did some sewing. Evenings he entertained them with stories of Mexico and New Orleans. Some of them had family from which they'd been separated, and he promised to take messages to anyone they wished to reach. None could read or write and some hardly knew English. He astonished them with what he could do. Most had never seen a free Negro before. He'd shaved his beard and looked in good spirits, far better than when Will had picked him out of Murchison's cotton fields.

"They're a good family, Will, nothing like that bunch in Henderson. These people are looked after. As slavery goes, I've seen worse. When the master's away the overseer is a slave himself. I talked to him, asked him if any ever run away. 'Where'd they run to?' he said. 'Never make it alive to Mexico.'"

Sunday clothes were scarce but they'd done their best. Jude had done some patching. When the contralto finished, Eugenia mounted the porch off the kitchen to lead them in hymns, which they knew and sang out in loud, stirring voices. The singing over, Anna Eliza stepped forward to read scripture. The slaves listened intently, chanting verses they knew when their turn came.

There'd been a murmur when the Reverend Staples went up on the porch with the women and seated himself on a chair. They knew who he was. The women were fine, but Staples in his black suit and white collar was the real thing. He was a strange-looking man, red-faced and physically intimidating for a preacher, nothing like the gentle Presbyterians Will remembered from Shelbyville and Cloverport. He was hard-eyed and intense, nearly bald but with a thick, black, well-tended beard and no mustache. He had a vigorous but oddly high-pitched voice when he joined in the singing and recitations. He'd left his cassock behind, and wore a simple churchman's collar under his black frock.

When Anna Eliza finished he stood up. There was some clapping, and he raised his arms to stop them. He knew what they wanted. As his reedy tenor voice began to sing the familiar words: *"Amazing grace, how sweet the sound, that saved a wretch like me,"* members of the congregation rose as one, clasped arms, and began singing and swaying together. They knew the words. They pulled it into their own key and took over.

*"I once was lost but now am found; was blind but now I see."*

They ran through all the verses, voices robust and true. Will heard Jude's voice rise among them, his clear baritone filling the air. His eyes found Will's and told him to sing and so he joined in as best he could. It was a joyful scene that he would never forget. Slavery did not have to be an awful thing.

The singing done, Reverend Staples turned to scripture, announcing Corinthians I.

"And Christ died for our sins . . ."

The chorus sounded: *"Ye-e-e-s-s, Lord!"*

"And that he was buried, and that he rose again the third day . . ."

*"Ye-e-e-s-s, Lord, y-e-e-s-s!"*

"And that he was seen of Cephas, then of the twelve."

*"Glory be to God!"*

"After that, he was seen of above five hundred brethren at once . . ."

*"Amen, Lord!"*

"After that he was seen of James, then of all the apostles . . ."

*"Pra-a-i-i-s-s-e the Lord!"*

The air was alive with clapping and hosannas surely heard from one end of Burleson Street to the other. The Reverend Staples beamed down on his black flock.


The dinner bell rang, and a Negro butler came out to escort them to the dining room. Place cards showed the seating, and they crowded around searching for their names. Everyone finally in place, Beverly rose with a welcome toast to the great state of Texas. Any reference to God or the Union would have to await the Reverend Staples, who did not disappoint. He invited them to join hands. Lucy was on Will's right, her hand warm in his. The parish lady on his left smiled as they joined hands. Hers was not as warm. The preacher began:

*Thank you Lord for the fellowship around this table,*
*for the good hearts that unite us in the love of Jesus Christ on*
*this Sabbath. As we prepare to enjoy the feast prepared by our*
*hostess, to whom our church and community owe so much,*
*let us raise our glasses to her, to her wonderful family and to*
*our guests from other states, to these young men who have*
*fought to defend the honor of our country and may one day*
*be called on again to defend the sanctity of the Union.*

The toast was unmistakable. As the guests raised their glasses to clink, he saw Elkanah hesitate until the plump lady on his left reached over and clinked for him. Anna Eliza on his right did the same thing.

They were a dozen at table, including two couples from church, friends of Eugenia. A light white Texas wine was offered, which kept the guests happily chattering. The main course was leg of lamb, and everyone had his fill. Two slaves in finery kept the glasses and plates filled. Will was surprised to find such elegance in Texas, which had always seemed a backward place to him.

"These two boys," Beverly said to the Reverend Staples as plates were being passed for seconds, "served together in Mexico but never met before coming to Wyalusing, Reverend. What do you think of that?"

"Ah came to Monterrey," drawled Elkanah, "with Jefferson Davis's Mississippi Rifles. Ah believe that Lieutenant Crittenden had already left to join General Scott."

With Lucy's help, he'd mostly managed to steer clear of Elkanah, who clearly had something on his mind but not yet found the opportunity to express it. With Will leaving the next morning, time was running out.

"*President* Scott, the Whigs would hope to believe," said Beverly, humorously. "Isn't that so, Lieutenant Crittenden?"

The patriarch's amiable face shined down the table on him. He'd had no tête-à-têtes with his host so far. If Beverly thought his young guest was likely to become his younger daughter's future husband, he'd shown no interest in interviewing him about it. He had all the markings of a gambler – secretive, elusive, asking no questions, giving no answers. Will suspected his marriage with Eugenia to have been arranged, for he'd observed nothing their two natures had in common.

The introduction of politics at Sunday dinner was a surprise, but Beverly had had time to enjoy his drinks while the others were in back singing and praying.

"I don't think so, Daddy," said Lucy, laying her hand on Will's arm and answering before he could say a word. "One president from Mexico – and it is General Taylor to whom I refer, God rest his soul – is quite enough. I believe Mr. Breckinridge will be the next president. Don't you agree, Lieutenant Crittenden?"

She was dressed in white satin and lace to her neck and wore a black silk collar with a cameo pendant. Her dark hair was pulled back in a chignon and parted in the middle. The effect was both elegant and severe and contrasted, as fully intended, with her playful manner.

"Mr. Breckinridge of Kentucky?" said Beverly, surprised. "That is news to me. Lieutenant Crittenden is from Kentucky. Does he have an opinion on that?"

Beverly seemed to have Cousin George's weakness and none of his strengths. From what Lucy said, her father was seldom home and not always "riding the plantation" as he pretended. She'd said no more about it, but the impression was that though Beverly tried to be discreet, his habits were well enough known to everyone. Eugenia, having no choice in the matter, tolerated it. Lucy did not, which created some tension in the family.

"Lieutenant Crittenden's uncle is governor of Kentucky," Lucy offered.

"I hear he has been mentioned for president as well," said the Reverend Staples, who as a former Ohioan knew something of Kentucky.

Political talk over the deal-making in Washington was at fever pitch. Would the former Mexican territories be slave or free? Texas wanted to spread its borders all the way to California. Zach Taylor, who'd threatened to hang the Texans if they tried it, had taken sick at a July Fourth celebration at the Washington Monument and died of the cholera, replaced by Vice President Millard Fillmore, a New Yorker about whom nobody knew or cared much. He certainly would not be re-elected in '52.

"Do you know Mr. Breckinridge, Lieutenant?" asked Beverly.

Customs in Marshall were clearly different from those in Frankfort, where no one dared talk politics at Sunday dinner. How could he talk of John Breckinridge, a man his own age and boyhood friend of Cousin Tom, but who as a Democrat had become a political rival of Uncle John? John C. Breckinridge, from one of Kentucky's oldest families, was a reasonable man, but was no Unionist and would go with the South if war came, no question.

It occurred to him that all these people at table knew where they stood on these matters and he alone did not. Counting on Uncle John and Henry Clay to head off conflict among the states, he'd pushed any thoughts of it from his mind, easy enough to do in a place like New Orleans. For weeks, his thoughts had been to Lucy and Jude. Politics had no place.

It was his mistake. In Washington, the two sides were trying desperately to put together an agreement to head off civil war, the agreement to be known as the Compromise of 1850. In Frankfort or Shelbyville or Cloverport, no one could talk of these things without tempers rising, thus they did not talk about them. In Marshall, where everyone, with the possible exception of the Reverend Staples, was in agreement, there was no risk.

His dilemma was the dilemma of every Kentuckian: Ohioans like Sam Grant, Texans like Beverly Holcombe, Mississippians like Jeff Davis, and Tennesseans like Elkanah Greer knew where they stood. Kentuckians, caught in the middle, did not, or if they did know mostly kept it to themselves to avoid rifts in family and community.

He thought his views closer to Breckinridge of Kentucky than to Grant of Ohio, but Grant and Breckinridge, reasonable men looking for reasonable solutions to the problem – like Uncle John himself – were not the problem.

The extremists were the problem, and he'd seen it in their first encounter: Elkanah Greer was an extremist.

# XV

He'd seen it in the eyes, felt it in the handshake, observed it in the twitch of the lips, heard it in the superciliousness with which he talked of the Mississippi Rifles. To be sure, the Rifles had a grand victory at Buena Vista, but then they went home. Zach and Jeff and Elkanah and the others at Buena Vista retreated to their plantations, leaving the dirty jobs at Puebla, Churubusco, and Casa Mata to the rest of them.

The Northern extremists, the abolitionists, were just as bad in his eyes. The South, after all, did not seek to change the North. The South asked only to be left alone. Most in the North were willing to live and let live, turn the argument over slavery toward the West and the new territories, making sure that the abomination that was plantation slavery stayed quarantined in the South. The abolitionists weren't content with that, but sought to remake the South in the Northern image, to do away with cotton, with plantation life, with Southern culture and tradition, the mind and way of the South.

But plantation life didn't have to be bad. For every Bobby Murchison there was a John Allen Crittenden or Eugenia Holcombe who took care of their slaves, kept families together, tended to their needs, granted manumission when deserved, even had slaves like Josie and Elias who turned it down. Hadn't he just that morning witnessed the civilizing mission of plantation life, slaves praying and singing so that even a man of their own race, a free man like Jude Freeman, attested that they were well looked after? What would these Negroes do if freed? They were not like Jude. They had not been educated from childhood to read and write, and some barely spoke English. Freed, they would be cast adrift with nothing to do but make trouble. It would take generations to teach and prepare them for something beyond the cotton fields. He thought of Grant's solution, mentioned during countless games of bridge: Send them to Haiti.

Easy enough said, but would Haiti take them?

He looked down the table to Beverly. By now the servants had cleared the table, brushed the tablecloth, laid out dessert plates and brought in two steaming pies, apple and cherry, which sat in front of Beverly, ready for slicing. But the master sat motionless, staring at him, eyebrows arched over his florid face, pie knife suspended in air, waiting, as were the others, for his response: Did he know Mr. Breckinridge?

Of course he knew Mr. Breckinridge.

"John Breckinridge is a fine Kentuckian and close friend of my family," he began, speaking slowly. "I had not known, however, until this very moment, that he was considered a candidate for the presidency of the United States. Mr. Breckinridge and I are the same age in addition to being from the same state. We have the same education, though in different professions. We are old acquaintances."

He paused to look around the table, finally turning to Lucy on his right. "Perhaps Miss Holcombe would inform us why she prefers Mr. Breckinridge in the White House and not me."

A split-second silence was followed by an eruption of laughter around the table, the Reverend Staples's tenor peals heard above all others.

"Well said, sir!" cried Beverly, slashing into the pies.

Lucy turned to face him when the laughter died down, smiling prettily: "I believe Mr. Breckinridge is a Democrat. Is that not reason enough to prefer him?"

"*And I am not?* And how do you know I am not, ma'am?"

Again laughter broke out. Lucy laid her hand on his arm. "I believe *all* the Crittendens are Whigs. Or am I wrong, sir?"

She loved to provoke, and he didn't mind at all. In all his life he'd never before met an opinionated woman, unless strong opinions on God and the Bible be counted. Even if he disagreed with her, he found it stimulating, arousing.

He smiled back at her, but before he could answer Elkanah Greer, who had been neither smiling nor laughing, intervened.

"I would prefer to see Mr. Jefferson Davis nominated."

The comment silenced the table. "No doubt because you served with him," said Beverly after a moment, starting to hand out dessert plates to the servants to be passed around. "But is that reason enough?"

"If you had seen Mr. Davis at Buena Vista, sir, you would say it is enough. It was the most splendid piece of fighting I have ever seen. I do not exaggerate to say that Mr. Davis put Mr. Taylor in the White House."

"None of us should thank him for that," said Lucy.

More laughter. "Well said, my dear," cried Beverly, "well said!"

"Indeed!" added Elkanah. "I do not believe that was Colonel Davis's intention in securing that great victory."

Perhaps he should have come to the defense of old Zach, a cousin, a Whig, a good general and the man Uncle John, not Jeff Davis, put in the White House, but he hardly considered Sunday after-church dinner at Wyalusing the place for serious political discussion. He let his eyes fall a moment on Elkanah, a humorless but worthy representative of the hard-eyed intractables of the Deep South, the ones who preferred war to the slightest intrusion on their ways.

For all his skill as a soldier, cleverness as a politician and charm as a man, Jefferson Davis would not win a single vote outside the South. John Breckinridge would not win many, but as a Kentuckian bought up in the compromising tradition of Henry Clay and John J. Crittenden, he might win some.

Elkanah stared back. Whatever was bubbling away in him had just about risen to the top. The others sensed it as well. The table fell silent, anticipating.

"Mr. Crittenden," he said, leaning back in his chair, stiff, formal, always the soldier, "I want to be fair with you, sir, so I will put my question directly. I have meant to do so for two days, but you are a hard man to corral." He paused to glance around the table. "Is it true, sir, that you came all the way from New Orleans to Marshall to take a nigra back from Texas with you?"

Will started to rise, but Lucy clapped him hard on the arm.

"*Mr. Greer!*" cried Eugenia. "Wyalusing is no place for such talk!"

"Begging your pardon, ma'am, it is a direct question posed by a direct man. I can do no less."

"You will not do so here in my house – *and at Sunday dinner!*"

Lucy held him fast, and as he looked from Eugenia back to Elkanah he understood that she'd kept him from doing something stupid. Elkanah was under attack. He was not. Eugenia looked down the table for a ruling from her husband and saw him frozen with a piece of pie before his open mouth. Closing his mouth without a bite, he looked not discomfited at all, but rather amused. Lucy's grip was surprisingly strong as she stared straight ahead, across the table, at Elkanah.

Laying down his pie, Beverly spoke: "Mrs. Holcombe, I yield to you as always. But can there be any harm in Lieutenant Crittenden answering the question that all of us have wondered about?" He chuckled. "These two gentlemen may be – and I emphasize *may be* – joining our little family one day. Would it not be best if they understood each other? We won't let the topic go any further, but if Lieutenant Crittenden has a desire to answer Lieutenant Greer it might be better for all that we heard it here. Wouldn't you agree, dear?"

He felt Lucy's fingers dig into him as she listened to her father's little speech, of which she clearly didn't approve. Eugenia gave a short jerk of her head to indicate she would not quarrel with the master. The Reverend Staples cleared his throat, aware of the rashness of his host's ruling.

"I am at Wyalusing, sir," Will replied slowly, "at the invitation of Mrs. Holcombe. I am honored to be a guest at this table. While here I had some private business to tend to, which now has been successfully transacted."

It was all he intended to say, but Lucy took up the attack. "Well stated, sir," she said, glaring at her future brother-in-law. "I do believe, sir, that Lieutenant Crittenden's business in Marshall is a matter for Lieutenant Crittenden alone. Why should you have an opinion on it?"

He wanted to throw his arms around her and cover her white neck in kisses. It did not pain him to have his cause defended by Miss Holcombe, whose disputatiousness was less likely to lead to unpleasantness than his own. The table remained deathly silent, not the clink of a fork on bone china or the tinkle of crystal glass to be heard. Beverly finally took his bite and posed his fork noiselessly. Greer's mouth was agape. He regarded himself as a match for any man; most certainly he was a duelist, but it was possible he had never before been challenged by a woman. Now he'd set two of them against him, though the third, Anna Eliza, poor girl at his side, looked hopelessly at sea.

"It seems to me," Elkanah began, surely grateful he'd picked the right Holcombe girl to engage himself to, "that . . ."

Still he felt the lady's hand clamping his arm. "But it is not your affair, sir," she said, interrupting. "Or am I wrong?"

*That* was the moment, *that* was his chance, a direct question, a direct challenge, press on with the matter or shut up. Eugenia looked ghostly pale, shocked at her daughter's audaciousness. Beverly's eyebrows arched high on his pink skull. The table waited for Elkanah, who was clearly disconcerted.

He looked from master to mistress, then to Anna Eliza who stared stonily forward, then back to Lucy. He closed and opened his mouth, seemed about to say something when he was struck with the impossibility of situation. This was, after all, to be his family. He shrugged and bit into his pie.

But the matter was not finished.

"Sir, you mentioned Buena Vista," Will said. "Were you there?"

Frowning, Elkanah looked across to him. "You know I was."

"My friend Henry Clay Jr. of Kentucky was there as well."

"Of course he was," said Greer, puzzled. "Colonel Clay fell at Buena Vista. The Kentuckians were on our flank. They fought bravely."

"The nigra, as you put it – the manumitted Negro freeman whom I have now rescued from his Texas kidnappers – was also at Buena Vista. He fought with Colonel Clay's Kentucky Volunteers. He was wounded on the day Colonel Clay was killed. The bullet is still in his hip. He is out back as we speak, freed from his abductors. I was in Mexico City by then, but I'm sure he would be happy to reminisce with you about that great victory if you had a moment."

Looking around the table, Will lifted his glass. "May I offer a toast to Henry Clay and to all the brave Americans who fought at Buena Vista; to all those who helped secure that great victory for the Union against Mexico."

"Hear, hear!" cried the Reverend Staples, raising his glass, breaking the tension. "To Buena Vista!"

Smiles spread around the table and one by one the guests raised their glasses. Elkanah was last. He knew what was being done, but still needed to negotiate marriage with this family. Up came his glass, slowly.

He was amazed at how she'd handled it, sending the man threatening to ruin Sunday dinner into a sullen sulk. His heart was engorged with love and respect for her. He turned to talk to her, but she'd already turned away to talk to the Reverend Staples. The church lady at his side asked something about Mexico and as he answered his eyes drifted across to Lucy's sister.

Anna Eliza was eighteen months older than Lucy, prettier, with more girlish features, also paler, clearly more fragile. Modest, maidenly, religious, she'd let the conversation swirl about her without adding a word. From time to time she glanced at her mother, who smiled back sweetly. Will wondered what could attract such gentle flower to a brute like Elkanah Greer.

How could these two girls, he wondered, whose lives had been nearly identical, have turned out so differently? With their slender builds, dark hair, and pretty faces they were alike in physical resemblance only. As young girls, they'd been sent to the Moravian Seminary, but Christianity seemed to have taken only with Anna Eliza. Lucy was an original, showing as little inclination for religion as he himself. Her passion was politics – politics and writing, telling him of the awards she'd won at school for composition. She was a free thinker, fearless, depending on no man or church for her tastes or ideas.

He recalled how her eyes had brightened on their first meeting at Monmouth, surely as much at his name as at his person. Perhaps she suspected that all Crittendens were not Whigs – or if they were, that she could do something about it. He'd seen her ambition from the beginning. But had he confused political with literary ambition? Women could not serve, could not even vote. But they could write. Why else would she show such passion for Cuba and for Narciso Lopez?

Dinner done, Beverly led the guests into the drawing room for coffee. Steering him clear of Elkanah, Lucy took his arm and guided him across the room, over the porch, and onto the path leading down the hill to the lily pond. It was well after four o'clock, the high heat of the day passed but still not the slightest waft of breeze discernable. He couldn't understand people living in a place like Marshall, flat, dry, and boring, with trees as scarce as Union flags. Lucy hated it. She was a city girl, a social and literary creature, someone bound to chafe under the tedium of the frontier, whatever its high pretensions.

The path descended between a few freshly planted birch and ash saplings, ending at the pond, nourished by well water and covered in water lilies. The gazebo was painted bright white, and they'd attached screens to keep out critters and insects. The interior was arranged comfortably, with low, soft-cushioned rattan furniture, tables with candles and a fireplace for wet or wintry days. Bookcases lined the walls. A desk was stocked with pens, paper, notebooks and letters.

"It is my place," she said, proudly. "Daddy built it for me. I come here to read and write. It is the only thing that saves me." Her hand gently touched his. "Many of the letters you see are from you – and from General Lopez, of course."

He must have frowned, for she pulled back, scrutinizing him.

"I hope, sir, with all my heart," she said, reaching for his hand, "that you will join his enterprise. I see you, dear Colonel, as my Lafayette, gone off to help an oppressed people gain their freedom. Oh, can anything be grander!"

He hardly heard her, though did not miss the word *colonel*. He lifted her hand to his lips and brought her to him and held her body tight against his own. She came willingly and they fell onto the sofa with the satin rustling as they came together in a passion he'd never felt before. She felt it too. Her body heat radiated through the satin. Whether she'd felt it before he could not have said, though he would not have doubted it.

"How I love you, Lucy!"

The words slipped out before he knew it. Even for a man firmly in control of himself, inured to show only emotions he intends to show, love removes the protections. She ran her fingers through his hair, and in the exquisite privacy and intimacy of her little place they kissed in the fading light to the music of the pond critters coming alive outside.

"Such a man," she said, leaning back from him. "A toast to Buena Vista, indeed! I do believe Elkanah will never live it down."

"Such a woman! I thought Elkanah would challenge *you* to a duel."

"And you would have stepped in for me, brave sir."

"It would have been my pleasure."

They fell back into each other's arms.

To have died without that afternoon would have been to live a wasted life. He'd known it from the first: She was a fighter. At that moment, he would have done anything for her. They were two of a kind.

# PART FOUR

✳

# DECISION

# XVI

From Wyalusing, he took Jude back down the Red River to New Orleans. After arranging an extension with the customhouse, he prepared to catch the steamer upriver. Instead of writing to Uncle John, he would travel to Frankfort. With the slow mails, there'd been a crossing of letters and confusion of facts but finally things were cleared up: Jude had been abducted and rescued; Josie had accepted manumission after Elias's burial and would come to New Orleans to join her family; he would meet her in Louisville and bring her back with him.

Beyond that, he had business in Memphis.

As he prepared to leave his rooms one morning, Madame Lucas came rapping, presenting him with two calling cards, which he inspected carefully:

**Cirilo Villaverde**
Attorney at Law, poet, novelist
Club of Havana
PO Box 15491
New York, NY

**Ambrosio José Gonzales**
Attorney at Law, professor of languages
Club of Havana
PO Box 15491
New York, NY

The cards belonged to two of the Cubans he'd met at Monmouth. He asked Madame Lucas to invite them up.

From postwar Mexico City, he recalled a certain type of Hispanic gentleman: educated, courteous, prosperous, one that didn't fit any type he'd previously encountered in Mexico. After Chapultepec, while Nicolas Trist moved to Guadalupe Hidalgo to negotiate a treaty with the new Mexican government, the American officers who remained in Mexico City under General Quitman found themselves sought after by Mexican society. They did not doubt the primary motivation for the hospitality: to ease the hardships of foreign occupation. But there was more to it.

War brings out the brutish side of people; with peace, gentler natures can resurface. The Mexicans they met during the occupation sought to put Santa Anna and the years of conflict behind them and reestablish good relations with their northern neighbor. These Mexicans knew of the "all Mexico" movement afoot in the States to annex their defeated country, and their purpose was simple: to show the occupiers that Mexican culture and society was distinct from anything north of the border. Many of them had been educated in Spain, possessed all the courtliness and flourishes of the Old World, and sought to impress upon their uninvited guests that while the two nations might live together, they did not fit together.

The Cubans he'd met at Monmouth, including the two now ascending to his rooms, were of the same sort, men of learning and achievement, perhaps not as prosperous as the Hispanics of Mexico City, for Cuba was not so rich a place, but men equally worldly, equally cultivated, equally determined to defend the rights and honor of their country. He remembered well their presentations at Monmouth.

He greeted them courteously, settled them onto his couch, and went to the kitchen to make coffee. While it brewed, he reflected that Cubans and Mexicans really were the same people, at least among the elites: All Spaniards at origin, some settled in Mexico, some in Cuba, some in South America. There were even some, like Lopez himself, who were part of all of it, Venezuela, Cuba, Spain, even the United States. He had no doubt about the purpose of their visit, and he would listen to them as attentively as he'd listened to Lopez. He could not deny that Cuba had been much on his mind since returning from Wyalusing.

Villaverde was tall, courtly, impassive, with a long face ringed by a black beard, the face of a prophet. His companion Gonzales was different in every sense. His card made him seem an academic, but his demeanor was that of a soldier, erect, clipped, authoritative behind the mask of a smile. Physically he was younger, shorter, darker, and clean-shaven except for a thin, well-tended mustache. He also seemed to be, from what Will remembered from Monmouth, the club's leader.

He wondered about the Club of Havana's attachment to Lopez. General Worth had come into contact with the Club, as had Quitman and Sigur, through a mutual connection to Freemasonry. But most Cubans, like most Mexicans, like most Hispanics, were Catholics. He recalled the golden cross around Lopez's neck. The conflict in Cuba had so far been presented to him as a purely political affair, but he wondered if other forces were at work as well. Freemasons and Catholics ordinarily don't make good allies – though sometimes natural antagonists will make common cause against a still greater enemy: Was that not how Europe rid itself of Napoleon?

Returning from the kitchen, he poured coffee, passed the cream and sugar, offered around a plate of New Orleans galettes, and settled back into the easy chair. Over the heads of his guests, through his front window, he could make out the treetops of Congo Square, bright in the morning sunlight.

"So good of you to receive us," said Gonzales, sipping his coffee. "We were not sure we would find you at home."

"Five minutes more and you would not have."

"We won't take long, Colonel," Villaverde said. "We are all busy men."

He smiled. Word of his promotion had got around.

"You have discussed the military plans with General Lopez," said Gonzales. "We are not military men. However, we want you to understand that our enterprise is not just a military affair. It is . . ."

Villaverde placed a hand on his younger friend's arm, stopping him. "Know, sir," he said, in an English that was accented but perfectly constructed, "that I am a man of letters, not a soldier. Know also that if I return to Cuba, mi patria, I will be executed." The eyebrows arched on his high forehead. "No, not shot – that is too good a death for a traitor – but strangled, garroted in the Spanish style."

He leaned forward to emphasize his words. "And what is my treason? I will tell you, sir: It is to fight for Cuba's freedom – fight not with arms, but with words, with the power of my ideas." He stopped a moment but never let his eyes leave his host's. "Can your country, the United States of America, live ninety miles from a place where freedom of speech and expression is denied; where people are murdered in the most barbaric way for daring to defend the ideas of freedom and liberty on which your country was founded?"

He stopped, and Gonzales began again. "It is our goal to drive Spain from the homeland – just as you drove the British from your homeland seventy-five years ago, hardly more than a lifetime. We are prepared to do anything . . . everything . . . to end the foreign tyranny."

A good team, the young man reflected: the politician and the poet.

"All America supports us," continued Gonzales. "We have travelled this great nation from Boston to St. Louis, from Chicago to New Orleans." He stopped a moment to emphasize what came next. "We have met no one who does not support us. No one! And not just with words – with action and contributions. You've heard of John L. O'Sullivan, of course: He has purchased a ship for us – the *Cleopatra*. O'Sullivan is coming to New Orleans. He has asked to meet you."

"*Meet me!* How would he even know of me?"

"He believes you can help us, Colonel," said Gonzales, softly.

The young man stood up and walked to the window, seeking to hide his annoyance. From all sides they came at him, the fox picked out from among dozens, pursued by the hounds until it falls. *But why me?* The men behind him were passing signs, wondering if they'd gone too far.

He turned to face them: "You say everyone supports you. You should say everyone except the President of the United States." "Ah," said Gonzales, "President Taylor, unfortunately he did not support our cause. President Polk, yes, I met with him myself. A pity he did not run again. As for President Fillmore – we will see. Perhaps he will agree with Polk."

*Gonzales had met with Polk!* He started to ask him about the meeting but was cut off by Villaverde.

"We cannot wait," said the poet. "The island cannot wait. Four years, eight years . . . maybe never . . . no, impossible! With a group of great Americans, some that you met at Monmouth, we ourselves will drive Spain from Cuba."

"And then?" said Crittenden.

"Ah," said Gonzales, smiling for the first time, "and *then*, you ask?"

"But we are democrats," said Villaverde, throwing his hands in the air.

"And General Lopez?"

Frowning, Villaverde was about to respond, but Gonzales spoke first. "You, Colonel, a military man like General Lopez, carry a great name. You bring military education and battlefield experience with you. We know from General Worth of your bravery. To have you by Lopez's side would be the highest of honors."

"Then seek out George Crittenden," he said, irritated with the diversions. "You want the name Crittenden, go for the son, not the nephew. George is the warrior!"

There was a silence while the men looked at each other. Did

they know of George? *What* did they know of George? It was Gonzales who spoke. "I believe General Worth has approached Captain Crittenden, who is not desirous, at this time, to leave the Texas military."

"It is the great issue of our time – of *your* time," said Villaverde, getting back on track. "Americans will look back on this in five, ten years as the French look back on the Bastille. Where were you on that great day, they will ask? What was your role in history?

When he came down the next morning, Madame Lucas intercepted him. She was a native Creole speaker but often spoke to him in French. That morning she used the clearest English.

"I've seen your name in the paper, Mr. Crittenden. Your uncle has been named attorney general by the new president."

He bought the *Delta-News* from a newsboy and found the story. So Uncle John had agreed to serve under Fillmore after rejecting the same position under his friend Zach Taylor. Eight years after serving President Harrison as attorney general, he was back in his old job because Zach was careless enough to stay out in the Washington summer heat and catch the cholera – certainly not the death the old warrior would have desired.

He had to get to Frankfort before his uncle left for Washington. He wrote immediately to say he was on his way.

The return from Wyalusing had plunged him into quandary. His heart was shredded, that much he knew. Deprived of the company of young women all his life, the romance with Lucy Holcombe had seized control of him. Day and night, thoughts of the gazebo floated through his mind, consuming him. He'd won her and already feared losing her. Throughout his life, even in the worst circumstances of war, he'd lived free of fear. Now, for the first time, he felt its sting, and hated it.

He'd fallen for a fierce daughter of the South, that much was certain. Beverly Holcombe had been raised on a Virginia plantation and built his own plantation in Texas; Eugenia Holcombe, for all her piety and gentility, was a daughter of Tennessee plantations and now mistress of one in Texas. Did he believe that restless, free-thinking Lucy, child of such a union, could accept a vacillating man, one who knew not where he stood on the great issues of the day – one content to plod on as a customhouse official with the country in convulsions all around him?

Did he really expect to bring a woman such as Lucy Holcombe into his rooms on St. Ann Street and support her on the wages of a customhouse official – wages already more than offset by debts? He'd chosen a military education and military career and then abandoned it. He'd thought that the life of a customhouse official in New Orleans, living in ease and surrounded by friends, would be enough and now no longer was sure of it. And even if it were enough for him, it would never be enough for Lucy. As much as she might love him, as much as she might wish to leave Marshall, it could not be for two rooms in a boarding house. How sordid!

Could he reenlist and take her to some godforsaken frontier post in the West? Would she come? Madness! She expected and deserved far more. Elkanah Greer, engaged to Anna Eliza, could offer his wife a Tennessee plantation; could he do any less for her far more ambitious sister? The Holcombes believed the name Crittenden meant he was a man of wealth. They had no idea of the truth!

Dismissing the Cuba enterprise as hopeless bravado, was he missing something? No one could accuse Quitman, Worth, and Davis of not being serious military men. Worth was military to the core, despite being a peacock. In Mexico, his break with Scott had come over Scott's maddening delay at Tacubaya, and Worth had opposed the suicidal attack on Casa Mata. He would not be involved if the Cuba plan were not serious, nor would Quitman and Davis.

For these men, the taking of Cuba would strengthen the South and put off talk of secession. Lucy had made the same point at Wyalusing. For three days she'd not said a word about Cuba, had been content to serve as his companion and occasional protector. Only in his arms in the gazebo had she brought up the subject, urging him to join the enterprise, flattering him with the name Lafayette.

She'd brought it up again the following morning. Walking the grounds together shortly before his departure, she told him that Anna Eliza had apologized for Elkanah, for what she called his "Southern sensibilities."

He'd had no desire to talk politics, but she had a point to make: did he know that the Union was divided into seventeen Northern and fifteen Southern states, giving the North a majority in both houses of Congress? With its smaller population, the South could never win the House, but by adding Cuba to the Union as two new states, the South would become equal in the Senate.

No longer could the North engage in the kind of political bullying – as in raising tariffs on goods essential to the South – that was pushing the nation toward civil war. It was bullying more than anything, she insisted, that led men like John C. Calhoun of South Carolina to press for the South's separation from the Union. A stronger South could not be bullied; could stand on equal footing with the North inside the Union.

He reflected on it all the way back to New Orleans. Why deny it? The idea of liberating Cuba had merit. Back to West Point, back to the political science classes of Major Desmoulins, the idea of booting Spain from the hemisphere had made sense to him. He'd thought the U.S. Army under Polk would do it, but Polk was gone and now other men had taken up the idea, dedicated and experienced men who wanted him with them. Lucy's involvement only made the thing more tempting.

But how could he go against something opposed by his uncle; opposed by the man he loved and esteemed above all others, the man to whom he owed everything?

• • •

The Mississippi meanders like no other river, and it is a grind going upstream, even in fair weather. The Ohio, from the junction at Cairo, is nearly as bad, hardly straight for a mile, at least until Louisville. It took him six days to arrive at Cloverport for a visit with Ma and to borrow a horse from Colonel Murray for going on to Frankfort. He wanted to see everyone, but especially Ma, who'd written about his brother Tommy, who was in his first year at Centre College in Danville and needed advice.

Every day he wrote Lucy, and every day she answered. He read and reread her letters, savoring each line, each clever phrase, each little rhyme and poem, affection pouring from the page as though she were there next to him. There'd be days without letters and his heart would sink. Then a packet of three or four would arrive and the world would be bright again. She always included something political: so sorry that Mr. Clay has taken ill, had he seen Mr. Breckinridge, could Mr. Douglas carry the bill, what did Governor Crittenden think?

Her curiosity knew no limits. How she was animated when she heard Uncle John was to become attorney general again, the enforcer of federal law! She wrote two letters the day she heard the news, the first of four pages; the second, with everything she forgot to put in the first, three more. How propitious, she said. What was General Crittenden's view on Lopez, she asked? As a friend of both Quitman and Jeff Davis, did he know of the plans? She never forgot Lopez nor let him forget.

More than anyone in the family his brother Tommy reminded him of Uncle John. There was a gentle, stolid equanimity to his little brother all the more remarkable because it was rare in the family. Pa had had it, but it is one thing to be generous and fair-minded in family matters and altogether grander to exhibit those qualities on the great matters of the day. Could a man like Uncle John, who'd devoted his life to bringing North and South together, prevail against forces that preferred war to yielding an inch? Each side to a quarrel has its principles – he'd seen that in Mexico. Yes, they went to Mexico to bring civilized values to a cruel and immoral place, but that's not how the cadets at Chapultepec saw it, the dark-faced boys who hurled themselves over the ramparts rather than face surrender.

Ma wrote that Tommy was floundering. He was a good Presbyterian (implying that not all her sons could make that claim), but had decided against taking the cloth. He was suited neither for farming nor the military. He talked about law and politics and following in the footsteps of Uncle John, but hardly knew his uncle, certainly not as Will did. Since he was coming up to Frankfort, why not meet Tommy in Danville and ride up together for a few days?

In the family, Tommy had always been the cheerful one, a bit stuffy but fair and tenacious. For such a temperament the military life was impossible, but were law and politics any easier? Was not war just another way to settle arguments, one step beyond politics and diplomacy, which had their own sharp edges? Could politics and diplomacy ever be successful without an iron fist behind them?

Had they not learned that at West Point – and from no less a teacher than Napoleon: "Bloodletting is one of the ingredients of political medicine."

# XVII

"Calhoun wanted to be King of the South, nothing short of it. His speeches were brilliant but treasonous. We were not personally close, though God knows I tried. Zach Taylor should have done what Jackson did: threaten to hang him. Or do it! Imagine that – a president hanging a senator, former vice president! Ha! Now there's a constitutional precedent! I need to be in Washington."

Lord, was he restless! The nephew saw it immediately. If his uncle regretted turning down Taylor's offer of secretary of state two years earlier he didn't say so directly but signs showed maybe he did regret it. The governorship of Kentucky wasn't enough, and he was grateful to Fillmore, a fellow Whig with whom he was on good terms, for calling him back to Washington. As he read the *Daily Journal* at the breakfast table he kept a running commentary on the national news. The day before he'd seen an item in the paper about a congressman named Abraham Lincoln giving a eulogy for Zach Taylor.

"Lincoln is a Whig," he said after reading Lincoln's homage aloud to his nephews, "from a Kentucky family that moved to Illinois. I met him when we both spoke out against Polk's war in Mexico. He has a rare eloquence for someone so young. I will write him about this."

The breakfast room had always been Will's favorite. Facing southeast toward the orchard, away from the street, the room was brightened by sunlight filtering through the trees enough to warm it without letting the sun in directly. In the garden outside, the birds chirped gaily away. The place settings had been carefully laid out before anyone was down – china, crystal, silverware, starched linen napkins standing in front of eight chairs. Fruits from the garden were set out in bowls and fresh flowers arranged. The Louisville newspaper lay ready by Uncle John's chair at the end of the table. There was no better place on earth to start the day.

The Frankfort house had once been as crowded as Ma's house at Cloverport, for Uncle John had seven children by his first wife, took Aunt Maria's three children as his own, and had two more with her. They'd been eight at breakfast the third day after his ride up from Danville with Tommy, breakfast presided over by Aunt Maria, gracious and lively and insisting the boys try the hot buns freshly baked that morning. After breakfast, sensing that Will had something on his mind, she took the others off so the brothers could be alone with their uncle.

He'd seemed genuinely happy to see them when they rode in, greeting them with hugs and inviting them to stay as long as they liked. Since Pa's death he'd treated them as his own children or maybe even better, for there were tensions in the Frankfort family. Ann Mary, the eldest daughter and Uncle John's favorite, was a champion of Calhoun's views, so adamant in her opinions that she'd moved out of the house, joining Cousin George in estrangement.

Sadness may have crept in, but Uncle John was in a good mood that morning, enjoying the company of his brother's boys, bantering with Aunt Maria about when she would be coming to Washington to join him in their house on Massachusetts Avenue, knowing he had but two more days at home before heading for Louisville to catch the steamer to Pittsburgh and then on to the capital. It was the start of a lovely day, the air clear and not yet heavy, trees losing their bright colors as the equinox approached. People were more than happy to be rid of oppressive summer afternoons of insects and thunderstorms.

Not much business was being transacted in the Kentucky capital beyond transition of power to John Helm, the lieutenant governor, and Uncle John was in no hurry to leave for the governor's mansion.

He didn't think much of Helm, who'd been elected with him two years before. Helm was a Whig but Uncle John called him "slippery," about the worst quality a man could have in his view.

He'd talked a good deal that morning about the new president, whom he liked well enough, finally lighting on Calhoun, who'd died a few months earlier. The *Daily Journal* carried an article that morning about him.

"Some say he was crazy," Will offered.

His uncle dabbed at his chin. He'd been eating soft-boiled eggs and some yolk had trickled down into the creases below his mouth.

"Crazy, no, though I have to say that Henry Clay differed with me on that. He was a brilliant, passionate man who was a secessionist. That was the whole story. He did not want the South to remain in the Union and opposed any effort at compromise. He hated the North, wanted a separate country. Most of the South never stood with him, though I concede that he was gaining ground." He grimaced. "Even in Kentucky."

"He opposed the war in Mexico, though. You stood with him on that."

His uncle took off his reading glasses and shook his head. "For completely different reasons. Calhoun believed Polk intended to annex Mexico as a non-slave state. He believed passionately in slavery, believed it was a positive good for both whites and blacks. Called it 'divine will.'"

"Slavery . . . God's will? Do you believe that, Uncle?" asked Tommy.

Uncle John looked to his youngest nephew, a boy he hardly knew. "I do not, Tommy. But it is an institution we must live with because the South will never give it up. The compromise I was working on in the Senate, still going forward thanks to Mr. Clay and Mr. Douglas and which has some chance with Calhoun gone, does nothing to touch slavery where it now exists. But it must not be allowed to spread beyond Texas. That is the important thing, don't you boys agree?"

"I agree with that, Uncle," said Tommy.

"I don't know," Will said. "If you'd seen what I saw in Mexico you might wonder if those people might not be better off under another system."

"Bah, annexation creates more problems than it solves, with slaves or without. The nation will spread to California, that's far enough. We don't need Mexico in the Union – or Cuba, and you know what I mean. It's why neither Henry Clay nor I wanted Texas. We have enough trouble as we already are. Zach Taylor was tough enough to deal with separatists like Calhoun. We'll see about Fillmore. He wants me back there to stiffen him."

"I wish you'd been on the ticket instead of Fillmore, Uncle," said Tommy. "You'd be president now."

The thin lips, perpetually turned downward, turned up a notch. He knew he might have been on the ticket. He was closer to Taylor than Millard Fillmore had ever been, but Taylor wanted a Northerner with him and settled on Fillmore, a New Yorker, whose main virtue was that he was unknown.

"Your ma writes me that you want a career in law, Tommy. That right?"

"I am interested in politics, Uncle, yes."

"Well, I'll tell you this: this country needs good politicians like never before, men who represent the people. The people don't want conflict. Politicians like Calhoun speak more for their ambitions than for the people. So, I have to say, do Northerners like Daniel Webster, who as secretary of state will be sitting next to me at cabinet meetings. People look to Kentuckians like Henry Clay to keep the peace. Kentuckians are not absolutists."

"Kentuckians like Henry Clay *and* John Jordan Crittenden," said Tommy.

"Well, maybe so, but time is running out on my generation. It's going to be up to you boys to keep the peace. What's your take on things?"

A shy boy, Tommy lit up, so pleased to be asked. "I'd follow your approach, Uncle. Do what you can to head off the trouble."

"What if it can't be headed off?" Will asked, pointedly.

"If you've done what you can you'll have no regrets."

"From what I've seen lately," Will said, "and it is Texas I'm referring to, Uncle, I wonder if you're right that the people don't want conflict. Some of them over there seem to be itching for a fight."

"If it comes," Tommy said, "they will be sorry."

"You're probably right about that," said Uncle John. "If it comes to it, I'd be inclined to let them go."

"You mean without a fight?" Will asked.

"Why force them to stay in the Union if they want out?"

"It cost us good Union blood to win Texas, Uncle."

"I know that. Texas didn't want to stay part of Mexico and now doesn't want to stay part of the Union. It is their right, you know, written into the Declaration of Independence: If people don't like the government they have, it is their natural right to leave it and form a new one. It is the reason we are no longer British colonies. We will do what we can short of war to keep this nation intact. But if the South insists on separation, I say, let 'em go."

"Kentucky too?" inquired Tommy.

"*No!*" said the uncle, louder than he meant to. He caught himself. "That's why the president wants me in Washington. Kentucky is not a plantation state, not the Deep South. We have nothing in common with those people. I will do everything I can to keep Kentucky in the Union."

"If we try to change the South," Will said, "the South will go. On that, I agree with Mr. Calhoun."

"But we are *not* trying to change the South, Nephew. No one will touch slavery; no one will touch Southern property. The issue before us is whether the plantation system will spread to the West. That is the issue being negotiated by Henry Clay and Stephen Douglas at this very moment. That is why Fillmore has called me back to Washington."

"Man for man, gun for gun," Will said, "the South cannot match the North. They are a brave bunch. I saw enough of them in Mexico to know that. But if the South goes, the South will be destroyed."

The sad blue eyes gave the old man away, and Will knew what was coming. His uncle was thinking of Ann Mary and George and how many others in his family he would lose if it came to separation.

"And you with them, Nephew?"

How many times had the question been asked, and how many times had he evaded it? It was the question being asked all over the nation, in every state, town and family: Where do I stand?

"It depends who is at fault," he said, equivocating. "I believe that if the South were better able to stand up to the North, it would make war less likely. We learned that at West Point: balance of power makes conflict less likely. For now, the South perceives itself as weaker, which makes the North more aggressive and the South more sensitive to slights. It gives audience to extremists like Calhoun."

His uncle looked away, turning outside, letting his gaze run over the gardens he'd planted years before. As a boy he would go out there with him, walk down the rows at his side, listen as he named each thing he'd planted over the years, every tree, every vegetable, every flower, down to the name of each rosebush – Alba, Portland, Noisette, others long forgotten.

He turned back to the table.

"Yes," he said, "that was Calhoun's view. He repeated it many times in the Senate: If the balance shifts any more against the South, it will lead to secession. It is why so many of them wanted to bring Mexico into the union. Now they're focused on Cuba – tie it to the South, strengthen the South."

"I heard something about that," said Will, recalling: "Thirty-two states represented in the Senate, seventeen North, fifteen South. Admit Cuba as two states, and the South equals the North, creating a balance of power and making secession less likely."

His uncle stared hard at him. "Hold on a minute there. You say seventeen Northern and fifteen Southern states. The only way I get fifteen Southern states is by including the border states in the South."

"Yes."

He leaned toward his nephew. "*You* may well count Missouri, Maryland, Delaware, and Kentucky as Southern states. We are all slave states. But slave or not, as far as Kentucky is concerned, as long as I have something to say about it, Kentucky will never leave this Union. And mark this: there are men like me in Missouri, Maryland, and Delaware as well. To be a slave state does not mean to believe in secession. If some in the Deep South choose to leave, I say let 'em go. It won't be long before they're back."

# XVIII

The boys fell silent, listening to the birds at work in the trees, watching the sun inch higher through the leaves, thinking on what their uncle had said, waiting to see if he had more to say. He turned again to look outside, toward the changing colors of his maple trees, then back to Will. It was then that the fateful turn was taken.

"Though I don't agree with your math, I know what you're getting at. You've written me about this man Lopez. So has Jeff Davis. Governor Quitman is involved, and Quitman is cut from Calhoun's cloth. I've given you my opinion of the business."

"I've made no commitment."

The uncle started to say something and stopped, scrutinizing his nephew. The look showed he did not believe.

"It is not a serious proposition."

He'd never had an argument with his uncle. There were things they disagreed on, but he refused to confront the man he loved so much. He understood the reason for their differences: Uncle John was a politician, a man who fought with words, not arms. He didn't understand what it was to be a soldier. But why then had he come? Why had he said he'd made no commitment? Why was he there?

"Uncle, do you not hold Jeff Davis, John Quitman, and William Worth to be serious people?"

The old man grimaced. "I believe them to be, on this issue at least, badly mistaken. It pains me greatly that Jeff Davis approached you on this matter – and in my house. In any case, with Worth gone, who's to take charge of it?"

*"With Worth gone?"*

"Somewhere in Texas. The cholera, I believe."

Why hadn't he heard? But who was to tell him? It was a blow to be sure, though not necessarily a fatal one.

"I had a high opinion of General Worth," he said, softly. "I served under him, you know. I imagine General Quitman will now take charge."

"So he will resign as governor."

"I expect so."

"But, Nephew, Worth or Quitman doesn't change a thing about it. Imagine I'd accepted Taylor's offer of secretary of state. Spain is a friendly nation."

"I think they should be gone, Uncle. Their time is passed."

Looking suddenly older, older than his age, tiring of the discord in his family, he sighed, and his head dropped. His life had always been intense; with age – he was already in his mid-sixties – the cheekbones had grown even more prominent, knobs ready to burst through the parchment skin. His eyes had sunk in so far that at times it was like looking at a living skull.

"Whatever you may think, it is a national matter, not a private one. As attorney general it may come to my attention and what then? I hope I can still persuade you against this thing."

The house fell dead still. Even the birds ceased chirping, awaiting his answer. He looked to his brother. Had Tommy even heard of Lopez or Quitman or Cuba? Did he know what they were talking about? He'd come up to Frankfort to talk with his uncle about his future and instead found himself in the middle of a quarrel he neither liked nor understood.

"It is too late for that, Uncle."

Eyes closed, sharp chin resting on his chest, the old man did not move a muscle. He seemed quite capable of falling asleep. Will knew that he didn't sleep well, had never gotten much sleep. How long did they sit like that, each man lost in his thoughts? Not a sound broke the silence.

"Consider this," he began after a while, slowly, intoning each word, like giving a legal opinion: "Much depends on England. England prefers to see Spain, not the United States, its principal sea rival, in control of Cuba. England has possessions in the Caribbean, as does France. Meddle in Cuba and you guarantee trouble with all of Europe. That is not in America's interest, certainly not with the other problems we face. God help us if civil war falls upon us."

"But Uncle, the idea is to *liberate* Cuba."

*"Don't you believe it!"*

He was awake again, head up, eyes wide, the vigor back.

"It will be up to the Cubans to decide. They have told me personally."

"*You think that's what it is* – that Jeff Davis and John Quitman are running off to Cuba to liberate the slaves? Is that what you truly believe? And Lopez himself, cashiered by the Spaniards . . . why are you involved in this folly of theirs?"

What answer could he give for it – ambition, vanity, boredom, the fear of losing Lucy? *Fear, no!* That he could never admit.

"Uncle, I was a soldier for eight years – thanks to you. You told me to stay in the army, and I believe you were right: I should have stayed in. I am not cut out to be a customhouse clerk. I believe in the liberation of Cuba. The army should have gone on from Mexico to do it, would have done so under Polk, but Polk is gone now and so some men have decided to do the job themselves. They've asked me to join them. It is a worthy enterprise. What happens afterward is up to the Cubans."

Will looked to his brother, who'd hardly stopped watching him since they sat down. He saw the pain.

"Have you told Ma?" Tommy asked.

"I'll write Cloverport before we sail."

"And how is your ma to find out about you?" asked his uncle, grimly. "If something happens to you, it won't be like Mexico, you know. The secretary of war won't be writing letters home."

"When we take Havana, the whole world will know."

They stared into each other's eyes for the longest time. Separated by four decades, united in their love for the lost brother/father, respecting and admiring the other and wanting to understand, they had reached an impasse.

Finally, it was the uncle who spoke.

"God be with you, Nephew. You always wanted to be a soldier. Perhaps there are things I don't understand."

The dreadful silence seeped back in. The birds had flown away. Surely Uncle will end this ordeal now, he thought.

But no. He looked to his other nephew, speaking up, trying to be bright. Having lost one debate, he was on to the next.

"It looks like you have something to say, Tommy."

"Yes, Uncle, thank you, I do. You said God help us if civil war comes."

He sighed, took a moment to answer.

"A figure of speech, Nephew. I tell you this, though: I pray to God that He keep us from civil war. I pray and your Aunt Maria prays and I know your Ma prays for the same thing. We must all pray, for if civil war comes it will be a catastrophe, the worst thing this nation has ever endured, and it might not survive."

"Uncle," he said, "will you stand for president in '52?"

The attorney general folded his napkin and put away his glasses. The translucent eyes shined from their deep sockets on his youngest nephew.

"You'd have me as president, would you, Tommy?" He stood up. "You boys come with me. I want to show you something."

He led them down the hallway, up the stairs, through his own bedroom and to the door of Aunt Maria's. He knocked on the door-frame, but they knew she'd gone out. Entering the room, he pointed at the bed.

"Have you seen that quilt before?"

They'd never been in Aunt Maria's bedroom before, nor seen the quilt. It was folded neatly at the foot of the bed.

"Come," he said, "let's have a closer look."

He unfolded the quilt and spread it over the bed. "Your aunt doesn't need it in this weather, but in winter it is a good friend to her."

It was larger than a double bed, painstakingly hand-stitched with pastoral scenes sewn into each square as bright as the leaded windows of a church on a sunny day. They saw riding scenes and country scenes and childhood scenes and multi-colored wreaths and bouquets, probably thirty in all. In the center, with a garland arched over his head like Julius Caesar himself, was the bust of a man whose thin lips and wry smile could belong only to Henry Clay.

"The ladies of the Lexington quilting circle presented this quilt to your Aunt Maria when I replaced Mr. Clay in the Senate. Henry resigned to run for president in '40, and when he was defeated by Mr. Harrison decided he would use all his energies to prepare for '44 and not reclaim his Senate seat. I'd come home after Harrison's death and found myself in the Senate again."

They had a good look before Uncle John began folding it up again. "It took the ladies, I'm told, a year to finish it. It is a masterpiece, and they brought it here one evening to present to your aunt." He stopped and turned away. When he turned back he was composed again.

"That, boys, is the way it once was in the Senate. There was a comity, and not just among those of us from the same party. We fought – oh, by Jupiter, we fought! But afterward we shared our Kentucky bourbon and moved on. I never agreed with Calhoun and rarely with Webster. I've had differences with Henry Clay and still more with Jeff Davis."

"Jeff Davis is passionate for slavery, Uncle. He would have brought Mexico into the Union as a slave state and now wants Cuba."

"You think I don't know that! We sat in the same Senate. We never agreed on slavery. Am I to have no friends in politics but with those I see eye-to-eye with on every point? Why, there would be no friendships at all."

His long thin hands fumbled with the quilt, poorly hiding his frustration. Straightening up, he grasped his nephew by the arm, looked him square in the eye. "I'd hate to have this Cuba business come between us."

They stayed like that, then turned and walked in silence back to the hallway and downstairs. By the front door he stood with them for a moment.

"Things have changed. That's my point, boys. The two sides are congealing with Kentucky caught in the middle. If I thought for a minute that as president I could prevent the confrontation, I would seek the nomination in '52 with all my might. But the time for compromise is running out. Calhoun's followers seek to provoke a great clash, and so do many in the North as well. Sooner or later they will have their way. Some event, and I don't know what it will be, will push us over the edge. War, if we are not careful, will be upon us."

He took his hat from the rack and stick from the stand for his walk down Main Street to the governor's mansion. Soon he would be off for Washington and his new job. He looked to his nephews and smiled.

Will wanted so badly to walk with him, one more time as he'd done as a boy, listen to the tap-tap of his walking stick as it poled his lanky body along the streets; to greet the good people of Frankfort, the Kentuckians, his kinfolk, keep on walking with him, talking to him, keep him in his sight forever, never let him go.

# XIX

He'd said nothing to anyone about Memphis, which had been on his mind for weeks. The more he thought of it the more he knew that having Josie along was a stroke of good fortune. Managing it alone would have been tricky. The plan involved some risk for her, but he doubted she'd refuse. Josie was practically his second mother. And she had her own history with Memphis.

As arranged, they met in Louisville to catch the Ohio steamer.

Josie was a woman of character, which is why Ma took to her so. She was biblical before she knew how to read and never forgot the stories she'd learned as a girl. Once Ma taught her to read she never would let go of her Bible. The stories he remembered from the kitchen were from her telling of them, stories like Joseph and the coat of many colors and Moses in his basket of reeds and Abraham and Isaac – who could forget that one! She took a snippet and gave it a thrill, and the boys never knew how much came from the Bible and how much from her imagination. For Memphis, her imagination would be useful.

He laid out his plan soon after they boarded. It was early morning and a brisk wind was up, so they left the deck to go inside. He'd seen her high spirits the moment he'd spied her coming along on the landing, and why wouldn't she be excited? All her adult life she'd lived in and around Shelbyville and suddenly was in Louisville ready to catch the steamer to a new life in New Orleans, eight hundred miles away, born again as a freewoman.

She listened carefully as she always did, recording the words as if she were memorizing a new part of the Bible. They found a bench at the rear of the main salon, out of the way, where they could talk privately. A boatman wouldn't let her pass until he was tipped, and some passengers eyed her suspiciously. Slaves were sent belowdecks unless their masters insisted they needed them. Free Negroes went with the slaves. He clearly didn't need her with him, but since he was armed and adamant and his name well-known, no one seemed inclined to press the point. For sleeping and eating, she would join the other Negroes below.

Memphis was where she'd lost her ma. It was the worst part of slavery. She'd cried for days, she said, and was such a miserable little thing that no one thought of buying her until Pa came along. The Lord has His ways.

She was about the same age as Ma, probably already close to fifty but still sprightly. Elias had always struck him as an old man, but maybe he wasn't so old, just aged fast in the hemp fields. Josie was a healthy and handsome woman, and his plan was to use her as a decoy. He believed she would be safe enough with him hovering about, but in Memphis, where all Negroes were slaves, you could never be sure, which is why he wore his revolver. In any case, she didn't seem worried, even seemed to like the idea of getting back at the people who stole her son.

He watched her as she stared out over the Ohio, back to some childhood memory, likely the time Pa brought her up on the river from Memphis. It seemed like he'd never seen Josie fretful. Ma went to pieces for a while after Pa's murder, and Josie more or less took over the household. Among the slaves, she was the one the women came to. Maybe she was born with it or maybe her strength was tempered in the hard early days or maybe it came from the Bible, for she was a strong believer and passed it on to her children, to Jude especially. Everyone on the farm believed, everyone except him, that is, and they worried about it. Ma talked to him about it, and finally had Colonel Murray take him aside.

He admired Colonel Murray. He didn't love him like he'd loved

Pa, but he admired him for who he was and what he'd done for Ma. He'd been a soldier but wasn't a real soldier, was happy to be done with fighting. His first wife, who'd died, was Ma's cousin and so it was natural they would meet, though who could have known it would turn out to be such a sweet marriage: two brave, peace-loving, God-fearing Presbyterians. Kindred spirits.

They went into the closet to talk. It wasn't really a closet, more a kind of den that Colonel Murray had used as an office and Ma made into a little chapel.

"Will, your ma is worried about you. She doesn't think you pray in earnest."

It was hard for Colonel Murray, inheriting so many children and he already had his own to worry about and then they had some together. He wouldn't have cared about Ma's godless son himself, though he was just as pious as she was, but Ma cared and so he cared as well.

"I pray," the young man said, "sometimes." He wasn't going to lie. "I truly do."

"But do you believe in prayer?"

"I probably don't, Colonel Murray."

"And why not?"

"I don't rightly know. Can you make yourself believe?"

They were on their knees on the prie-dieux Ma had brought over from the Shelbyville farm because John Allen didn't want them. Presbyterians don't kneel in church, but at home Ma liked them.

"I don't reckon you can make yourself believe, Will," he said, "but that's not the important thing."

He was like that, Colonel Murray, nothing fraudulent or pretending about him. He could have said that of course you can make yourself believe, you're just not trying hard enough, but he was too sensible for that. Colonel Murray knew his stepson didn't believe and probably never would believe but that was not the important thing. Will knew right away what Col. Murray meant, though let him say it himself.

"The important thing is not to upset Ma, wouldn't you say?"

Of course, he agreed with that, and so did his best from then on to make Ma believe he did pray and did believe, though he doubted she ever swallowed it.

They were on the *Spirit of Saint Louis*, bound from Pittsburgh to Saint Louis, changing boats at Cairo for the *Memphis Belle*, which carried them to Memphis. The *City of New Orleans*, which would take them on to New Orleans, was due at Beale Street Landing three hours after they arrived in Memphis, giving them time for the project he had in mind.

Beale Street Landing was chaos every time he'd been there: a jumble of smoke-belching boats, frenzied docksides, screeches of humans, animals and machines and the blend of a dozen different stinks. The gangplanks off the steamer bows were long and narrow, and passengers had to maneuver carefully to avoid lines of slaves toting cotton bales and sacks of goods and produce. Occasionally traffic stopped to bring new slaves, roped and dazzled by the sun, up from below to head off to the pens to await their fate.

Memphis stayed with you. The air was foul. The horse and mule droppings from carts along the quay didn't add to the atmosphere, nor did the slaves, who didn't bathe much. There was dirt and dust and stink and flies and rats and nothing to be done about any of it. Memphis was a hellhole.

They checked their bags at the depot and headed down Beale Street toward Market Square.

Negro restaurants didn't exist, but there were places for them to buy food. Slaves brought the cotton and produce into town and sometimes their masters gave them a few cents to buy Negro food instead of toting their own. The places he'd seen were always around the markets. Some enterprising owner would fix up a stall, hang a sign saying "coloreds only" and serve grits, bacon, and coffee.

Jude had given him a precise description of the place, a shack with bright colored beads dangling in place of a door. A sign said: "Colored-Eats." It stood nearby to a greengrocer on the lower side of Market Square.

They walked along Beale for about ten minutes, stopping a while at Auction Square and looking into the slave pens, which were empty, waiting for a new boatload up from New Orleans. Josie stared into the pens and beyond to the shed and he could see her eyes turn inward as she thought back on events. She probably wasn't ten years old when she'd seen her ma dragged away from this place, but her look told him she'd forgotten nothing.

They walked on and he asked again: "You sure you're up to this?"

The weather was turning and people were covered up. There was nothing odd about them on Beale Street. If people noticed them at all they likely took them for master and slave heading to Market Square for provisions. Josie was dressed in blue and white calico with a matching bonnet. She carried a little red purse and a dark blue shawl covered her shoulders.

"I *am* sure, Will Crittenden. You are a good man."

"Nonsense."

The place was exactly as Jude described: a shack on the south side of Market Square a few doors up from a greengrocer. "Colored-Eats" was painted in red on a plain board hung above the beads at the entrance. Slaves can't read, but word gets around and the sign warned whites to stay away.

They walked around the market, a sprawling, bustling, dusty place selling everything imaginable. Chickens squawked, pigs squealed, and carts squeaked. He verified that no other place fit the description. Back outside, he checked to be sure there was no rear entrance. They posted themselves outside a feed store across the way and watched.

It was a busy day on Market Square, but no one entered "Colored-Eats." Then two men came up from the greengrocer's and pushed through the beads. As planned, Josie went in right behind them. After a while the men came out and returned to the green-grocer's. She was alone with whoever ran the place.

Time crawled. One way or another he'd expected the operation to be over quickly, but ten, fifteen minutes went by. The plan was for her to enter with others, order something and wait until she could speak alone with the operator. She was to tell him she was the mother of a free Negro who'd gone missing after being seen in this place and was desperate to find him. The people running "Colored-Eats" would be slaves, but the owners would be close around somewhere.

He watched and waited. Josie was to offer $20 in silver coins for information, an immense sum and temptation for any slave. Perhaps they would tell her themselves; perhaps they would leave to consult; perhaps the two men from the greengrocer's already were talking to someone who knew. There would be interest for there was money to be made. Another possibility – remote, he thought – was that they would try to rob her or drug and abduct her. He kept a close watch.

A Negro man with a limp and wearing a red tasseled cap came out of the greengrocer's along with the first two men, and they made their way up to "Colored-Eats." Were they customers or part of the operation?

The shack could not have been more than twenty feet square, likely no more than a kitchen and small eating area. He thought he might be able to hear voices or see movement through the beads, but could see or hear nothing. His nervousness increased. He glanced at his watch. Could there be a rear exit he'd missed? Five more minutes, he told himself, and he'd go after her.

Not a minute had passed when the first two men pushed through the beads holding red tassel between them. He was slumped as if drugged or drunk. Josie's shawl was draped over his shoulders.

*But why . . . ?*

They saw him coming, shouting at them, drawing attention. They let go of Josie, who crumpled to the ground, and they ran down the way. Red tassel, sans tassel and carrying Josie's red purse, came out through the beads, took in the scene and limped after them, fast as he could go. He shouted after them, and a crowd gathered. As he bent over Josie, he saw two market guards stop the three men. A man emerged from the greengrocer's, said something to the guards, slipped them something, and led the three men back into the shop.

He called to the guards, who turned and walked away. Was everyone in on the foul business?

He helped Josie to the rear of the feed store where she was laid out on a sofa. A doctor was summoned. Someone in uniform pushed through, eying him closely, noticing his revolver.

"Sergeant Johnson, Memphis police. Who are you?"

Before he could answer the doctor arrived, opened Josie's closed eyes and took her pulse.

"She's been drugged," he said.

"Drugged and robbed," said Will.

The police station was on South Main, overlooking Beale Street Landing. They took Josie to a Negro infirmary while Sergeant Johnson led him back to the landing, planting him in a waiting area while the captain was informed. The *City of New Orleans* was due in any moment, but it was clear they would not be leaving anytime soon. He watched a steamer come in, pushing two coal barges down from Pittsburgh and starting up Wolf River. A new line of horse and mule carts had pulled in to await the next boats. Slaves sat in the carts eating or sleeping. Some played dice.

Captain McCloud was a blond, red-faced fellow who came no higher than Will's shoulders and was near as broad as he was tall. He looked closer when he heard the name Crittenden, but said nothing. McCloud didn't like looking up to him and told him to sit down. He paced and listened to the story without a word, his frown growing along with the story. Will finished. Still McCloud said nothing.

Finally: "You expect me to do something about this?"

"I expect you to enforce the law. Kidnapping is illegal in this country. So is drugging and robbing people. The people running the operation are at the greengrocer's. I saw it all. So did the guards. They have her purse. My God, come to think of it, they have her manu-mission! What more evidence do you need?"

McCloud sat on the edge of his desk, peering down at the visitor.

"Kidnapping has to be proved. Takes time. Don't know about Kentucky, but slaves in Memphis don't like to talk against their masters. How long you in town?"

"Not long."

"Too bad."

He started walking again. "Kidnapping usually applies to white folks."

"White folks and free black folks. The man was manumitted, is now a U.S. citizen. So is the woman. Both were drugged and robbed."

"Manumitted in Kentucky, not Tennessee."

"Come on, man, what's the difference? His owner, my brother, gave them both their freedom. They earned it."

"What you do in Kentucky don't mean nothin' in Tennessee."

Will fought to stay calm, knowing the danger of an outburst. "Strange, Captain, but you don't seem surprised by any of this."

McCloud turned and stared. But instead of taking offense, he smiled. "Oh, no, sir, we appreciate citizens' information. And we'll surely look into it. Unfortunately, it's likely to be after you've left town. Assuming I let you leave, that is."

Will stood to face him. "Crimes have been committed here, Captain. Do you want me to march up there and bring that greengrocer back myself?"

The eyes were not friendly. "I don't reckon I'd do that if I were you, Mr. Crittenden. They might not like it up there. They might ask me to arrest you. I might have to agree."

"What law have I broken?"

"Oh, we could find something."

He felt his blood rising. "Captain, there is an illegal kidnapping operation in your city – an operation that sells into slavery manumitted Negroes who fought in this country's war against Mexico. Have you no interest in stopping it?"

He considered the question. "I think I'd take the greengrocer's word over a bunch of niggers."

"It is *my* word I am giving you!"

They faced each other. McCloud held all the cards and had no reason to be careful, though in a different situation his reply would be a matter of honor.

"You know, if you were from New York – or Ohio, or Pennsylvania – I could understand you making a fuss like this, but man – *you are from Kentucky!* I know your name. You are a man of the South."

"The law is the law."

McCloud waited a moment before replying. The banter was gone from his voice. The eyes narrowed. He held the cards and he played them.

"For how much longer?"

# XX

Through fall and winter, they trumpeted the mission. More publicity meant more money, more recruits, more notification to the Creoles in Cuba that help was on the way. In France, the Revolution of 1850 brought to power a government promising to free French slaves in the Caribbean. If the weak Spanish government followed suit it would spell disaster for Cuban landowners, for the sugar and tobacco plantations and the Club of Havana. Newspapers wrote that Cuba was ripe for annexation as never before, and Lopez's friends traveled the country to drum up support. "Cuba must be ours," Jefferson Davis announced in the Senate, "to increase the numbers of slave-holding constituencies."

Following the Mexican War, America's imperial enthusiasm was transformed into jingoism. Manifest Destiny had taken root, and few Americans believed Spain had any business in Cuba or anywhere else in the hemisphere. Everywhere he went, Lopez was greeted as a hero, the next Bolívar. Cuba was in a state of quasi-revolt, he proclaimed, and if Spain would not abandon the island and Fillmore would not fulfill Polk's promises, all that remained was for patriots to do the job themselves. Spain was done in America, he told cheering crowds. It was time for Spaniards to pack up and head home, their colonial adventure in the New World ended.

The young man was fully into it now. If there'd been doubts before Frankfort, back in New Orleans months of daily customhouse routine proved that the sedentary life would never be enough for him. He hated thinking back on the dispute with Uncle John, but too many forces were pulling him toward Lopez.

In her correspondence, Lucy was relentless.

"Stay strong, dear heart," she wrote. "In your last, I detected lingering doubt. Finally, you have found the mission to suit your ambition and talent. It is what we all dream of: to do the one great thing. *Carpe diem!*"

She stiffened him, no question, and soon he was even recruiting on his own. Robert Downman, a veteran army colonel up from the ranks in Mexico, answered an ad in the *Delta-News*, and publisher Laurent Sigur sent him around to see him at the customhouse. He remembered the man from Cerro Gordo, a giant of a man in the frontline of every charge. Downman soon had brought other Mexican veterans along with him. New Orleans was teeming with young men who'd come to rebuild the levees following the great flood of '49 and now sought more rewarding work.

He met with Lopez weekly. Quitman, who'd resigned as governor after Worth's untimely death, came down from Natchez, staying with Sigur in his house on Customhouse Street and taking charge of planning. By March they had three hundred men signed up and were ready for their first maneuvers. Quitman wanted more men, at least five hundred, he said, and they continued to recruit.

For a while they had no ship after federal agents blocked the *Cleopatra* from leaving New York harbor. It was a blow, and he wondered if Uncle John, now settled in as attorney general, had a hand in the impounding. But John L. O'Sullivan, their good fairy, located another ship, the *Pampero*, in Jacksonville, and with another check from Laurent Sigur, she was purchased and brought to New Orleans.

They found little support in Washington, but the South was another matter. Enthusiasm in New Orleans was palpable. Everything pointed to a July sailing.

Never in a hundred years would he have broached the subject in the presence of those women, nor with Jude, who as far as he knew, knew nothing about it and wouldn't have cared if he had. Nor would

Lucien have mentioned it, for he hated everything about the idea. It was a careless slip, nourished by good conversation and brandy and the happy household of the Freemans. It was out before he knew it and could not be undone.

It was to be an entirely social evening, one of those events that could take place only in New Orleans. If anything similar ever happened in the North, where Negroes were theoretically free, he'd not heard of it. Such a meeting in the North would be a patronizing affair, not done in friendship but because Northerners liked to display their moral superiority. As for the South, New Orleans was different that way.

The grandmothers, Josie and Liliana, took the children off to bed, leaving five of them in the sitting room over coffee and cake. Lucien had brought a bottle of French brandy. At dinner, the mission to Memphis had come up. Jude had nothing to say, but Mary Jane scolded her mother – certainly not for the first time – for taking such a risk. Will knew the criticism was directed at him.

His rooms on St. Ann Street suited his needs, but Jude's place on Phillipa was home, especially with Lucien along. The doctor had always treated black patients as well as white, in New Orleans as in Shelbyville. His New Orleans practice was growing faster than expected and now included Jude's expanding family of two grandmas, two young women, two little girls, and Jude.

Lucien's practice was three blocks away on Royal, and Will would pick him up on his way for the ten-minute walk to Phillipa. Will's job was on Customhouse Street; Jude, Mary Jane, and Dominique all worked at couturier shops along Chartres, and so it was that all of them lived and worked within a square mile of each other. The Vieux Carré, called the French Quarter by some, was their village, a considerably livelier village than Shelbyville.

After dinner the talk got around to Uncle John, who'd arrived in Washington and taken up his new job as attorney general, the same job he'd turned down, along with that of secretary of state, under Zach Taylor.

"Why turn down the job under Taylor and accept it under Fillmore, a New Yorker?" Mary Jane asked.

"One more story of Kentucky and Tennessee," Will said, "goes back to the election of 1824 when no candidate won a majority and the decision went to the House of Representatives. Henry Clay was Speaker and threw his votes to J. Q. Adams, not Jackson. Adams named Clay secretary of state; Jackson called it a corrupt bargain and took his revenge on Kentucky when elected president four years later."

He sipped his brandy. "Uncle John didn't support Clay in '48; he supported Taylor. It caused some hard feelings between old friends, not to mention the wives, but he didn't think Clay could win and he wanted to be rid of the Tennesseans – remember that Van Buren was running as a Jacksonian that year. He didn't want to hear of another corrupt bargain and so refused everything Taylor offered."

"And so now," said Mary Jane, who followed politics closer than the others, "Attorney General Crittenden has advised President Fillmore on the new slave bill."

Will knew where she was going. "Not just the slave bill, but the entire agreement, yes."

"And what was that advice?"

"For that information perhaps Dominique will bring out her cards," said Lucien, who hated politics.

"It is beyond the power of the cards," said the Cuban girl.

"Are we to believe that Mr. Crittenden advised Mr. Fillmore, who they say opposes slavery, to sign the Fugitive Slave bill?" asked Mary Jane.

He had great affection for Mary Jane, the pretty, sassy, pig-tailed girl he and Jude used to take on treks to the Shelbyville lake. The Fugitive Slave bill, obliging Northern states to return slaves escaped from the South, was an abomination, but if Texas was to be denied slavery expansion into New Mexico and California was to be admitted as a slave-free state, the South needed something in return. With Uncle John in the administration and Henry Clay leading the Senate, the compromise was something only Kentuckians could have put together.

"At the price of avoiding civil war," Will said, "maybe he did offer that advice."

It was Lucien who responded.

"Something I have never understood, Will – being a political naïf, as you know – is why the departure of a few Southern states would be so dramatic."

It was the question often thought, never asked. He recalled a class at West Point when poor James Woods, who later fell at Monterrey, put it to one of the instructors, a gruff old major named Bouchard, who happened to be writing on the blackboard when the question came. Bouchard froze as though struck by lightning, chalk stuck on the board in mid-scratch.

Finally turning, his face matching the color of his scarlet ascot, he said:

"Cadet Woods: Is there a provision in the Constitution for separation from the Union?"

"There is not, sir."

"Therefore, any separation from the Union is a violation of the Constitution and shall be prevented by all means the government has at hand. Would you agree with that statement, Cadet Woods?"

It took longer than Bouchard would have liked for a response, but Cadet Woods was deep into the matter of whether the humiliation for agreeing to such an outrageous formulation would outweigh the demerits he would receive by disagreeing. Finally, he agreed and sat down. The matter never came up again.

"If you are a political naïf, dear Lucien, then so is Uncle John. You have expressed his position exactly."

It was a gentle answer, and the matter might have died there – except for Mary Jane. Jude's sister was not inclined ever to back down and had never hidden her view that the Fugitive Slave Act was criminal.

"And when war does come, Will Crittenden, as it surely will, which side will you take?"

She was sitting back in the sofa, Dominique by her side, both girls handsomely dressed in bright colors and looking to him more than ever like twins.

She wasn't the first to ask and wouldn't be the first to have the question avoided. But he did it in the wrong way.

"Perhaps I won't have to choose."

He glanced at Lucien, the only one understanding his meaning, who remembered Lopez well from Monmouth and hated everything about him, calling him devious, imperious, and sinister. The doctor was scowling. He knew Will's view of the Cuba enterprise was changing, but did not know how much it had changed. Will observed his shake of the head, but ignored it.

"Explain," demanded Jude.

The dinner, a spicy chicken and rice dish made by the Cuban women, had been excellent. The coffee, cake, and brandy warmed him. He was relaxed and content and off his guard. Among people he would have trusted with his life, why wouldn't he be? He was in love. Life was good. The Lopez mission was advancing smartly – the *Pampero* refitted, recruitment going well, and the date of departure fast approaching. He could not keep the thing secret from his friends forever.

"You've heard of Narciso Lopez?"

He saw their surprise. Lucien's head dropped.

"You're part of *that*?" said Jude, incredulous.

"*Liberating Cuba?*" said Dominique, eyes wide in astonishment.

Why wouldn't Dominique, as a Cuban, have heard of Lopez? Why wouldn't they all have heard? It was in all the newspapers. The cat was out of the bag, disinclined to climb back in.

"Well . . ."

"Count me in," said Jude, standing up.

"*What?*" cried Mary Jane.

"*Jude!*" Dominique shouted.

"*No,*" said Mary Jane. "*No!*"

Lucien slumped in his chair. Jude walked behind the couch where the women couldn't see him.

"If you're going, I'm going too," he said, aroused. "It's time we did a mission together. I've heard about Lopez – where can I find him, I wondered, how can I join up? Liberate the slaves, the Cuban slaves! Negroes can't do anything about slavery here. Nat Turner tried and look what happened. But an army of liberation for Cuba – *yes!* Take Dominique home someday to a free Cuba, *yes!* Imagine it! I am a veteran. I can help over there, Will. I had no idea you were part of it."

He was in full flight.

"Jude . . ."

"*It is in the cards!*"

The girls, shocked, grasped hands. Jude came away from the window where his large body was blocking light from the *réverbères* outside. His guileless, generous face appealed to everyone for approval, at least for understanding. Mary Jane glared at Will, exhorting him to say something. Dominique sat rigidly on the edge of the sofa, staring at her husband.

Damn the cards! Jude should leave the voodoo to his wife, the young man thought. He was mad at himself for having clumsily brought discord into their happy home, blurting out something without thinking. The fact is he'd been dying to tell someone, anyone, get it off his chest. Did Jude really think they would take him on that leg – a hip with a bullet in it? He needed to defuse a bad situation. But how? He could hardly say Jude couldn't join up because he was a cripple.

There was one thing he might have said: that no one knew the end plan for Cuba and its slaves: liberation and emancipation might be the goal – and again might not be. *Independistas* and *annexionistas* – starting with Villaverde and José Gonzales themselves – had strong differences. As for Lopez, he was inscrutable.

But if the adventurers disagreed on the ultimate status of the island, they did not disagree on the mission. For that, they were as one: The job was to throw Spain into the sea. As Napoleon always answered when asked about military strategy:

"Start fighting and see what happens."

In heavy silence he trudged with Lucien along Phillipa, turning on Common, heading for their favorite bistro in Pirate's Alley. Lucien was far from his amiable self. His young friend had blundered badly and must find a way out of it.

They leaned on the beer-stained oak counter at the Jean Lafitte, nursing their pints in silence. The Lafitte was impossibly noisy, reeked of sloshed beer and garlic, was too dark to see into the corners, which was just as well, and never closed.

"It is bad enough that you bullheadedly insist on going on this insane mission yourself," the doctor opined, "despite your uncle's sound advice; despite having assured me that you had no intention to do so."

He laid his hand on his friend's shoulder and squeezed. Will would never forget the eyes, as serious as the day he lay on the kitchen table at Shelbyville and prepared for Lucien to cut him open.

"But Jude must not sail with you," he said, eyes shining. "You got yourself into this mess – now get out of it! If you won't think of him, think of that beautiful family. Imagine that he didn't come back."

# XXI

James Freaner sent his card around and called on him at the custom-house. Freaner had seen the ad in the *Delta-News* convoking members of the expedition to the river fields by the old Marigny plantation at eight o'clock Saturday morning, May 24. The plantation was still in shambles from the great flood; its fields were vast and empty but finally dry, a perfect place for maneuvers. They headed to lunch around the corner on Basin Street. Freaner was in a fine mood.

"I've covered a few battles in my time," he said, "but planning is usually kept secret from the enemy. This is the first time I've seen a newspaper advertisement announcing maneuvers."

It felt good to see him again, the reporter they'd come to esteem through countless games of whist outside Mexico City, the man who carried the peace treaty back to Washington after Polk fired Nicholas Trist, the ambassador who negotiated it, surely one for the history books. Freaner was a Northerner who, like Quitman, had done all right in the South, maybe not as well as Quitman but done it without the help of a dowried daughter of the plantations. Northerners in the South seemed to fare better than Southerners in the North, who proved less adaptable.

They ordered beers and wasted no time finishing them off. Gulf weather gives a man a thirst.

"And just why are you telling me this?"

"Don't be coy with me, Crittenden, I know more than you do."

"So tell me what I don't know."

"Sigur showed me the list of officers. Your name is at the top,

Colonel W. L. Crittenden, West Point, '45, star of the show – fast promotion, I must say. Half of them are Europeans, mostly Austro-Hungarian refugees from the '48 revolts – including a general, Pragay by name, who came by the newspaper with a fastidious little peacock in pince-nez named Major Schlesinger. Everything is public."

Will shook his head. "The names of the officers are not public. What Sigur showed you is private, as I'm sure he explained."

"I have to say I was surprised to see your illustrious name on that list."

"It is a long story."

"The idea is pure madness."

"It better not be: You're coming with us, you know. Sigur tells me you've been looking for a war to cover."

"So you're palling around with my boss?"

"He's part of it, you know."

"You bet I know."

They were in a big, noisy place called the Bayou House. They ordered chicken croquettes and bouillabaisse. And more beer. The newspaper had sent Freaner off to cover the Indian campaigns in Texas, and he hadn't seen his whist-playing friend since Mexico City. His name came up each time he ran into Sigur, who had genuine affection for his shambling reporter, who didn't look as robust as he had in Mexico.

"You've lost some weight."

"I'm fine." The beers came and they clinked. "To your success."

"*Our* success."

"You know that Lopez already was prosecuted once for invading Cuba."

The young man smiled. "Old story, Freaner, prosecuted and acquitted, along with Sigur and a certain Governor John Quitman."

"I covered those trials. Lopez may not be what you think."

The smile was quickly gone. "What do you mean?"

"I mean the man has reasons to hate Spain."

"Which are . . ."

"Something that happened back there, not exactly clear at the trial, promotion going to someone else, personal resentments, that sort of thing."

"Are you impugning the gentleman's honor?"

"And then there's the Hungarian general. Where did you find Pragay?"

"Schlesinger found him. The European revolutionaries all seem to have settled in New York."

"Pragay doesn't speak English. Schlesinger does all the talking."

"Pragay is a professional. I'm not sure about Schlesinger. He's Hungarian – though they all speak German. He serves as the general's interpreter. Probably bought his commission."

"I see you don't like him either."

"No comment."

"Where are the other West Point veterans of Mexico? Or are you alone?"

"Downman was in Mexico. We're still recruiting."

"You're the only West Point officer. Where are your old whist buddies – Grant, Pickett, Kirby Smith . . . sorry, I forgot about Smith."

"I bet old Kirby would have signed up too. He was a professional."

"So where are the others?"

"General Worth was West Point."

"General Worth is dead."

"But he signed up. That's the point."

"So there were two of you. I suppose your name helps."

He didn't like that but wasn't going to quarrel. For all he knew Freaner was working on a story. He sat back and drank his beer.

"How's your whist game?"

"Don't change the subject, Lieutenant – sorry, Colonel. Anyway, you asked if I'm coming along and I suppose the answer is yes since the thing's backed by Sigur. But I don't like the smell of it. How can five hundred men push Spain out of Cuba where it's been for three centuries? If it were that easy don't you think the U.S. government would do it?"

"With the right man in the White House, yes. Not with Fillmore."

"Polk didn't do it."

"Polk would have done it."

"How do you know that?"

"He told certain friends of mine. He offered Spain $100 million and when they wouldn't sell, was ready to invade. We all thought we'd go on to Havana from Mexico City – *you know that, Freaner!* But Polk wouldn't run again and so we got Taylor and Fillmore and you know the rest."

"Do you really have five hundred men?"

"We will when we sail."

"I hear Quitman wants to delay."

"No comment."

"What do you think France and England will do?"

"You tell me."

"Wouldn't be surprised if they declared war."

"Look – France and England and Spain are European nations. If any one of them tries to tell us what to do in America, they can have their war. This is our hemisphere, not theirs. Little thing called the Monroe Doctrine."

"What I'm saying is that Fillmore, like Taylor, has good reasons not to rattle the cage. What president wants trouble with Europe when he's got enough problems at home? And don't forget the Neutrality Act. If the Spaniards don't get you the Americans will. You're creating a problem for your uncle, you know that, don't you?"

"Is that why we're having lunch – so you can write some ridiculous story about Crittendens fighting each other? Forget it. There is no story."

The waiter arrived with their croquettes, spicy, crispy, and golden, New Orleans style.

"Who said anything about a story?"

"To go back to the Neutrality Act: Do you really think the American people would stand for our conviction under some archaic law once we've thrown Spain out of Cuba? We'll be greeted here as heroes, Freaner . . . with flowers and confetti and a parade down South Rampart Street . . . *and* Pennsylvania Avenue . . . *and* Fifth Avenue! The people of this country showed what they thought of Lopez three times in acquitting him. Fillmore would be impeached if he tried such a thing."

"And another thing, and forgive me for mentioning it, but do you truly believe that Cuba wants to throw out the Spaniards only to be taken over by Americans? Have you thought about that?"

"It will be up to the Cubans to decide."

"You disappoint me. A majority of Cubans *with guns* will decide, and that majority backed by you and Lopez consists of plantation owners."

Freaner reached down into his bag and brought out a folio, handing it across the table. It was in Spanish, but the title was clear enough: *Ideas Sobre la Incorporación de Cuba a los Estados Unidos*, José Antonio Saco, 1848. The frontispiece identified Saco as a Cuban exile living in Paris.

"I take it that Señor Saco is an *independista*."

"He and many others. Read it – you might change your mind."

"This is not news to me, Freaner. Some of the Cubans involved with us are *independistas*. I have no call to change my mind. I am committed."

The reporter had a malicious look. "Did it ever occur to you that John J. Crittenden might be prosecuting his own nephew one day? Now that's a story."

"You never give up, do you?"

"As I said. I'm not writing a story. I invited you to lunch as a friend."

• • •

The young man sat back with his beer. He drank and wiped foam from his lips. Never had he felt better. He loved everything about New Orleans. The city was irrepressible, bubbling with energy and enthusiasm from two years of rebuilding. He'd not yet joined the levee brigades, a task Jude was constantly pressing on him. Jude's leg kept him from heavy physical work, but didn't keep him from recruiting. Even the girls pitched in. The levees were every New Orleaner's civic duty, they said.

The waiter cleared the table and brought the bouillabaisse.

"Sigur puzzles me. What's his interest in Cuba, anyway?"

"He's French," said Freaner. "He hates Spaniards."

"To the point of buying two ships and bankrolling an army to invade Cuba? There's more to it than that."

The reporter surveyed the restaurant, spying a few familiar faces from the quarter, elegant slavers up from the pens on Royal Street to enjoy a boozy lunch. Some of the gentlemen were accompanied by ladies, though he doubted any were wives, at least *their* wives. He was troubled, pained to have found his friend's name at the head of an operation he believed had no chance to succeed.

"Sigur's an expansionist," he said. "He believes in Manifest Destiny."

Will dipped his spoon into the creamy gumbo, extracting a fat gulf *gamba*. "Talk of empty phrases . . ."

"You asked a fair question, and I'll give you a fair answer: The author of your empty phrase, one John L. O'Sullivan, a member of my own esteemed profession, just happens to be a friend of one Laurent Sigur, just happens to drop by the *Delta-News* every time he's in town.

"I've heard of O'Sullivan."

"Do you know that John O'Sullivan just happens to have spent his honeymoon in Cuba where his sister just happens to live because she just happens to have married a Cuban plantation owner? My thought is that maybe O'Sullivan looked around and decided that Cuba could use a little Manifest Destiny."

The waiter collected their plates and brought coffee. Will offered his friend a *puro* and was refused. He lit his own and glanced around the room. A sweet-faced demoiselle with bare white arms made him think of Lucy, though she wore a feathered hat Lucy would have put on her horse – or mule. He smiled, and she smiled back. Her companion wouldn't like it but he was too busy eating to notice.

Freaner glanced over at the lady. A light went on.

"I told you about Sigur. Now you tell me something."

"Gladly."

"How exactly does a certain Lucy Holcombe fit into all this?"

*"Good God!"*

"I'm listening."

"Is that why we're having lunch?"

"Listen, Crittenden. I happen to like you, happen to have liked you ever since Mexico, though God knows why. Maybe because you are young and reckless and ambitious, all the things I am not – at least not anymore. We're having lunch because I saw your name on a list where I didn't think it belonged. Maybe I still have hopes of making you into a decent whist player and would find it painful if you didn't come back. Anyway, I've told you what you wanted to know and now it's your turn."

"How do you know about Lucy Holcombe?"

"How do you think?"

"Sigur."

"Correct."

"Do you intend to write any of this?"

"I do not. Not yet, anyway."

"What do you mean, not *yet*?"

"Just in case, let's say."

"Just in case . . ."

"Exactly."

"Put it this way," he said after a moment's hesitation: "Lucy Holcombe is a friend of the Quitmans – or rather her mother is a friend of Mrs. Quitman and thus Lucy has spent time with some of the people involved, including Quitman and Lopez. She supports the project, but is not involved. How could she be? She is a woman."

"Sigur says she is . . ."

"*Yes* . . . ?"

"I'm trying to recall how he put it – I believe 'inspiration' was the word."

"I wouldn't disagree with that."

"But why?"

"*Why?* I don't know, Freaner, and that is the truth. She has a passion for the thing. Lucy is a writer, a romantic. Calls me her Lafayette."

Freaner did not comment. But he would remember.

"You say she is a writer?"

"I believe it is her aspiration."

"Ah."

He did not like the turn in the conversation. "It has been a most agreeable luncheon," he told the reporter, looking to change the subject. "Let's hope the food is as good in Havana as it is here."

"It's the same, you know. Half of New Orleans comes from the islands. More *gens de couleur* here than whites. New Orleans, my friend, is the future of America."

"I believe you are wrong about that. What they have here cannot be duplicated – and thank God for that!"

"From the population I see in this city there must be a lot of white boys sleeping with the slaves. Or maybe it's the white girls with the slaves."

"Freaner, you are foul."

"You know any other way to make *gens de couleur*?"

"Everything about New Orleans is distorted. It is like some kind of separate universe. Reality is that North and South *should* be separate. I see it more clearly every day. What does a Mississippi Cracker have in common with a diehard Yankee like you? I just hope it can be done short of war."

"North will never let South go."

"It should, though. The two parts of the country have nothing in common."

"What about Kentucky – you a Cracker or a Yankee?"

It was a curse, really, being from Kentucky. For everyone else it was easy: I'm right, you're wrong; I'm a slaver, you're not. In New Orleans three-quarters of the people had forgotten completely about slavery. They just threw everything together in the bouillabaisse and asked what all the fuss was about.

He sipped his coffee. Those three-quarters likely had Negro blood in them and so why would they give a damn? Half the free blacks in the South, about 15,000, he'd read, lived in New Orleans. In their hearts, North and South alike hated a place like New Orleans, hated the thought that a city of mulattoes, a nation of quadroons and octoroons, could be the answer. New Orleans had its answer, but it was the wrong one.

"Maybe we'll just draw a line through the middle of Kentucky and split it up like the rest of the country."

"I thought they did that when they made Tennessee."

"Might have to do it again."

"Even if you draw that line, can you extend it all the way to the Pacific?"

"That's what the Compromise was all about."

Freaner shook his head. "The Compromise of 1850 no more solved our problems than did the Missouri Compromise. Everything just got pushed a little farther down the track so that when the crash finally comes the locomotives will be going ten times as fast. Tell me this – all that New Mexico and Utah Territory – it going to be slave or free?"

"Let the people decide, says Senator Douglas. Popular sovereignty."

"Bet on this, Colonel. Bet on it that the North will never allow slavery in any new territory. There will be war before that happens."

"It is for the people to decide. Even Whigs accept that now."

"Whigism is dead. Fillmore will be the last Whig."

"They haven't gotten the word in Kentucky."

"They will."

"So why worry about it? We'll be in Cuba, you and me, riding down the Malecon in Havana when the great fight comes. We'll stay there until it's over and come back and offer everyone a bottle of rum and a big box of Havana cigars. We'll all be friends again."

# PART FIVE

✳

# PREPARATION

# XXII

They'd met before, here and there around the city, company commanders bringing men together for drilling and arms instruction, but this was their first assembly as an army. They planned more maneuvers before sailing, but the first meeting was crucial for assessing what they had and what they did not. Their numbers were still growing. The ads in the *Delta-News* were not just calling together men who'd already signed up, but inviting new men to join. They'd raised the money, bought the ship, laid in the stores, arms, ammunition, and equipment. They would take to Cuba as many qualified men as wanted to fight. They would have more than enough to take on the Spaniards and liberate the island.

They recruited men who'd been in battle before: American veterans of the Mexican and Indian Wars; Cubans like Lopez who'd fought with the Spaniards and now turned against them; revolutionaries from Austria-Hungary, Poland, and Germany who'd opposed the monarchs in '48 and now sought revenge against the crown of Spain. Seventy-five years after the Declaration of Independence, America still was refuge to the world's refuse, above all to those who rejected the European way, the divine right of kings – or queens, as was the case in Spain.

It was a war of different things to different people:

For most of the volunteers, men for whom war was a profession, it was a simple business transaction: war as a job like any other.

For Lopez supporters around the country, ordinary Americans who read the editorials, heard the speeches, and offered money, it was a matter of America's right to rid the hemisphere of imperialists whose oppression had brought them to these shores in the first place. From the Northeast, we had driven out the British and French; from the Northwest, the British and Russians; from the Southwest, the Spaniards and Mexicans. Remained only the Southeast, the Caribbean.

For a key group of Lopez backers, the war was more calculated: For Laurent Sigur, John Quitman, Felix Huston, Jeff Davis, William Worth, John O'Sullivan, the Club of Havana – all those who would have backed Polk's taking of Cuba had he stayed in office – it was a war of annexation. For them, the objective was to bring Cuba into the Union as a slave state (or two slave states) to balance California's admission as a free state and guard against the possibility that states formed from the New Mexico and Utah Territories would choose to be slave-free under the popular sovereignty provision of the Compromise of 1850.

Cuba was asking to be annexed, and Lopez was the means. Maybe some members of the Club, men like Villaverde and Goicuría, were *independistas* rather than *anexionistas*, but they knew Cuba could not liberate itself without a slave revolt, an idea they loathed more than they loathed Spain. In backing Lopez, they would drive Spain from the island and see what followed. Think of Texas, they said, ten years a republic before joining the Union. It would work just as well the other way around. No one could foresee the future.

Let history mark the time and place: At eight o'clock Saturday morning, May 24, 1851, the Lopez army assembled in full for the first time on the Marigny fields along the north bank of the Mississippi River as it cuts across New Orleans.

Weather clear, spirits high, prospects bright, they began early to beat the heat and finish in time for anyone who had Saturday afternoon business. Three sergeant recruiters sat at camp tables along the riverside taking names and directing recruits to their units. The 1st Battalion, commanded by Col. Robert Downman, assembled on the south side of the field, nearest the river. Next to it was Colonel Crittenden's unit, the 2d Battalion, in charge of artillery.

No artillery was present that day, nor was ammunition, though each soldier was issued a musket. Quartermasters handed out blue denim shirts; boots would come later. Company sergeants met with recruits and broke men out in groups to go over instructions for handling the muskets. At 9:30, troops assembled into companies and squads for discussion of tactics. At ten, drilling began. At eleven, the men were brought together into battalions to prepare to pass in review.

Included in Downman's battalion was an independent Cuban unit, the 1st Regiment of Cuban Patriots, commanded by Capt. Ildefonso Oberto, formerly of the Spanish army. Also assigned to the 1st Battalion was a company of Germans and Austro-Hungarians under Capt. Herman Schlicht. Assigned to Crittenden's 2d Battalion was a company called the Guards of Sigur, a group of tough fighters recruited and paid for by Laurent Sigur himself. By this time everyone knew that Sigur represented both the organization and the bankroll behind the expedition.

The Guards of Sigur were commanded by Capt. Robert Ellis. Colonel Downman's second in command was Lt. Col Thomas McClelland. Capt. James Sanders, another veteran of Mexico, served as a company commander. Answering to Crittenden were Maj. David Martin and Captains John Kelly and Victor Ker.

Flags and colors whipped, and a band of New Orleans highsteppers hired by Sigur filled the air with march music, thrilling even the most seasoned veterans. As the morning passed, crowds along the levees began to grow. The music halted, and the general staff and aides stood off at a distance to watch as the battalions fell in behind the band to prepare to pass in review. For a first day's full maneuvers no one could be too unhappy. They'd begun to look like an army. None would forget this day of hope and promise.

Lopez stood at the center of things, flanked by chief of staff

Gen. John Pragay, who wore his medals. Pragay was a dour veteran who'd risen to the top of the Austro-Hungarian Army before escaping to America when the people's revolt against the Habsburgs failed. Alongside Pragay stood Col. Max Blumenthal and Maj. Louis Schlesinger, both in uniform of the Austro-Hungarian Army. Gen. Felix Huston of the Texas militia was there. Col. John Pickens and Maj. Thomas Hawkins, both prominent Kentucky militiamen and friends of the South, were present. Recruited by Crittenden with Sigur's financial help, they would form a Kentucky regiment to sail for Cuba as reinforcements once the beachhead was established.

Taken together, their army's officer corps, in its gallimaufry of uniforms, was more experienced and abler than anything the Spaniards could bring against them. They were sure of it.

Resplendent in white linens, Panama hat, and Havana *puro* clamped between stained teeth, Laurent Sigur stood by Lopez with a group of civilians that included the Cubans from Monmouth. U.S. and Spanish agents mingled freely with the crowd along the river, most of them easily recognized: Sigur had made every effort to advertise the maneuvers, daring the federal government to try to stop them, knowing it wouldn't.

By noon, the path along the levee was crammed with the curious. New Orleaners would use any occasion to have a parade. A small army preparing for war against Spain was more than enough.

Crittenden joined the other senior officers – Lopez, Pragay, Blumenthal, Downman, Schlesinger, Dr. Fourniquet and others – waiting for the band to start up again and the troops to pass in review. Unlike the others, he was dressed in simple fatigues, sans insignia. The mood was of great expectation, even exhilaration. How could conditions have been more perfect? Staring down the river, he felt the presence of Cuba just over the horizon, almost in their sights, almost in their hands.

Bedecked in an enormous red and white hat, the drum major gave the downbeat and started the band off in slow march tempo.

Wearing a variety of hats and trousers, close to three hundred men were marching, all in blue denim blouses. Most of them were veterans of one campaign or another, a good many familiar with band music and able to keep in step as they headed in high sunlight toward the far end of Marigny to prepare to turn and pass in review.

"*Terrible*," intoned Major Schlesinger.

Heads turned. Crittenden didn't like the man, but couldn't have said exactly why: something "slippery" about him, like what Uncle John saw in John Helm. Or maybe it was the pince-nez, which seemed an affectation.

"What, Major – you don't like the music?"

"I don't like the marching, *Colonel*."

The young man didn't like the emphasis. "We won't be marching in formation in Cuba, Major. This isn't Europe. It's not how you look. It's how you fight."

It took a moment for Schlesinger to respond.

"Sir, just what do you mean by that remark?"

"I mean I don't appreciate your opinion of these men on their first day. Give them time. I'll be glad to turn my battalion over to you for personal march instructions if you'd like."

"I wasn't expressing my opinion; it was General Pragay's."

"Then let him express it himself."

"See here, are you doubting my word?"

"*You* said it, Major, not the general. It was your comment I heard and it is to you that I addressed my comments."

"I think you owe me an apology."

"Sir, you are insolent. I will give you satisfaction if you insist."

"You would cross swords with a Hungarian?"

"*Gentlemen, gentlemen*," cried Sigur, "you're not here to fight each other. Save it for the Spaniards."

"I have been insulted," said Schlesinger.

Pragay whispered something, and Schlesinger turned to face the general. A brief discussion in German ensued before he turned back to Crittenden. "I was wrong," he said briskly. "I should not have taken offense where none was given."

Will nodded. The matter was set aside.

As the band and battalions waited at the far end of the field. Sigur motioned to him. A Creole of friendly aspect whom he'd come to know through countless planning sessions, Laurent Sigur was a man born to Louisiana wealth and privilege. He'd inherited two sugar plantations from his father – an immigrant from Alsace when Louisiana still belonged to Spain – and still spoke with a French accent. His business was politics and planting; the *Delta-News* only a hobby. His gregarious manner helped him get his way with people, as did his wealth.

He took the soldier by the arm. "Colonel Crittenden, I have a friend in Havana, a man I would like you to look up when you arrive in the city."

The music started at the far end of the field.

"His name is John Thrasher. We've not yet met, but have long corresponded. He publishes a newspaper, *El Faro Industrial*. Our friend Villaverde writes for him. Thrasher will be a useful for communicating with the Club of Havana."

He handed him Thrasher's business card.

"We are all members of the Club. Every Cuban you have met in New Orleans represents the Club. Thrasher will put you in touch." His voice dropped to a whisper. "As a fellow American it will be easier for you to approach him than it would be for Lopez, if you get my meaning."

He nodded.

"The Club of Havana is crucial to our enterprise."

He turned to go and stopped. "You are not a Freemason, are you, Colonel? Pity. It would help. Perhaps when you return we can address that."

Again he turned to go, and again he stopped. "Oh, yes . . . and at some point you will have affair with Mr. Allen Owen, the U.S.

counsel general in Havana. A word of warning: do not regard Mr. Owen as a friend."

As Sigur drifted away, the young man spied James Freaner in the crowd and crossed to join him. From the end of the field he heard orders barked out. Freaner looked worse than he had at lunch a few weeks before.

"Rough night?"

"No worse than the others."

He looked closer and for the first time understood. It was not fatigue or liquor or overwork that afflicted his friend or anything else he could have corrected: Freaner was consumptive, something likely picked up in Mexico. He shouldn't be in New Orleans, let alone planning to sail for Havana. The man needed a dry climate. He wondered if Sigur knew. He said nothing more, but clapped him on the shoulder and started to move off.

"Hold a minute, Colonel – somebody missing today, no?"

"Who's missing?"

"Where's General Quitman?"

He wouldn't get into it with the reporter. "Maybe he's just late."

The formation was nearly upon them, drums pounding, trumpets blasting, the army looking as good as it ever would. As it reached them and the 1st Battalion did "eyes right," he saw a face that had no business in the ranks, a face he'd forgotten during weeks of preparations, forgotten though he shouldn't have.

Jude Freeman was marching at the head of his squad in Captain Sanders's company, leading the line like the other corporals, looking as proud as he'd looked in Monterrey coming in with Henry Clay's Kentucky Volunteers. The stripes he'd won in Mexico were sewn onto the blue shirt of the Lopez army. As a member of Sanders's company in Downman's battalion, Jude had so far escaped Will's scrutiny.

At eyes right Jude spied him and fixed on him a second longer than he should have done, turning his head when it should have been still. Will immediately noticed the limp, but he was looking for it.

Another man might not see it or might take it for something passing, like blisters, certainly not something to cause recruiters to reject him. You don't throw a man like Jude Freeman from the ranks because of blisters.

He knew what he was going through to hide his limp, to keep in step with parade march. How would it be when they hit the beaches or made a forced march into the mountains? What if he was assigned to haul a howitzer or dig trenches awaiting the Spanish charge? The Spaniards had horses. If they formed a square to repel a cavalry charge could Jude Freeman hold his ground on that leg?

His eyes swept the crowd along the path by the levee. Did the women know he'd come? Would they have followed him? He saw a woman standing off alone. The other women had come with men or children to enjoy the parade, but this woman, who could have been either Dominique or Mary Jane but might be neither, was by herself on the grass, her face shielded from the sun by her parasol.

He stared long and hard, couldn't see the face but recognized the yellow parasol. He started over. As he neared, the woman's face came out of the shadow of the parasol. She signaled to him. It was Dominique.

"We couldn't stop him."

She'd been crying and had tried unsuccessfully to put her face back in order. Seeing him brought more tears and she dabbed at her eyes. "Mary Jane wouldn't come. She is furious, the house in turmoil. We tried everything, even the cards. Please, Will Crittenden, you must not let him go with you."

He waited until the parade made its final turn and came to rest. The sun was beating down. He approached the 1st Battalion. The men stood at ease in their separate companies, addressed by their captains. They were to be dismissed by 12:30.

Could anything have been more delicate? He knew how much Jude wanted to come, how much he wanted to participate in the liberation of Cuba and, he believed, its slaves. Jude knew his brother would never reveal his war wound, never ask him to be removed from the corps over his badge of honor.

But there was another way.

They didn't recruit family men. They had no strict rule about it, didn't look too deeply into the personal affairs of the men, but preferred it that way. With other officers, he'd gone down the rosters. Some men had surely lied about it, and they signed them up. What else could they do? Theirs wouldn't be the first war where men signed up to escape family situations. But if a man freely admitted he had family to support, he was turned down. The risks were too great.

As for the Europeans, none was married that he knew of. Most had escaped the Continent alone and one step ahead of the firing squad, if not the noose. The Americans like himself were mostly restless war veterans with no time for families. Some came for the adventure, some for the promise of spoils, some were simple soldiers who would rather fight Spaniards than Indians.

He approached Capt. James Sanders, who saluted smartly.

"Captain, there are to be no married men in these units. The risk is too great."

"These are single men, Colonel. I've been down the roster."

"At least one of them is not single, for I see his wife standing in the crowd."

"And which man would that be, sir?"

"The corporal of the second squad – the big man. Jude Freeman is his name."

"Ah, the Negro, Mexican War veteran. He said he was not married."

"He lied. He has a large family to support."

"Pity."

# XXIII

She knew the moment was approaching. He didn't know how she knew, for the one thing they'd kept secret was their schedule. But she knew. The navy also knew and was paying close attention to ships heading down the Mississippi into the Gulf. Already the government had seized their first ship, the *Cleopatra*, but that was in New York. New Orleans was more sympathetic to the cause, and the *Pampero* was faster. As a customhouse officer, he had access to the navy's patrol schedules, which was an advantage. At times he wondered if it wasn't his access as much as his name that had secured his promotion.

In her letters she tried to pry out every detail. She'd become passionate about the expedition, lyrical, romantic, comparing it to the Crusades. No more Lafayette, now he was Ivanhoe bringing light into a world of darkness. Her imagination exceeded anything he'd ever come across, her letters full of allusions to a Cuba already liberated, islanders prostrate with gratitude at America's feet:

> *That beautiful emerald isle with its coconuts and mangos, so close we can smell it, almost reach out and touch it, and oh, I can see you dearest, walking in your white uniform under the bougainvillea, climbing into your carriage for the ride to Government House, people clapping as you pass. "Libertad, libertad," they sing out; finally, we are free! In the evening we will sit under the palms along the Malecon and watch the moonlight shimmering on the Caribbean. I am filling notebooks with delirious thoughts of adventure.*

• • •

Reading over her poetic flourishes, it was clearer than ever that she had in mind to become a published writer. Hadn't she told him of winning prizes for composition at the seminary school in Pennsylvania? How else to explain the reference to "filling notebooks?" Why else her passion for something ordinarily so far removed from the feminine mind; her passion for war? However it turned out, Cuba was to be her theme. Dull, dry, uninspiring East Texas had turned her to a life of literary imagination and escape.

Was he no more than a character in her play?

How he hated the thought! Everything she'd ever told him, ever written him, every gesture and action gave it lie. The gazebo, the gazebo! The image came to him day and night, popping into mind as he worked over papers in the customhouse, tipped beers with colleagues at the Jean Lafitte, even floating through his mind in the deepest sleep. Once it came as a dream turned nightmare. They were together in the gazebo, and when he reached to embrace her she slipped away and began to evanesce, a will-o'-the-wisp fading away up the misty path into the arms of a sneering Elkanah Greer.

In June she wrote that she was coming to New Orleans. Eugenia had been invited to stay with her friend Victoria Raynaud in Royal Street, and of course they refused to let Maman come without them. They would stop off in Memphis to visit Elkanah on his nearby plantation. She was not looking forward to visiting the Greers, but there was no avoiding it. Anna Eliza knew of her feelings for Elkanah. It was a delicate matter between sisters, but she'd gone as far as she dared go.

She knew how busy he was, but of course expected to see him every day, if only for a few minutes.

So loving were her letters that he spent days wondering if he should seize the moment. Everything about the situation was new to him, exhilarating but frightening as well. As much as he longed to ask for her hand, he had doubts. Would she accept him? Wasn't it better to live in doubt than to suffer a refusal? Speculations about her literary ambition had plunged him into dreary confusion.

What kind of life could he offer this high-spirited woman who surely had a brilliant future ahead of her? She opposed her sister's marriage because Elkanah was a boor and his prospects mediocre, but his own, those of a mere customhouse officer renting rooms on St. Ann Street, were worse than mediocre. Eugenia, intoxicated by his famous name, may believe in his bright political future and Lucy may fantasize about him as a modern Ivanhoe, but reality was another matter.

And what of the risks that lay ahead? She might write of sitting under the palms on the Malecon, but all of them who'd signed on knew they faced a battle. How could he expect a woman to accept his offer when the risks were real that he would not return? And what if she accepted and he did not return? Was that not why they rejected men with families? The burden on survivors was too great. How many women would be left with children and no means of support?

Though Lopez expected a great Creole rallying to the liberators, he knew the Spaniards would fight. Lopez's earlier expedition to Cuba, the adventure at Cárdenas, which he called reconnaissance, had beat a swift retreat to the ship when word came of Spanish forces on the march from Havana. Spain had two thousand troops on the island, a force that could be dealt with by a smaller, better trained and equipped U.S. force once the Creoles rallied to them. But anyone who believed Madrid would quit its last major foothold in the Americas without a fight did not know Spanish history.

General Quitman was arguing for delay, insisting they raise more money and recruit more men before sailing. Lopez disagreed, and members of the Club of Havana, whose views would be decisive, were still to be heard from. Ambrosio José Gonzales, at the center of Cuba's liberation movement since the Mexican War, convoked a meeting to resolve the matter. In a letter to the principals, Gonzales made his own position clear:

*Any delay past the time specified in the contract with Gov. John A. Quitman puts our project at risk. In previous communications I have indicated my reasons for opposing any delay past August of this year. My position has not changed. We will meet July 4 at Raynaud House (U.S. Independence Day: could anything be more appropriate!) to allow each of you to give his opinion on the matter. We will proceed by consensus as always.*

Will wrote to inform Gonzales of his complete agreement. Past summer, how could they keep the men together? For that matter, how could monies be stretched to pay them? How much longer could they ward off interference from the navy? Spain knew they were preparing to sail; how could they keep Spain from using the time to accelerate her preparations for defense? He recalled General Scott's insufferable delay (on Polk's orders) outside Mexico City, a delay that eventually cost them hundreds of casualties and threw the war's outcome into doubt. They dare not run the same risk in Cuba.

He had another worry, one he did not share with Gonzales: Having lost General Worth, they could not afford to lose General Quitman. It was a damnable situation, and presented him with a dilemma: Quitman insisted on delay, which they could not grant; yet they dare not sail without Quitman. Without Quitman, Col. William Logan Crittenden of West Point, former lieutenant, would be the senior American officer.

Victoria Raynaud, widowed grande dame of Royal Street, lived in a garden mansion less than a mile from the corner of the city's busiest intersection, Royal and St. Louis Streets, where the Hotel Royal, formerly the Hotel St. Louis, catered to the Louisiana elite. Royal Street, like most of New Orleans, had been drowned in the great flood of '49, caused by a levee break a few miles upstream at Pierre Sauvé's plantation, the break known as Sauvé's Crevasse.

At Raynaud House, it was said, the waters rose to the top step of the front porch, but dared not enter.

The house consisted of two elegant colonnaded stories plus a third story dotted with dormers, all whitewashed in the New Orleans style. Eight pillars marched across the façade, and the second story was distinguished by a lace iron balcony running its length. The house was shaded, hidden really, from prying eyes by a canopy of magnolia and willow trees extending to Royal Street.

The privacy afforded by the canopy was no accident. Jean-Baptiste Raynaud, Victoria's late husband, had been the city's leading slaver, always careful to cover his affairs, and above all his visitors, in a mantel of secrecy.

One end of the house, where the salon was located, was built in the form of a domed turret, with picture windows giving onto the gardens. The turret salon, as it was called, was where Victoria gave her parties and receptions. It was said that Jean-Baptiste had built the city's grandest house on its grandest street for its grandest dame, who, like so many in the city, had come down from Tennessee, where life was not so grand. To be invited to Raynaud House was to have arrived; to be uninvited was to dwell in the city's social shadows.

He called on Lucy each day, usually in early evening when he was done at the customhouse, always finding her surrounded by a houseful of guests. For days, he found no moment alone with her. It was maddening, as if she maneuvered to be surrounded whenever he came – one day off with Victoria or her daughters, another with Eugenia and friends or gliding about with Lopez, or in deep tête-à-tête with General Pragay who spoke no English but was pleased to chatter away in French free of the oppressive company of Major Schlesinger. She even had time for the detestable Texas General Huston, a slaving colleague of the late Jean-Baptiste.

One day he arrived to find her deep in conversation with a handsome officer of the U.S. Navy. His heart thumped. Not only was the enemy inside the walls, but Lucy's hand lay on the young man's arm!

He approached and was relieved to be introduced to Lt. Christophe Raynaud, childhood friend of the Holcombe girls and a man who, despite his uniform, supported their enterprise.

"I can tell you sir, I am not the only naval officer in town who believes in what you are doing. Some would even like to sail with you."

"Then why don't they come, Lieutenant?" he responded, laughing. "We soldiers have nothing against the navy."

"The navy will arrive to support you in victory."

"Support us or arrest us?"

They both laughed. Christophe, Victoria's only son, would turn out to be useful for their enterprise.

After several frustrating days during which he became certain she was dodging him on purpose, he finally found himself alone with her. Impulsively, he'd bought a diamond ring he couldn't afford and carried the little box in the pocket of his jacket, constantly running his fingers over it. He'd begun to wonder if he'd ever have her alone long enough to offer it.

"I've been trying for days to ask if we might have lunch together."

"Of course," she said, with a lovely smile. "I wondered why you had said nothing."

Mystifying.

# XXIV

The men arrived separately and were shown upstairs. It was Independence Day and for once there was no effort at secrecy – New Orleans had other things on its mind. Firecrackers had been popping since sunrise, and by ten o'clock the sound of drums and cornets could be heard across the city, from Metairie to Algiers Point across the river. Parades had already begun in the Vieux Carré, the center of things, though fireworks would have to wait for nightfall. New Orleaners intended to make it a joyous full day of celebrations on America's seventy-fifth birthday, our diamond jubilee.

The turret office was immediately above Victoria Raynaud's turret salon. When the grande dame gave receptions, the office was where Jean-Baptiste's friends repaired when they could not stand it a moment longer without a smoke or a libation stronger than the *gentilles breuvages* offered downstairs. Professionally, the turret office was where Jean-Baptiste met associates when he had slaving business to transact. To avoid interruptions, a dumb waiter sent up whatever visitors might require from the kitchen below.

It was to be the decisive meeting. The sole item on the agenda was the timetable for operations, the date on which the *Pampero* would be fully loaded and ready to set sail, direction Cuba. The consensus had long favored early August, with the precise date to be fixed in function of preparations.

But General Quitman now sought delay.

Ambrosio José Gonzales was the Club of Havana's director in the United States. His efforts to free Cuba from Spanish control were known from Madrid to Havana; New York to New Orleans. On working terms with Cuba's *independistas*, Gonzales's sympathies lay with annexation. Along with John L. O'Sullivan, he'd met with President Polk on Cuba while American troops still occupied Mexico City, a meeting intended to persuade Polk to move on Cuba once the treaty with Mexico was signed. Polk's desire to annex Cuba was no secret.

But instead of dispatching the army to Havana, Polk instructed Secretary of State James Buchanan to buy the island from Spain for $100 million. By the time Madrid rejected the offer, Polk, unwell and unwilling to run again, had left the White House. When Zach Taylor, his successor, showed no interest in Cuba, Gonzales and O'Sullivan turned to Gen. William Worth, recently back from Mexico. If the business could not be done officially, it would be done unofficially.

Worth gave his word to join Lopez in leading a private army to take Cuba. When Worth fell to the cholera, the club offered the job to Quitman, who signed a handsome contract and resigned as governor of Mississippi. A few months later, President Taylor died of the same disease, removing an obstacle to their plans. Fillmore, his successor, who signed the Fugitive Slave Act, was friendly to the South. Everything was falling neatly into place.

They were ten that morning, ten coconspirators climbing the spiral stairs of Raynaud House to the steady rattling of firecrackers, reminding of gunfire, a sound familiar to all. After enjoying coffee and biscuits sent up on the dumb waiter, they took their places around Jean-Baptiste's large mahogany table.

Gonzales, a brusque, no-nonsense militant who'd recently become a U.S. citizen, immediately gave the floor to Quitman, the reason for calling the meeting. The man with the lion's head glanced once around the table. Speaking slowly, almost mournfully, he explained that he'd come to the conclusion they would need at least one thousand men to take and hold Cuba against the stronger Spanish force, and that therefore they could not possibly sail in August.

His words were met with stony silence. Crittenden glanced around the table and observed people looking anywhere but at Quitman, each man waiting for someone else to respond to the commander-in-chief who'd just rejected the war plan. The one man who did not look away, but stared Quitman in the eyes, was Narciso Lopez, who finally spoke, the tone firm.

"I regret to say, General, it is too late to reach that conclusion. We are but two weeks from sailing."

Quitman shook his head. "Lamentably, sir, I cannot agree with the schedule."

Sigur: "The problem, General, is that you have a contract with us stipulating that the invasion will take place during the summer of 1851. That leaves us scarcely two months before summer's end to recruit five hundred more men to reach your thousand, an impossible task."

Quitman ignored both Lopez and Sigur and turned toward José Gonzales, the chairman. "I thought we'd have more men by now, Ambrosio. It is a failure of recruitment for which I bear no responsibility. We cannot launch a premature invasion to satisfy a contract."

He would not get off so easily.

"It has nothing to do with recruitment, General," said Domingo de Goicuría, who, like Cirilo Villaverde, was a club member but not a plantation owner. Goicuría's long, lugubrious face and pointed white beard gave him the aspect of the wayward hidalgo from La Mancha. "No one ever believed we could have a thousand men by summer. You yourself could not have believed it."

"I agree," said Miguel Teurbe, another club member in exile. Teurbe wrote editorials for James Gordon Bennett's *New York Herald*, which was a vigorous defender of Manifest Destiny. "With the Cuban people behind us, we don't need a thousand men. We have more than enough for the task."

"It was never a question of numbers," said Lopez, "but of will."

The Hungarians were whispering.

"General Pragay observes that it is not a matter of numbers *or* generals," said Major Schlesinger. "Why must we have three generals for five hundred men?"

"See here, Major," said Crittenden, who found the comment insulting to Quitman and wondered if Pragay had actually said it. "We're talking here of experience, not numbers. The majority of our men are Americans. They expect to be commanded by a general who has led American troops in action."

"Does that mean, sir," said Schlesinger without waiting to confer with Pragay, "that you doubt the competence of Generals Lopez and Pragay?"

"Does that mean, Colonel," said Lopez, not waiting for the young man to respond to Schlesinger, "that you support General Quitman in arguing for delay?"

He would not take the bait. "We need General Quitman with us," he said, simply, looking squarely at Quitman.

"But that is not the issue," insisted Schlesinger. "The issue is that we cannot put off the invasion beyond August. General Pragay believes delay would be disastrous for the morale of the army."

It was Quitman's time to answer, and he leveled his predator's eyes first on Schlesinger, then Pragay. He knew that the European troops, who made up a third of the force, were essential, but looked on Pragay and the Austro-Hungarians as political revolutionaries, not battle-tested fighters. He sensed, as the others did not, or did not yet, that they would be a problem.

"We can have one thousand men under arms by early spring," he said. "What does the delay of a few months matter if it guarantees success?"

"Impossible!" said Sigur. "And what if it guarantees defeat?"

Quitman frowned. "Just how could it do that, Laurent?"

"It is indeed a possibility," interrupted Gonzales. "Fillmore is no Polk. I've heard rumors that the attorney general will order the *Pampero* impounded."

"Attorney General *Crittenden*?" said Quitman, eyes going to Will.

"It is something we must consider if Colonel Crittenden cannot persuade his uncle to desist," said Sigur. "I refuse to pay for another ship."

"I am dismayed," said Gonzales, holding up his hands to quiet a table that was becoming raucous. "General Quitman, you have been central to our plans since General Worth's unfortunate death. It has never been a question of delaying past this summer. Speaking for all of us, I beg you to respect our contract."

The room fell silent. Crittenden doubted that Gonzales spoke for everyone, at least not for the Hungarians and perhaps not for Lopez. He glanced at the portraits ringing the walls, all of similar size except for a larger one in the center. The brass plate was too far away to read, but the fat man with muttonchops and a crooked smile could only be Jean-Baptiste himself, clearly a man used to the comforts of life. He'd fallen in a duel, it was said, though the topic was forbidden at Raynaud House. Strange, he thought, to be planning a war of liberation at a slaver's table.

"I sincerely regret this, gentlemen," said Quitman, shaking his head. "In Mexico, as you know, General Worth and I shared responsibility for the battle of Mexico City, the battle that decided the war." He paused to glance around the table. "General Worth was above all a prudent general – prudent to the point of resisting General Scott when he thought our forces were put unnecessarily at risk. I can tell you with no fear of contradiction – and with certain support from Colonel Crittenden who was there with us – that if General Worth were here today, he would echo what I have said."

"What you fail to appreciate, General," said Lopez, calmly as always, "is that our forces serve only as the spark. Ignited by the spark, as Señor Teurbe rightly says, the Cubans themselves will feed the fires to take our country back from Spain."

"Would that it were so, General," said Quitman, quickly. "But as a military man, I cannot base my planning on contingencies. Gentlemen, in all good conscience I will not do it. I will not do it because it should not be done. I beg you to extend the contract another six months – no more, I promise."

All energy was sucked from the room. More discussion was pointless. No one but Quitman supported delay. Even the young man, as much as he wanted Quitman's presence – or rather feared his absence – was itching to get underway.

Unhappy meeting over, they made their arrangements and slipped separately downstairs and out onto the street. Waiting in the foyer, Quitman clapped him on the shoulder and wished him luck. Outside, he headed down Royal Street toward the Vieux Carré. The streets were busier now, and somewhere a band was playing, several bands even, a cacophony of sounds filling the air like cries from competing flocks of noisy birds.

He needed time to reflect on the turn of events. Losing a man like Quitman was a blow, no question, but the operation was based on the proposition that Cuba already was in a state of quasi-revolt, and that the Creoles needed only a little outside help to rise up and throw the Spaniards into the sea.

With the islanders behind them, they didn't need a thousand men and they probably didn't need Quitman; without the islanders even a thousand men and Quitman might not be enough.

Quitman's loss presented him with his own problem: He was now the senior American officer, subordinate not to an experienced American general but to a cashiered Spanish Army general of unknown reputation and a Hungarian on the run from Europe. He did not fool himself into believing he had the experience or the authority to replace Quitman.

Lost in his thoughts, he'd soon covered half the distance down Royal to Saint Louis Street. The music, drifting down from Bourbon, grew louder and more cacophonous at each cross street. Past Canal, without realizing it, he'd halted in front of a handsome, white-washed, two-story edifice, its lace-iron balcony covered in bougainvillea, a building little different from others on the street.

Still, he knew the place. He read the brass plaque.

### LUCIEN HENSLEY
### DOCTOR OF MEDICINE
Second floor, right

He climbed the stairs and turned right. A sign on the door told him the doctor was out. Odd that the doctor would be making house calls on July Fourth, though perhaps not: births, deaths, disease do not take a holiday.

He would return later. He needed to talk to Lucien, always full of common sense. Now that Jude's enlistment had been terminated, at least his friend had stopped trying to talk him out of his own participation. The matter was settled between them. He wondered what Lucien would say about Quitman's defection and his own promotion to senior American.

And he had something else to tell his friend. Descending, he resumed his walk down Royal, heading for Pirate's Alley, the crowd pulling him along with it like the river. As he went, his hand slipped into his coat pocket to find the tiny square box, snapping it open, feeling inside, finding the ring, running his fingers over its sharp, polished edges, smiling at the touch. Yes, he had done it, and why not? Lucy had given him every indication that it was what she wanted. Everything was up to him.

He stopped into the Jean Lafitte, pushing his way through to the bar, ordering a sausage and beer. Lucien would be thrilled, able for a moment to forget his opposition to Cuba and share the joy of his friend's engagement. In his life had he ever been happier? Surely not. The unfortunate meeting at Raynaud House was forgotten and his mind turned to the coming rendezvous with Lucy. It was to be a double triumph: the new American commander wins the beautiful princess! His doubts were gone. He'd kept his fingers wrapped around the box all the way down Royal Street and into Pirate's Alley. He would show Lucien the diamond, and when the doctor was done with his patients they would walk together up to Bourbon and join the parades and fireworks and have dinner and drinks and celebrate the first of many Independence Days to come in the city that was now their home.

Lucien had had the kind of morning only a doctor can have: a three-a.m. knock on the door followed by an endless walk through the narrow streets of the Vieux Carré and the baby's delivery; not enough time to return home to bed and so on to surgery at the hospital and a completely unexpected death on the operating table leading to turmoil with the deceased's family and to the extended – and dreaded – hospital death formalities.

Exhausted, he was not back in his office until well after noon. Two patients were waiting, as was his cheerful young friend, whom he motioned into the consulting room ahead of the others.

Still standing, he opened the box that was presented and stared down at the ring. He stared for some time. What followed was unrelated to his mood or fatigue or the waiting patients. Reflecting on it later, he was sure of it. Even tired and dejected, his physician's lucidity never deserted him. His first thought was that neither the diamond nor its intended recipient could be afforded on a customhouse salary.

But that was not what most troubled him.

"Have you thought this through?"

The tone was hard. Will was taken aback.

"Why did you reject Jude? Why have you excluded married men?"

Will waved his hand. "But all that is different, Lucien."

"You know the hazards of this insane mission; do you want that poor girl to lie in her bed wondering what happened to her fiancé when it is perfectly possible that if you fall no one ever hears of you again?"

The young man was chilled to his core. The doctor's voice was loud enough to be heard in the waiting room.

"Have you even thought about that? Where would it leave the lady? If you fail you won't be the gallant band of warriors come to liberate Cuba, but a band of brigands either shot in the dust or marched off in chains to the execution block. What does that make of your fiancée?"

He was too stunned to reply.

"Why do you need to hear these things from me? It is caddish behavior, unbefitting a gentleman."

"Lucien, I . . ."

Then, with real anger:

"Imagine that instead of murdering you, they throw you in jail to rot away the rest of your life – what is your fiancée supposed to do, wait ten, twenty years until the bloom is gone and the flesh sagging?"

"Good God, Lucien!"

"Still worse than any of that – yes, still worse I say – imagine you come back mutilated or blinded or shell-shocked and raving like a blithering idiot. I see them all the time, these once brilliant young men brought to me after some terrible event. I may save their lives but no one can restore them to what they were. I see the wives when they come to fetch them, envisaging the years of misery ahead of them, the calamity in their eyes as they lead them away."

And then the worst blow of all: "Do you believe that Lucy Holcombe is the kind of woman to deal with any of that?"

# XXV

Dressed for the city, the Holcombe ladies were waiting when he arrived at Raynaud House. Did they not understand? Would he never be alone with her? What could he possibly say or do with her mother and sister along? Surely Lucy expected the offer, as did Eugenia. Was that not even why they'd come to New Orleans? And that was the problem. Everything had been so clear until his meeting with Lucien. He hadn't had a worse night since Mexico.

They laughed at his surprise, which apparently he had not well concealed. Lucy laid a hand on his arm.

"Surely Colonel Crittenden won't mind dropping Maman and Anna Eliza in Chartres Street for some shopping?"

He flushed. Surprise gave way to embarrassment.

She looked different from any time he'd seen her. To him, Lucy Holcombe was a study in contrasts: black hair and pale blue eyes; soft, sensuous mouth and sharp tongue; firm convictions and flirtatious manner; animated yet composed, elegant yet simple. Everything she did was capable of surprise. Anna Eliza was the prettier one, but see them together and you fixed on Lucy because she was so much more electric. You could almost see her mind working through those pale blue windows. She was exotic and unpredictable. The effect was intoxicating.

Eugenia and Anna Eliza were dressed in very correct white ruffles, high to the neck and sprouting little collars. Compared with them Lucy was a bird of another species, colorful in blues and reds, wearing yellow beads instead of the usual ribbon at her neck and with a yellow ribbon tied in her dark hair. She'd abandoned the high-necked flounces of the others and wore a V-necked pale blue frock under a little red vest. Whatever the other women had done to their faces, she had not, nor did she need to.

To the other contrasts he could add this one: She was a girl in a woman's body. Or was it a woman in a girl's body? He reflected that she was but twenty years old, seven years his junior. He'd never had that thought before, always regarded her as a contemporary. Never had he known anyone so young and accomplished. On the first day that they would be alone together since Wyalusing, she had decided to abandon her serious salon self – the one that conspired with generals and punctured pomposity – and become the girl of the gazebo, the dazzling romantic.

The sisters had been up past midnight. Victoria had given a going-away dinner for her guests, who were leaving in two days to return to Marshall. Afterward the party went into the garden to watch the fireworks and listen to the music still rising over the city. Back in their room, unable to sleep, the girls lay in nightgowns staring at evanescent figures dancing on the ceiling, kept in motion by the flickering candlelight, keeping time with the distant drumbeats.

"You are expecting a proposal."

Anna read her sister's mind like a clairvoyant, a maddening gift that made it impossible to hide anything. Lucy no longer even tried.

"It is what they do, you know. All week he's hovered about trying to catch me alone. He knows we're leaving."

"And you will accept?"

"If you know he will propose," she teased, "you must know as well how I will respond, n'est-ce pas?"

Anna didn't answer at once. Lucy turned to face her, puzzled that her sister would not have a ready reply.

"I think you will accept," she said finally. "He seems like a good young man."

"He is a good young man."

"And he takes you away from Wyalusing."

She looked quickly over again, surprised Anna would be quite so cynical. Lucy liked to stay in control, but with Anna never bothered. From the earliest age they'd shared a bedroom and even at the seminary been allowed to share a room. Striving in public for dignity and composure, they knew that at the end of the day, when at last alone, they could let go. They giggled, told made-up stories never to be repeated, and sometimes even threw things. It was their moment of total freedom, the one time they could revert to the little girls still hidden inside.

Now, with one engaged and the other expecting to be, they had more serious affairs to discuss.

Lucy snuffed the candle. The room fell dark, the dancing over.

"How can I possibly go back when you're gone? I'll have no company at all. Still . . ."

"Still . . . ?"

"We'll see."

"You'll still have your writing."

"Which needs inspiration."

"He is a fine young man. He positively sparkles."

"My Ivanhoe – sailing off to battle."

"It makes a better story."

"What do you mean?"

"Weren't Ivanhoe and Rowena engaged?"

"Anna, dear girl, it is not your nature to be so cynical. Please stop. It does not suit you at all."

"I am certainly not cynical. I am spelling out all the reasons for marrying."

Lucy considered that. "But you haven't mentioned the main one."

Anna sighed. "Ah yes, *that* one."

"My goodness! You *are* cynical. Are you going to tell me that you're not in love with Elkanah?"

Had the candle been lit Lucy would have seen her sister blush. "Of course I love Elkanah!"

Anna thought about what she'd just said, the first time she'd said it, aware how perfunctory it sounded. She didn't like talking about Elkanah with Lucy, who did not like her fiancé. And she was a little frightened of the novelist in her sister.

"True life is not a novel," she said, pedantically. "There are other reasons to marry – practical ones. Elkanah is dependable. He is solid. I know he doesn't sparkle – at least not like your young man sparkles. It doesn't bother me because I don't sparkle. You are the sister that sparkles."

"What nonsense you talk. You're the pretty one. Everyone says that."

"Everyone does not say that – and even if it were true, which it is not, you're the clever one."

"Too clever to fall in love, is that what you mean?"

"I hadn't thought of it like that. That is too cynical for me. Are you in love with the young man?"

It took a while for Lucy to answer, as Anna knew it would. She did not interrupt her sister's meditation. Love was not a subject often discussed by the sisters. As young girls they'd naturally talked about it, but never at the seminary. Since Anna had accepted Elkanah's offer, neither sister cared to introduce it.

"Oh, drat, Anna! How can you ask such a thing?"

"Ah!"

Lucy was on an elbow staring at her sister, whose outline she could see under the sheets. "What is 'ah' supposed to mean?"

"For the girl who doesn't like young men I believe you have just made a confession."


He dropped the shoppers on Chartres Street, and they proceeded on to the Hotel Royal, where he'd reserved a table. Nothing in Kentucky, even Louisville's famed Galt House, came close to the

Royal. Connoisseurs said it exceeded in every way the old St. Louis, lost in the fire of '41: The Royal's dome arched higher, its ballrooms glittered brighter, its tropical birds were more exotic, its food tastier, its rooms, with their French windows and lace iron balconies, more elegantly appointed and offering a superior view onto Royal Street and the slave market below.

Lucy stopped in the lobby to admire the birds, whose colors were fully matched by her own. Entering the dining room, she took his arm and pointed to the chandelier of a thousand glittering crystals falling from the glass dome like raindrops. The dome, crisscrossed by arched iron girders, was supported by green iron pillars laced into colorful arabesques. Porcelain vases of flowers and tropical plants dotted the room, waiters maneuvering artfully around them with platters of food and drink.

The buzz from several dozen tables fused into a single hum rising up to the dome. The maître d'hôtel escorted them to their place as dozens of eyes followed along. Dressed as the other women, Lucy still would have been admired. Bright as a Creole market girl, she was the center of attraction. He was thrilled.

As much as he'd done in his life, he'd never been in a place like the Hotel Royal alone with a woman, much less a woman he loved. He was nervous, unsure of himself, regretting that pulled by emotion he'd blundered into a situation that could have no good ending. As much as he was used to danger, romance was new to him, a deep, dark, dangerous mystery.

He'd rushed off to buy the ring, taking an exorbitant loan to afford it. Then came the awful meeting with Lucien.

The elegant setting only added to his confusion. How did he fit into such a place? Lucy, of course, fit in. Born to places like the Hotel Royal, Lucy was meant to command attention wherever she went. And what of him, a former army lieutenant turned clerk with more debts than income, living in rooms off Congo Square and used to beer and chips with mates in Pirate's Alley?

His name was all that entitled him. He saw that more clearly than ever. Looking around the vast room, he spied New Orleans' best – the wealth, the high tailoring, the crisp uniforms, navy flag officers in dress blues and foreign uniforms with stars and heavy gold braid, far more suitable companions for Lucy Holcombe than he. How many men in the room shared that same thought? No lieutenants in the crowd that he'd noticed. Two years after leaving the service he still felt naked in civilian clothes. He was awed by the surroundings and unsure of himself.

She would accept his offer, he was sure of it. Since Monmouth she'd been as true as any man could expect, writing constantly, standing up for him, inviting him to her home, visiting him, *leading him on*. It had nothing to do with her ambition as a writer. How could he question her affections after Wyalusing, after the gazebo? Such collaboration, such intimacy, had formed an unbreakable bond.

*Lucien was a fool!*

A waiter took their order for jambalaya and tea.

She was irresistible. "You are, my dear Lucy, the most beautiful woman in New Orleans."

Smiling, knowing what was coming, eyes bright as the glittering crystals overhead, she let her gaze sweep the room. "How you exaggerate, Colonel. Have you not noticed that beautiful blond creature a few tables away? Have you ever seen such radiance?"

"I see it before me."

She did not blush. "I am very happy. You cannot know what it's like to travel constantly with mother and sister. And Victoria . . . bless her heart . . . Raynaud House is like a sorority . . . like the seminary in Pennsylvania. I have almost no time alone. It's the first time I've been out of the company of women since we arrived in New Orleans."

The waiter poured tea from a glistening silver pot.

She fell silent, slowly sipping, watching him over the rim of the cup, wondering when he would make the offer.

He started to say something and stopped, fiddled with his

napkin and glanced around the room, unable to meet her eye. His mind returned to the meeting with Lucien, going over each phrase, each terrible word. She eyed him closely, puzzled by his reticence, touching on discomposure. He was nervous, perhaps deciding to put it off until dessert, she thought. Determined to show no sign of disanimation, she muddled on.

"You can't blame Maman, you know. You can't possibly understand how difficult it is for a mother. It's the same with Anna Eliza – no, I should say it's worse with Anna, for Maman does not feel half the affection for Elkanah Greer that she feels for you, though that can hardly be news to you. It's just that we have been with her for so long. We are her companions, her only ones. Oh, she knows it will end someday, that it must end someday, and that is her quandary. Daughters must marry and move away. It is our fate. Imagine we did not! But it is always so wrenching. I am sure it is different with sons."

He was stunned. Had she just proposed to him? The waiter interrupted his thoughts by rolling up a small table with a steaming cauldron of jambalaya. Chattering away in Creole argot about shrimp and sausage and delectable bits of this and that only to be found in New Orleans, he proceeded to ladle, with great flourishes, generous portions into their waiting dishes.

Still watching him, awaiting his response, she took up her spoon.

He was in an impossible situation, like an advancing army that had failed to secure its flanks, inviting inevitable disaster.

In his pocket he felt the little box he no longer dared bring out.

# XXVI

Jambalaya cleared, fresh strawberries were ordered for dessert. Mistress of every situation, Lucy was nonplussed. She'd given him every opportunity to proceed with what she presumed was the purpose of their luncheon and nothing had happened. He sat mutely, expression distant, mind clearly elsewhere. Her confusion had gradually progressed into annoyance. She was not used to people's minds wandering off in her company. Had she let her writer's imagination impute designs to the gentleman that he did not have? Had something happened that she didn't know about? Had his mother or uncle advised him to await his return from Cuba? Did they even know about Cuba? She could hardly question him about it, hardly say, "Dear Colonel, isn't there something you wanted to ask me?"

The gazebo had made its impression on her too. Never before had she been so intimate with a man. In the flush of the drama of the day, she'd heard the hero of her story confess his love for her. It was impulsive and more than she expected, but the day had been full of emotions. She was thrilled. She let herself be swallowed in his embrace. The situation was too perfect!

The strawberries came, and she dipped the reddest, fattest, juiciest one into her little dish of powdered sugar and devoured all but the stem in a single bite. She could not imagine that he would not make the offer, but whatever happened she would not flag, would not lose sight of the essential thing, which was that she had found the perfect hero for her story: strong, handsome, brave, bearer of a distinguished family name, decorated in one war, about to sail off to another. What did it matter if they were engaged or not? Were Ivan-hoe and Rowena engaged? Only in their hearts. And whether he real-ized it or not, *she* was responsible for it all. Without her, he would not be sitting with her in the Royal, would not be a colonel, would not soon be riding side by side with Narciso Lopez on their triumphal march into Havana.

"This mission of yours, sir," she pronounced, finishing off another strawberry, dabbing at her lips and gathering herself, "can anything be more glorious? Liberating these gallant people. General Lopez is a saint; I see him as nothing less. Your endeavor – my God, if only I were a man! You are a saint too, my dear Colonel. Oh, how I love the sound of it. And you must love it as well: Colonel William Logan Crittenden, how proud your family must be of you. Don't you long to be back in uniform?"

He was completely derouted. Yes, he said softly, he did long to be back in uniform, not adding his other thought – *what* uniform? The uniforms of their little army were not meant for the Hotel Royal, and he doubted he'd ever wear a U.S. Army uniform again. His eyes went to a naval officer across the room, rows of brass buttons gleam-ing, crisp and confident in his captain's blues with its gold braid, a man who knew his place.

Lucy was hungrily devouring the strawberries while talking at the same time, something about Cuba tipping the balance more toward the South. Her attitude had somehow changed. He scarcely heard her.

". . . Only right that Kentucky and the name Crittenden be pres-ent at such an historic moment; what a magnificent honor! How I envy you!"

She paused and stared. "Sir, are you listening?"

"Yes, yes, sorry, thinking about what you said – well said, of course."

"The North has become so aggressive and overbearing . . . surely we must do something about it . . . I get letters from my friends . . .

my former friends, I should say . . . girls I went to school with in Philadelphia . . . you would not believe some of the things they say about us . . . that we are warmongers . . . that they hate, absolutely hate the fugitive slave provisions of the new bill – the bill you brave Kentuckians helped to write and in which your uncle John J. Crittenden, advising the president, played such an important part. They say that no one in Philadelphia or Boston or New York has the slightest intention to send back any slave who might escape . . . that on the contrary that such a provision only hardens their determination never to return any slave who comes their way."

Amazing, he thought, practically as if she were making a speech, her voice rapid and elevated, and he had the impression that people at the closest tables, those behind the potted plants, were listening, no doubt surprised that such a handsome young woman would have such political passion.

"It is awful! Absolutely awful! I answer them all, of course, each one, no matter how insulting they are, no matter how much they presume on my good will and my tolerance, I answer each one, painstakingly pointing out how they are wrong about the South. They truly believe that we all live down here riding the fields with whips in our hand. They won't believe that I myself helped rescue a Negro from slavery. You, my dear Colonel, saw how we treat the slaves at Wyalusing. Would they have a better life in some disease-infested swamp in Africa? Some of these girls were my closest friends. I fear that they are lost forever."

"I quite agree," he said, trying a strawberry for which he had no taste, his mind stunted. "The North has become overbearing."

"Senator Calhoun's last speech, like he knew it was his valedictory. Absolutely masterful. Did you read it?"

"I did read it, yes. I believe I did."

"What did you think?"

He did not care to speak ill of the dead and for the moment didn't care about any of it. He was perspiring, couldn't control it.

"Calhoun's speech in the Senate, yes. Well, I think I should say this: that if we are going to criticize the North for its extremism, we must avoid extremism of our own. We in Kentucky, we . . . well, let's just say we don't think South Carolina should be the model."

At once he had her attention. Was it the first time that day she'd paused to consider what he'd said? But he hadn't said much, had he? She might have been talking across the table to almost anyone, certainly not to a man with a diamond ring in his pocket – a ring in a box nearly squeezed flat and that he would gladly have smashed to smithereens if he could have afforded to do so.

"That is well said, Colonel. I do believe you have a point." She smiled nicely. "I get carried away, I know I do. It is what Maman tells me all the time, but I really can't help myself. You have to understand that my family has almost no political sense. I have to have enough for everyone. Daddy is content to run his plantation and visit his – well, you know. Maman doesn't even read the newspapers and Anna Eliza believes anything anyone tells her, mostly Elkanah, unfortunately. I form my own opinions. I am always learning."

He nodded, trying to bring himself back to the table. "I confess that my family is the opposite. We probably talk politics too much."

"How I do want to meet your family, Colonel. Do you know that I have hardly set foot in Kentucky – unless you count stops along the Ohio on the way to Philadelphia. I quite agree that South Carolina can't be the model. It would be like making New York the model, or Pennsylvania. Much better that a state like Kentucky, a *Southern* state like Kentucky, take the lead, wouldn't you say?"

Again he nodded.

"But you must never compromise your principles," she continued, "which is why it's so important that Kentucky belong to the South: With the border states and Cuba joined to the South, strengthening us in our determination to defend our way of life, we will avoid the war Senator Calhoun so greatly feared."

• • •

He was miserable on the ride back, wanting to take her hand, wanting to hold her, wanting to tell her the truth about his feelings, knowing it was only a short ride and that she would not invite him in. She was looking into the shops, watching the city pass by, chattering, bearing up as always. While he was a wreck. He could not read her. He'd seen the confusion in her eyes at the Royal, but now it was gone. She was back to herself, the girl who never flagged. She was returning to Wyalusing the next day and had an afternoon of packing in front of her. Fortunately, Victoria had girls who would help her, she informed him. He wished the carriage would slow down long enough for him to arrange his thoughts.

Of course they would write each other, she was saying.

He was frozen into a paralysis he did not know how to escape. He was passionately in love and afraid of losing it all. He was trapped, unable say what was on his mind, yet unable to explain why he could not say it.

Dread lay on his heart; or was it panic? It was a battle unlike any he had ever been in.

What if Lucien was wrong?

But Lucien was not wrong. He remembered it from Mexico, remembered sitting in his tent writing the families of the dead and the missing, or sitting in the field hospital writing for the men who could no longer see or hold a pen to write themselves, maimed men they'd picked up from the killing fields, men ready to abandon everything, for whom death would be deliverance.

His hands were too moist to touch her. He was stricken with the thought that he would never see her again. The day before, a mere 24 hours, he'd been walking down this very street, Royal Street, in the opposite direction, heading for the Jean Lafitte with a ring in his pocket, love in his heart and spring in his step.

Now the day lay in ruins, perhaps his future as well, and there was nothing to be done about any of it. Lucien had spoken the truth, the terrible truth of war and death that he knew from Mexico and could not share with her. She would know the truth only if he survived to tell it.

If he did not, she could end her story any way she chose.

# PART SIX

✳

# CUBA

# XXVII

*Last days of July, 1851*

The navy was watching. Richard Lewis, the *Pampero*'s captain, a veteran of the Mississippi and the Gulf of Mexico from New Orleans to Campeche, took the ship out each day, steaming down toward the bayous, leaving at different hours with different passengers, returning to New Orleans to tie up at a different place, trusting the navy to lose track of him and interest in him. Will accompanied him when he could get away from the customhouse, curious to know more about the strange swamp landscape of the lower Mississippi, so close to New Orleans, so much of another world.

It was the land of the Acadians, the Cajuns, the isolated French people with their ancient French language that no one understood but themselves. Driven by the English from Acadia, in New France, those who survived the horrors of deportation, deprivation, and death along the treacherous 2,500-mile journey from Canada found refuge in the bayous of Louisiana. Settling down in the swamps to nurse their chagrin, they never came out again.

Lewis never went more than fifteen or twenty miles downriver, ignoring the young man's pleas to go down farther toward the Gulf, to see more of the river and turn into the bayous, which Lewis abhorred.

"Seventy-five miles to the Gulf. You'll get there soon enough."

He'd heard stories about the lower river, about the bays and bayous, thousands of little islands and cays where you couldn't see ten feet inland for the weeping willows and cypresses. People lived in there with the swamp critters, never emerging. They said the Cajuns were as isolated as the Amazonians, with their own laws and language and strange customs; they said the Cajuns didn't know when Louisiana passed from France to the United States and wouldn't have cared if they had. At the Jean Lafitte one night he'd heard of a bayou murder a few years back: Two Plaquemines policemen went in to investigate and never came out again. They sent a boatload of gendarmes in after them, and they never found trace of crime, criminal, or policemen. They left those people alone now.

With gunrunners and slavers and smugglers of all kinds coming up from the Gulf, the navy sought to keep watch on anything moving on the lower river. He learned from Christophe Raynaud that an order, signed by Fillmore (had it carried Uncle John's signature as well?), had come down to keep a special watch on the *Pampero*, which the president feared was bent on starting a war with Spain. Raynaud reminded him that more than a few officers did not mind what the *Pampero* was about, promising to keep him informed of navy communications and maneuvers.

On occasion they were hailed by a navy cutter pulling up alongside so the crews could exchange pleasantries. On one occasion when Will was along, the navy captain came aboard to sit on the bridge with Captain Lewis and share coffee laced with Louisiana rum. They chatted about life on the river. If the navy knew what was being planned, they said nothing about it. Lewis had been around New Orleans for a while. He was well-known and liked.

Even with navy sympathizers, getting down the river, past the bayous, and into the gulf fully loaded with arms and men would be a ticklish affair. Had they been anchored on Lake Pontchartrain, it would have been a simple matter to steam through Sawmill Pass and slip into the Gulf through the Rigolets, but just as simple for the navy to sight them, for the Sawmill lighthouse signaled constantly to the cutters. Thus the many feints by Captain Lewis on the river: bore the enemy, lull him to sleep. The delay gave them more time to recruit and train; it gave Lewis more time to make the *Pampero* shipshape.

It was nearly a month since he'd seen Lucy, who had returned to Wyalusing. The ring to be hers had gone to Lucien to hold in safe-keeping until the right time. Despite the disaster of their last meeting, Lucy continued to write, never dispirited, her letters full of all the little phrases of affection he'd grown used to. He'd been desperate and depressed following their lunch at the Royal, feeling he'd ruined everything. But then a letter came and then another and soon the gloom lifted.

Her resilience amazed him. She took no offense, somehow came to understand that his wretched performance at the Royal was due to consideration for her, not to a change of heart, not to rejection.

Her letters even offered military advice, prescient as things would turn out:

"You will be outnumbered," she wrote at one point. "You must keep your forces together."

He smiled as he read it, remembering Napoleon's precept: "Never split an already inferior force."

By the end of July, he'd had a month more of letters, the army a month more of training, and he was back to his usual high spirits. The Marigny parade had been for show and recruiting, nothing more. There would be no parades and high-stepping bands in Cuba, but instead marshes, mountains, and rains, and if it was at all like Mexico, insufferable heat and mosquitoes. For two weeks in July they moved upriver to Sigur's plantations at Franklin and Iberville to train in squads and companies, learning to move in small units through swamps and deltas, to keep arms and powder dry and to sleep in the open, often in the rain, with only small tents for cover.

It was meant to be grueling, but esprit de corps remained high. If they lost some men during maneuvers, they signed on just as many new ones. Pay was modest, though not modest enough to keep their purse from nearly running out. If Quitman had won his delay, if only until the end of summer, they would not have had enough to cover.

Money came in, for John O'Sullivan, José Gonzales, and the Club of Havana kept beating the drums around the country, where enthusiasm for the mission was higher than ever. Manifest Destiny, the phrase coined by O'Sullivan, was destined to have a future far longer than its author could have imagined. It had become the new national motto, as symbolic as "Don't Tread on Me" during the Revolution. Ever more newspapers, and not just in the Deep South, supported the cause of expansion, and few opposed it. Victory in Mexico had changed the national mood.

Money came in, but went out even faster. What kept men from defecting was not their paltry wages, but the promise of the spoils of war, a promise never made specifically, but understood by every soldier, as it always is.

The last letter from Lucy arrived 48 hours before departure:

*My dearest Will,*

*As I sit to write today, my mind overflows with tender thoughts for you and with joy and pride for the thrilling mission you are about to undertake. My intuition tells me this may be the last missive you receive before sailing; if so, please know, dear Colonel, that I will be with you every hour of the day, every mile of the way. O, to be with you at this historic moment! But if I cannot be there in person, know that in heart and mind I shall not rest until word comes of your success. I have not ceased thinking of you since our sad farewell in New Orleans. I count the hours and days until we are together again in Havana, under the palms of the Malecon.*

*I write today while sitting in the gazebo. If once it was my place, forever it will be our place. When I am here now, it is like some part of me is missing, a bold and courageous part, the handsome gentleman from Kentucky who would be here with me now, were he not set to sail off on the great adventure soon to be acclaimed by all America – yes, and in the nation's capital as well!*

*Know, dear heart, that you are with me constantly in spirit.*

*Outside, the birds chirp and bees buzz and the music they make is for you alone! They wish you, as your dear Lucy does as well, Godspeed and a safe voyage for you and your men to Cuba.*

*Until we meet again in Havana,*
*I am, affectionately yours as ever,*

*Lucy Holcombe.*

He was thrilled! He had not lost her. He folded the letter carefully into his billfold, which went into a corner of his kit. He would read it every day.

# XXVIII

Captain Lewis tied up downriver, near St.-Bernard, farther south than he'd moored before, out of sight of the navy even if they were looking. According to Christophe Raynaud, two cutters would be on patrol that night, downriver near La Hache and Venice. Raynaud did not know if the captains were friendly or not: Best to steer clear of them, he advised.

It was the dog days of summer, the sun still late to sink. Arms, stores, and munitions had been quietly loading for days. Arriving at different times in small groups and from all directions, men began boarding the *Pampero* soon after sunset, slipping on with kits and blankets. He went below to share the camaraderie and good humor, the same pre-mission enthusiasm he remembered from Mexico. Was it not always like that? "The moral," said Napoleon, "is to the physical as three to one." Soldiers need to convince themselves that they are invincible.

Below decks it was hot and crowded with little comfort. The *Pampero,* three decks and 110 feet, was built to carry cargo, not passengers, and certainly not four hundred men, though most of these men would have known worse. They had only mats for sleeping on the boards. Soldiers, unlike sailors, are never comfortable in hammocks. Arms were stowed in the hold. Artillery, coming from Biloxi, would join them at Key West.

In all, they were 451 men and officers, a well-trained, well-armed fighting force in two battalions, more than enough to spark the uprising and deal with the Spaniards once the Cubans rose up against them. Successfully landed and with a solid beachhead they would be joined by a third battalion under the command of Kentuckians John Pickens and Thomas Hawkins. Word would be sent back to New Orleans via Key West, where Lopez had confederates. They'd been over it dozens of times. Everything was meticulously planned.

The officers were satisfied. The men were well trained and equipped; the ship was fit and ready. If they could make the Gulf, they would have clear sailing to the Florida Keys with little chance of being detected by the navy. Once arrived in Key West, they were practically in sight of Havana's Morro Castle. He went back on deck to join the other principals as the loading continued.

Shortly after ten o'clock, they readied to hoist anchor. Back on deck, he felt elated as seldom before. To the last minute he'd hoped to see Quitman's bushy head among those come to wish them Godspeed. Sigur, Freaner, Huston, Gonzales, Teurbe, Villaverde, Goicuría were there. Quitman was not. Freaner threw his arms around him before he left the ship, and he thought he saw a tear in that good man's eye. *He wants a war but not this one. Besides, he's too sick.*

It was a date to be marked in history: The day the liberation of Cuba began. For the young man, it was the culmination of a process begun at Uncle John's Christmas party twenty months earlier. He could not have said when it was or how it was or why it was that he rallied to the cause: simply that everything that argued against it shifted in its favor. What seemed at first a lost cause, pipe dreams clashing with hard reality, became a noble undertaking. The rational arguments of the opponents, Uncle John and Lucien Hensley above all, gave way to the passion of the champions. *What chance has reason in the clash with passion?*

He heard the boilers start up and felt a thrill as powerful as the day Zach Taylor's army set out for Monterrey: The same two words rang out in every soldier's mind: *At last!* At last the interminable waiting over! At last we are under way!

Hardly were the boilers going when sounded a huge explosion, one that rocked the ship, tearing through her like struck by a bomb. The noise and shock were sudden and ferocious. He'd gone back below decks to help the men get settled when he heard the crash above, the sound of iron tearing through wood, the sound of a ship's mast falling. But they had no mast! The men leapt to their feet, certain they were under fire, rushing for the hatchway and fresh air, certain they'd been hit before even hoisting anchor.

Would the navy have dared? Or Spanish sabotage?

He ran up prepared for the worst, but it was neither bomb nor cannonball. *They had blown a pipe!* One of the ship's two smokestacks was splayed across the deck like a dead whale, steam jetting from the hole where it had previously stood, men leaping back. The pipe had taken down part of the bridge and driven into the deck as it fell. Miraculously, no one was injured. Captain Lewis stood calmly inspecting the damage. He'd seen it all before. The *Pampero* had been around the block a few times.

Lopez was another matter. He stood nearby the fallen whale, muttering, cursing in Spanish, certain everything was lost, trying to communicate in English with General Pragay, who, separated somehow from Schlesinger, understood nothing. Sigur and the others had already debarked and stood dockside gaping in disbelief. Captain Lewis, a true professional, approached him, nodding toward Lopez.

"Calm him down, Colonel. Get the men back belowdecks. I'll soon be back with a new pipe. Better this happened now than at sea."

The damaged pipe was dragged ashore. With five others, Lewis slipped into a shore boat and was off into the night. Fortunately, it was dark and they were out of sight of the city. With the mate in charge, the crew went to work repairing damage to the deck.

Finding a pipe in the dead of the New Orleans night seemed a preposterous proposition, but the man knew his way around the ship-yards. He was back with a replacement by midnight and the engineers soon made it fit. The delay meant they would be in total darkness all the way to the Gulf, a serious danger without a skillful captain, but one that may have been a boon in disguise.

It's a long haul from New Orleans to the Gulf and for most of the time they motored slowly in the darkness, lights out, moving along with the flow of the river. It was smooth and quiet, the men sleeping as only soldiers can. He went below from time to time to check, but mostly stayed on deck near the captain and didn't once shut his eyes. Quitman's absence still ate at him, frustrated him. He should be with them. He'd been paid to take command. He hadn't repaid the money.

Above Pointe à la Hache, Captain Lewis cut the motor and they drifted along in silence. He'd seen enough of the terrain to know this was no place to get lost. Lewis said it was unique on earth, swamps formed by the river back to prehistoric times and populated by critters just as ancient. He stood on the bridge and could make out nothing, though the captain looked ahead as though seeing everything. The river seemed fairly straight as it headed for the Gulf, though who could be sure? Even in the gloom the captain navigated with a sure hand.

Thirty minutes into their silent drift, Lewis pointed to starboard and they saw the dim lights of a cutter, the only lights they'd seen since New Orleans. Bayou people lived on both sides of the river, but showed no sign of existence. It's a strange feeling to drift noiselessly in the blackness like that – ghostly, sinister, like drifting through the Stygian underworld, no return possible.

Past the cutter, Lewis restarted the motor. "Another thirty miles to Venice," he said, his voice livelier. "After that, if young Raynaud is right, done with the navy and smooth sailing to the Gulf. Why don't you catch some sleep?"

Instead, he walked the deck, making out vague shapes along the starboard riverbank. It was a marvel that Lewis could see anything, but the mate said he could navigate the bayous with his eyes shut, which they might just as well have been. He encountered Lopez several times asleep in a deck chair.

After Venice, the river widened. Captain Lewis cut the motor again, but they saw no lights, saw nothing nor could be seen. Twenty more miles to Loutre Pass, but they were far too heavy to risk it or even South Pass, Lewis told him, and would head west into Southwest Pass, deeper and wider but adding a day to Key West. Hours later, with Eos awakening and night fading, they entered Southwest Pass, moving briskly along and out into the Gulf of Mexico, finally free of land, the sea as vast and clear as the sky above them. Soon an orange sliver appeared in the east, and as the sun grew the water began to change color, from gray to green, finally to blue. Slowly men drifted up for breakfast, finding the magnificent day and sprawling in the sunshine. They might have been a yacht heading out for a day of deep-sea fishing instead of an army sailing into battle.

The day was a startling contrast of yellow and blue, and before long a few lines dropped in the water. Gulls squawked overhead, anticipating a meal. Flying fish leaped and sailed. Marlins were sighted. It would remain like that for nearly three days as they steamed the Gulf, the only noise coming from the pistons below and occasional flocks of squawking birds. They headed southwest toward Mexico to evade any navy ships that might be searching, then turned eastward toward their first destination, Key West.

If losing their exhaust pipe in New Orleans had been a stroke of luck it was the only one they would have.

# XXIX

*August 7–11, 1851*

Napoleon: "Give me lucky generals."

But what is luck – a star, intuition, coincidence, a good guess? The young man remembered a Bible passage Josie read in the kitchen at Shelbyville: The race is not to the swift nor the battle to the strong for "time and chance happeneth to them all."

Time and chance! Nothing is foreseeable, predictable, even for Napoleon, not in the fog of war. The trick is to find lucky generals.

Was Waterloo lost because of bad luck – Grouchy's misunderstanding his orders, Blücher's arrival in the nick of time to save Wellington, the horrible weather that limited French maneuverability? At West Point, every instructor had his theory about Waterloo. He held with Major McClendon, who taught modern European history: Napoleon ran out of lucky generals.

May history tell the truth! As Waterloo was a close-run thing, so was the Bahia Honda campaign. History would see the mistakes, the key mistake above all. It would also see how things might have gone differently.

The first sight greeting them coming into Key West was the thing called Fort Taylor, a great mound of rocks offshore named after old Zach. If the rocks' aspiration was one day to become a fort, they still had a way to go. But there they sat as the *Pampero* approached the harbor, something for every visitor to contemplate, like the stones of Egypt before they became pyramids. If army engineers were working to complete it, no one saw a workman. Captain Lewis remarked that it was to be part of a ring of forts built around the Caribbean to protect the Southern states, though he offered no opinion who or what they might protect them from.

To a new visitor, Key West was not much, a rustic little beach cay among dozens, somewhat more populous, somewhat busier than most. Once the harbor came into view, Lewis ordered the men below. It was unlikely that word of the *Pampero's* disappearance from New Orleans had reached Key West, but the island patrol, active because of a strong U.S. Navy presence on the island, would grow suspicious of any ship carrying so many men. The ship rode low in the water, but that could be any heavy cargo. They did not care to be searched.

They anchored in the harbor, and six of them – Generals Lopez and Pragay, Colonels Blumenthal, Downman and Crittenden and Major Schlesinger, all dressed as common seamen – took the dinghy ashore. If they were observed, they were not challenged. Why would they be? Led by Lopez, who knew the way, with Pragay walking beside him, they headed in pairs down Duval Street toward the south shore. They might be six sailors from any ship with business in port.

Populated mainly by fishermen, the island appeared prosperous enough. The houses were neat and clean, of stone foundation and sturdy wood construction to withstand hurricane weather, mostly clapboard and shingle painted bright white against the salt air and topped with dark planked roofs. The cay could not have been more than a mile wide, though longer east to west. The main avenues were broad and vegetation sparse, plants having difficulty in the poor soil and only the hardiest palm able to withstand the hurricanes. Flat, sandy, and dry, Key West had a desert feel rather than a tropical one.

The walk, uncomfortable in the hot weather and on sea legs, took them across the width of the island, past a variety of shops, most with signs in Spanish, marking the heavy Cuban fishing presence. Their destination was a little bougainvillea-covered cottage on a small cove looking out toward the open sea, a strangely peaceful setting for a council of war.

A Creole named Escobar, representing the Club of Havana, met them at the door, the two Cubans embracing and chattering away in Spanish. An attractive young woman watched silently from a rear doorway, apparently the only other person in the house. Escobar was built like Lopez, short and solid, but was younger, more vigorous and darker. He wore sandals and a loose-fitting tropical shirt bursting with chest hair. He smoked a *puro* and offered the box around, tobacco from his own plantation, he said, which abutted Lopez's plantation at Frias in Pinar.

It was late afternoon, and Escobar led them outside where a table was set on a sheltered porch. The woman, silky and sultry in a multicolored sarong and smelling of coconut oil, brought them fruit and juices and disappeared to the back under the devouring eyes of the men. She was not introduced. After three days of bacon and hardtack on the *Pampero*, the nectars were manna from the gods.

It was there, on a steamy day in a cottage on a leeward Caribbean cove dotted by a few small boats at anchor, that the fatal decisions were made. Immediately Escobar offered bad news: the artillery had not arrived. The bazookas were to have been waiting for them.

"What have you heard, José Maria?" asked Lopez.

"*Nada*," said the Creole. "Ship leaves Biloxi two days ere you leave Nueva Orleans."

"Intercepted?"

". . . or stolen."

"A sinking?"

He shook his head.

It was stunning news.

"We cannot sail without artillery," said Crittenden. "We must wait."

Troubled, Lopez said nothing.

"Not wait for something not come," said Escobar, shaking his head again. "Not two days to Biloxi."

The Hungarians were whispering. "General Pragay agrees," said Major Schlesinger. "We cannot wait."

"We must wait," said Colonel Downman. "The bazookas level the field. The Spaniards have no artillery."

He'd come to like Downman, an older man, maybe even as old as Lopez, and a veteran of Mexico. A brawny fighter, Downman was gruff and taciturn, up from the ranks, a man who spoke only with something to say. They'd grown closer as Lopez came increasingly under the sway of the Hungarians. Downman might have had grounds for resentment, but the young man, who had recruited him, saw none. He saw him as a man who did not flinch. They would need each other.

"No!" said Escobar, with feeling. He spoke a mixture of Spanish and English with some Creole thrown in. "Time *imprescindible, imprescindible!* Plantations fear Spain follow England and France and free slaves. They fear *una revuelta,* general . . . like Cárdenas . . . murder . . . white people dead . . . women and children. Worse . . . Haiti! Dessalines's massacre . . . another slave republic. Every plantation in Cuba with you, General. No wait!"

There was a pause while Schlesinger translated for Pragay, who was intently watching Escobar. The Hungarian general, with several days' gray beard, was dressed in dungarees and sea shirt and bore no resemblance to a senior European officer. He held up his hand so they would not continue. He spoke in a low voice to Schlesinger who said the following:

"Let it be clear. We of Austria-Hungary, who fought to bring down the tyrants of Europe, did not join this mission to protect slavery. You have your views, Señor Escobar, which are irrelevant to our mission. General Lopez and I are in perfect agreement, which is the essential thing: The goal is to drive the Spanish monarchy from the Americas. And that is an end to it."

Lopez turned his inscrutable face toward Escobar and nodded. "*Asi es.*"

So it is.

After a short hesitation Lopez added: "What becomes of Cuba after the Spaniards are gone is for the Cubans to decide. What Señor Escobar failed to mention, but which should be clear to all, is that the Club of Havana prefers joining Cuba to the United States. About this, the club has been clear from the beginning, back to its initial meetings with President Polk."

Crittenden brought the meeting back to the affairs at hand.

"I am the artillery officer," he said. "It is the artillery that is *imprescindible* – essential: We cannot proceed without bazookas."

There was another pause for Schlesinger to translate while Lopez, frowning, stared out past the cove, direction Cuba, some ninety miles away. It was a hard decision, perhaps a telling one, and Lopez did not respond immediately. The constant arbitration between Europeans and Americans was taking its toll. It was not how he had envisaged it.

"Three days," he pronounced, finally. "We wait seventy-two hours. No more."

But Escobar was not finished: "More you wait, more you risk. Spanish spies everywhere. You know Creoles, General . . . they know you. Plantations . . . the island rise up to greet you. Everyone waiting."

"Three days," repeated Lopez.

Escobar dropped his head onto his hairy chest, frustrated but apparently deciding to press no further. He called out a name – Maria something – and the young woman appeared from the back with more refreshments. The eyes of the hungry men did not leave her. Was she a servant, a daughter, a wife? No matter: She was female. Drinks were poured around the table, and again Escobar waited until she was gone. Crittenden looked to the cove and saw a ketch push off, making for open water and a day of fishing. Blissful scene. He envied them.

Escobar looked to Lopez. He had another surprise:

"You land at Bahia Honda and march to Pinar, General. I arrange friends to meet you at Bahia Honda with horses, carts, oxen."

Lopez was startled. "*Bahia Honda?*"

The plan, drawn up after months of discussion, was to circle the island and come in from the south, near Punta de Cartas, on the isolated south coast. They had considered Bahia Honda, for it was an easier path to San Cristóbal de Pinar, their initial destination, but rejected it. Bahia Honda lies on the windward side of the island and would put them at the mercy of tropical rains. Even with the strongest oxen, carts laden with heavy arms risked being lost in the mud.

"*Sí*, Bahia Honda," said Escobar. "Gift from God no artillery. Circle island, you seen. Concha wait with men."

Lopez visibly winced at the name Concha. It was unmistakable. De la Concha was the captain-general of Cuba. Was there something between them? Was that the "promotion going to someone else" that Freaner had referred to?

"*Perdóneme*, General," muttered Escobar.

"More likely Enna," said Lopez, softly.

"*No importa*," said Escobar, recovering. "At Bahia Honda you meet friends, not Spanish."

He had trouble believing what he was hearing. First the Creole had informed them of the missing bazookas, then opined that it didn't matter, further opined that it was even a good thing because on his own he'd changed the operation to land on the north shore rather than the south.

"You are no soldier, sir," he said bluntly to the Creole. "You are no soldier or you would not thank God for making our bazookas disappear. Artillery is a soldier's best friend. We have less than half the men the Spaniards can bring. As Colonel Downman said, bazookas level the field. Now, as to this business about changing where we make land . . ."

Lopez laid a hand on his arm. The young man looked to him

and saw a weariness he'd not seen before. The dashing figure from the salons of Natchez and New Orleans, the general who seemed lifted from the pages of Alexandre Dumas to charm the ladies and inspire the men, suddenly looked his age, more than his age, whatever it was. The face was drawn and the eyes half closed. He suspected the old body had had enough of hardtack and water and sleeping in deck chairs.

And now he was called on to deal with two completely unanticipated problems. The compromise on artillery was easy enough: wait three days and see. There was no way to compromise between two sides of the island.

They had not drawn up their plans lightly. Weeks of discussions had led to the decision to come in from the south. They knew the risk of being sighted rounding the island, but calculated it was a lesser risk than losing their artillery in the mud of Bahia Honda. *But that was Escobar's very point!* Without artillery, why not land at Bahia Honda? If they were lucky with the rain ("Give me lucky generals") Bahia Honda would be to their advantage, for there were no mountains to cross.

Again the Hungarians whispered. The others waited.

"General Pragay never liked the idea of circling the island," said Schlesinger. "In Europe, we know how to fight in the rain."

It was a vexing comment, and Will thought he noticed Colonel Blumenthal smile. Did the comment come from Schlesinger and not Pragay, who he did not remember opposing the original plan? Blumenthal, nominally Pragay's chief-of-staff, would know, but despite a decent command of English, Blumenthal rarely spoke up at staff meetings. He was a courtly man, the friendliest of the Austro-Hungarians, never without his sword, a soldier of the old school who carried a dueling scar on his left cheek running down to his mouth, giving it a tendency to close in a fixed smile, making it impossible to tell when he was truly amused.

In any case, if the bazookas did not come, a wrenching thought, it made sense to head directly for Bahia Honda. He did not argue the point.

"Enough for now," Lopez pronounced. "We wait three days. If artillery does not come, we decide if our plans should be altered. If it comes, we keep to the southern landing."

For the next two days they saw nothing of Lopez, who stayed with Escobar in the cottage while the rest of them remained on the ship. If the navy was searching for them, doubtful since Washington would not yet have received word that the *Pampero* had quit New Orleans, it was not looking in Key West. They allowed the men to take shore leave in small groups, depending on them to keep silence about the mission, which, as he explained, was in their own interest. No one doubted that the Spaniards knew they were coming. What they could not know was where and when – for the simple reason that they did not know themselves.

When they returned to the cottage for the final meeting it was hardly a surprise to learn that the bazookas had not come. Lopez, attended by the young woman, who treated the old general more affectionately than the first time, informed them that Escobar had left the day before for Cuba to alert his friends that they would be landing at Bahia Honda.

He had long hours to ponder it all. Artillery or not, it was too late to back out. The lots had been cast, impossible to know how they would fall. He wondered how Quitman would have handled it. What had really happened to the bazookas, without which they would have followed through with the original plan to land on the southern shore? Why was Escobar not as concerned as the others that they had not come? Did he know something he was not telling? Was he playing a double game? In view of what was to happen, the question must be asked.

# XXX

*August 12–13, 1851*

They made good time in smooth waters. The men lay on deck watching the great dreadnaught called Cuba grow ever larger before them. The place that had previously been only a name and an idea, the island they were to conquer, loomed large as a continent, covering the horizon one end to the other, a formidable challenge. From his vantage point the young man watched the island shapes come slowly into focus – dark mountains turning to woods, specks of color growing into houses, an indistinct gray dot transforming itself into Morro Castle above Havana Harbor, built to defend against Drake's English fleet. Behind Morro, he spied the even more formidable La Cabaña, built following the capture of Havana by the English in 1761, a battle they studied carefully at West Point for its elements of siege warfare. He moved his glass slowly, side to side, missing nothing.

Capt. Victor Ker, the massive Creole he'd come to admire, a man fully his equal in size, approached. "I've looked forward to this glorious day all my life, Colonel," he confided, a broad smile illuminating his dark face. Ker's mother's family came from Cuba, nationalists forced to flee for opposing the Spaniards. He would clear the way for her to go home again, take back the island that belonged to America, not to Europe. As the day wore on, men disappeared belowdeck, escaping the sun, investing in sleep. For soldiers, sleep is so precious that you learn to drop off at every chance. The men were fully prepared and brimming with confidence. He could not remember a battle in Mexico where enthusiasm ran so high. But then, few men had gone to Mexico by choice.

All hands were on deck when Bahia Honda was sighted and called out by the mate from the bridge, the bay lying some fifty miles west of Havana. There was some whooping, nothing excessive, just the relief of soldiers knowing that action soon would begin. For Crittenden, who'd fought his way across half of Mexico, arriving at the sugar island might have been routine, but he found himself as exhilarated as the others. Inevitably, his mind went to Lucy, wishing she could witness the glorious scene unfolding in front of them. He reached for her last letter, which he carried in his breast pocket, reading it over one more time, savoring each loving word before replacing it over his heart.

The liberation of Cuba! How different it would be from Mexico, where he'd been a lowly second lieutenant trained to die in one more mad charge against Mexican fortifications. If he'd survived Mexico it was thanks to the bad muskets and aim of the Mexicans. The soldier who shot Kirby Smith likely was aiming at him! Bad muskets, bad aim, and good luck: Every soldier knows to worship at the feet of lady luck. Here in Cuba he was a commander, with his own battalion, the senior American officer in an enterprise soon to reward his country handsomely.

Still five miles off the coast as dusk closed in, they spotted a small Cuban fishing boat returning to port, heading for Mariel, lying between Havana and Bahia Honda. They closed quickly, Captain Lewis bringing the *Pampero* to grappling distance. Lopez ordered the helmsman on board, and they lowered ropes. He would not come until a group of soldiers went over the side to encourage him. He was told to guide them into the bay after nightfall.

"*Piratas, filibusteros!*" shouted the fisherman, fearlessly spitting his words and clearly wanting no part of them. The man was no

Spaniard. Why would he oppose them if Cuba was in a state of revolt?

The *Pampero* carried two six-pounders. Lopez pointed to the canons and snapped some words to the man. One ball from either would send boat and crew to the bottom. The man grew sullenly cooperative, looking around, taking everything in. He was no friend. What would they do with these men afterward?

They spied a faint plume of smoke in the distance, barely visible in the fading light. The Cuban identified it as the Spanish warship *Pizarro*. Captain Lewis shut down the engines, and in silence they watched. In the growing darkness, they could not tell which way the ship was moving, though Lewis, glass glued to the ship, remained unperturbed. Soon the plume disappeared. The ship was returning to Havana.

Night fell, and the Cuban guided them to the entrance to the bay, where Lopez sent in a boat to reconnoiter. After a while, they saw lights and heard shots, and the boat quickly returned. Why were they fired upon? Lopez's tawny face remained inscrutable. Already their presence had been noted by Cuban fishermen and guards at Bahia Honda, and they'd barely escaped being sighted by the *Pizarro*. It was always the risk of landing on the north shore.

They decided to put in outside the bay, near the village called Morillo. They met to discuss the fishing boat. Lopez would have shot the crew and scuttled the boat. There were some tense words exchanged for Captain Lewis, still in command, would have none of it. For lack of a better option, the Cubans were sent off.

Approaching shore shortly after ten, they hit a sandbar. More bad luck, more cursing, and they could proceed no farther. They sent a picket ashore led by Captain Kelly to procure flatboats. After several circuits by the flatboats, the men were landed. Her load lightened, the *Pampero* moved gingerly off the sandbar and disappeared into the night, heading for Key West and thence to New Orleans to prepare to bring reinforcements under Huston, Pickett, and Hawkins, expected within the week.

Without a single casualty, their little army of 451 determined men was landed on the shores of Cuba, historic island possessed by Columbus four centuries earlier in the name of Spain, a possession they intended shortly to terminate. The beachhead was secured. They stood together in the moonlight, listening to the lapping of the waves, quietly exulting. In the shadows they observed the little village spreading up from the beach under a ring of palms, but saw no light or movement. Resplendent in his uniform of indeterminate origin, General Lopez raised his sword as Columbus must have done. He fell to his knees and intoned words in Spanish.

"What's he saying?" asked Major Martin.

"'*Dios, Dios, Dios,*' is all I understand," Crittenden said. "He is talking to God."

"I hope God is listening," said Martin.

Nine days after setting out from New Orleans, they set up tents along the playa, exhausted but satisfied. A periphery was established and sentries posted. The moonlight shone down on them, not a cloud visible. So far the risk of landing on the windward side had paid off, but he knew the gulf weather well enough from Veracruz. Great storms arise in a trice. He pitched his tent and crawled in, tired but content. The crossing had been uneventful, the landing successful, the weather propitious. So far all signs were favorable.

Dawn brought more good news. He looked down the beach, past the rows of four-man tents, well-aligned, well-spaced, an army that knew the virtue of order and organization. He saw men clamoring out, rubbing their eyes, scratching, heading for the field canteen. A detail was at work on a latrine. A light drizzle, more like a mist, greeted him, no problem, but the sky was ominously dark for five o'clock in the tropics. Beyond the tents he saw four horses being tended. Close by, on what must be the road to Las Pozas, stood two oxen and a heavy cart. Not much from the Creoles, but a start! Apart from their camp, he saw no sign of life. The village of Morillo either still slept or preferred to stay hidden.

At 5:30 the commanders gathered in Lopez's field tent. Camp chairs had been set up, and an orderly brought coffee, fruit, and hardtack. Inside was dry enough, but the sand was saturated from earlier rain. A lamp was lit.

As always on the first day, the mood was light, spirits ran high, though a sky showing no sign of brightening did its best to put on a damper. Just a little sunshine, he prayed, sensing that minds were on the weather, each man wondering if the decision to change the landing would prove a mistake.

He was peeling a mango when Major Schlesinger grabbed his arm.

"It is not yet ripe enough to eat, Colonel. Unripe mangoes are poison."

He said it with a smile, and the others laughed as Schlesinger commanded the orderly to dispose of the unripe mangoes and bring fresh ones.

He was disinclined to trust Schlesinger on anything – how could a Hungarian know anything about mangos? But poison or not, the little man with the pince-nez had gotten their minds off the weather.

Not for long.

As they sat quietly over breakfast, nourishing stiff and aching bodies with fuel they would need for an uncertain day, suddenly the skies opened up like sluices on a great dam, the sagging balloon of water hovering over them punctured and buckets thudding down on their tent, bending but not collapsing it, leaking in at the folds and sloshing under the canvas. The noise was staggering enough that they might have been under attack from artillery, the pounding drowning out all other sound. Waiting for Lopez to open the meeting, they looked from one to the other, each man wondering.

Shouting over the din, Lopez opened by passing around a sheet of paper extracted from his breast pocket, informing them he'd dispatched a picket that morning from Captain Oberto's Cuban company to Las Pozas, a village some ten miles inland on the way to San

Cristóbal, which was their objective. The picket carried a *pronunciamiento* under the heading:

## LIBERTAD! INDEPENDENCIA! DEMOCRACIA!

It was a single page, printed in New Orleans, to be distributed wherever they went. To Crittenden and to Downman it was new. The others seemed unsurprised.

The document invited all Cubans to join the liberating army in driving the Spanish occupier from the island. Volunteers would be supplied with arms, ammunition, and uniforms. Each man joining up was promised the just rewards of a conquering army.

He asked Lopez if the *pronunciamiento* was meant for slaves as well.

"But they cannot read, Colonel," he said with a laugh.

It was not a happy laugh, for the deluge had turned the mood dark as the sky. He remembered the rains of Mexico City, faithfully arriving each afternoon and quickly gone as clouds evaporated in the thin air. But Mexico City was a mile high; at Morillo they were at sea level.

Lopez fell silent, waiting for some sign from the weather. What marching orders could he give if the road was impassable? Artillery or not, starting up mud roads to Las Pozas in these conditions was absurd. They carried several thousand pounds of arms, ammunition, and stores, too much to be dragged through the muck by two beasts and a single cart. They needed more transportation.

"The rain complicates things," muttered Lopez.

"The road already was mud," said Colonel Blumenthal. "I inspected it this morning. If rain doesn't stop . . ."

"It will not stop," said Schlesinger, interrupting the senior officer.

Though clearly well informed, Blumenthal seldom offered an opinion. Pragay, it seemed, preferred the counsel of his outspoken translator to his laconic chief-of-staff. There was a rivalry of some kind at work among them, perhaps personal, perhaps social, perhaps national, no doubt reaching back to events in Europe.

"We cannot wait," said Lopez. "The goal is to reach Las Pozas before the Spaniards are at our heel."

"We must divide our forces," said Pragay through Schlesinger.

"Split our forces . . . *impossible!*" said Crittenden, with force. "We cannot split an already inferior force."

He'd thought much about the Europeans. Yes, they were important to the operation, but beyond their failure to understand American military tactics, he feared that so many foreigners speaking unknown tongues would make the Creoles wary. The further problem was that Lopez paid more heed to the Hungarians than to the Americans. It was where the absence of General Worth or General Quitman was most telling. The error they were about to make, fundamental, would never have been made by an American general.

Lopez remained silent.

Lest anyone misunderstand him, Crittenden repeated: "You cannot divide an already inferior force. Every plebe at West Point knows that cardinal military rule."

He looked to Lopez for support and then to Downman. He glanced at Blumenthal, hard to read but who seemed to agree with him. As a colonel, normally a brigade commander, Blumenthal, like Downman, would understand.

The torrent weighed heavily on them. Armies hate rain. They could not move supplies in this weather. Bahia Honda was always a risk. He thought of Napoleon waiting out the rain at Waterloo, but Belgium is not the tropics.

Lopez was about to make the fateful decision.

He turned to Crittenden. "But where *is* the superior force, Colonel?"

The Hungarians were whispering. "And will we be inferior when our forces are augmented?" said Schlesinger.

"No one has joined us yet," said Downman. Like Blumenthal, he was a man of few words, but one who understood the folly of unnecessary risk.

"Our supporters are all around us," said Schlesinger, not waiting for Pragay. "Did the Americans not observe the equipment delivered during the night?"

"One cart will not carry a quarter of our equipment," said Downman.

Lopez's chin sank to his broad chest. He was in shirtsleeves and braces and his silver hair fell down across his brow. For most of them, days of stubble had turned into scraggily beards and mustaches. Only Schlesinger looked well groomed. Lopez took his time. He might have been asleep. The nephew's mind went to his uncle.

"I believe General Pragay is correct," he said at length. Addressing Crittenden, "Do we have a choice, Colonel? Either we split forces or wait for rain to stop, which it shows no sign of doing. It was the risk we took to avoid being sighted. Soon General Enna will come. Ships are not bothered by the rain, nor are horses. We cannot defend ourselves against cavalry on this beach."

He would berate himself for not protesting more vigorously.

"We will march inland gathering forces as we go," continued Lopez. "Since supplies cannot move in these conditions, Colonel Crittenden will remain behind with two companies. The rest will march to Las Pozas from where we send back carts and oxen when the rains are stopped. Colonel Crittenden will then come ahead. We will wait in Las Pozas until he comes. We must be reunited in time to confront Enna, who cannot possibly be here before tomorrow."

An hour later, he watched as senior officers mounted up on the horses delivered during the night. Rain or not, they looked quite magnificent as they set out down the beach, covered in caps and ponchos. He imagined visions of Bolívar dancing in Lopez's head. Did it rain on Bolívar too? A few expressionless faces from the village finally peered out among the palms, but no one came down to greet them, much less to join them. Perhaps it was the rain.

The Hungarian company led off, followed by the mounted officers. Next came the Cubans of the Sigur company followed by the Americans under Colonel Downman and the Germans under Captain Schlicht. Downman had declined the horse that went to Schlesinger. The sand was solid enough, but the men's boots would be tested in the mud of the road. They took nearly three-fourths of the force. He was left with two companies, 120 men, 3,000 muskets, 100,000 cartridges, 700 pounds of powder and most of the food stores and supplies for 451 men.

His officers, Martin, Kelly, and Ker, came up to him, seeking explanations that he could not give. Where were the Creoles? Where was the Club of Havana? Where was the state of insurrection? Above all, why were they being left alone?

He thought of Grant at Monterrey, a supply officer so frustrated at being left behind that he grabbed a horse and rode off into battle. He had no horse, but instead of waiting for wagons from Lopez, he set out to find his own, eventually locating two more carts and two teams of oxen, easy enough to commandeer as all Cuba remained indoors, sheltered from the storm.

Night fell before they finally set out on what had become a nearly impassible road. It would be a night without sleep. No word had yet come back from Las Pozas. How could he know that the *Pizarro* was leaving Havana with eight hundred men at precisely the moment he was leaving Morillo? Lopez believed they had a full day's advance on Enna. Again, Lopez was wrong.

# XXXI

Never had he seen worse physical conditions. All night they slogged through the mud toward Las Pozas, making barely a half-mile an hour. Where was Lopez? Why had he not sent back more carts and oxen to lighten the loads? The rain abated, but sometime toward dawn the skies opened up again and soon the legs of the oxen were thick with mud to the knees. He felt sorry for the poor beasts, pulling more than they could manage in such conditions. The wheels of the carts sank below the hubs and had to be repeatedly wedged out.

He was as low and tired as he'd ever been, fully as much as his men, though unlike them he could not show it. Progress in the mud seemed impossible, but they kept at it, prying, lifting, pulling, dragging, like Sisyphus hopelessly pushing his stone. Stopping a moment, he looked at the men and saw more than fatigue on their faces. He saw disgust. This is not what we signed up for, their faces said. Sit and wait a while, Colonel, they said; wait for the mud to harden so the wheels can roll again.

But he could not sit and wait. Imagine that the Spaniards, mounted and unburdened by carts and oxen, came upon them, cutting them down as they stood knee-deep in the mud, unable to take positions, unable to move or maneuver. They must not stop. It was up to him to reunite the army *that should never have been split.*

Branches were laid so the carts didn't disappear into the earth as if into a sinkhole. Men dropped out, thinking they wouldn't be noticed, desperate for the sleep they'd been denied by rain and mosquitoes and an all-night march. He sent back patrols to bring them up, aware for the first time how undisciplined these men were, wondering how they would fare when faced with Spanish regulars. In battle, cohesion is everything. Stragglers would have no chance with the Spaniards. Already they had the aspect of a defeated army and had not yet encountered the enemy.

As dawn broke they arrived at the place called San Miguel, less than halfway to Las Pozas, he calculated. All night to go four miles! Still no sign of the others. Had he not located the carts on his own, they would still be waiting in Morillo!

Ker reported that neither men nor beasts could go farther. The rain had stopped. A few cocks crowed. The town was still asleep. Why get up to a world of mud? He saw a dozen houses with a *tienda* in the middle. The store's windows were broken. In the mud he saw sodden copies of Lopez's *pronunciamiento*, another inauspicious omen. Some of the houses had chairs or benches in front, giving his men a chance to rest and take breakfast. He posted sentries at each end of the street, found a chair on the porch of a little house and collapsed into it. He laid his head back against the boards and closed his eyes.

Lost, abandoned, hopeless, the words of defeat floated through his befogged mind. In two years in Mexico he'd never seen anything like his first day in Cuba. He thought of Napoleon's adage: "I have destroyed the enemy merely by marching." Yet his men were incapable of marching, were collapsed in a ramshackle village, splayed across it as if mowed down by cannonshot and hardly more alive.

He reached for Lucy's letter, letting sleepless eyes run down the now-memorized page, filling his depleted soul with her expressions of affection, anything to escape the morass. He replaced it and closed his eyes again. How had it come to this? He saw the mistakes. As the senior American in an army dominated by Americans, as the only West Point officer, he'd been thwarted at every turn by motives of men he did not like or understand. He was disgusted with himself.

As his men sat to breakfast they could not know that the *Pizarro* at that moment was landing eight hundred infantry at Bahia Honda. No, she'd not sighted the *Pampero* off the coast and sent word to Havana. It was the fisherman they'd brought on board to steer them into Bahia Honda – *the Creole fisherman!* He'd gone on to Havana to advise Captain-General de la Concha personally of the Americans' arrival at Bahia Honda. All would come out later.

The captain-general knew nothing of Bahia Honda. Intelligence – surely from spies in New Orleans – had informed him the *Pampero* would circle the island and land on the south shore – the original plan. Imagine it! But for a Cuban fisherman, Spain's main force would have been under steam three hundred miles around the island as the Americans marched unopposed to San Cristóbal.

Had he known the *Pizarro* was landing at Bahia Honda as they sat to breakfast in San Miguel, he would not have stopped. Though they could hardly walk, he would not have stopped. Though beasts will not move nor men fight on empty stomachs, *he would not have stopped!*

At some point he came out of his doze, fought to clear his mind, and called for coffee and a mango from an orderly. A *pronunciamiento* lay under his foot and he kicked it away. He was peeling the mango with his bayonet when he heard a sentry call out and saw Corporal Hernandez of Captain Oberto's Cuban company riding in on the road from Las Pozas on one of the horses delivered during the night. Hope surged in his breast! He dismounted, saluted, and handed him a message, the first word he'd had from Lopez since he'd ridden off so magnificently twenty-four hours before.

> *Colonel Crittenden:*
> *Come ahead immediately. The road to Las Pozas may be closed at any moment. Leave arms, ammunition and supplies where you are. Have each man pack as many cartridges as he can carry. We are waiting. Full speed at all costs!*
> *General Lopez*

He burst out laughing, a bitter, sleepless, semi-delirious laugh that crackled through the silent town. Heads turned.

Nothing he knew of Lopez had suggested such blunders:

- To have come to Cuba without artillery.
- To have taken on board the Cuban fisherman.
- To have divided the army.
- To have delayed in reuniting it.

And now to abandon arms, ammunition, and supplies – *the very reason for dividing the army in the first place!*

Hernandez, handsome young Cuban he remembered well from New Orleans, stared at him, puzzled by the idiotic laughter.

"At ease, Corporal. Now tell me where you have come from."

"Las Pozas, Colonel. General Lopez is waiting for you."

"*But I am waiting for him, Corporal!* Where are the carts and oxen that might lighten the load of these poor animals?"

Hernandez shook his head.

"Did you see enemy on the road?"

"The road to Las Pozas is clear, Colonel, but you must hurry."

"*Hurry* . . . in this mud . . . are you joking?"

He called to an orderly for more coffee. "We're happy to have you join us, Hernandez, happy to have your horse. Now sit and rest a moment."

He reread the message. Surely he could not follow such an insane order. Already they were without artillery, what chance did they have if deprived of arms and ammunition? How long could they hold out without supplies? How could they survive until reinforcements arrived from New Orleans? How could they equip Creole fighters – and *where were the Creoles?* Where was the Club of Havana? Why had no one come to join them?

As he meditated, the door to the house creaked opened and an old woman dressed in a colorless sack emerged. She looked first at the sky and then up and down the street at the soldiers flopped on any dry spot they could find. She examined Corporal Hernandez. "*Cubano?*" He nodded. She spat, some of the spittle landing on Crittenden. Aching, frustrated, disgusted, furious, he grabbed her wrist as she spewed a toothless volley of incomprehensible argot at him.

"Corporal, for God's sake, what's she saying, what does she want?"

Hernandez waited until the tirade stopped. "She says the others broke into houses here, robbed the store. She tells us to go away. She tells us to go to hell.  A crazy old woman, Colonel. Pay her no mind."

"Ask her why no one will come. Ask her if she doesn't want Spain gone."

A wicked smile sliced across the woman's coconut face as Hernandez translated. She went up to Hernandez, thrust her toothless face and shapeless body at him and ranted at a speed such that Crittenden could not catch a single word. If this was Spanish, it was not the Spanish he knew from Mexico.

Finished, she spat again and disappeared inside.

He looked to Hernandez, who shrugged. "She says one devil's the same as another."

"Surely she said more than that."

"Yes sir, she said more than that. She said that yesterday another group of devils came through, a larger group, and that some of them stole things, including from her house and the store. She asked me why I was fighting with the devils."

Strict orders to respect discipline had been given to all the men.

"She said that one of the leaders – a white-haired man who spoke Spanish – caught one of the thieves and was ready to run him through when the man raised his musket at him. Another man with a sword had to intervene."

"Lopez and the Hungarians," he said.

"Most likely."

"Madness. These people won't come to us if we rob them."

"*My* people, Colonel."

"Your people, yes, Hernandez."

He sat back down to consider his options. Nothing could be clearer: To follow the order from Lopez was to abandon all hope of success. Was Lopez the cause of it or was it General Pragay, recognizing his initial mistake and seeking to rectify? Surely both generals understood they could not prevail without arms and ammunition. Surely Lopez saw that! Any plebe at West Point would see that!

But how could he defy a direct order? How could he take it upon himself to ignore a direct order from the commander-in-chief? Yes, Lopez had made a grievous error in splitting the force, but as commander-in-chief that was his prerogative. In war, officers are shot for disobeying a direct order.

But this was not the U.S. Army. Lopez was not commander because he'd been nominated by the president and confirmed by the Senate. He was a former Spanish Army general who for reasons of his own had turned against his clan. He would not be in command if General Worth had not died and General Quitman not defected. Could he allow Lopez – or was it the Hungarians – to compound their initial mistake? Should he try take command himself? The Hungarians would surely shoot him.

How long did he sit there, carving on the mango, debating with himself?

Finally making up his mind, he ordered the troops to finish up breakfast and be ready to move out. He heard no complaints. Men and beasts had their rest and food and were ready to go, ready to join the main force, ready to join the battle, ready to do the job they'd come to Cuba to do.

Two companies, 120 strong, they formed up, prodded the oxen to their feet, and hitched them up and began to move out. Finally, the wheels of the carts could get a grip. They would get on with it. They would not abandon their arms and ammunition. They would not be killed by their own guns.

# XXXII

They were not fifteen minutes from the village when shots rang out from the hills in front. Surprised, his first thought was of irregulars, Creoles for some reason opposing them instead of fighting with them, but the firing indicated a disciplined military force, not large but clearly Spanish. Somehow the Spaniards had gotten between him and Lopez without passing him – a full day before anticipated! He moved his men off the road, into position and blindly opened fire into the hills. The enemy laid down a heavy sheet, then stopped. He heard shouts and sounds of withdrawal. No more than scouts, he determined, a picket. So where was the main force? How far away could it be? The picket should at least have done the service of alerting Lopez that Enna had arrived sooner than expected.

A mile outside the village, the road narrowed, heavy growth pressing in from both sides. The marks of several hundred boots stretched out before them, Lopez's men having stuck to the sides where grass grew, where the ground was harder. It had been easy enough for the main force to pass by, a different matter for carts and oxen. He could not help but curse the man for leaving him with barely enough men to defend the supplies let alone mount a serious attack on the enemy.

They resumed their trek, direction Las Pozas. The sun was trying to fight through the blanket of clouds. The road, with grass to bind it, was firm in places. They had every chance of making better time. He expected to meet Lopez on the road, to unite the forces before the main Spanish onslaught began.

They were not two miles out of San Miguel when shooting broke out in front again, and this time it was no picket. There had to be another road, one not marked on his map. They were cut off in front, could hear horses through the trees. His only option was to fight through, counting on Lopez to hear the battle and come back. Enna had discovered that they'd split their forces and that the smaller unit, laden with heavy carts, had not yet reached Las Pozas.

United, with superior weaponry and help from the Creoles, they'd have been a match for an enemy twice their size, horses or not. Divided and without support, the situation was critical. He could not deny it: The delay in San Miguel had given the Spaniards time to circle around and get between him and Lopez, which was always the danger. They took heavy fire, the *whoosh* of musket balls filling the air. The enemy had deployed in the hilly woods on the west side of the road. They'd not had the time or men to occupy both sides, indicating it was still not the main force.

Where was it?

He ordered the men to take cover on the east side and return fire. It was a devilish ambush with Spaniards holding the high ground, laying sheets of fire downhill on them. He heard men cry out as he'd not heard since Casa Mata. Without Dr. Fourniquet, who was with Lopez, there was little they could do for the wounded. Hospital steward John Fisher patched up the men as best he could until he took a ball in the neck, screaming as he slapped his hand to the bloody wound and fell into the mud, writhing and suddenly still with no one to treat him.

The woods crackled with fire, yellow tongues lashing out from behind the trees above. He heard shouts in several languages as men were hit. The oxen, lowing in fear, were shot dead, straining in their yokes and letting out blood-curdling cries before sinking down on their knees in the mud. Poor beasts. Any hope of saving supplies and ammunition now depended on Lopez. Corporal Hernandez had taken his horse into the woods, and his plan was to send him forward to alert

Lopez. First, though, they had to break through the ring of fire.

He motioned to Major Martin, behind a tree some twenty yards away. The idea was to send Kelly's 2nd Company through the woods, flanking the enemy and breaking through to Lopez as the main force charged across the road and up the hill. Judging from the firing, the enemy was not much stronger than he was, a battalion at most, and he might as well find out if his men could execute a charge. Major Martin was no more than five yards from him when a ball opened his head. His eyes went huge for a moment, he shouted a vile curse, dropped his musket and fell into the bramble.

He pulled him to cover and held him. Martin was gone, his luck run out. The look on his face was raw and fierce. He knew the man, understood the cry, that last loud GODDAMN! His own would have been no different. You got me first – YOU DUMB LUCKY BAS-TARDS! He closed Martin's angry eyes. He thought of Kirby Smith at the Molino. One more good soldier dead in his arms.

Kelly made it over, and he told him the plan. He could not sit there letting his men be picked off one by one. It was the only chance to reunite the army that had been wrongly split.

He sent Hernandez back to inform Lopez and pulled Kelly's 2nd Company from its position to follow Hernandez through the trees, direction Las Pozas. He heard some firing off the left flank when they were gone, but then it stopped, an indication the flank was not cov-ered and they'd made it through. He ordered ceasefire and slipped through the trees toward Victor Ker, a musket ball slamming into a tree just as he stepped behind it – alive by a millisecond. Why his luck still held he did not know. Since Casa Mata he didn't ask.

They were pinned down by the enemy's superior position. He looked down the road as far as he could see, the woods grown thick to the edges. They would have to break out, cross the exposed road and charge up the hill taking fire all the way. As he considered the situation, the enemy fire stopped.

Silence oozed back, the deadly silence soldiers fear as much as battle for it means the enemy is regrouping.

Ker agreed with the plan. "Why they haven't charged down the hill already I cannot understand," he said.

"We'll beat them to it."

Ker's dark Creole face, so often smiling during training for the liberation of his homeland, was solemn with worry and fatigue. "Either we charge or wait here to be wiped out. Look up there – see the movement – the charge could come any second and we are finished. From the firing I judge their strength to be about the same as ours. I believe the men have it in them. We'll find out."

"How many have we lost?"

"About twenty men down."

"We'll lay down a heavy volley, load up again, fix bayonets, and I'll give the order to charge. We knock them out and proceed on our way."

"And the carts . . ."

"Would you like to pull one?"

"And the dead . . ."

"No time for that now."

"And the wounded . . ."

"Those who can move will come with us."

"The others . . ."

"We'll come back for them, Victor. First things first, you know that."

"Aye, Colonel, I know that."

The Spaniards had managed to get between him and Lopez. It was a brilliant stroke, the work of General Manuel Enna, second on the island only to Captain-General de la Concha himself. Lopez had often talked of Enna, a young officer with him back in Spain. He knew de la Concha, too, though never mentioned him. "Personal resentments," Freaner said. Is that what this was all about?

He watched as word to prepare the charge was passed along the line. He could see few of his men, but knew the face and story of every American, Cuban, German, Hungarian, Pole, every man gathered from around the world to risk his life in an enterprise that few of them understood. By now they would all have their doubts. It was not the situation they'd been promised.

No one thought any longer of Creoles or the spoils of war. It was beyond all that. Survival was what mattered now: kill or be killed. Yes, some Creole friends had slipped in at Morillo to leave them oxen now dead, carts now useless, and horses serving no purpose other than to preen the egos of a few officers. By now the men knew, as he himself knew, that they'd been deceived.

### *"CHARGE!"*

It is the word every soldier waits to hear, waits to hear however much he fears it, waits to hear because whatever is to come cannot be worse than the dreadful wait, the anticipation that is worse than the confrontation. *Get it over with!*

Muskets loaded, bayonets fixed, they tumbled forth from the woods, shouting, screaming, faces red with fatigue and anger, murder in their hearts, ready to make someone pay for their misery, across the road and up the hill toward those licks of flame hiding behind the trees. They ran smack into a solid wall of fire, volley after volley, the enemy prepared and ready, perhaps surprised just a bit because it was preparing its own charge as the invaders dashed across the road to the tree line and started up.

The noise was deafening, muskets cracking all around, men shouting in strange languages, some hit but if not mortally wounded still going because to go down was the worst thing of all; scrambling through the bramble, up the hill, around one more tree, toward those deadly tongues of fire slashing out like dragon breath cutting through flesh and bone; trying for the top, trying to reach the blue sky of victory visible through the trees at the summit. The Spaniards held their ground and fired into them point blank, like the Mexicans at

Chapultepec, but his men were killing more than they lost for the Spaniards tended to aim high and their muskets were slower to load.

Suddenly he stopped climbing. Listening intently for a moment, he shouted at the top of his lungs: *"Hold your fire!"*

Shouts in Spanish told him the enemy had broken. *"For-ward!"* he shouted, waving his arms and bringing his men out from behind their trees to resume the scramble up the hillside.

Reaching the summit, they came upon the most glorious sight soldiers can behold: a valley dotted with the fleeing enemy, men and horses alike. His men fired after them until he gave the order to cease fire. They dare not waste ammunition.

He looked around at the dead and groaning Spaniards and saw his own company at half its former size.

Strange as it was, the firing hadn't stopped. Beyond the valley, behind the hills, in the far distance, they heard the blasts of many more muskets, signs of a far greater battle. So that's where Enna had gone, circling around to come in behind Lopez's main force. Finally, they meet again, former compatriots, former colleagues, perhaps former friends, going toe-to-toe.

Now he understood why Lopez had not come back: Enna had bypassed San Miguel entirely, sending his main force to meet Lopez at Las Pozas after learning from his picket that the Americans had split their forces and that the smaller unit was bogged down in the mud outside San Miguel. The force they had just routed was meant to deal with him, and he had turned the tables.

He stood listening to the battle for several minutes, trying to discern some sense of the action. Spanish and American muskets make different sounds, distinguishable ones, and to his ear the Americans were getting the best of it.

Then it stopped. The symphony reached its loudest crescendo, every instrument sounding at full force, and with the wave of a baton – *fine!* What had happened? One moment a great din driving rabbits into their holes and birds into their nests; the next, rabbits peeking out again, birds taking wing.

He stood still on the hill surrounded by men who'd just faced their first real test of fire and won. It is what every soldier lives for. After twenty-four hours of misery and discouragement, they had met the enemy and they had prevailed. None of them knew what was happening in the distance, what the clash of the main forces would produce or how it would affect them. But based on what they'd achieved themselves there was every chance of victory. They had the enemy on the run.

He turned to his men, seeing the pride written on their faces. Only hours before, slogging in the rain and mud into the place called San Miguel, they were a demoralized group, a unit cut off from the main force, isolated and burdened with carts that wouldn't move and men too tired to fight. Now they were revitalized, ready for the next challenge.

But what had happened on the far side of the hills? One thing was certain: Lopez had reached Las Pozas, first stop on the way to San Cristóbal, and there run into Enna. A battle had started and stopped, indicating that one side had either won or withdrawn. But Lopez had not come all this way to withdraw. Suddenly his heart was thumping. Was this it? Had they won and he didn't know it? Could it be? Had they somehow overcome the splitting of their army? Was the war over?

He had no time to exult. He needed to move his men up the road either to join Lopez or close the pincer. Whatever had happened, Enna was battered and likely trapped between them. If Enna had somehow gotten beyond Lopez, unlikely since Las Pozas lay at the foot of the sierras, he would now join Lopez to bring the full weight of their reunited army against the Spaniards.

He led his men back down the hill, over the trampled brambles, through the blackened trees, jagged stumps, and broken branches, nature once again despoiled by man and his quarrels, gathering up the wounded, picking up the dead. He ordered his men to take as much ammunition as they could carry from the carts. They were off again into battle. They would not tarry.

# XXXIII

A horse came snorting through the trees, and Will looked up into the face of Corporal Hernandez. Kelly's 2nd Company had gotten through to Lopez, he reported, and together they'd felt the full force of Enna's attack, which had surprised everyone. They'd fought well, he said, his voice flat, body crooked in the saddle. Will looked closer, saw that the man had been hit. The field was littered with the dead, he said, including General Enna himself.

*"Enna dead!* So we have won?"

His heart leapt.

Hernandez tried to answer, but his eyes blurred and he almost fell from the horse. At once he saw the torn shirt and the shoulder oozing blood underneath. He helped him down, laid him out and called for an orderly. None left. He took the blanket from the horse and placed it under his head.

"They're coming this way."

"Who's coming this way?"

"The enemy . . ."

"But you said . . ."

"Down the road from Las Pozas."

"Lopez in pursuit?"

"Lopez gone into the mountains."

*"But who won?"*

"We were winning, Colonel. I watched from the hills. Then I was hit."

"But the fighting stopped."

"Maybe Lopez ran out of ammunition."

*"Ran out of ammunition!"*

He fell to his knees, astounded. Moments before he'd felt only elation, and now this! Hernandez had to be wrong. They could not have been deprived of victory for want of ammunition. It was not possible.

Mind churning, he cut the man's shirt open with his bayonet. The ball had gone through his right shoulder and the arm dangled. It was a miracle he'd stayed on the horse. A soldier came up with bandages. It would stop the blood but the arm would have to come off to save him. They had no one to do it. They gave him morphine. He was a goner. His eyes said he knew.

"So Lopez didn't win."

His eyes were closed. "The enemy withdrew after Enna fell, Colonel. Is that not victory?"

Victor Ker, his only surviving officer, stood over them, shaking his head. "I'd take his arm off myself, Colonel, but it would do no good."

They moved off to consult. He'd lost more than half his force, down to fifty men who could still fight. The wounded who could not walk would be left behind, made as comfortable as possible and left with muskets, ammunition, and provisions in hopes Spaniards proved more merciful than Mexicans. No commander faces a worse decision than to abandon his wounded, but he had no choice. With or without Enna, the enemy was between him and Lopez. It was one thing if Lopez was on his tail, but if Hernandez was right, Lopez had retreated into the mountains. The enemy had broken off with Lopez to concentrate on the smaller force.

He put himself in their shoes and understood immediately. Why take casualties from a direct attack on the main force in the mountains when you can wipe out the smaller force and seize the enemy's ammunition and supplies in the process – *without which the main force is helpless?*

But how to explain Lopez's actions?

With a personal score to settle, Enna might have fought to the last Spaniard, but the second-in-command saw the situation more clearly: Deprived of half his force and all his supplies Lopez would be cast adrift in the mountains with no better prospects than to shoot rabbits and eat berries until he was tracked down.

Unless his friends in Pinar rallied to him; unless, reinforced, he could prevail against Concha in a showdown in the mountains.

"No good options, Victor."

"None that I see, Colonel."

They stood in the shade of a mangrove tree and looked out on the miserable scene, one he'd witnessed too many times before: cries of the wounded, moans of the dying, men bandaging themselves and bandaging those who could not do it for themselves, men lying so still you didn't know if they were dead or alive, so easy for the ghost to slip away unnoticed. *And they had won their battle!* The elation of a half hour ago, the fresh smell of victory, was gone. He looked at Ker, a man of courage and character, and saw defeat in the eyes of the man called Victor. If there was something better than what he was considering he knew he'd hear it from Ker.

Slowly Victor Ker shook his head. "Fifty against five hundred – we owe the men better than that."

"Could not Lopez have let the Spaniards go in order to trap them between us? If he's on their heels, we'd have them in our own pincer."

Ker's eyes showed a hint of humor. "If Lopez is on their heels, wouldn't we know it, wouldn't we hear it, wouldn't Hernandez have seen it?"

"I believe I would have tried it," he said. "It is the only chance."

"You, Colonel, yes. Lopez, no. He wants to be in the mountains."

"That was always the goal, wasn't it – to be up there with his friends."

"It's not gone as planned, has it Colonel?"

Ker went off, and he stood a moment by himself.

Retreat? He'd never retreated before. He'd never seen a retreat before. For all the blood spilled in two years in Mexico, they'd never retreated, even against the worst odds. Taking the Monterrey fortress, the Black Fort, they called it, had led to the worst day of Zach Taylor's career, but he didn't retreat, just redeployed his forces the better to attack again. General Worth pulled them back from the slaughter at the Molino, but only to regroup.

You don't much study retreats at West Point. The assumption is that if you've planned your battle correctly it is the enemy who retreats. Retreat means defeat, and West Point only studies enemy defeats to learn what went wrong so it doesn't happen to you. He'd won his battle; why should he retreat? His men had made a magnificent charge and dislodged the enemy from a superior position. Every man would have his medal when this war was over.

But Ker was right. Fifty against five hundred! The same as Thermopylae, but the Greeks were not in open country. They were defending a narrow pass against the Persians. And they were at home.

*And they lost.*

He had no intention of being annihilated by a force ten times his size while waiting for Lopez to execute a maneuver he wasn't even considering. They'd seen no sign of a Spanish rear guard. Enna was so intent on crushing Lopez that he'd brought his entire force forward. He cast one final forlorn look at the dead oxen, ordered the men to take water and stores from the carts, and they set out for the coast, the silent cries of the men left behind ringing in their ears.

They moved back through San Miguel. Unlike the first time, it was late morning and it was dry and people were up and going about their business. His men moved faster than the first time but not that fast, and people watched and they saw defeat. He looked for gloating, at least for satisfaction, for these people, the Creoles to whom they'd come to help lift the Spanish yoke from their shoulders, had done nothing for them. They paused in their work to watch the soldiers pass through town and their faces were masks. People were sweeping and repairing broken windows and picking up soggy *pronunciamientos* from the dirt road. The old crone stood statue-like with a broom on the porch where he'd eaten his mango. The town was deathly quiet: no celebration, no satisfaction, not a gesture, smile, or frown. They watched them pass as they might watch a herd of goats driven down the road.

They'd heard the battle, at least his part of the battle, for it was just up the road. They saw his unit half the size it had been and with no carts or oxen. As bad as his men looked the first time through, they saw it was infinitely worse. They saw the blood and bandages and slings and makeshift crutches and they knew these were not signs of victory. They did not know and would not have cared that this company, Crittenden's company, the 1st Company, 2nd Battalion of the liberation army, had won its fight. What did it matter? The villagers saw only retreat, and where there is retreat there is defeat.

He thought of Lopez. With Enna dead, Lopez could have attacked the main Spanish force. One never knows the effect on an army of losing its commander. What chance did the English have after losing Harold at Hastings or the French after losing Montcalm at Quebec? If Lopez had pushed them down toward Las Pozas they could have smashed the enemy in a vise. Is that not what they came to Cuba to do: defeat a stronger Spanish force? Had he not seen himself that morning how the Spaniards ran when attacked?

Whatever Hernandez believed, it was unlikely Lopez had run out of ammunition; more likely he took advantage of the ceasefire after Enna's death to head for Pinar and into the arms of his friends, to await the great rallying of the Creoles that he expected – the Creoles and the Spanish defectors: How many times had he heard Lopez say it? He even named the colonels and units of the Spanish army he expected to join him in Pinar.

What did he care about Crittenden's puny force of 120 men –
now reduced to remnants?

Lopez never intended to go toe-to-toe with Enna, but things
changed when Enna fell upon him a day before expected. *That* was
the moment they paid for splitting the army. Lopez expected their
forces to be reunited before Enna arrived, but Enna, alerted by the
Cuban fisherman – the fatal mistake! – surprised him. So now Lopez
would head for Pinar, perhaps even make it to his own plantation at
Frias with what was left of his force, there to await de la Concha, the
man who took the job that should have been his.

# XXXIV

*August 14–15, 1851*

They reached Morillo unopposed, commandeered three fishing boats and with provisions from the abandoned carts put to sea at dusk. The sun sets late in the tropics, too late for their own good if the Spaniards got word and came after them in their steamers. A nose count showed 51 men left from his 120. Loaded onto three single-sail fishers with arms and provisions, they couldn't outrun anyone.

The boats moved north as the sun moved west, neither moving fast enough for anyone's taste. Victor Ker was in the second boat, and about a mile offshore they brought the boats together for a powwow. With dusk approaching they were likely safe for the night, but he worried about morning. If the wind didn't come up they'd be lucky to be ten miles out at daybreak. His idea was to head west rather than north, direction Yucatán instead of Key West. The Spaniards were more likely to search the Florida Channel rather than west toward Mexico.

Victor Ker changed his mind.

"The loop current, Colonel, you've heard of it?"

He confessed he had not.

"Heading west, we'd be moving against it. With this load and no wind, we'd be dead in the water. "

"And north . . ."

"Heading north the loop will carry us straight to Florida."

Like most Louisiana Creoles, Ker knew tides and currents.

Florida was closer anyway, and the closer they got the better their chances of running into an American ship, maybe even the navy. As much as they'd sought to avoid the navy coming out, nothing would have heartened him more than the sight of the sun coming up on the great gray mass of a U.S. cutter out from Key West. At least they should be in international waters by sunrise. The Spaniards would have no right to detain them. Their chances were decent.

They lay crammed against each other on deck, tending their aching bodies and minds, smelling the fish whose place they'd taken, most men asleep after the awful day, a few disinclined to sleep while any light remained, any chance of still being sighted. Each boat carried seventeen men, keeping them low and slow in the water. They kept watch to the south and west, on sun and sea. He stared into the fading mouth of Bahia Honda until his eyes blurred. If a ship came out they were finished, for it could easily run them down in the twilight. His eyes tricked him, showing distant shapes in the water, like mirages, that quickly evanesced.

Gradually he could no longer see the bay and so relaxed. Soon he could not see Cuba but as a jagged silhouette cut against the dark sky. The moon came up and would shine high and bright as it does in the tropics, but the Spaniards would not search for them in the moonlight. He took Lucy's letter from his pocket but could not read it in the gloaming. No matter, he knew it by heart. "Until we meet again in Havana," she wrote. Not this time, my love, he thought. Maybe next.

He drank some water, ate some hardtack, set the night's watch for the tiller and shoulder-to-shoulder with the men sank down to sleep on the boards. The smell of fish was overpowering, but nothing could have kept them from sleep after what they'd been through. The boat rocked side to side as he drifted off, but he had little sense of forward movement.

He sank into a sound sleep that lasted a few hours. At one o'clock he was up to relieve the tillerman but did not wake the next watch. Let the men sleep until sunrise. He sat in the moonlight and listened to the waves slap at the bow. The sail luffed in the warm breeze. He couldn't make out the other boats. From time to time they called across to stay close. The Cubans put three men on those boats, and even with a good fishing day they wouldn't reach the weight of seventeen armed men. A big marlin could sink a boat like this. They probably kept to mackerel and bass. With Jude, they'd sometimes hooked a bass at the lake. The fish would migrate down Clear Creek from the hills that fed all the mid-Kentucky lakes. Mostly they caught catfish. Jude stuck in his mind, lazing under the sassafras with his line in the water. He'd be fast asleep now on Phillipa Street, his arms around pretty Dominique.

He sat for hours, dozing off and on, leaning on the tiller, his mind electric. Lucy was everywhere, her rosebud mouth on his. When would he see her again . . . how could he face her . . . would she still want him? How could he face Uncle John? He had to get to New Orleans before Pickens and Hawkins sailed . . . meet Quitman and start planning again. Get it right next time. No more mistakes. First they had to get home. Needed a little luck. The Bible phrase popped into mind: "Time and chance happeneth to them all." They could use some of both.

Night broke, and the gray dawn came crawling in, the world slowly waking with the sun still hiding. Distant shapes forming. A marlin jumped in the misty gloom, black eyes on him all the way, could easily have landed in the boat, spearing it, sending it down. How do fish know day is coming before a single ray of light penetrates their briny depths? He saw the tiniest golden speck appear in the east. The lamplighter got the wick to take and soon there was light.

He had no desire to look behind him, but turned and there it was, a great shadow rising from the sea through the salty mists, the place called Cuba, still much larger than he'd hoped. Had they moved at all? Where was the loop current to carry them to Florida? The boats had drifted maybe half a mile apart.

He stood by the tiller and looked out over his men, jammed asleep in all positions, enjoying dreams he hated to end with the hard reality of another day. His shout broke the silence with the force of a foghorn. Men awake quickly as they might for reveille, pain in their drawn and untended faces: pain from wounds, fatigue, retreat, the misery of remembering where they were and knowing this day would be no better than the previous one. Why were they here, they'd be asking? In the distance he saw movement in the other boats. He waved them to approach. They were fifty armed men at sea and had to stay close.

A morning waft touched the sails but soon died. He looked to the water and saw motion. Or was it just current? What he'd give for long oars to get this thing moving. He doubted they were even ten miles off Cuba, close to international waters, but they would need luck. Time and chance. Carefully, the men rose, seventeen in a boat meant for three. They had some breakfast, straggled apart for a little privacy, and set to work on their muskets. Small boats at the mercy of almost anything, at least they would be prepared.

He could see Morro Castle, its ramparts and towers stretching along the hills on the east side of Havana Harbor. He stared until it began to blur, longing for it to vanish completely. My God, could it only be three days since they'd lain on the decks of the *Pampero*, 450 jubilant men certain of victory, watching the flying fish, watching Morro grow larger as they came in, less than seventy-two hours since victory turned to retreat and . . . suddenly his mind went to Lopez: Lopez in the mountains at Pinar, waiting for the Creoles to join him. Why had he not come after the Spaniards? They had them trapped between them. They would be marching on Havana by now.

Could he, Crittenden, have acted differently? Separated from the main force with the enemy marching to annihilate him, he'd done what any commander would have done: saved his men to fight another day. He knew nothing of Lopez's motives or of his fate, but wished him Godspeed. He'd love nothing more than to be with him at this minute, fight it out to victory. Land under his feet, not Davy Jones's Locker. Why did Lopez listen to the Hungarians? Was it because he himself was at heart a European, a Spaniard, a member of the very people he was trying to chase from the hemisphere?

*"Colonel!"*

His drifting mind was brought back by the sharp voice of Victor Ker knifing through the mists. The sun was up now, lying like a golden ball bobbing on the distant sea. Everything dull and dead; no wind, no sails, no flying fish. No land anywhere except where he didn't want to look. Ker made him look, pointing to something too dark and black to be a cloud. He looked closer and saw a smoke plume rising over Morro Castle, only it wasn't from the castle. It was a plume rising from the water, trying to hide the castle. The direction told him everything, and the stab went straight to his soul. It was what they most feared. They'd slept soundly, laid their heads on the clammy boards with hope that when they awakened Cuba would have disappeared from the face of the earth. It was not to be.

His little boats had no plume but had masts. The ship's captain would have a glass, would be running it side to side across the horizon and it would not be long before he spotted them.

She was bearing down on them, and for the first time in his life he felt desolation, the hopelessness that comes with no escape, worse than at San Miguel or Monterrey or even Casa Mata where it was kill or be killed and you had no time to think. On land, the order comes and you charge, knowing your chance is as good as theirs – even better if you fight well. At sea you're a sheep, frozen in dread, watching the wolf bound down on you. They could not run and could not fight for the steamer would send them down with three good shots and not bother with survivors.

Her plume of black smoke grew thicker and uglier by the second, defiling the beauty of everything around it.

"Make sure all arms are dry and loaded," he shouted, loud enough for everyone to hear, loud enough so the cracking in his voice might not be noticed. "It looks like we're not quite done with these people."

Should he believe an escape west toward Mexico would have succeeded, that he'd chosen the wrong route, that his luck had failed when he needed it most? But they'd have fought the current and likely been no farther off Cuba than they were. He gave the order to maneuver the boats closer, but not too close. They would stagger themselves at twenty-five yards distance. Don't make it too easy.

Twenty minutes later they were looking straight into the mouths of a row of black canons, twelve pounders at least. She was not the same ship they'd sighted as they headed into Bahia Honda three days before, the ship the Creole fisherman called the *Pizarro*. This ship was tighter, smaller, faster.

The dull guns grew larger, and then they heard them, warning balls whistling overhead. He looked at the other boats. Fifty muskets were trained on a Spanish steamer that carried cannons ready to send them to the bottom. He thought of the fishing boat at their mercy off Bahia Honda: muskets against cannons.

The ship stood off at fifty yards. He ordered the men to put down their guns. The wait was interminable. He supposed the captain was making up his mind whether to be done with them or not. Finally, they saw a boat manned and lowered and slowly rowing toward them, a Spanish lieutenant looking for a sign. He waved him over, accepted his salute and returned with him to the *Habanero*.

Surrender was offered after long parlay with Admiral Bustillo, who could not have been more courteous or solicitous of his men. He offered his guest lunch, and when it was refused sat to take his own lunch with sherry and talk of Spain and Cuba and the United States, where the admiral had visited as a young officer and where he hoped to visit again. His guest, miserable and starving but unable to eat with his men languishing in the boats, listened quietly and waited for him to get to the point, which was to give his word as an officer and a gentleman that his men would be accorded all the rights of prisoners of war.

Without that promise, there could be no surrender. Without surrender, they would be blasted from the sea, and the admiral could return to his sherry. *Amor fati,* said Napoleon: if you can't change it, embrace it. Over dessert, the promise was given, the two officers rose and shook hands and he returned to his boat. His men were brought in small groups onto the *Habanero*. Spanish sailors were dispatched to the fishing boats to return them to Bahia Honda.

The prisoners' hands were tied and they were put in the hold for the return to Cuba. Now, if ever, he would need Uncle John.

# XXXV

*August 12–16, 1851*

The *Pampero* brought word of the landings at Bahia Honda back to New Orleans, but nothing more. Captain Lewis, counting on returning to the island almost immediately with reinforcements and still worried about the navy, did not advertise the achievement, though anyone wondering where his ship had gone likely had a good idea. Thanks to the *Delta-News*, Lopez's designs for Cuba were known to anyone who bought a newspaper.

Lewis's first appointment upon his return was at the *Delta-News* offices on Canal Street. Laurent Sigur was there, along with James Freaner, John O'Sullivan, and various members of the Club of Havana. John Quitman was invited, but did not come. Before O'Sullivan and the others could set out around the country for more fund-raising, they needed information on the battle in progress. Sigur had sent no reporter with Lopez, depending on John Thrasher of Havana's *El Faro Industrial* to provide him with news by ship, which had not yet come.

The telegraph had existed since 1844. Wires were furiously being strung between cities and would reach New Orleans via St. Louis, Memphis, and Natchez in the fall of 1851. The first cables would not be laid under water – under the English Channel – for two more years.

For Sigur it was the most frustrating of situations: a public hungry for news, and a newspaper that knew next to nothing. He knew no more than Captain Lewis could tell him, which beyond the facts of the landing on the north shore instead of the south was not much. He was distressed to learn of the missing bazookas: he'd paid for those weapons, and they had disappeared, bad enough in itself, but what if they had fallen into the hands of the Spaniards, to be turned against Lopez? From what Lewis informed him of the meeting in Key West and the unexpected change of plans, nothing could be excluded.

Newspaper silence did not mean that the public knew nothing of events. New Orleans is a port, and where there are ports there are ships, and where there are ships there are sailors, and where there are sailors there are bars, and where there are bars there is talk. Sailors have an urge to do three things when returning from sea duty, and two of them are drinking and talking. Captain Lewis urged his crew to keep mum about where they'd been, what they'd done, and what they might be doing in the future, but it was like asking the birds not to sing.

Even if the birds had not sung, it was hard to keep planning secret. Colonel Pickens and Major Hawkins were in town with their regiment of Kentucky volunteers, drilling and waiting to embark, when news came from Cuba. With just under two hundred men, the volunteers formed less a regiment than a battalion, but sufficient with enough bazookas to hold any beachhead controlled by Lopez and prepare for reinforcements. General Felix Huston, a bon vivant and old slaving colleague of Jean-Baptiste Raynaud, was in the bars of Pirate's Alley every night, gabbing and looking for more men. The navy was paying attention to all these activities, but it was half-hearted. President Fillmore (and his attorney general) was more concerned about Lopez than anyone in New Orleans, where Lopez was a well-known figure and his cause a popular one.

Fillmore, a New Yorker, had been put on the '48 ticket with Zach Taylor because Whigs feared that the more popular William Seward, a strong anti-slaver, would be rejected as vice president by the South. Taking over upon Taylor's death in '50, Fillmore was sympathetic to slavery and to the South, though not to point of starting a war with Spain over Cuba, which he feared would break the nation apart, with history blaming him. He did not know of the navy's indifference to his orders to keep close watch on the *Pampero*. He did not even know the *Pampero* had disappeared. How could he?

The navy knew the *Pampero* left New Orleans on August 4, but it did not send the information on to Washington until she returned on August 15 and it was discovered where she had gone. From August 15, the news took a week to reach Washington by ship and another week for instructions to arrive back to New Orleans. Thus everyone in the Fillmore cabinet, including Attorney General John J. Crittenden, remained in the dark about events in Cuba even as they unfolded.

In any case, the *Pampero's* business with Spain and Cuba was the business of the secretary of state and the secretary of war, not the attorney general – which is not to say that Mr. Crittenden did not have a personal interest.

Returning to Wyalusing, Lucy began to write, drawing on several notebooks of material. Although she was unclear about the construction of her novel – having no idea how it would end – she had outlined a few chapters set in New Orleans, laying out the motives and inspiration for the mission and introducing the principal characters. She knew her story would change with time, but like any writer carrying a long and complex narrative and a good many characters in her head, she was desperate to get something down on paper.

She had hated leaving New Orleans. The departure outside Raynaud House had been sad enough without the additional grief of returning to a place she thoroughly disliked, a place soon to be deserted by her sister, her only confidante. The frustration was intolerable. There was a war on that she knew nothing about. Wyalusing was far away from New Orleans, and when news came from Cuba, how would it come to her? Everything was days away by exhausting river travel, and she almost never saw a newspaper.

In the meantime, she had to do something.

So she wrote.

Each day after breakfast, in the cool of the early morning, she came down to the gazebo, installed herself at the desk, and began the task of transforming her notes into a story. She wrote all morning, went back to the house for lunch with her mother and sister, followed by a nap, returning to the gazebo when the heat of the afternoon had passed to resume her work. Sometimes in the afternoon Anna Eliza came down to join her, not to talk, for she knew Lucy demanded silence, but to sit quietly with book in hand and be the supportive presence for her younger sister that she had always been and soon would cease to be. Lucy had been cranky since returning to Wyalusing, which was unlike her. Anna understood that she had much on her mind.

Her writing, Anna saw, was the principal cause of her petulance, and she wondered how to help. She knew nothing about writing, but was puzzled how a writer could start a story without an idea of its ending. It was not her notion of how stories were told. Don't you need to know where you're going before you set out on any journey? She was dying for instruction.

Her chance came after lunch on an especially hot mid-August afternoon. They'd come down from the house together, Anna taking her place on the sofa and Lucy at her desk. As Anna read, she glanced up from time to time, noticing that her sister was not writing, but sitting motionless at the desk, staring out the window, pen in hand, never moving. Anna watched for some time, then turned back to her book, waiting to hear the scratch of quill on paper. Instead, she heard only the loud emptiness of East Texas silence. Lucy stayed like that for some time, as if in trance. Was she even breathing? Anna could not see her face, but had no doubt that it was frozen in a mask of angry frustration.

It was her opportunity. She dared ask the question that had been on her mind for days.

Lucy spun as if slapped. "Oh, don't you see that the ending is unimportant? Of course, I don't need to know the ending. It is the nobility of the act itself that matters, the human spirit doing the grand thing. The ending will come in its time. It's like the Crusades, don't you see, chivalrous knights called by something higher to do what they must, summoned by their most noble instincts, gentlemen soldiers doing what pusillanimous governments refuse to do: undertaking to rid the world of tyranny and evil. What could be finer?"

Anna Eliza closed her book. The world of Emma Woodhouse seemed far too tame. She believed her sister had quite lost touch.

"The ending unimportant . . . you mean you don't care . . ."

Lucy came over and stood above her. She was flushed. Anna saw little beads of moisture formed on her upper lip.

"But is that not the very definition of heroism?" she cried, moving around behind the sofa where Anna could not see her. "A band of virtuous men striving against insurmountable odds, ignoring the risk of failure?" She came back around, and Anna saw that the beads were gone. "Of course, risk is there. In war there is always risk." She paused. "But without risk, where is the glory? Tell me this, dear Anna: How would failure diminish the magnificence of the motive? I see their action as divinely inspired, like the Crusades, a holy war!"

"My goodness!"

To Anna it made no sense. And she knew something was wrong. The wastebasket had accumulated as much of the manuscript as the desk. Lucy did not even try to hide her failure. She was the very essence of frustration, of thwarted ambition, of emotional annihilation. She was like a ship decked out in full sail and crew and lacking even a breath of wind to get out of port. Despite her grandest literary efforts, without information she could not advance. Anna understood the cause of her mumpishness and knew she must do something to help.

They walked back in silence to the house. Anna believed that Lucy was near collapse.

"This won't do, you know," she told her the next day. She'd arrived at the gazebo to find Lucy pacing and actually talking to herself.

Lucy turned on her, flushed, agitated. "Anna, what am I do in this place if I can't write? I'm going quite mad, you know. No one ever visits, I've read every book in the house and you're on the point of deserting me. I shall be quite daft if news doesn't come soon."

"And how is it to come?" asked Anna softly.

"They've all promised to write as soon as they know something."

"Who has promised to write?"

"All of them – Victoria, Lucien, Laurent Sigur, the minute they've heard."

"And you are depending on them?"

"What else can I do?"

"*Go, Lucy, go!* Go to New Orleans where you'll know the minute that word comes. You owe him that, you know."

Lucy stopped pacing long enough to observe her sister on the sofa, occupying the very spot where she'd lain with Will. Of course she was right! Why had she skulked back to Wyalusing after their departure instead of staying on in New Orleans where she could be in touch? It was insane to sit in East Texas pretending to write a story when she had no facts to put in it. She was waiting for a letter that might never be written.

She wrote Victoria that day asking if she might spend a few days with her at Raynaud House. She wondered if Christophe was home. She wrote to Laurent Sigur and to Lucien Hensley, advising them that she was returning to New Orleans, asking to meet with them.

She began packing. She was desperate. She had to find out something.

# XXXVI

*August 15, 1851*

One person who did know something was John Snyder Thrasher, owner of *El Faro Industrial*, a popular Havana daily. Steaming toward Havana with her distressed cargo, the *Habanero* flag-signaled to Morro Castle that she was arriving with prisoners; Morro, its telescope fixed on the steamer, set off its guns to announce the news to the city. Hearing the guns, Thrasher climbed into his carriage in Havana Centro and ordered the driver to the Malecon, the coastal road that parallels the sea as it reaches eastward toward Castillo la Punta, then turns sharply inland and runs along Havana Harbor. Once on the Malecon, Thrasher ordered the driver to wait until the *Habanero* came into view.

He wasn't the only one heading for the Malecon. Havana's newspapers had kept citizens well informed of Lopez's attack on the island. Word of the arrival of American prisoners spread quickly. Masses of people began to funnel toward the Malecon from the dozens of little *callejuelas* that crisscrossed the old city on their way to the bay and harbor.

It was late afternoon by the time the *Habanero* approached. Thrasher, refreshed by the breeze off the sea, was comfortable for the first time that day and in no hurry to move. He waited for the ship to pass him and ordered his driver to keep pace as she moved in from the sea, rounded la Punta, and entered the harbor. The crowd was streaming toward the harbor from all directions, the ship beckoning to them like the Lorelei.

Having arrived on the island as a child with his parents, John Thrasher knew Cuba, its people, and its culture as well as any native did. He was a successful newspaper publisher, Freemason, member of the Club of Havana, and friend of the Creoles. He had published articles written by members of the Club. Cirilo Villaverde and Miguel Teurbe were among his contributors, and Thrasher had had his clashes with the censors. He was not popular with the Spaniards, particularly with the captain-general, Don José Gutiérriez de la Concha, marquis of Havana, viscount of Cuba.

A year earlier, Thrasher had purchased *El Faro Industrial* over the objections of de la Concha, a faithful member of the one true church and a fierce enemy of Freemasonry. De la Concha demanded that Thrasher renounce both his U.S. citizenship and Freemasonry to buy the newspaper, a demand that Thrasher, a well-known figure in Havana, rightly declined. His acquisition of the newspaper was a private business transaction that de la Concha had no legal right to interdict.

He would pay dearly for his obstinacy.

At first, the *Habanero's* course puzzled him. She steamed by Castillo la Punta, where he first thought she would drop off her cargo, but did not cross the harbor toward the twin fortresses that guard the north side, Morro and Cabaña Castles, where most prisoners of the Crown were sent. To set course for the fortresses – no more than a mile across the mouth of the harbor but ten miles around by land – would have meant the crowds accumulating along the Malecon could not follow.

Next the ship passed Castillo de la Real Fuerza, headquarters of the queen's royal forces, another common destination for prisoners. That left only Fort Atarés, deep inside the harbor, as the ship's destination. Thrasher's carriage rolled along with the ship, slower now, hardly faster than the crowd pressing in on it. The ship, too, had slowed. The publisher concluded that the captain-general, a fierce patriot of Spain and a man addicted, like most Spanish Catholics, to ceremony and celebration, had decided to put on a show for the population.

He knew what it meant and silently cursed the man.

As Thrasher passed Castillo de la Real Fuerza, another carriage rolled up alongside him. "Good evening, Mr. Thrasher," a voice called.

The voice belonged to Allen Owen, U.S. consul general in Havana.

"Good evening to you, sir," he called back, putting more bonhomie into the greeting than he felt. The horses' clip-clop over the cobblestones added to the clamor from the masses around them and made it necessary to shout. "We seem to be heading to the same place."

"And where would that place be, Mr. Thrasher?"

John Thrasher had lived in Havana for twenty-five years; Allen Owen, President Fillmore's personal representative in Havana, fewer than two years. It did not surprise Thrasher that Owen would ask him where they were headed.

"By the process of elimination I'd say we are headed for Fort Atarés."

As the crowd pressed in on them, the horses slowed to a walk and the two Americans found it easier to converse. It was as though a single powerful tide flowing in from the Gulf had lifted everything in Havana and was carrying it inland – horses, carriages, the *Habanero*, her prisoners, and a large part of Havana's population.

"Do you have any idea who is on that ship?" asked Owen.

Thrasher looked over to him. He did not like the consul general, who he knew returned his feelings. Since arriving in Cuba, Allen Owen had refused all contact with the Club of Havana. What's more, without giving a reason, Owen had not supported Thrasher's bid to buy *El Faro Industrial*, which, as an American, he should have done. Since then, the publisher had had little contact with the consul general, who seemed more interested in sharing Rioja wines and Havana *puros* at the captain-general's table than in helping Americans in Havana, which was his job.

"The ship is the *Habanero*. I believe she signaled that she has prisoners aboard."

"They would be American prisoners, would they not?"

"It is a safe assumption."

"Lopez himself?"

"That I cannot say."

"The newspapers say Lopez arrived with a force of a thousand."

"That is not the figure my newspaper has published."

"I am aware of that."

"The captain-general has reasons to exaggerate."

"What have you heard?"

The thing that most irritated Thrasher about Owen was that the man did not understand his job. Newspapers and diplomats are in the same business: They gather information and report it, albeit to different audiences. In foreign lands their common interests normally lead them to share information. Of all the consuls general Thrasher had known, Owen was the single exception: He shared nothing. He was said to be a personal friend of President Fillmore, which Thrasher believed explained his churlish incompetence.

"I'm sure your sources are better than mine."

Owen laughed. "Oh, I doubt that."

Thrasher smiled. He would give the counsel general something. "I hear that Lopez is still out in Pinar somewhere."

"You see, your sources are better than mine."

"If the prisoners on the *Habanero* are Americans, Mr. Owen, you will have work to do."

The carriages had practically stopped, as had the ship, easing in behind a much larger ship along the docks at the foot of Fort Atarés. Thrasher recognized the second ship as the Spanish man-of-war *Esperanza*.

Owen looked across at him, trying to suppress a look of annoyance and not succeeding. "I suppose so, Mr. Thrasher, I suppose so."

• • •

The consul general and the newspaper publisher were not the only Americans watching the *Habanero* steam into port that evening. Anchored at the foot of Mercaderes Street about halfway between Real Fuerza and Atarés was the USS *Albany*, a three-master with a crew of ninety, thirty-two guns and two companies of Marines, a ship more than equal to anything that Spain had in the Caribbean, including the *Pizarro*. Havana was a traditional port of call for U.S. ships on Caribbean duty, and the *Albany* happened to be in port on a routine visit.

Commander Charles T. Platt, captain of the *Albany*, knew more about Lopez than what he'd read in Havana's newspapers. Platt had taken over the *Albany* the previous year from Commander Victor Randolph, who had tracked Lopez's prior expedition to Cuba, at Cárdenas, the expedition that led to U.S. charges against Lopez for violation of the Neutrality Act. Randolph had fully informed Platt of Lopez and his ambitions, how after his failure at Cárdenas he had vowed that the next time he would have the men and means to succeed. Platt knew of Lopez's preparations in New Orleans. He was on deck with members of his crew as the *Habanero* steamed into harbor. Like Thrasher and Owen, he'd heard the guns from Morro Castle and knew what they meant.

The captain's eye wandered up and down the harbor. He counted a half dozen U.S. flags flying from commercial ships. All of them would have seen the *Habanero* and understood the canons.

It was a damnable situation, and Platt pondered it for some time. Washington did not know Lopez was in Cuba. How could it know? He knew that Allen Owen, the U.S. consul general, had sent out word of Lopez's arrival on the island, but it would be a week at least before the information reached Washington. The *Albany* had no orders. Spain and the United States were friendly nations. The last Platt heard was that the two countries were negotiating the possible purchase of

Cuba, so it could hardly be a question of prisoners of war. The situation was anomalous. No standard operating procedure existed.

Though he liked nothing about it and briefly considered putting to sea to avoid complications, he decided to remain in port. With so many U.S. commercial vessels as witnesses it would be awkward to leave just as the *Habanero* arrived with a boatload of American prisoners. A cautious man, Platt dispatched a Marine detail into the city to round up Marines and sailors on shore leave. Finding them in the labyrinthine streets and alleys, bars, and bawdy houses of Old Havana would take time. He needed to be ready for anything.

The fifty-one men lying miserably in the hold of the *Habanero* knew nothing of any of this. They heard the clamor outside as the ship approached port, heard certain sharp but incomprehensible shouts rising above the general din made by the crowd. But they could not see and could not know what any of it meant. They could not know that they were not alone, that hundreds of American residents in Havana were part of the tide flowing in from the sea with the ship, that at that very moment they were passing a U.S. fighting ship that just happened to be in port.

The residents watched; Platt and his men on the *Albany* watched; the captains and crews of the half dozen U.S. commercial ships in harbor watched; Consul General Owen watched; John Thrasher, furiously taking notes for the story he intended to write, watched.

All were witness to the events shortly to unfold.

# XXXVII

*August 15, 1851*

They reached Havana at seven o'clock that evening, less than three days since they'd landed in Cuba, eleven days since they'd sailed from New Orleans. It was not how they'd intended to arrive in the Cuban capital. The sun was still bright. The Spaniards brought them up from the hold, and as his eyes adjusted he looked out on a sight he never could have imagined. An enormous mass of people stretched along the quays and up the grassy hills toward the fortress at the summit. Looking up the Malecon toward the mouth of the harbor he saw people running along toward the ship, carriages rolling, palms swaying, boys scampering as the ship tied up. The glint of the falling tropical sun had turned the water into a shimmering mass of golden specks on sapphire blue. His eyes ran along the harbor, the green hills, the monster fortresses across the way, ships docked at their wharfs, some flying the stars and stripes. He spied the navy three-master. He looked closer. Yes, he knew that ship. He had been on her! His heart lifted.

He looked to his men, roped like slaves, waiting to debark. His mind went to Memphis: So this is how it felt!

The crowd continued to swell as they stood on deck, already thousands and still they arrived, spilling out of little streets and pushing down toward the harbor. Had the whole city been alerted? He saw white faces in the crowd – Americans, perhaps, come to help? Spanish soldiers lined the quay in their green blouses and high, plumed hats, standing with muskets at parade rest as the prisoners were led unsteadily led down the gangplank and prodded along the quay toward a much larger ship, *Esperanza* written across her bow. To the man they tried to march as soldiers do, erect, heads high, chins up. In their condition of depletion and desperation, it was impossible.

The mob pressed in closer as they shuffled along, shouting, trying to push past the guards to get at them. If there were Americans among them they stayed silent. Someone spit and a great gob landed on his face. With hands roped behind him he could do nothing but shudder and curse as it trickled down. Blows were landed. The soldiers laughed and pushed the crowd back to let the prisoners pass.

These were Cubans mocking them, the very Creoles Lopez claimed were in a state of revolt against Spain. What had these people been told? He looked to Victor Ker beside him, brave man, standing tall, defiant, eyes straight ahead, a Creole himself, come to Cuba to liberate his people. No man could feel Lopez's duplicity more than Ker. Where was the revolt? They were deceived, but so was Lopez, who wished to be Bolívar, out there in the mountains somewhere. The young man could never forgive Lopez, who had turned tail, something no U.S. commander would do.

Herded like cattle, they were brought onto the deck of the *Esperanza*.

Two tables, each with a logbook, pens, paper, and ink, had been set up beneath the bridge. At first taken by surprise by what he saw, he quickly understood: There had to be trial and sentence before contact with Washington was established and negotiations could begin. At least it was to be in full view of everyone, including the U.S. ships in the harbor. His eyes settled on the USS *Albany*. Her officers would be watching through binoculars. It was even possible that some would remember him. The *Albany* had carried him, along with General Worth and the 1st Army Division, from Brownsville to Veracruz to begin the march on Mexico City. Would they had marched on to Havana!

His mind drifted as they were pushed into lines and ordered to attention, unable to reconcile the beauty of the surroundings with their grim situation. He looked at his men, a few smiles, winks, fear covered up as soldiers always do, brave men, most hurting badly but holding up. His eye caught the rows of palms stretching up the skirt of the hill off the bay, dates and coconuts, ripe for picking. How he'd love to crack a coconut and drain its delicious milk.

Finally, the Malecon! Ah, Lucy!

They'd given them water on the *Habanero*, but no food. He'd trusted the word of Admiral Bustillo that they would be treated as prisoners of war, but watching an exchange taking place at the tables between the admiral and a cold-eyed man whose full-braided uniform meant he could only be the captain-general himself, Don José Gutiérrez de la Concha, changed everything.

"*Palabra de honor,*" said the admiral, red-faced under his black bicorne, clearly angry and speaking loudly. He'd given his word to the Americans.

He knew enough Spanish to translate the captain-general's response:

"Why did you not sink the boats and save me the trouble of a *pelotón de fusilamiento?*"

A firing squad? A chill bubbled along his spine. With the *Albany* tied up a few hundred yards away, they did not dare. War would be declared the next day.

He saw it was to be a drumhead court with de la Concha, now seated, to be the sole judge. Spanish soldiers formed a semicircle around them to keep anyone from going over the side, though with roped hands it would be suicide.

While a lieutenant went down the lines taking names, he studied the captain-general, marquis of Havana, viscount of Cuba, the man of whom he'd heard so much. Clearly all business, he sat erect, uniform pressed, bicorne heavy with gold braid, decorations aligned, cold eyes marching down the lines in step with the lieutenant, thin lips under a noble nose and trim mustache: the picture of a serious soldier who neither asked nor gave quarter.

The captain-general began writing. Time crawled.

The lieutenant was a Spaniard who spoke decent English and was painstaking in his effort to get their names right. Crittenden identified himself as commander and asked to be presented to the captain-general to give his testimony. The lieutenant shook his head. He asked about the civilian dressed in American clothes standing by the captain general. Again, he received no answer.

Finished, the lieutenant took the names to de la Concha, who went slowly down the list. When he came to Crittenden, he looked up, pronounced his name, and pointed at him. Will nodded toward him. De la Concha said something to the civilian standing beside him. He heard the name, "Mr. Owen," and understood that the counsel general of the United States was witness to the deadly farce. Owen served under Secretary of State Daniel Webster, who sat next to Uncle John at cabinet meetings. Owen whispered something to de la Concha, informing him if he did not already know. Owen looked straight toward him and they held each other's gaze a moment, before the consul general looked away.

*Now*, he thought, de la Concha knows who I am, knows of Uncle John, knows that the authority of the United States stands on this very deck watching him. He knows that anything he does runs the risk of war. He knows how close we've been in recent years to taking Cuba by force. Whatever he does will be done in consultation with Madrid, and Madrid in negotiations with Washington.

After talk of a firing squad, he felt some relief. Uncle John soon would know.

It did not last long.

De la Concha handed the list back to the lieutenant, now seated at the adjoining table, who began transcribing the names into his log. Meanwhile, the captain-general returned to his writing while the prisoners remained at attention. Time stood still. The high heat of the day was passed or some of the men surely would have collapsed. The smiles and winks were gone. It was an endless, grueling ordeal. The sun had sunk behind the hill stretching out to the west above them and now cast long shadows over the harbor. He heard groans and saw legs trembling. His own continued to hold steady.

Finally, de la Concha stood up. In a strong clear voice that sounded nothing like the Spanish of Mexico or Cuba, the captain general read out the sentence. He read slowly, giving the lieutenant time to translate the words into English:

It was long and tedious, but two phrases stood out:

"Pirates who dare profane the sacred island . . ."

"Persons arrested belonging to the horde headed by the traitor Lopez . . ."

"*Pirates! Horde! Traitor!*" He wanted to shout out in protest: *We are soldiers!*

He waited for his moment with Owen.

Reading in a loud, steady voice that carried to the ears of every Spaniard and Creole along the quay and allowed them to whoop at every outrageous phrase, slow enough to allow the lieutenant translating to get every word right, de la Concha came to the end of his statement.

"All persons whose names are attached in the subjoined list," he called out, "will suffer death by firing squad at sunrise."

From the crowd, a still louder whoop went up.

"*No, no,*" someone behind him shouted.

Another voice: "*You dare not!*"

"*Let us go, you bastards!*" someone cried.

"*At ease, men!*" he called.

"Señor Lieutenant Rey, of the Plaza de Armas, will have the honor of directing the execution."

Clearly impossible! Clearly bluff! Madrid would never allow it. De la Concha was dealing with a casus belli. He could not take it upon himself to murder American prisoners of war. No officer can take such a charge upon himself. And in sight of the American consul general and a U.S. warship. *Impossible!*

More whooping, and a lieutenant standing to the captain-general's right, who would be Lieutenant Rey, snapped his heels and inclined himself toward the captain-general.

As they were led toward the hold, he called to Mr. Owen. The sun was finally disappeared, the bright tropical colors fading in the dusk. He saw Owen turn toward him, an inquisitive look on his face. As the counsel general seemed about to say something, the butt of a rifle cracked the prisoner's head.

The lights turned bright for a millisecond, then everything went dark.

# XXXVIII

*August 16, 1851*

Do they think no one knows? All New Orleans knows the *Pampero* was bound for Cuba. Freaner has surely written about it. Would they have put him down here, too, shot him in the morning, too, a newspaper reporter? What about Sigur's friend, Havana publisher, what's his name . . . can't think . . . Thrasher, that's it. Was he up there with Owen? What will Thrasher be writing? What about Quitman . . . would he be down here with us . . . an American general, a governor? Ha! But things would have gone different with Quitman, wouldn't they? Owen, Thrasher, the *Albany*, every American in Havana knows. They'll do their duty. Owen will do his duty or be tarred and feathered when he gets home. The captain of the *Albany* will be cashiered. How many guns does a ship like that carry, thirty at least? Imagine they let it happen, unique in American history . . . fifty-one soldiers shot like dogs while the consul general and the navy looks on. War would be declared the next day! Fillmore would be impeached! Why did old Zach have to die and give way to the likes of Fillmore? Uncle John might be president now instead of Fillmore. You can bet he'd get us out of this.

*But does he know?*

His mind churned like a kaleidoscope. He had no idea how long he'd been out – an hour, two, three, hard to distinguish consciousness from unconsciousness in a black void that stays the same with eyes open or shut. At some point he remembered calling to the guard at the door and asking to see Mr. Owen. He heard laughing, and the consul general did not come.

Fifty-one of them sprawled in the gloom, hands still roped behind. He thought of rats – rats that live in the dark holds of ships, feasting on whatever cargo they can find. Were rats crawling around them? He listened for squealing. Without hands they were at the mercy of the lowest of the beasts.

He called out to the men, tried to reassure them. The sentence was a charade, he said. The risk for Spain was too great. They did not dare carry out the sentence. Negotiations were already underway.

"What about the letters, Colonel?" a voice called out.

"What letters?"

"The lieutenant said we'd be able to write letters home."

"I heard nothing."

"You were out cold."

Concussion? The dried blood on his face told him his head had been opened. He could do nothing about it.

"Part of the bluff, I'd say."

His brain was spinning. What would Grant think? Damn fool, he would say, let yourself be talked into a thing like that. What's the objective, Crittenden: Bring Cuba into the Union? A quarter million more slaves, that what you want? Balance North and South and head off war. Ha! Turn Cuba into another Negro Republic, whites massacred, like Haiti? *That what you want?* We can't run our own country so how can we run a place like that? What got you into something so hare-brained? The objective, Crittenden. What is the objective?

How would he answer? We came out of Mexico with California and Texas – why not try for Cuba? Polk would have done it. What business does Spain have ninety miles off our coast? If Lopez deceived him, he was ready to be deceived. *Seduced* is a better word. Seduction precedes deception, doesn't it? They'd get onto slavery because Grant had his ideas about that. Re-colonization, he called it. But he didn't come to Cuba for the slaves. It was always to drive Spain out. Manifest Destiny, they call it.

Deathly quiet as night wore on, only a few mumbles, maybe prayers, hard to tell. Hard to talk when you can't see who's next to you. Sleep? Who could sleep? Every mind busy fighting off thoughts of death. He thought of the letters. He hadn't known about the letters. He couldn't write to Ma, not if they were serious about it. A letter from beyond the grave would surely kill her.

Lucy? He could not do that. Nor Jude.

He would write to Lucien: Dear Lucien, you were right, you old dog.

Let the doctor, who knows how to communicate bad news, deal with it.

And if there was time, a note to Uncle John, just in case.

The tide flowed and the ship rocked. Creaks, not squeaks. Everything moving but time, which was standing still. Telegrams had surely gotten through – but were cables even laid to Havana? People had been running lines for years – but underwater? New Orleans still wasn't connected. They'd asked about it at the customhouse: Later in the year, they said, or maybe next. The *Albany* watched, her guns more than a match for anything the Spaniards had. He imagined her captain had already paid a visit to the captain-general. No sherry at that meeting. A warning from the *Albany* was all they needed.

His hands were swollen numb, like frostbite on winter bivouac at the Point and you feel the cold in your fingers and toes and after a certain point the pain lessens and you know what it means and it is not good and you'd better do something fast. Bad without hands. How could he write letters with hands like that? His body itched and cramped. Head ached. Nothing to be done. Momentary panic. His mind flew backward, back to Shelbyville, back to Cloverport, and suddenly tears were falling, angry, frustrated tears. He felt them running down his blood-encrusted face and could not stop them.

Not a ray of light penetrated. Couldn't be more than three o'clock, night inching by. *Madrugada*, the Mexicans call it, the wee hours. *À quién madruga, Dios le ayuda*, they say, God helps those who rise early. Shouldn't want morning to come if it is to be your last. He wasn't afraid. He wouldn't let himself be afraid. In battle he never gave a moment's thought to dying. No time for it. Dying is not the hard part. Dying is easy. Everybody does it. Just don't let yourself think about it.

I don't believe he will do it, he repeated to himself. I don't see the logic in it. What soldier can run such a risk? Imagine the headlines in every American newspaper: "Fifty-one U.S. soldiers murdered in cold blood!" The whole country would rise up in arms against Spain and Cuba. Why give Fillmore the provocation he needs? What president could stand by after such an act?

He tried to stay lucid, keep his mind steady, but he wasn't ready for this. You don't train for this at West Point. You learn that war is the noblest of endeavors, honest combat among principled men to settle real differences. You win or lose, live or die, on the battlefield. Politics by other means, said Clausewitz. What does murdering the wounded and executing prisoners of war have to do with the nobility of fair combat? Are these people barbarians? Are we back to the Huns?

He couldn't pray. At Shelbyville they'd said prayers every night, and now he couldn't do it. Four of them in the kitchen, Ma, Josie, Jude, and him reading the Bible, and now he couldn't pray. Pray to whom, to what? What would he say?

He was different from Jude. He never found consolation in prayer. Ma came to wonder about that, took him into the room they called the closet at Shelbyville and pushed him to his knees. "Oh, my blessed Savior, protect all my children in their youthful years and shield them in other days from the sins of the world."

He never minded church as long as there were friends or family. At West Point he went to chapel with the others (fifteen demerits for missing chapel), but for him it was the camaraderie of the thing, not the religion. *The corps! The corps!* He was on his knees down there with the others but didn't know where to look, what to say, what to think. Some of the others didn't know either.

A person has to trust himself, not some fantasy in the sky – himself and his family. Family is everything, the one true thing that matters and endures. How blessed he was to have been born into his family, to carry the name Crittenden! What a privilege! If his life was to be short, at least it was full. He thought of Ma, Pa, his brothers and sisters, Uncle John, Aunt Maria. He thought of Jude, their destinies severed. He thought of Lucy, her bright eyes shining across the table at the Royal.

Was he here because of Lucy? Ridiculous! Mind like a grasshopper. It was the right thing to do and they damned near pulled it off despite Lopez's mistakes. Would she have come to him? *Colonel Crittenden!* How she loved the sound of it: Colonel Crittenden walking his beloved along the Malecon . . . Colonel Crittenden in Government House . . . Colonel Crittenden joining Cuba to the Union . . . Colonel Crittenden changing history.

Better this way . . . give her a better story . . . hero dies in the end.

Or maybe is rescued in the nick of time.

He smiled for the first time in the dungeon.

# XXXIX

"Hey, Colonel."

He recognized the voice but couldn't put a name on it. Still couldn't see a thing in the blackness.

"Your uncle going to get us out of this?"

"Who's that talking?"

"Private John Stubbs talking, Colonel. Just curious."

"The men to help us are down there on the *Albany.* Thirty guns at least. You saw her as we came down, didn't you, Stubbs?"

"Yeah, but how many guns do they have up there in those forts?"

"Sam Reed here, Colonel. Pretty funny to be saved by the navy after all this."

"We'll owe every man on that ship a drink," someone said.

He heard some chuckling and felt good about it.

"I'd say a bottle for each one," someone said.

"You're paying, I hope."

More laughter.

"That light I see through those boards?" someone asked.

"You better damn well hope it's not," came the reply.

More chuckling, nervous this time. Men bearing up, feeling funny talking in the obscurity.

"Get this thing over with one way or t'other," said the voice.

"That's light, all right," someone said. "Must be close to five o'clock out there."

"Say your prayers, gentlemen."

"What do you think I've been doing all night," said a voice.

"Who you praying to," called someone.

"Prayin' to the United States Navy, I am. First time I ever done it."

Laughter.

"Don't think I want to be shot," someone muttered.

"Who dat don't want to be shot?"

"Bill Hogan don't want to be shot."

"What's to be done about it, Bill Hogan?"

"No one got a knife?"

"Bastards stole my knife."

"Nobody slipped his ropes?"

"Nobody slips sailors' knots, even Spanish."

The ship rocked. Noise of movement above. Silence in the hold as the ray of light through the boards gradually grew brighter. Time inches by.

"What happened, Colonel?"

Someone else picked it up.

"That's the bloody question, all right, Colonel, what the devil happened?"

"I'll answer that," sounded a new voice.

It was the growl of Victor Ker. "I'll tell you what happened. It was the Hungarians. From the first the Hungarians who wanted to split us up. Tell 'em, Colonel. Tell 'em how you opposed splitting us up."

"What's the point, Victor? Why go over it? We're in here, and the best we can hope is that the U.S. Navy gets us out."

A noise at the door and it is thrown open. Lieutenant Rey of the Plaza de Armas stands at the threshold. Fifty-one men, some who would gladly exchange death for a drink of water, are commanded to stand. Without arms and hands it is an impossible task. The open door lets in some light from outside, and as Lieutenant Rey stands watching, his guards laugh at the spectacle of men writhing on the boards like snakes.

"Untie these ropes, you rotten bastards," someone shouts.

Corporal Hernandez translates the first part of it, though the lieutenant has understood everything.

He gives a command and his guards help ten men to their feet. Their ropes are undone, and they are led away. For forty-one men, the wait begins anew.

"Lieutenant," Crittenden calls out before the door is slammed again, "a little mercy – *misericordia, por favor*. Untie us. Bring us water. These men have reached their limits."

"In due time, Colonel, in due time."

Time crawls. The guards return, and another ten men are brought to their feet and led away. He wonders about it but has heard no shots, so at least executions have not begun. Time creeps by, and the guards are back again and then again until the last men, including the young man himself, are led from the miserable hold. On deck, the sun works its way up in the east.

It could not have been six o'clock, not a time of day you'd think many people would be up and around, but this was the tropics, where people keep time with the sun. Many in the crowd had followed the *Habanero* in from the sea the previous day and spent the night under the palms on the grassy skirt of Fort Atarés, taking their rum and water as the sun went down, not stirring until it poked up again in the morning. What Cuban could miss a great day like this? A *peloton de fusilamiento* is a rare event in Havana, and as for fifty-one men – and *yanquis* at that – never!

In groups of ten, the untied men are shown to the desks occupied the previous evening by Spanish officers. Two more tables and more chairs have been brought up. They are allowed water from a tub on deck. It is ladled into them and over them to quench and refresh depleted bodies. Wretched, clothes covered with foul stains, faces hollow, bodies wounded and aching, hope fading, they are supplied with quills, ink, and paper and told to write. So swollen and numb are their hands, some can barely grip the pen. Some have no one to write to, but most write something to someone, hoping it will be received, hoping it can be read. What to say? How to say it? Who rehearses for a moment like this? Understanding, the Spaniards give them the time they need.

The letters are to be addressed at the top, but not sealed. The Spaniards will read them and seal them. They are to be kept personal. The deck is ringed with soldiers, so no untied man can make it over the side. As they stand from the tables, the men's hands are retied, and others are untied and take their places. The young man stands watching his men: fear, fatigue, anger at the hopelessness of the situation, he reads the faces. Reprieves would not require letters to be written.

His time comes toward the end. He's had time to consider it, and writes to Lucien, charging him with passing the news. The letter is detailed and precise, though scrabbled with difficulty with a hand that can barely grip the quill.

"*In a half hour, I, with fifty others, am to be shot,*" he begins. He looks up at the Spaniards watching him, no one pressing him to hurry. Why would they?

"*If the truth ever comes out you will find that I did my duty and have the perfect confidence of every man with me.*"

He is writing easier now, the hand responding to movement. He is onto a second page and then a third, writing about Lopez's failures.

"*We saw that we had been deceived grossly, and were making for the United States when taken.*"

He finishes the third page and is on to a fourth, wondering how to end it.

"*Write to my mother,*" he instructs Lucien. "*I am afraid that the news will break her heart. Farewell. Love to all my family. I am sorry that I am to die owing a cent, but it is inevitable.*"

He finishes, hands the pages off to an orderly, and starts a second letter to Uncle John.

"*Do me the justice,*" he begs his uncle, "*to believe that my motives were good.*" He has barely finished three lines when Lt. Rey commands him to finish.

They are led down the gangplank, pushed through the mob along the quay, and then up a grassy hill, moving slowly under the palms, toward the fort at the pinnacle, Fort Atarés. The sun is higher now, rising up over the twin forts to the east. It shows every sign of being a splendid tropical day, not a day when you want to die. Someone kicks a fallen coconut, and he hears the milk slosh inside. Ah, to drink it down! Walking in twos, they are fenced in by grenadiers unable to keep in step because of the slow pace of the prey. The mob tries to press in, but the soldiers keep them away. Knees and legs are stiff and weak, bladders have emptied, but every man does his best to stay erect. Make your last minute your best, soldiers say. Though not all the men would have heard it, they understand, and to a man they will try. What does it matter, someone might ask, but a soldier knows. Whatever demons are sapping his legs, choking his throat, opening the pores of his body, whatever filthy fate awaits him, the desire for dignity endures.

The crowd, the mob, the rabble that has waited all night to witness the dreary spectacle is all around them, laughing, joking, cavorting, searching faces for signs of weakness. Why is it not as solemn for them? the young man wonders. Death should be a solemn business.

They come to a crest behind which the heavy woods begin, stretching up to Fort Atarés at the top. A dozen Spanish soldiers, silent, immobile, rifles at parade rest, stand waiting behind a crisp-looking Lieutenant Rey. There is a ditch, freshly dug, long, narrow and deep. Shovels lie behind it. Anyone who still believed in bluff knows now it is over. They are commanded to stop. He looks around at his men. Heads are high. They will do it right. Terror of the mind is not for soldiers. It is why armies take them young, take them single, take men who've known war before, like Victor Ker, like William Logan Crittenden.

Even the rabble, held now at a distance, has fallen silent.

Six men are brought forward. The grenadiers don't push or shove, silently separating them from the others. It is triage, the word all prisoners hate. The Spaniards mutter in low voices. They don't like this day's work either. As his men turn to face their executioners, he sees them talking, bucking each other up, helping assure that each is strong to the end. They stand before the ditch.

"You dirty bastards will pay for this!" spits Pvt. Bill Hogan, whose knife was stolen. Some men watch, others cannot, looking down, mumbling prayers. Curses are shouted out as the lieutenant cries: "*Apunten, listos, fuego!*"

It is horrible but goes quickly. Everyone wants it over with. Lieutenant Rey uses his pistol for the necessary coups de grace. Bodies are pushed into the grave as more men advance.

His mind has taken flight: back to Shelbyville, back to Frankfort, back to Pa and Ma and Uncle John. He thinks of Jude. His time comes toward the end. His gift of time has run its course. He decides to die looking at the sun, already halfway up the blue sky. No use worrying about his eyes now. He thinks of the letters. His last thought is of Lucy.

Brief moments of success, raindrops in eternity, it's all we get; moments that sparkle and dazzle in their brightness as, exhilarated, we soar ever higher, ever closer to the golden eye, to truth, wisdom, perfection, making our mark. We are Gods, Icarus, free, brilliant, unique, approaching fiery extinction.

# XL

*August 21, 1851*

Lucien Hensley, still under the shock of the letter, had finished with one patient and was ready to see another when a messenger arrived with a note from Lucy Holcombe. She was at Raynaud House and would call on him that afternoon if he would specify a convenient time. While the messenger waited, he wrote out a quick reply: She should stay where she was. He would come by Raynaud House at two o'clock.

He had patients to call on, but must get to her before she saw the afternoon newspapers.

A steamer had brought the letter the previous day, along with Havana newspapers. Hensley's Spanish was imperfect, but he did not need perfection to understand the news articles, which were perfunctory at best, recounting little more than the fact of the executions and the information that the traitor Lopez was still at large. For the story in *El Faro Industriel*, Hensley didn't need much Spanish at all: Blank spaces covered half the front page.

Will's letter had surely been read by the Spaniards, but not censored, for nothing was inked out. Reading it, he saw there was nothing that Spain would not want known. On the contrary. The steamer had also brought letters from men executed along with Crittenden, letters Hensley had learned about earlier that day in an urgent message from Laurent Sigur:

*Sir:*

*Letters from members of the Lopez expedition, addressed to friends and family, have been brought by same to my office with the most terrible news. I fear all is lost for our friends. It is my intention to publish the letters in a special afternoon edition, accompanied by an editorial blaming Spain and declaring the executions a matter of national honor: a casus belli. All America, all the world, must know the truth, and the sooner the better.*

*The letters are from members of Colonel Crittenden's 2nd Battalion, but I have received no letter from Crittenden himself. I cannot imagine that his men would have written without Crittenden writing as well, if he was still alive. Do you, sir, know anything of a Crittenden letter? If such exists, I would wish to publish it as well.*

*Know, sir, that I remain your most humble and respectful servant,*

*Laurent Sigur*

Neither Sigur's bellicosity toward Spain nor Hensley's own feelings about the folly of the Cuban expedition could influence the decisions he had to make. Crittenden's letter was addressed to him alone, asking him to communicate with several people. It carried no specific reference to Lucy Holcombe. Its author referred to his mother, to Jude, to Lucien, to the Reverend Whistlar at Shelbyville, even to people at the customhouse, but not to Lucy. Most likely, the doctor reasoned, his friend chose to spare her the pain, trusting him to communicate the news to her at the proper time and in the proper manner.

He could not allow her to learn of events through the newspaper. But should he show her the letter, a letter with such a terrifying beginning? And should he allow it to be published by Sigur and to serve the cause of the warmongers?

He sat for some time pondering the matter. It was a heart-wrenching missive, poignant, courageous, and defiant at once, exactly capturing the man. The doctor kept his tears from falling until the final phrase, "*I had better have been persuaded to stay.*"

It wasn't for want of trying!

He had no idea if Will would want it published. Possibly not, since it was so deeply personal, even intimate. On the other hand, if letters from his men were published, should not the commander's letter be there as well? How could he withhold it in such circumstances? Did Americans not have the right to know the truth of events, especially since Spanish newspaper accounts either were censored or said nothing of value?

If he allowed Sigur to publish it, he must show it to Lucy before she saw the newspaper. He had no special sympathy for Lucy, who had played a pivotal role in an enterprise he thoroughly despised. Moreover, he doubted that she had ever reciprocated Will's love, doubts that had led him to dissuade his friend from offering his ring before sailing.

He would not, however, allow his feelings to affect the decisions he had to make. He had already considered the risk of the Kentucky family learning of the tragedy through newspapers, already taken pen in hand to write to dear Anna Maria in Cloverport, fragile enough to be felled by news of her son read in a newspaper. A messenger had come for it. He trusted the mails would get there first.

He arrived at Raynaud House precisely at two, knocking and being admitted by a Negro butler who showed him into the well-appointed turret salon. He'd not had the privilege of visiting Raynaud House previously, nor of meeting Victoria Raynaud, who, he understood with relief, would not be present for the interview.

He found Lucy alone on a settee, awaiting his arrival. She rose and crossed the room to take his hand. They'd met once before, at Monmouth, but had exchanged no conversation. He had no doubt that he remembered her better than she remembered him. His knowledge of her was considerable, both from his friend and from his own observation and investigation.

She was dressed conservatively in plain indigo velvet with an ivory cameo at the neck, not at all the devastating presence he remembered from Monmouth. But much had changed since those days, had it not? They sat on opposing ends of the settee, and she made polite talk as the Negro butler served coffee and cake and quietly withdrew. He observed her closely, determining, as doctors do, how much he might safely tell the patient. He saw immediately that she knew nothing of events. But how could she?

Even subdued and dressed in old maid's clothes she was a beautiful specimen of womanhood. Poor Will, so easy to see how he'd lost his heart. She sought to hide her anxiety, though his trained eye saw everything. Perhaps he'd misjudged her feelings for his friend. She'd come to New Orleans, she said, to stay in touch; so she would know as soon as word came.

He'd brought the letter, which remained for the moment in his breast pocket. He listened as she talked, explaining how she could not have remained another day in Marshall without knowing something, nervously playing with her hands, allowing no silence as if sensing in the doctor's demeanor that he'd brought news she did not want to hear. Pretty blue eyes, he thought, but strangely turned inward. He could see the writer in her, someone who was present but not entirely, always thinking of her material, anxious to get her fingers back in the clay, back to work, molding, shaping, creating her story.

He saw a strong young woman, intelligent, passionate, clearly ambitious; a woman determined to make her mark. He listened, reflected, and decided not just to speak of the letter but to show it to her. Then he would take it to Jude. Only after both had seen it would he take it to Sigur.

He produced the letter.

Her hands were steady. Had he made the right decision? She was slow in extracting the letter from the envelope. He could see that she sensed what was coming, though still hoping it was not the worst. Reading the first line, she gasped and dropped the missive to her lap. She looked up at him, and their eyes held as the tears fell. With a sigh, she took it up again and read to the end.

# HISTORICAL NOTES

Published in the *Delta-News* and other New Orleans newspapers, the letters from Havana became front-page news across the country. The dead men praised Crittenden and blamed Lopez and demonstrated astonishing presence of mind for men facing imminent death. Will Crittenden's letter to Lucien Hensley is remarkable in its calm, compassionate exposition of events.

The nation reacted with fury. Poems were written, as was at least one song, "The Death of Crittenden." Marches and demonstrations were held in cities from New Orleans and Louisville to Philadelphia and New York. Democrats in Congress denounced Fillmore for cowardice and demanded the recall of Counsel General Owen, who'd done nothing to help the Americans, in fact had conspired with Captain-General de la Concha to make the situation worse.

In Baltimore, an effigy of the counsel general was burned, and Fillmore finally had to recall him. Editorials in newspapers, North and South alike, insisted that America could not honorably tolerate such provocation, and that Cuba must now be taken. If Fillmore had acted as Polk would have done, they opined, there'd be no need for patriots like William Logan Crittenden to act alone. It was time to deal with Cuba as we had dealt with Mexico.

As for Fillmore himself, he was finished. The Whigs wouldn't re-nominate him, preferring General Winfield Scott, the last Whig, who won only four states in the '52 election (including Kentucky), crushed by Democrat Franklin Pierce. Jefferson Davis became Pierce's minister of war, militating to bring parts of Mexico into the Union as slave states, ending up only with the Gadsden Purchase. Caleb Cushing of Massachusetts, a Northerner with Southern sympathies, was named attorney general to replace John J. Crittenden, who had supported Scott for president.

Public disgust only increased when de la Concha's official report of the executions was published in Havana and excerpts printed in American newspapers. The captain-general praised Consul General Owen and Commander Platt of the *Albany* for their cooperation. Owen had turned away two delegations of Americans seeking his intervention, informing them that President Fillmore deemed the men traitors who had lost their nationality and could be offered no protection.

Commander Platt's actions were judged equally disgraceful. When a delegation from American ships in the harbor came to the *Albany* on the fateful night urging him to intervene, reminding him that the Marines on his ship were there to assist Americans abroad in danger, Platt sent them away. He did the same to a delegation of sailors and Marines from his own ship that came to protest the injustice of the sentence and to beg his intervention, all to no avail. Platt lost command of his ship the following year, disappearing from history.

After dealing with Crittenden, the Spaniards turned back toward Lopez, sending a regiment to Pinar, flushing him out of his plantation at Frias and wearing him down. Relentlessly, the Spaniards tracked survivors, rounding up 167 men during the last days of August – all that remained of the original 451. Lopez was the last to be taken, eluding the enemy until sniffed out by bloodhounds ten miles west of Bahia Honda on August 30, bitten in the leg when finally captured.

Of the 167 men captured, 166 were transported by ship from Mariel to Havana and taken to the city prison behind Castillo la Punta, which stands guard over the south side of the harbor. Among the captured men, six American officers (among them Capt. John Kelly, who'd left Crittenden to join Lopez) were pardoned and returned to the United States. De la Concha alone knows why he spared them – just as he alone knows why he murdered Crittenden's fifty-one.

Of the remaining 160, which included Major Schlesinger (but not General Pragay, Colonel Downman, or Colonel Blumenthal, all killed in battle), all were found guilty of insurrection and sent as prisoners to work in the iron mines of Ceuta, in Spanish Morocco. Publisher John Thrasher, accused by de la Concha of aiding the insurrection and abandoned, like the other Americans, by Counsel General Owen, accompanied them as a prisoner to Ceuta.

The 167th prisoner was Narciso Lopez.

Judged a traitor to his country by de la Concha and not worthy of the iron mines or a firing squad, Lopez, dressed in a white shroud and holding a crucifix as he ascended the scaffold, was garroted on Havana's Plaza de la Punta on September 2, 1851, a day proclaimed a national holiday. "My countrymen, forgive me for the evil, if any, I have caused you," he called out to the thousands gathered for the festivities. "My intention was not evil, but good. I die for my beloved Cuba."

Lucy Holcombe recovered from her chagrin. Returning to Wyalusing, she threw herself into her novel, *The Free Flag of Cuba or the Martyrdom of General Narciso Lopez*, published in 1854 under the pseudonym H. M. Hardimann. The book found a wide audience, and was especially well received in the South, where it was recognized as the antidote to *Uncle Tom's Cabin*, which was detested in the South. The book was praised by one reviewer as "redolent of female fancy, taste and sentiment. A gifted, spirited, pure-minded and warm-hearted Southern woman alone could have so handled such a theme."

For the rest of her life Lucy romanticized about the young man she'd encouraged to join Lopez, claiming they were engaged, describing him in her novel as "tall and good-looking, with cold, quiet manner, and large commanding eyes – a perfect prince of knowledge, at whose feet I would sit with timid wonder and love." The book was dedicated to Gen. John A. Quitman, who even after the Lopez debacle continued raising money and recruiting men for the next invasion of Cuba, which he intended to lead himself.

Events, namely Quitman's death and the Civil War, would intervene.

Lucy Holcombe was a firebrand, a true daughter of the South, never letting go of Cuba or anything else that might help in the coming showdown with the North. Having rejected many suitors her own age, she married Francis Wilkinson Pickens in 1858, a man thirty years her senior. Pickens was governor of South Carolina and Lucy Holcombe Pickens his first lady when Jefferson Davis, provisional president of the Confederate States of America, gave the order to General P. G. T. Beauregard to begin firing on Fort Sumter on April 12, 1861, the first shots of the Civil War.

Lucy's portrait appeared on the $100 Confederate bill, earning her the title "Queen of the Confederacy."

Returning to the Senate, John J. Crittenden did not give up his efforts to head off civil war. The Crittenden Compromise, introduced in December, 1860, in the turbulent days between Lincoln's election and inauguration, sought to bridge the North-South gap by banning slavery north of the Mason-Dixon Line, extended to the Pacific. The Compromise of 1850, as well as the Kansas-Nebraska Act of 1854, had allowed popular votes on slavery north of the line. The Kansas-Nebraska Act, the work of Senator Stephen Douglas of Illinois, Lincoln's pro-slavery nemesis, made Lincoln's rise and Civil War inevitable.

Senator Crittenden's sons, Tom and George, comrades in arms of cousin Will Crittenden in the war against Mexico, opposed each other as generals in the Civil War, facing each other in the Battle of Mill Springs in January, 1862, when General George led a Confederate force north into Kentucky from Tennessee and was repulsed by Union forces that included his brother. Important at the time, the battle faded in importance weeks later when Gen. Ulysses S. Grant, another colleague from Mexico, captured Forts Henry and Donelson, assuring that Kentucky would remain in the Union and opening up Tennessee to Union forces.

Neither Crittenden general particularly distinguished himself in the Civil War. The Crittendens of Kentucky were the only family to have generals on both sides of the war.

*William Logan Crittenden*

"Tall and good-looking, with cold quiet manner and large commanding eyes – a perfect prince of knowledge, at whose feet I would sit with timid wonder and love."

*Free Flag of Cuba*
Lucy Petway Holcombe

# Crittenden Family Tree *Revolution through Civil War*

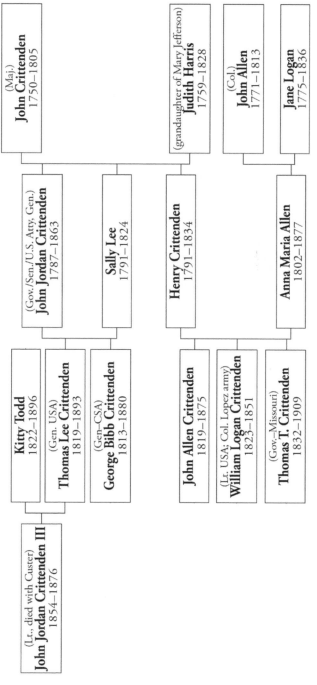

(Maj.)
**John Crittenden**
1750–1805

(Gov./Sen./U.S. Atty. Gen.)
**John Jordan Crittenden**
1787–1863

**Sally Lee**
1791–1824

(grandaughter of Mary Jefferson)
**Judith Harris**
1759–1828

(Col.)
**John Allen**
1771–1813

**Jane Logan**
1775–1836

**Henry Crittenden**
1791–1834

**Anna Maria Allen**
1802–1877

**Kitty Todd**
1822–1896

(Gen. USA)
**Thomas Lee Crittenden**
1819–1893

(Gen.–CSA)
**George Bibb Crittenden**
1813–1880

**John Allen Crittenden**
1819–1875

(Lt. USA; Col. Lopez army)
**William Logan Crittenden**
1823–1851

(Gov.–Missouri)
**Thomas T. Crittenden**
1832–1909

(Lt., died with Custer)
**John Jordan Crittenden III**
1854–1876